Sue Woolfe is the author of three novels, including the bestselling *Leaning Towards Infinity*, which won the Christina Stead Award for Fiction and the Commonwealth Writers' Prize for Best Book, Asia–Pacific Region, and was shortlisted for almost every other major Australian prize and for the Tiptree Award in the US. It has been translated into French, Italian and Dutch.

Sue has adapted both *Leaning Towards Infinity* and her first novel, *Painted Woman*, for ABC radio and for the stage. Her third novel, *The Secret Cure*, is currently being adapted as an opera.

Sue Woolfe teaches Creative Writing at Sydney University, and is the author of *The Mystery of the Cleaning Lady: A Novelist Looks at Neuroscience and Creativity* and, with Kate Grenville, *Making Stories: How Ten Australian Novels were Written*.

Also by Sue Woolfe

Painted Woman
Leaning Towards Infinity
The Secret Cure
Wild Minds (editor)
Making Stories: How Ten Australian Novels were Written
    (with Kate Grenville)
The Mystery of the Cleaning Lady: A Novelist Looks at
    Neuroscience and Creativity

The Oldest Song in the World

SUE WOOLFE

FOURTH ESTATE

Fourth Estate
An imprint of HarperCollins*Publishers*
First published in Australia in 2012
by HarperCollins*Publishers* Australia Pty Limited
ABN 36 009 913 517
harpercollins.com.au

HarperCollins*Publishers*
Level 13, 201 Elizabeth Street, Sydney NSW 2000, Australia
31 View Road, Glenfield, Auckland 0627, New Zealand
A 53, Sector 57, Noida, UP, India
77–85 Fulham Palace Road, London W6 8JB, United Kingdom
2 Bloor Street East, 20th floor, Toronto, Ontario M4W 1A8, Canada
10 East 53rd Street, New York NY 10022, USA

National Library of Australia Cataloguing-in-Publication entry:

Woolfe, Sue.
The oldest song in the world / Sue Woolfe.
ISBN: 978 0 7322 9499 1 (pbk.)
Aboriginal Australians – Fiction.
A823.3

Cover design by Jane Waterhouse, HarperCollins Design Studio
Cover images: Australian Desert © Nicole Périat, www.iconico.net;
all other images by shutterstock.com
Typeset in Berthold Baskerville Regular by Kirby Jones
Printed and bound in Australia by Griffin Press
The papers used by HarperCollins in the manufacture of this book are a natural, recyclable
product made from wood grown in sustainable plantation forests. The fibre source and
manufacturing processes meet recognised international environmental standards, and carry
certification.

5 4 3 2 1   12 13 14 15

To everyone who taught me

Part One

Chapter 1

In an open-air café in Alice Springs, beside a river that was nothing like my river, there was a blue-shirted man in his forties, reading, but I wasn't sure it was him. Oh, I'd known I wouldn't see the young man who was my every second thought, the boy on the mudflats with the silver river nibbling at his thin amber feet, always about to swallow him, always about to take him away from me forever, but this man was old, surely too old. His wild hair that once fizzed into blond curls was now a grey ponytail held in an elastic band, his face was scrunching into double chins – surely that wasn't him. I paused, waiting to see his eyes, if his eyes were the silver I remembered. But he didn't look up. He wasn't curious about me. He didn't seem to be waiting; he was absorbed only in his reading.

I sank into the nearest white plastic chair, reddened with dust and pooled with crackling brown leaves curled up like foetuses. I leaned my trolley bag against the chair, and hooked my workbag around the handles. I'd just flown three and a half thousand kilometres from a cool southern city, unprepared for the menacing sun that argued with my certainty. It said: you were a fool to have come.

A waiter called through a hatch from inside.

'Want a menu?'

He wasn't going to leave his air conditioning until he had to.

'Just coffee. Short black,' I said, appeasingly, as if its shortness might be less trouble. I was always appeasing. Though one day, very soon, I promised myself, I'd find a way to change.

I moved my chair under the umbrella, and then I made my first discovery about the desert: the air seemed remarkably cool whenever there was a small circle of shade; as if the air, as conciliatory as me, was trying to make up for the heat. I repropped my bag and looked anywhere but at the man. Of course it wasn't him. I wished I'd suggested we meet in an air-conditioned hotel lobby.

Black women passed the café at that moment, their red, purple, pink and yellow skirts swinging over thin brown legs and bare feet. As they trod, I glimpsed pink soles. They seemed so vulnerable, the pinkness of those soles. I listened to the way their voices rose and fell and paused, and tried to hum along with the rhythms. I was doing quite well, considering the heat. She surely would be impressed that I was already hard at work. Da-da-der, da der, der.

At the university, she'd been suspected of an irregularity because of me. She'd taken a risk with me, and I'd got her into trouble. That's why I was here. Though that wasn't entirely true, of course. Perhaps not true at all.

The café owner had called his establishment 'The Waterfront Café' and the joke made me cranky. The last time this was a waterfront must have been in the Ice Age. Huge trees grew in the corrugations of the river's dry bed, like trees sprouting out of a brain, a dried-up brain. Even the riverbed made me cranky.

My river, in my memory, always floats silver with a promise that it would bring drifting into my reach something I longed for, or that it would drift something painful away. Although that had failed me, too.

Suddenly, it came over me again, the terrible loss of that childhood, that river, those people, that luminous woman, that almost transparent boy with the silver eyes. That loss hit me like a blow on the plastic chair in the heat, and it almost felled me.

4

The stranger at the far table turned a page. Even paper crackled in the heat. I wished he'd look up. People can't change silver eyes. Oh, his eyes might've faded, but surely something would've remained, something of that strange silvery fire.

I'd met the woman who saved me at a suburban library when my job was to gather up books people had left behind. It had got very dull, picking up books, hundreds of books covered the way libraries cover them, with worn blue or maroon covers, the titles and authors almost faded to invisibility. I was only ever allowed to work in the non-fiction section, amongst the serious, boring books – or that's how I thought of them. I found myself wondering how dull a book could be without causing the expiration of the reader. At least it'd be something to do, it'd be a game to find this out and, since no one else was around, the guinea pig would have to be me. I took to secreting away from the sorting shelves the books most likely to cause my expiration and, when the librarian was busy, I'd open them and wait to cease breathing. In this way I lumbered through the opening chapters of *The Descent of Man* and *The Meaning of Meaning*. If anyone were to notice me, I planned to claim that I found the books irresistible. As indeed, in my boredom, I did.

But after weeks, despite having the *sensation* that my heart was slowing down, I was still as strong as a horse. One afternoon I came across *A Critique of Common Postulates: Our Indigenes*, authored by somebody pompously cloaking their identity with initials: E.E. Albert. I set myself up in my corner, checked that the head librarian was trying out her new eyeliner in the Ladies, and I must have been reading for a good half hour when a sensation prickled me. Someone was watching.

I wheeled around.

'What's it about?' a voice asked. It belonged to a woman around the age that Diana would've been. She was red in the face as if she'd just been scrubbed, she was motherly hipped and very buxom, so I felt reassured she wasn't some library administrator come to check on me. They were always skinny with caved-in chests, which meant, poor things, that they didn't have many opportunities with men, I believed, or had to work harder to get them. But I had given up love affairs, and mentally slapped my hand.

The woman came over and stood beside me, touching the book's cover as if she might like to read it, too.

Something about the way she then looked at me, her face tilted on one side as if it was pinned up by a star, made me take a breath and I began to talk, not about expiring but about the book. Here I have to remember what had happened to me while I'd been reading, even while my index finger had felt hopefully for a faltering pulse. I'd experienced a dizzying phenomenon familiar to more sophisticated people but never before to me: it was as if, while I read, I'd been looking down the barrel of a microscope, and not only looking down it but travelling down it – I could almost hear the echoing of my breath as I slid down it, down down down, to land like some errant bacterium on the book's microscope plates. I swear, as I read, I'd heard the whistling of the desert winds and the scrabbling of tiny insects in the grey scrub, just as E.E. Albert had described, and the receding thud of a startled kangaroo, and I'd wondered, without stopping to check, if the sounds were coming from the book's pages, or from inside the library. I'd smelled the native ti-tree, its perfume stronger in the scorching dust at midday; I'd shivered as the sand under my feet chilled to a frozen powder at night.

So despite my confusion, I found an answer for the woman standing beside me: I explained that the book said that Indigenous people were misunderstood because their language led them to see their homeland, the desert, in a way totally different from the Western world, or perhaps what they'd done was to invent a language which reflected what they knew – in any case, their language was part and parcel of their world and their beliefs – and non-Indigenous Australians assumed, because city people saw other things, city things, that Aboriginals were dull-witted, whereas they weren't.

'For example?' she asked.

To my surprise, I found I could keep going. 'Well, in their languages, they don't have a future tense –'

'Not at all?' she asked. 'No idea of the future?'

'Not the distant future,' I corrected myself, because I realised that this was a person who mightn't accept my usual sloppiness, 'but the near future – nothing further than halfway through next week. So, if you don't have words for the future, you probably don't think about it. At least, not clearly. Of course, many people dispute whether the limits of your language are the limits of your world. That's a much-discussed theory.'

I paused then because I'd remembered this line straight out of the book, without quite understanding it, but as she nodded, its meaning came to me.

'It makes sense, doesn't it!' I said. 'In a sort of way. You can't think clearly about things you have no words for.'

'Perception's a strange thing,' she said.

I thought about that for a moment. I thought about Diana and my father and a suspicion I'd long been harbouring, almost without knowing it, that Diana's beauty might've just been the way *I* saw beauty – and my father, of course. Her skin was amber, like a felt lampshade with a light under it. Definitely not my mother's taste. No one before this stranger had ever brought anything like that so clearly to my mind before, no one had reached in and touched an unfocused suspicion that had nudged against the walls of my insides, pulled it out onto the surface and put it into words.

Then I remembered I was in the library talking when I should've been tidying up, and looked around guiltily.

'Maybe you don't think about the future when you're living hand to mouth in the desert,' the woman beside me said.

'Maybe,' I said, unsure, because where I lived was in the past. To cover my confusion, I turned to the front page where there was a photo of a group of near-naked men and women, the women carrying plump children on their hips, the men holding weapons. 'They're not skinny, are they?' I said. 'They lived well. The book says so.'

We examined the photo together, admiring the desert babies, almost like the children in a Rubens' portrait.

'I suppose they had to think enough into the future to plan to walk to where the good food would be,' I said. 'The future would be very connected to the past.' I startled myself by adding: 'Maybe ours is, too.'

She was nodding, her eyes on me, thinking along with me.

'But anyway –' I continued, because I really wanted to keep her with me, this person who could think along with me, thinking was usually such a lonely thing to do, and those eyes on me were crinkling with warm approval, like two dark lagoons I could dive into, lagoons in the mountains and ravines of her face, 'without an idea of the distant future, it probably means that you wouldn't think of putting things by for the future, like possessions, you wouldn't need possessions for some future time.' I turned back to the photo. 'See how they don't have much to carry around, just their babies and the spears – so you wouldn't need a manager to organise the possessions you didn't have, or figure out systems to store them like people have done in this library.'

I paused because the head librarian had tried to explain about Melvil Dewey and his system till she was blue in the face, she said, because I was such a slow learner. I hoped I wouldn't have to explain Melvil Dewey to the woman because I was still getting it wrong, especially when there were lots of digits behind

8

the point, or lots of digits and no point, or lots of digits and letters and a point and a second line of digits – I was always putting books in unfindable places. Readers often complained.

'You wouldn't need mayors and councils to administer things,' said the woman. She kept nodding and smiling, and I kept finding more to say to her, so she'd stay with me and keep this warm feeling going.

'Or shops,' I said.

Each thing I thought of to say seemed like a victory. I'd been a thin awkward child with round shoulders, my parents said, definitely not the sort of person anyone noticed when I entered a room, so for years I'd wondered if I was invisible, and could with impunity pick yellow crumbs of sleep out of my eyelashes or adjust my panties under my skirt in public. Even when I'd been in a school play, walking across a bare stage as a donkey, I wasn't absolutely convinced I could be seen.

'You wouldn't need administrators!' the woman continued, as if she really was aware of me standing right there beside her. I was beginning to feel so noticed.

'Or cupboards to put the things in that you didn't have. Or shelves or drawers!' I said. 'You'd be very different from what the book calls Westerners,' I added, pronouncing the word self-consciously because I'd just now read it in E.E. Albert, and I'd only used it before about movies with heroic men on galloping horses and pretty singers in saloon bars – but I'd noticed that the author's word had an extra bit on the end. The woman didn't wince, so I went on: 'You'd have very different worries from people who lived in the one place all the time, like farmers have to.'

Now I could tell the woman what Diana had taught me when she showed me how to sow summer vegetables in the spring, and winter ones in the autumn.

'Farmers have to gather seed and sort it so they know which seed is which and from what year, and ways to store it through the winter. And they have to stay where the soil is good. Nomads don't have to think about that.'

'So you'd have no worries?' she asked. 'You'd be a happy savage?'

'Oh no,' I said. 'You'd just have different worries. Like, knowing what trees fruited when, and where, and how to get there without roads or footpaths, and when fish spawned and snakes were born and eggs were laid, and because you don't write things down you'd need to teach someone else to remember these things, maybe in songs, and what to do if no one wants that job, no one wants to learn the knowledge, and you can't write it down.'

The kindly woman brought me back to where I was by putting her finger to her lips. The head librarian had returned from the Ladies' with black-rimmed eyes, and was glaring at me.

'That isn't in the book,' the woman said. I should've noticed it wasn't a question. But I was enjoying myself too much. I wished I could tell her that this conversation was the most interesting thing that had happened to me in years, but I didn't.

'This isn't the sort of thing every young woman muses on,' she said. 'Are you studying this in a course?'

I was so startled, I forgot to whisper.

'Not me! Never! I just clear up books after people leave.'

The head librarian began clearing her throat meaningfully. As if we were conspirators, the woman gestured that we should go out to the lobby. Without a thought, I followed her outside, I was so unmothered.

'Why are you reading about this?' she asked as soon as we were leaning against the wall.

I blushed. Her question brought me back to my ordinary life.

'I like to know things,' I thought to say. It was sort of true.

'What an interesting young person!' she said, and suddenly excitement swept through me, a delicious wave of possibility about myself. No one had ever thought of me as interesting before, no one at school, no one in my childhood, no one in all my thirty-six years of living. They'd always thought of me as someone who'd forgotten to do this thing, or failed to do that. Or made a mess: 'Kathryn, was it you who made this mess?' they'd say, until I got to hate my very name.

But to be thought of as interesting – ah, then! It'd make up for not being beautiful like Diana, it'd make up for not doing well at school, it'd make up for my disaster of a love life. I wanted to stay in the company of someone who thought me interesting, so she'd keep making this delicious wave go through me. She might be right. I might be interesting, after all. It was almost like falling in love, except I was falling in love with myself.

'Ever thought of studying, to find out things?' she asked.

'No,' I blurted. 'Study's boring.'

Then I stopped, because I shouldn't have said that; the good impression I'd been making up till then was ruined. Now she'd find out that I wasn't interesting at all. But she seemed lost in her own thoughts.

'At a university, for instance,' she said.

'I'm not the type for university,' I said.

'Would you like to see if that's really true?' she asked.

I said no again but she didn't seem to hear. She fussed about what month it was, and whether it was too late in the year, and slowly I realised she meant too late to enrol in a university course. I was disappointed at this turn in the conversation, and all my excitement faded away.

'I'll have to go inside,' I said, trying not to show how I felt. 'I'll be in trouble.'

'I'll send the forms to the library,' the woman said.

Afterwards I had to tell the head librarian what I'd been talking about. She snorted. She was ten years older than me and often snorted.

'The woman's probably mad,' she said.

But the forms turned up the very next day. I had to pass a test.

'Do you think I should do this test?' I asked the head librarian. At that moment, I decided that I would do the opposite of what she advised.

'Definitely not,' she said. 'You're not the type for university.'

I had to go to a special building in the university. As I passed a group of actual students, I hoped they'd comment approvingly on me to each other.

In the test I found myself able to remember all sorts of things I didn't know I knew. My mind was suddenly like the river eagle flying over my life, swooping down on succulent baby crabs before they scuttled away to their holes in the mudflats. Perhaps I might turn out to be an interesting person, after all.

It was only as I addressed the envelope to send back to the woman that I found out her name: she was E.E. Albert. So I found myself at university. I chose her course, linguistics, a word I could scarcely pronounce. It didn't sound very promising, not like other subjects I saw listed which made me feel dreamy – psychology, philosophy, ancient history. I chose linguistics to be near her.

You'd think I'd have gone to see her immediately, you'd think I'd have made myself a cabin in the corridor outside her very door, but every time I went to visit her, my hand fell away just before I knocked. Partly it was because the door was labelled Dr Elizabeth Edna Albert, not E.E. Albert. She wasn't mine after all. Partly it was because I was jealous of the other students, who seemed to have more access to her thoughts, the way they so ably wrote down everything she said in a vast old-fashioned theatre with raked seats. She was one of those lecturers who still felt allegiance to her academic gown, black with crimson edges to show her fellowship with an ancient tradition of learning. Her booming voice was filled with certainties, not at all like that warm, probing, encouraging woman in the library. She drew on the whiteboard a cross-section of the human mouth and throat, with esoteric labels like 'the glottis'. I knew she was mistaken, I knew that mouths were enticingly warm and moist and filled with kisses and words and food and drink, that a mouth wasn't anything like this diagram. It wasn't until we were filing out of the lecture room that I realised the two identical bumps I'd drawn above a downward tube were tonsils.

But the worst was the reading list she gave us, for they were the sorts of books that in the library I'd thought could cause my expiration. I argued with myself that she wasn't to know that, but the list seemed a betrayal.

So I made no headway with them, and I couldn't visit her until I had.

As the months went by, I knew I had to take action. I began with the first book on the list, and borrowed it for the longest time we were allowed, which was a week. By week's end, I'd got through the first page fifteen times and couldn't have told her what I'd read. I returned it and waited for the librarians to put it away, then I scurried back and borrowed it again, resolving that this time I'd bribe myself with an adventure when I got to the end of every chapter. I spent time planning the adventure instead of reading: Adventure Number One, to find some stranger in a bar and sleep with him. I hadn't given in to my old sex addiction for a long while; but now, to continue as her student, I must. I put the book in a big tote bag and went to a bar and propositioned the first man I saw who leaned on the bar counter in a lonely way. He was endearingly chubby with lanky hair and he had a way of laughing that made me laugh too. I told him I'd sleep with him just as soon as I'd read a chapter of the book in my bag. 'It must be erotica! Let's read it together!'

he kept saying. I took them both home, him and the book. We all got into bed together, him, me and the book. His body was rounded and furry like my memory of a childhood teddy bear. I loved the weight of his furry thigh on me as he slept, holding me in his arms. I hardly closed my eyes for two nights, the hours swelling in delight, becoming playthings. Perhaps, I thought, this will continue. The book toppled on the floor and didn't get opened.

I'd been determined when my demented father finally died his lingering death to find love, an anchoring love, as he'd always put it. Diana had been his. So I'd left the river, and worked in a city job filing and scanning dull documents, in a grey air-conditioned office smelling of white plastic machines. I felt like those machines, waiting for someone to bring me to life. Suddenly there were crowds of people all around me but I didn't know how to be with them, and no one knew or cared how to be with me. Every time I went to the tearoom, people much more senior than me came in, whispering confidences to their friends, and oblivious of me, because I was too unimportant to be visible. I'd hurry out, my teacup slopping in humiliation. From that moment on I swore a lifetime of revenge on people who made me feel invisible.

I'd eat home-made lunches in a meagre triangle of a park outside the office block, sitting on a bench on a green lawn with meticulously clipped edges, and chewing carefully in case something about my sandwiches might betray me. If work colleagues strolled by, I'd take another bite and seem to consider some weighty, knotty problem that demanded solitude and a furrowed brow. In fact, I'd learned over the time I'd been alone, which sometimes seemed forever, to protect my solitude even while it shamed me, so that if a colleague did shout Hi, I'd only nod, because what if, after all this yearning, the colleague found I had nothing to say? Sometimes I wondered if there was a medical condition where people had no words inside their heads.

On the way home, I shopped for little packets of food in a supermarket where no one spoke to anyone else because it was assumed everyone was hurrying away to their families. I walked home with my head bent, too, so anyone would think I had a lover there, like a light unfurling down a tunnel – that was how I imagined the man, it was always a man, waiting for me. He'd have pulled on a sweater, something in soft grey wool with carelessly bunched sleeves and his cuffs undone, he'd be padding about in my apartment in his socks, and tapping long fingers on my dining room table as he gazed out the window watching for me at the traffic lights. Sometimes as I hurried I would begin to believe he really was there, this man with a listening face, head bent to mine as he considered what I said, and afterwards we'd make love, true love. But the shadowed stillness of the lonely apartment would always rush up at me like a resentful yapping dog when I opened the front door.

Yet I had company of a sort. The walls of my apartment were so thin that I knew all about my neighbours. I knew when they awoke in the morning because I could hear their alarm clocks, and I knew the exact ripples and explosions of their snores, and the exact time of their shaving because of the chinks of shaving mugs on bathroom benches, and the exact pitch of joy and pain when they made love. When I first moved in, I forced myself to say hello once a week in the lift to a stranger, since everyone stood so close, but every time my shy voice had been drowned in the lift's asthmatic creaks and sighs, for all the world like the old kangaroos back home when drought forced them down to our place.

I became a flirt, in the deliberate, industrious way that thin, awkward women must who haven't the breasts to do the work of searching for love. As a matter of course I flirted unflinchingly with every man I met. I'd flirt on my deathbed, I began to think. I'd flirt with the doctors, hoping one would fall in love with me. I'd even flirt with the angels if I was allowed. I knew that there was to be no flirting with God.

But flirting leads inexorably to sex. Even while the furry man slept, I counted the men I'd slept with, my fingers one by one tapping the silent sheet, like a child doing a difficult addition in the hope of impressing a teacher the next day, though who my teacher was, I wouldn't have been able to say. It seemed to me that a morally good person would remember the names or at least the faces of the men she'd slept with, and in what sequence their faces had hovered near to, usually above, her own. I remembered a thin muscular neck here with a gold necklace slipping on it, a wide-nostrilled nose there, but then the faces blurred. All I could remember clearly was my longing for transformation, and afterwards, when they left, an appalling loss. Remembering an exact number, at least, seemed proper, if not faces. But on one counting I remembered seventeen, on another, twenty-three.

It was a sort of counting of sheep, although I was a shepherd hoping to find out that her flock was small.

I wasn't quite sure if I had to include my husband in the count. He was the first man I'd slept with. I'd met him in a bar and got pregnant on our first night. He'd been excited at the prospect of having a child – a son, he was sure. He'd have someone to take to football games, he said. We married within a month, scarcely knowing each other. I took his name, eager to put an end to my childhood. Then I miscarried, and our marriage fell apart. It seemed he hadn't wanted me at all, just his child.

Eventually, I'd got as exhausted by sleeping with strangers as if I'd fallen out of a boat and had to swim to shore for years, not knowing how to call for rescue, not knowing if I had any right to be rescued, or if rescue was possible. I told no one, and there was no one to tell. I knew men would say, 'You must've had a good time,' and even in conjuring up this comment I blushed in the dark, because wasn't that why I'd had sex with so many men, seventeen or twenty-three, to have a good time? I should've had a good time. A proper person would have. But that was the trouble. Certain experiences leave you emptier than ever.

So I deliberately stopped flirting, and kept myself uneasily in check, resigning myself to waiting like an office machine.

Then I went for an interview for the job in the library. At least books would talk to me – some of them, at least.

And then E.E. Albert arrived in my life.

On the third night with the furry man, just when I was beginning to hope it'd last, he told me he was married.

'That hurts,' I said. I was embarrassed to admit it, for somehow, like my mother, I always felt in the wrong.

He turned his back.

We were in bed. I got up and showered, and cried under the rush of water. I didn't know how to matter to him; I'd never known how to matter to anyone. Some people are very good at mattering to others. Even if their only problem is being held up in traffic, they could make others weep for them.

I fell asleep from weeping, but when I awoke, I reached out for him. There was a long moment while I remembered why his space was cold. I hoped against hope that he'd just gone to the bathroom. But the front door was ajar, the street outside was wet and grey, a dismal drizzle was settling like a cloud over the garden, the front fence, the footpath, a drizzle that felt it had set in and would go on forever. At first I thought he'd stolen something, and panicked for days when I mislaid an earring, a new blouse, a screwdriver. After a few days the gap he'd left closed over, like paint does in a tin. Whatever he'd stolen, I couldn't name, and the unreadable library book remained unread.

I took it back and borrowed it a third time, then a fourth. That time, the librarian checking it out was a classmate of mine, in fact a man I often sat near to admire his handsome profile and muscular shoulders. He looked at my record of borrowing and asked, sardonically, 'This book's a favourite of yours?' I blushed with shame, from my toes to the roots of my hair, for my ineptitude.

In fact, the unreadable book convinced me I didn't belong in the university. When my classmates boasted that they'd got to the end of the reading list, I took to hiding in the toilets until the next lecture. Amongst the tinkling of the cisterns I had to admit I'd come to the university not to find out about the world, but to get again that warm delicious wave of excitement merely about me. It was like a small child's longing for home.

Chapter 2

When you put something off, when you say: 'I'll do it next week', then the week further on seems acceptable, and then the next week further on seems fine as well. But then suddenly you can't do it because you've left it too long. So I couldn't visit E.E. Albert.

One day, however, after the semester-end exams, I got an email message from her that broke this cycle: *Come to my room.*

I feared the worst. My time was up. Now she was going to find out that I wasn't interesting at all.

I even put off going for a few days until she wrote again: *Did you get my message?*

I knocked at the door, and she opened it, Dr Elizabeth Edna Albert. However, this time she looked almost like my E.E. Albert again, not a forbidding stranger in an academic gown, but a comfortable woman in street clothes – a long grey checked skirt that ended in girlish blue shoes, and a blue twinset whose cardigan hung almost to her knees.

'Sit down,' she said, indicating a chair on the other side of her desk in a friendly way. But from the way she leaned back and tucked her hands under her weighty breasts, I knew what was coming was serious. Then I noticed that her library wasn't at all friendly: around us books were crammed on shelves grimly, pushing against each other, not letting any others in, and a few orphaned books sprawled sideways on top of the others. There were also piles of books on the floor waiting to be auditioned, hoping to make it one day onto the shelves.

She came to the point immediately after we'd both enquired about each other's health. There'd been a notice on the board for weeks bearing a most unusual request: that the university send a woman student linguist to a desert Aboriginal settlement in the Northern Territory, to the hottest part of the country, at the hottest time of the year, in the long summer break, all to record the song of one old woman. Only a woman was permitted to hear the song, so only a woman could record it. The notice by now was hanging by one pin. No one had volunteered to go.

'So the task is yours.'

I heard my backpack flop to the floor.

'But I'm one of the worst students.'

She nodded. 'That's why.'

Her office didn't have proper air conditioning. It was summer and the heat in the air was almost liquid. I felt compelled to keep talking, so I wouldn't have to take her seriously.

'Summer in the desert?'

'That's why the other girls won't go. They're spending summer with their lovers at the beach.'

I'd have done that, too, in the old days.

The desert loomed in my mind as empty of hope and joy as the car park of a shopping mall after closing time. A giant car park, the size of Europe. A void at the centre of our country, at the centre of our heart, instead of what should've been there, which was a wide blue bottomless ocean busy with grand and important ships of commerce plying from one far shore to another, and little storybook sailing boats bouncing over it, and tiers of houses gazing over it. That's what it was like in proper countries, at their centres. My father had taught me it was something to be ashamed of, to belong to a country with a void at the centre, as if it revealed his own emptiness, and mine.

My voice came almost in a squeak. 'Why do they insist on living out there?'

She sighed, decided the question was foolish, and reached across the desk to a pile of papers. She pulled out a letter.

'The woman in question is dying. She might not last till the weather gets cooler.'

'But doesn't she know we're whites? Why would she want a white woman recording her? Couldn't she teach a daughter or someone?'

'There may be cultural reasons why she can't.'

It wasn't only E.E. Albert, it was the river I couldn't leave, though I no longer lived beside it. And not for an empty desert.

'Her daughter might have always refused to learn it. The song might have been handed down through the father's line, so only her brothers' children were allowed to learn it. Of course, there might not be a daughter at all. There might be only sons. Or nobody.'

Curiously, her voice broke then, and she cleared her throat. I should've noticed that, and adjusted my ideas, especially about the ready availability of love for the big-breasted. I only thought about it in the months afterwards, the way she cleared her throat as if some strong feeling was obstructing her voice.

'But shouldn't you send someone who speaks her language?' I asked.

'It's an endangered language,' she said. 'There are only a few hundred speakers. It's true that whites have known their language for decades; an American linguist went there in the 1920s and learned it but kept his notes in his attic for twenty years; someone else went out in the 1940s and said –' here she struck a pose to amuse me, '"It has all the marks of Divine Origin."'

We both laughed. My laughter was a little too loud.

'Even the CIA's been out there to see if it would be useful for a code,' she added, and we laughed again. 'Can you imagine? A language without our technology and hardly any abstract nouns!' The very idea of the CIA's misconception sent us both into hysterics.

She seemed worried about our laughter, and got up and shut the door. Her academic gown flew out from its hook where it had been hanging, like the flurrying wings of a great bird, to remind me of her authority over my life, and then it settled down again to rest.

She sat and leaned closer to me.

'You're in trouble,' she said. There was a low intensity about her voice that made my heart thump with guilt. I hadn't expected guilt. After all, I reminded myself, it was only me I was letting down. I wasn't letting her down. She must've read my mind.

'Your marks don't look good,' she said in the same low, deep voice. 'Your essays are shoddy. Your exam papers are half-hearted. You're heading for failure. I championed you because you seemed so full of promise, you seemed to intuitively understand so much – do you remember when we met?'

'Every day,' I breathed, her eyes on me.

'Did I misunderstand you completely?' she asked.

'No,' I breathed.

'Your entrance test, your marks weren't in the top band but I argued for you, I said: "This student is brilliant, she's unused to the exam system, she doesn't know how to present herself, let's give her a chance –"'

'I'm sorry –'

'The trouble is – in that gloomy little library, you listened, no, you astonished me with the way you listened, your eyes almost protruding from their sockets. Every teacher becomes foolish because of a dream; perhaps the same dream: that one day a student will come along who connects with what you say, more than that, whose life can start over again because of what you say, their potential which had been imprisoned till then can shoot up like a fountain into their life, the way it was meant to.'

She shot her hands up in the air and we both followed the imaginary sparkle of water thrusting up to the ceiling, which I noticed was stained and peeling from neglected leaks in the roof, as if she wasn't important to the university, after all.

'That's a teacher's hope, that what has inspired you might inspire someone else, your knowledge will become theirs, and the way you share this precious thing will waken them like –'

She laughed wryly, her lips twisting at one end, and she paused, searching for an analogy.

'Like the prince kissing the sleeping beauty?' I asked.

She laughed again. She seemed to do a lot of laughing, as if somewhere inside she was crying.

'No. Yes. All right. Yes, I'll admit it; I wanted to be the prince. Your prince,' she said. 'There you were, spending your employer's wages reading my book instead of whatever you were paid to do, a simple uneducated reader whiling away a dull afternoon, but you were hungry, weren't you?'

I didn't know whether to nod or not. I decided to nod.

'Starving,' I said, and then blushed because of the untruth.

'Do you remember, you wondered how to pass on knowledge if it's not written down and no one is ready to hear it? My book has caused much academic debate, oh, I'm not short of readers, I've lectured in great halls all over the world – but there I'd stumbled across a young woman standing on one leg in a suburban library, speculating on my ideas. This young woman reminded me of why I teach, of what's worthwhile.'

'I'm sorry,' I said again, wondering if indeed I had been starving, though for the new life that love might bring. Not knowledge. I'd never been very interested in knowledge.

There was a pause.

'Now I look like a sentimental fool,' she said. Sweat was pouring down her forehead, and I wasn't entirely sure she wasn't crying, the way she got out a crushed handkerchief festooned with green and yellow flowers, like an English teaset, unbundled it and mopped her cheeks.

'You're too important to be in trouble,' I said.

'Questions are being asked,' she said, her voice sinking to a whisper. 'Particularly by my Dean, who, incidentally, wants to use the data that the song might reveal.'

'What for?'

'His research. It might provide a missing link.'

I wasn't interested in his research. I'd seen him before, stalking hunch-backed in his black gown between the gold sandstone arches, absorbed in his thoughts.

'What questions are being asked –?'

She dashed her hand across the desk, pushing the letter towards me.

'My judgement,' she said. 'In paving your way. The place I insisted you have, that could've been given to someone else. So, live up to that promise I glimpsed in you. Show me, show everyone, I didn't make a mistake. Give the Dean what he wants. Agreed?'

I knew I was supposed to leave, but I didn't know how to. I couldn't say yes, I couldn't say no. I couldn't leave the coast. I couldn't go to a desert with no river, not a barren and lonely desert. But I couldn't resist the insistence in her eyes.

I tried to talk myself into it: if there really was something surprising in an ancient language I could help reveal to the world, then I'd be less ashamed of my country. My country would have something mystical at its heart, almost as good as the frescoes of Europe my father had coveted. I could put off my search for anchoring love until summer ended.

'We're told this song is known as the "Poor Thing" song,' she said, as if this could persuade me. I was startled back into attention.

'"Poor Thing?"' I repeated. 'Who's the poor thing?'

She ignored me. 'It's a very ancient song, said to be from the

Dreaming, so the Dean hopes it might have ancient grammar preserved in it. Like an extinct butterfly preserved in amber.'

At that moment, as if on cue, there was a peremptory banging on her door and before she could open it, the Dean popped his head around.

'I must have that report for the five o'clock meeting,' he said, speaking exclusively to her, and without excusing himself.

'Of course,' E.E. Albert assured him. 'We'll be finished here soon.'

His grip on the door was white-knuckled.

'Perhaps less laughter?' he said.

'Of course.' She nodded and smiled like a doll. He stared at her a long moment. She kept smiling.

'This is the student we're sending to the desert,' she said, to distract him from his stare.

'Fine,' he said. His eyes retreated but not to me.

He slammed the door on us, on me. I had been made invisible again.

His footsteps down the corridor were adamant. I kept wondering if he'd come back, apologise, say, I'm sorry, I wasn't thinking, how silly of me. But his footsteps said: How dare you waste her time in gales of laughter.

'But – for his research – won't he have to listen to the recording of the song, even though he's a man?' I asked.

'Of course! No! I'll help him, of course!' E.E. Albert amended quickly. 'There are protocols in place.'

I swallowed. I didn't want to go, and especially I didn't want to go for the Dean's research. It was the mention of grammar that tipped the balance. My notes in the grammar lectures were full of sleepy doodles, one more proof that I was a failure, not only in the university but in life. This woman in front of me was the only person who'd ever thought otherwise. I'd keep being a failure. It was my lot.

I can't go.

Say it, say it. Stop appeasing.

'I'm sorry, I can't go,' I murmured.

She didn't hear me, or she pretended she couldn't. She would make me speak my refusal clearly. So that then I'd feel guilty. I looked down, hoping the wood grain on her desk would help me to say it, admit to her that I couldn't do it, I was inadequate, I'd be found out, I'd be exposed as the uninteresting person I really was.

The air conditioning finally expired. Sweat was dripping down me, too, down my face onto my shirt. My sweat was rippling the letter that she'd pushed towards me; I gazed at those ripples. That's when my vision cleared. I saw where the request had come from. And from whom.

There are moments when you turn a corner, look in a particular direction, glimpse through a gap in a heavy velvet curtain, and in that moment everything turns on itself. My moment came with a crescendo of full-throated romantic music straight out of a Hollywood film. I couldn't think or see or reason. My reasoning was effaced by a thousand violins and several oboes and a French horn and somewhere a piano tinkling high up in the heavens. Then a banner floated across the screen. There was a single word on it: *Destiny*.

The letter was from a health clinic in the remote settlement of Gadaburumili. That name. I'd known that name almost as long as I'd known him. Of course it was the only place in the entire country he would've gone to – I'd often thought that. I'd ricocheted between certainty and uncertainty about it, and in the certain periods, I'd nursed fantasies of going after him. But what would I say when we met? And what if he didn't remember me? What if that childhood meant nothing to him? And if I meant nothing? So, year after year, I'd found a reason, many reasons, not to go.

And there was his signature – Adrian, though with a different surname. My silver-eyed boy on the river had been Ian. You could say that there was an Ian inside Adrian. It was all so inevitable that on one level, I wasn't even surprised.

You. I was always talking to you.

No one had been able to contact you for the funerals. I didn't inform anyone where I thought you could be, because no one asked me. Their deaths excited no interest, not even from my father. There was no one else to be interested, even the police. It was a common boating accident to them, two women who didn't know to slow down in the treacherous rips near the bridge pylon. Except that Diana knew everything about the river.

You might be Adrian of Gadaburumili.

I touched the signature that might be yours.

I must've gasped.

'He manages the clinic,' she said, indicating the signature, a surname that was unrecognisable, that he might've invented. 'No doubt he speaks the language.'

I found something to say. 'I thought the letter was from a linguist.'

'This Adrian –' she checked his surname, 'is writing on behalf of the linguist.'

*

Mother doesn't say she's going out on the boat with Diana until she's getting dressed.

I'm bewildered. 'On a boat-trip? With Diana?' My mother's intimidated by your mother, she always has been, I suppose because she reasons that her husband's mistress must be much more womanly than she is, and that's what my father wants, a woman to be a woman, and my mother, rather than being angry, feels she's in the wrong.

I expect the worst, no, not the worst – I expect that Diana is taking her out on the boat to abuse her, to tell her to give her lover back, that he should die in her arms, not my mother's. I should insist that my mother refuse to go.

It'd be easy to hold my mother back. I could run in to my father's room and beg him to call out to her from his sickbed, where his mind is dying. 'Don't leave me,' I could coach him to call – he's become a puppet to us, after we've been his – and my mother wouldn't leave his side. But I don't. Why don't I? I have my own plans. I want to be alone with you, after your years of absence. You've only just returned, a figure with a backpack, yesterday. After all, while they're out, while Diana is giving my unassuming mother a bad time, you'll be alone at your house. I want to plead with you to take me away with you – wherever you live. So I say nothing to my mother. I watch silently as Diana skilfully manoeuvres her new deep-keeled boat against our little jetty with scarcely a bump. She can do something that's impossible to do in our heavy old boat – she throws the steering so the stern slides compliantly into place.

Mother, who hasn't been on a boat since we got here all those years ago, lifts up her skirt and lumbers over the side. She's become almost as wide as she is high. She needs my hand to steady her, my traitorous hand.

'His pills in half an hour,' is all she says to me.

Perhaps those words tip the balance because Diana hears. Her mouth sets in a thin grimace that I later realise is hate. Hateful determination. How wise I am, afterwards. Still I say nothing, only wave goodbye, but they are gazing past each other at the river and neither of them waves back. They've scarcely turned the point when I untie our boat, motor to your house, pull over to your jetty. I clutch at the pylon and call.

'Ian. Ian.' No answer. I tie up. Still no answer. 'Ian. Ian.' Nothing. I climb up the cliff to the house, calling your name all the way. You don't answer my knock. Diana's left the door open, as she always does. My voice echoes through the rooms. You aren't in the living room, not in the bedroom, not in your sleep-out. Slowly, I have to admit it: you aren't here. I work it out: You must've left. You can't have gone visiting – you have no friends along the river, as we don't. We aren't respectable enough. The gossip's rife about Diana and my father, the condemnation of us all.

The sole possible explanation for your absence is that you left at dawn, as soon as the tide came in high enough. It was an unusually high tide that morning for our mudflats, a 1.98, how indelibly these details are inscribed on my mind – your mother must've quietly slipped her new deep-keeled boat off its mooring, the boat she was later to take my mother away in, slipped it out so quietly that only the ducks and pelicans heard – we were downriver and usually heard all the boats coming in and out – until you were far out in the open water. She'd have taken you to the station for the dawn train, returned, waited for the tide to turn, to become the dangerous running tide, and then come to pick up my mother. But why had you left so soon after your return?

*

I took a deep breath, came back to the shining desk, the impassioned eyes of E.E. Albert. It was essential to go to you at Gadaburumili. If it was you.

'Yes,' I breathed.

The film music was still sounding in my ears; your name was still pounding in my heart. I heard her words 'next week' and 'read'. It struck me that this all might be a plot, that she might know more about me than I'd realised, that she'd chosen me for this moment, that she was in cahoots with someone, maybe even with you. But all she was doing at that moment was jotting down a reading list, on and on, author after author, ripping off the page, handing it to me. I searched the page for Diana's name, for a message, for a clue. Her pen was sketching circles in the air as she considered out loud how her worst student must prepare herself – in a week.

'What reading have you done this year?'

I struggled to recover.

'Your book,' I said quickly. It was true that I'd read it several times, but only so I could imagine clever things to say to her about it.

'I suppose,' I said, struggling then to be the right person, the one who should be sent, now that I knew I must go and find you, 'you want me to form an opinion on why she is dying – if she's not all that old – why government money and health plans don't work.'

'Why would I want that?' she asked. 'That's sociology. Social work. Journalism.'

I blushed. I tried again: 'You want to know when this song is from? When exactly the Dreaming was?'

'What's that got to do with it? Goodness, young lady, we're not historians! If nothing else, this task will teach you to be a linguist.'

But my question lingered, and she added, in a fretting way: 'The Dreaming is in all their creation stories. Who knows its age? Some white scholars say 20,000 years, some say 60. The Aboriginal people would say that the song, like their stories, was given to them by the Ancestors. But it's only the grammar we're interested in.'

She put into my hand the page she'd written, and then took it back.

'There's something else you must do. The recording session mightn't go smoothly. Since the singer is old and sick, she might stop and start the song, or ask you to come back a couple of times. You might have to edit the recording and cut the parts together so they make sense the way you heard it. You'll have to edit it by the grammar. You won't understand the language, of course, but it'd be best if your recording could make grammatical sense by the time you send it back to us. Do you remember Toolbox?'

I tried to look as if memories were cascading through me.

She sighed. She wrote down a web address.

'It doesn't translate Djemiranga – it's not for translating, and anyway, it's for another language in the area, but it will help you figure out Djemiranga's grammar – that's the language of Gadaburumili.'

She added: 'I've realised why they asked us.'

'Because of me?' I asked, I almost shouted.

She was impatient enough to scoff. I blushed.

'You think an important linguist in the desert knows about your essay attempts?'

When I said nothing, she explained: 'Because of me. This linguist who approached us – I've spoken with him at conferences. He's internationally significant, Collin Collins, a Catholic missionary. You'd have noticed his journal articles on the reading list. You would've read how he's found an 1840 translation into Djemiranga of St John's gospel, done by a wandering remittance man, a poet, who built himself a hut and died there translating it – Collins found his bones still clasping the hand-written pages. He finds the differences startling between it and modern Djemiranga –'

She paused, gave up the thought, then went on.

'I suppose he remembered us because of the Dean's interest in Djemiranga, of course, but I've footnoted it as well, as you'd have noticed, and he would be aware of that. It's quite a feather in my cap – in our cap, of course, that he's asked for one of our students!'

I realised suddenly that she was preening herself, that she didn't have many opportunities to preen herself, despite being read all over the world. Despite her breasts.

31

'He's been out there for ten years,' she was continuing. 'He knows the language back to front. He's not allowed to listen to the song, of course, but he'll know which woman sings it. He'll be there all the way, helping you. He'll have to be out of the room during the time of the recording, and he won't be able to help you edit it.'

There seemed nothing more to be said. I wanted to be alone, to marvel at this sudden twist of fate in my tedious life. I got up.

'Oh – silly me! It might help you to know what grammatical point the Dean's particularly interested in,' she said, so ironically that shame flushed through me like a drink of water. Now that I would really be found out, I plopped down.

'It's called the travel affix,' she said.

'The travel affix!' I cried, nearly fainting with relief. I swallowed. Knowing about something at last was mottling my face with red, as if I was revealing my secret life.

She'd learned to be ready to make excuses for me. 'My lectures haven't covered it yet.'

So I spoke up.

'It's where a particular language – is it this one? – is uniquely careful about saying where the speaker is, the place an event happened – the way English is always concerned at showing exactly when things happen,' I burst out. 'So, for example, if the "Poor Thing" song was about me walking across a creek when a man suddenly appeared out of nowhere and tried to touch me –'

I was so excited to show her, I let my fingers walk over her desk, between her framed photos, and only then cursed myself for coming up with a sexual example – why did I always think of sex? 'I'd rush home to tell my mother, and on the way, as I went over in my mind what had happened, I'd use a particular affix – there's not one, there are at least a dozen of them – about exactly where I'd been in relation to him.' I stopped, I checked her face to see if she thought me cheeky because I was being too intimate with her desk, perhaps students shouldn't play with her photos, but she was watching my fingers so I picked the photos up and arranged them in a triangle.

'Then when I got home, because my orientation to him had changed, I'd use a different affix to describe where he and I had been standing when he touched me.' I stopped, checked her face again; it was still watching my fingers. So I rearranged the photos, this time in a circle. 'And if she told me to go and tell my grandmother about it, and my grandmother was over by her fire –' I moved the photos into a straight line, 'I'd have to use a third affix because my orientation to him had changed again. If then I was sent to tell her sister, who was gathering berries nearby, I'd have to use a fourth affix. I'd have a constantly changing map in my head as I described what the man had done, which I suppose any speaker in any language would have subconsciously, but this language is meticulous about it – it's so meticulous that in a car, a speaker wouldn't just say "move over" not even "move left", they'd say "move south-south-west", adding one of a dozen points on the compass. It's considered uncooperative or childish if you don't use it. It might've come about because they were always travelling in a vast and hostile place – you'd have to be meticulous about where you saw a goanna egg or a bird looking at a tree root for witchetty grubs.'

I took a breath and worried whether I'd remember the proper places for her photos.

'Sorry,' I said, blushing all over again.

But she was sitting back, beaming.

'That's one way to explain it,' she said.

'Am I looking for that?' I asked, pleased. 'You footnoted it in your book. I followed up some of your references.'

I didn't add that I'd been killing time in the library, hoping to catch the handsome man when he came on duty at the borrowings desk, which happened to be in sight of my desk. But

I got absorbed and forgot where I was until it was too late. By then he was chatting to a girl much prettier than me. But that didn't matter, because I'd given up sex.

'You're the student I thought you were,' she smiled.

Warmth bounced between us across her desk. Her approval was like a warm liquid poured right down into my body. I was almost panting with relief.

'I'll get this done,' I said, a little incoherent now that I was basking in her smile once more.

'I'm sure you will,' she said. 'I'll tell them you're coming, Kathryn.'

This with only the slightest inclination of her head towards a note on her desk of my name and student identification number.

'Could you call me Kate from now on, tell them that Kate is coming – Kathryn seems to belong to my childhood, to my old self, and I'm turning over a new leaf –' I was thinking ahead, thinking that perhaps I needed a disguise.

'Of course,' she said. She amended the record, and beamed at me.

'This mission will turn me into the perfect student,' I said. I could've sat there all day and all night basking in her smile, but she got up.

'Were you alone in your childhood?' she asked me. 'Is that how you developed your unusual mind?'

I didn't want to talk about that childhood. I was the only one left who remembered. Me, and, of course, you.

I couldn't help myself blurting: 'Can I ask – who chose me?'

'Haven't I made that clear? Me!'

The film music began again in my head. Chance had taken my life, and turned it around.

Far off across the quadrangle, the pealing of carillon bells argued with us all.

I took one last look at the framed photos on her desk, still awry, and pushed against each other. They were all taken in the inner city, and the only person in them was her. She was surrounded in all of them by well-fed cats, only very well-fed cats.

In preparation, first I had my long blonde hair cut – it had always been long, right from when Diana stopped cutting it, suddenly, as if I'd done something she disapproved of. I kept growing it, hoping she'd get exasperated and pick up her scissors like she'd done in the old days – but something was finished, something was broken. In the city, my long hair had become a veil, something to hide in. I looked down at my ropes of hair on the beauty salon floor.

'You needed that off!' said the hairdresser. 'Now you can start a new life.'

I had it coloured raven black, and my sandy eyebrows dyed to match. I had my fair freckled skin sprayed a golden brown.

'How long will the tan last?' I asked.

Her gaze at my nakedness wasn't flattering.

'Six weeks. Is that long enough to impress someone?'

'Plenty,' I said.

I bought black-framed spectacles with clear glass in them. I considered a prosthetic nose but feared I wouldn't be good enough at fitting it, not every day, every hot morning.

Then I rang the man I'd tried to read the textbook with, and asked in a voice I couldn't stop from trembling to meet me in the bar where we'd first met.

'But I'm back with my wife,' he said.

I sighed. I'd had one last vestige of hope, that he'd say he couldn't live a single day more without me – then I'd be able to refuse E.E. Albert's demands, and instead lie all summer on the beach with him.

'There's something I need to check with you. It'll only take ten minutes,' I said.

So I sat in the back of the bar with a newspaper folded up in front of my face as if I was short-sighted, and a drink beside me. When he appeared at the door, my heart leaped in the way it had before, but it seemed to go back to a different place inside my chest. He made a self-conscious, dramatic entrance, framed by the doorway, the light behind him, his elbows a little turned out from his body as if to allow for the width of his chest, which I reminded myself was fat, not muscle. I lowered the newspaper. He threw his long hair back and I watched his eyes travel over the bar, over me. He decided I wasn't there, bought the bartender a whisky, drank two himself, and left.

My disguise seemed excellent.

I also read. I downloaded Toolbox. At last, but too late, I became a student. I was suddenly able to concentrate as I hadn't all year, despite the fact that I was to be met in Alice Springs, the nearest town to the dying singer, by Adrian, head of the health clinic, and maybe my childhood love.

E.E. Albert made all the arrangements.

And so, in the Waterfront Café in the middle of the desert, I explained myself and my life to you for the thousandth time.

The sun had shifted. I stood, moved my chair, sat in the new shade. I was to be driven out to the settlement, find the old woman, get her trust, record her, and then go home, back to E.E. Albert's warm approval. It'd be easy, surely, just the effort of a few days, yet the university had sent me there for a whole month. I could only think that everyone was allowing for the unforeseen. Things can change in the desert, E.E. Albert had said, although she admitted that she'd never been there. She'd never got further than Alice Springs. Reading about it was enough, she'd said. She was a book person.

I didn't think the black women passing by would be speaking Djemiranga, the language I was heading towards, but mine would surely be a little like this, with family resemblances, as we linguists call it. (If I kept repeating that, I'd come to believe myself: 'we linguists', meaning myself and E.E. Albert.) Her friend, or perhaps it was her sister, could be asking her a question: I mimicked it, humming, Da-da-dum da. I was so engrossed in my humming that I didn't notice that one of the women had broken away from her group.

'Welcome to my land,' she said, her face wreathed in smiles.

'Your land,' I repeated, so startled that I thought like the city person I was, and so made my first embarrassing mistake. I looked around for which might be her land. I had no memory of passing a fence. There was only the annoying non-river in front of us, and a tarred road beyond, with a scattering of houses, and the inane squawking of chooks nearby as if they were trying to remember what was on their minds.

'Is it all yours?' I asked, eager to be friendly because it would take me away from my memories. These were the first real-life Aboriginal people I'd ever been near.

'My mob's land,' said the woman. She held out her hand and I took it, more a grab than a shake, and I captured it too long, so that the woman had to slide it out of my grasp.

'From up there,' she said, making a graceful gesture with her reclaimed hand, and her body bent in the gesture's direction, almost as if she was listening to it. Her skirt swayed around her bare calves as she bent. I noticed her bare toes, the way they gripped the ground, untroubled by twigs and small stones. It was as if she worked the entirety of her foot, whereas mine, always encased and hidden away in stiff shoes, could only have one purpose and that was to clamp me down.

'From the mountains?' I asked, suddenly aware that I had no idea how near or far any mountains might be. Perhaps the water ran underground, and swelled every now and then to the surface in small ponds. Why hadn't I looked at a map? That's what any proper scholar going to a remote community would've done; they would've looked at the lie of the land. Why was my mind always anywhere other than where it should be?

The woman didn't answer, but looked back over her shoulder to her group.

'Where does it end?' I asked. 'Your land?'

She gracefully gestured again, but in the opposite direction, anxiously this time.

'Thank you,' I said, realising that the conversation had run its course, like a waterless river. 'It's a beautiful river,' I lied.

She swayed in her intent walk as she headed to her group. The waiter arrived with my coffee. It slopped against the sides of the tiny white cup, and the grains looped like veils. The waiter plonked a menu down as well.

'The wife thought you might be hungry, after all,' he said. 'They only feed you rubbish on the planes. The eggs are from our own chooks.'

His lips opened lopsidedly, which gave him a confiding air.

I looked at the menu politely, though it was too hot to think of food. He was dressed in an old, shapeless yellow t-shirt and grey shorts fanning out in a star-burst of wrinkles from his crotch, but there was a starched white serviette over his arm. I imagined his wife ironing its sharp folds and arranging it just as he stepped out the door.

'Sugar? We only have it in little packets because of the flies.'

'No sugar, thanks,' I said.

He was glad of a chance for a chat, I could tell, the way he propped his bottom against the neighbouring table, which slid slightly under his weight, and he swayed but didn't topple. He gripped the table firmly with both hands. We both pretended not to notice this.

'We're starting a cabaret tonight under the stars, all you can drink,' he said. He leaned the upper half of his body forward.

'Nothing cultural.' He laughed and took a chance with his balance and my beliefs, holding up a hand and making a halt sign with it. 'We don't do cultural.'

'Culture's fine by me,' I said.

He laughed because he thought I'd misunderstood.

'I mean a particular sort of culture. We don't do that.' He paused, waiting for me to get his meaning. 'Are those people bothering you?' he asked.

The Aboriginal women had sat down in the dust at the perimeter of his café, which was marked out with rangy little potted bushes, and were chattering as they unrolled canvases covered with paintings.

'No, not at all. I'm fine.'

'Often tourists don't know how to take them.'

'Oh, I'm fine,' I repeated.

He took his folded serviette and ruined the impression his wife meant her ironing to give by wiping the sweat off his face.

'I can tell them to move on,' he offered.

'Oh, no, really, I was charmed –'

But he was turning and calling out: 'Eileen, get going. Off you go.'

He flapped his serviette towards the group as if he was swatting at flies.

'She's a little drunk,' he said loudly enough for her to hear. 'It's shocking, at this hour.'

'The lady said she's fine.' A voice suddenly boomed from the far table.

The waiter's serviette drooped.

'She's fine. They're fine,' repeated the blue-shirted man.

'I've got a café to run,' the waiter told him angrily. 'I can't have them scaring off my customers.'

Even from this distance, I saw that the man had silver eyes.

Chapter 3

For weeks after you left, for years after, I measured the date, even the time of day, against the last time I saw you. I grew up measuring it. 'It's ten days, it's fifteen days, it's a month, it's ten months since your voice, it's ten years. It's been one decade, it's been two, soon I'll be into the third.' There'd always been in my heart a quiet, sad anniversary.

'You're not Adrian?' I managed to produce the name.

'You're the one from the university?' the man called. 'Why didn't you say so before? I've been sitting around here, wasting my time and everyone else's –'

'I didn't – I wasn't sure – I'm sorry,' I said guiltily.

He came over and stood, towering above me, arms crossed. Tendrils of curls had escaped his ponytail and frilled around his high forehead like a curtain around a stage, just about to open on a performance. He was a tall stocky man who gave the impression of unbounded energy and unhesitating authority, the way he stood straight-backed, with strong square shoulders and a wide deep chest above his slender waist, his slim jeaned legs tucked into tough, heavy-duty boots scratched by desert life to the colour of bones.

The waiter left, his head ducked between his shoulders.

Surely this wasn't Ian. My Ian was always taller than me, but more slender, like a sapling that could fall over in a wind, not a man's man, a boy caught somewhere between a girl and a man. There was no girlishness about this man at all. He was almost a cowboy in the way he'd swaggered over to me. Had the years taught him to act like that? No, surely a swagger comes naturally. But he did have silver eyes.

I couldn't depend on silver eyes. Many people have silvery eyes; they're not unique to him. And – the thought almost attacked me, almost made me slump back into my chair – was it really Ian who had the silver eyes? Or were his silver eyes just the river reflected in him, and might he have had ordinary grey eyes, or even hazel, or anything other than silver? Or, worse, did the silver eyes belong to another man, one of the seventeen or – admit it – twenty-three I'd slept with? Had I superimposed another man's silver eyes on him, just as I'd always tried to superimpose him on all men – my thin man-boy standing skinny-legged on the jetty, the river moving beneath him, taking him away from me. We all have our own madness.

Perception's a strange thing, she'd said.

This man was the wrong man. I'd made yet another mistake. I'd come all the way into this heat for the wrong man. I'd accepted E.E. Albert's demands – and worse, the Dean's – for the sake of this stranger. But of course, I'd had no choice.

'I'm a busy man,' he was saying. 'You're lucky I even made it into town. Often I make arrangements to come in, and then there's a funeral out there, or a death, or a crisis, so I can't. I've been promising to cook dinner for a friend here in town for a year and I keep cancelling it.'

'I'm sorry I didn't speak,' I repeated, confused by his eyes and the heat. 'Can I order you a tea? A coffee? I might have another one,' I said.

'Never touch the stuff,' he said.

He turned at a noise and caught the waiter standing at his doorway flapping his serviette at the women again.

'Has it occurred to you that a visitor might want to talk to them?' shouted the silver-eyed man who might be my Ian to the waiter.

'Do you?' he demanded of me, eyes skewering me. 'Do you want to talk to them?'

Everything about him was burnished with indignation and energy – those eyes, his mobile face, even his freckled skin. His energy was infectious; it flared off his skin like smoke.

'Of course,' I said loudly, smiling, because I wanted to assure him we were on the same side.

'She wants to talk to them!' he shouted at the waiter. 'She's a language expert – what do you call yourself?'

He didn't wait for me.

'She speaks language,' he told the café owner. 'Will I call them over?' This to me: 'Then you can talk to them.'

'No,' I said. Something about his intensity and his eyes made me forget who I was.

'Why not?' he demanded.

'I can't,' I said. As he looked impatient, I added: 'I don't speak their language.'

He laughed with incredulity, and his laughter became high-pitched.

'But they told me they'd send a linguist!'

I was opening my mouth to explain, but he was interrupting again.

'I've brought in one of our mob with cataracts. There's a visiting specialist from Adelaide at the Alice Springs Hospital, but before he could do the operation, he had to test Brian's eyesight with the eye chart. But Brian's never been to school so he had no hope of reading an eye chart! When the doctor pointed to "L" and asked him which way the leg of the "L" goes, Brian didn't know what he was talking about! The hospital as usual had no translator for Djemiranga, so the specialist couldn't legally do the operation, and now I've got to take Brian home, still blind. It'll be three months before the specialist's back. So maybe you could translate! Maybe the doctor's still at the hospital! Maybe they could reschedule Brian for tomorrow, you never know! How do you say, "Which way does the leg of the 'L' go?"'

When I said nothing, he prompted again: 'What's the word for "leg"?'

I still paused.

'You won't help out a blind man?'

'I can't,' I said at last. 'I don't know how to say it. I don't even know the word for "leg". However, I do know how to say "not". As in "not this direction". You put the "not" in the middle of the verb,' I explained, pathetically relieved to at least know that much. I hoped it made me sound like I knew my stuff.

I made the sound of 'not' in Djemiranga.

He was unimpressed.

'I can't believe it!' he scoffed. 'You'd learn parts of the body first off, wouldn't you?'

'Language isn't just a list of words,' I said.

'Isn't that what linguists do? Talk in a language's words?'

His voice was ringing with suspicion. Then his high-pitched laugh of incredulity came again. My Ian never laughed like that, or never at me. He never laughed at me. Only sometimes. Some moments make the certainties of the past, the ones you depend on, sway like weed under water, so that you can't quite touch their strands. You think, maybe it's there, no, maybe it's there …

Suddenly it was this that filled my mind, the way I was trying to impress you, the way I was always trying to impress you, claiming to have caught dozens of tiny crabs, claiming to have dashed to death hundreds of mosquitoes, claiming I'd rowed further than I actually could, anything to make you notice me. Hadn't that always been the way with me and men? Hadn't

I always been trying to impress them? I had to be the sexiest woman they'd ever seen, the most willing, the most compliant, anything but the most beautiful because Diana was that – and did it make me happy? Never. With you, in our childhood, I learned to be an appeaser.

'Linguists study languages,' I said. 'How they work.'

'But after all your study you only know "not"?'

And he repeated 'not', gesturing to the sky, and the ridiculous excuse for a river in front of the café. He mispronounced it, making it sound like 'onion'.

'Onion – onion – onion,' he mocked. Then he dropped into silence, and looked down, as if he was suddenly bored with me, so that all I could see of his eyes were his eyelids with their horizontal folds.

I must harden myself against him, I told myself, or I'd be lost in him. Something about the grandeur of his energy made my concerns puny.

'The reason is –' I took a breath so I could reproduce E.E. Albert adequately. With her firm, clear voice in my head, suddenly I was making sense of what I'd heard all semester but only then seemed to be taking in. 'People think in other languages in different ways from ours. It's not just a matter of swapping one word in your language for a word in another language.'

He was still looking down, his whole body contracted with impatience, as if at any moment he'd spring up much larger. Something about him – the energy flaring off his skin, my uncertainty, his mockery, the damned heat – he was one of those people who enticed – no, forced – people to perform, or he would draw away, leaving them crumpled, like a blanket thrown aside, less than human. I became nothing when he looked down, it was like the ocean sucking the tide out, the water rushing out across the mudflats, little black crabs poking out fearfully and scuttling into their neighbour's hole. When he'd left, that was how I'd felt, that was how I'd lived my life after him.

Whether they were Ian's eyes or not, I found myself prepared to do anything to make them rest again on me.

'It's like this,' I began. Now even the waiter was peering out through his window, listening. Suddenly, I – of all people! – felt I had to uphold linguists, especially E.E. Albert, though never the Dean. I put the palms of both hands together, though I wasn't sure Ian – if it was Ian – was watching me from his downcast silver eyes.

'European languages match each other, more or less, like this.'

I turned my hands sideways so he could see my matched palms fitting onto each other exactly. 'But for desert people, their experience doesn't match ours, and their language doesn't match ours. We call it mapping. The way languages map each other. The language of these people doesn't map ours.'

I let one palm slip down lower than the other, and was rewarded by his eyes following my hands.

'So, for instance,' I went on, encouraged, 'there isn't a word in their language for "democracy". It's a concept that doesn't match their way of thinking. You'd have to use a lot of words to try to explain it, and even then there'd be a lot of meaning lost.'

I let my palm slip further down.

'What's more, the words that do seem to match, why, even then a whole lot of other meanings and people and places crowd in.'

He looked up with that flash of silver I knew so well – didn't I?

'It's like the word "land",' he said. 'You misunderstood that woman when she said "my land".' You thought she was talking about owning real estate.'

So he had been listening! And it was true, how easily I'd been caught out, with such scant knowledge, so recently acquired. In linguistics, I was only a few pages ahead of him.

'That's true,' I said encouragingly.

'Language is a way of thinking!' he repeated, interested.

'Yes!' I said again, delighted with his interest and remembering what had first intrigued me about E.E. Albert's book. 'That's why I was sent here.'

He was gazing at me, and for a moment I allowed myself to believe that he'd been carried away by my words.

'I'm here to record the song – the "Poor Thing" song – because it might have fossilised inside it a –'

I wasn't up to it, I couldn't keep pretending I was. But his eyes were forcing me to keep going.

'Some grammar they used to use, they still use it, to specify exactly where they are if they're going anywhere –' I petered out because it didn't sound like the sort of thing that anyone in their right mind could possibly be interested in. I needed E.E. Albert beaming at me, I needed her, her desk, her photos, my fingers walking between her photos. I needed to explain about the creek and the man who touched me –

'So what's the poor thing?' he asked. 'Maybe it's their country. They worry over their country as if it's a relative.'

I didn't want to be deflected: after all, E.E. Albert hadn't been.

I tried again – this was my first test and I had to pass it.

'I'm looking for the remains of the most ancient form of their language, to see if it's stayed the same or if it's changed, if it was once, say, a language only women could use, or if it reveals a particular thing they did, or even its antiquity …'

He wasn't looking at me. He was no longer interested. His energy had left me. I wound down. I made one last try to impress him.

'There seem to be five patterns for other world languages, and the song might show if Djemiranga conforms to them. After all, our own ancestors might have spoken in the same way when we were hunter-gatherers. The song might tell us who we once were,' I said. 'The way we used to think.'

But wafts of doubt were coming over me, as if doubt was part and parcel of being near this man. I felt absurd, vainglorious, to be struggling to impress a man who wasn't my Ian, after all.

'So you're of no use to us,' he said.

'Use?' My voice was a cry.

He shrugged.

'Academics are worse than useless.'

Then it's lucky I'm not a proper one, I wanted to assure him, but I didn't have time before he said: 'We've got to leave town soon.' He was changing the subject, as if all I'd said was completely irrelevant. 'I've got a troopie full of patients anxious to get home.'

'Sorry, I –'

'Let's get going.'

He glanced at my bag.

'Have you brought food for your month? No? You'd better go and buy yourself a boxful of food. There's a shop out there in the settlement, only one, and it won't stock fancy food, the sort you'd want. Spices, sauces. Your globalised cuisine.'

This he almost spat out, as if he'd turned his back on the globalised world.

As I reached for my belongings, he said: 'Don't worry about your bag.' He'd grabbed its handle. 'I'll load it on the troop carrier. And that little bag as well.'

'Is it you who's taking me out to the settlement?' I asked.

'Who else? There's no bus. No train.'

'How do people out there get in and out?'

'Their car – if it's working. Usually it isn't. They have old bombs, at best. Most of the time, there's only me.'

He grabbed the handles of my workbag and threw it effortlessly over his shoulder.

'The supermarket's down there,' he said. He waved his hand in the direction I was to go. 'I'll meet you in front on the footpath in one hour. I brought in patients from the settlement this morning, early, in the troopie – it doubles up as an ambulance. Many of them are sick. They need to get back home. They won't want to wait around for you.'

'Of course not,' I said. 'I'll be there. In one hour.'

He began to wheel my suitcase, and in that act he became a gentleman, suddenly deferential, it was as if he was the student trying to please his teacher by carrying her books. The switch confused me, as if his acting a part now, the part of a gentleman, made him alter inside.

But he was pointing to a large jeep parked nearby, its once-cream duco barely showing through a powdering of dust so that the duco was pink and orange, with yellow ochre forged by the wind into the shape of waves. I was to wonder about this again and again: that so much of the desert reminded me, ironically, of the sea.

'That's our troopie. If I have time, I'll join you in the supermarket.'

He downcast his eyes again, and when he looked up, his thoughts had returned to me.

'I know I told your boss that Collin Collins would be there, but it's turned out he's had to visit his family in Perth.'

Alarmed, I stopped walking.

'He's not out there? But I was assured he would be!' I cried out.

It was my turn to be agitated. Collins was the reason that E.E. Albert believed I could do the work. If he wasn't here, I might not be able to. In fact, I would barely know where to start. I'd have to go back with nothing. And that would ruin everything.

Adrian kept walking.

'He'll be back soon. Soonish,' he threw over his shoulder. 'He had family to attend to. It's the way out here. Everything is provisional. Not like your city timetables.'

By now, he was ahead of me. I almost stumbled in my distress.

'Collins was going to explain all sorts of things,' I said. 'For a start, do you know which old woman sings the song?'

'What song?'

'The one you invited me here to record!'

'Lots of ladies sing, don't worry,' he said.

'But there's one old lady who's dying! The only one who knows this song. Your letter said so. You signed the letter!'

'Collins was humbugged by the relatives about it and he humbugged me. To get them all off my back, I signed it. But to tell the truth, the women are quite healthy. Because of my work.'

He saw my face.

'Don't worry, Collins will come back, sooner or later.'

'But I only have a month.'

'I said, "soon".'

I tried to calm down. Adrian, who was too self-engrossed to be my Ian, walked beside me. Though he said he was a busy man, he came with me all the way to the supermarket.

'You seemed a little lost,' he said in explanation.

'I'm getting over your news,' I said. I was ruing my time as a student, ruing how I didn't spend the hours working that I should have, didn't read the books that would've paved my way, a pathway of stepping stones. The books I'd ignored were lining up in the bookshelf of my mind, spine out, thin, upright and accusing. I didn't learn enough about Aboriginal languages, I hadn't found out if there were experts in Alice Springs who could give me advice – I'd been too busy worrying about what I looked like.

But we'd arrived at the supermarket. He stopped in front of two young black women with beautiful, deeply set eyes, high cheekbones and glossy skin. They were holding babies in their arms, and speaking what I assumed was Djemiranga. They fell silent as soon as they saw him.

'You can shop, but only for an hour,' he told them.

He showed them on his watch.

'An hour, then you are here. Understand? An hour,' he repeated. 'Here.'

He was pointing down at the very bit of cement footpath we all must stand on in one hour. He pointed so fiercely that I glanced at my watch anxiously, and checked exactly what square of cement we were to stand on, and looked for help at the shop window nearby, and memorised its display of cherry-flavoured cough mixtures. I said to myself like a child: I must stand exactly in front of the cough mixtures. The young women nodded obediently, but I noticed even then they didn't wear watches. However, I would keep assiduously to his timetable, and be standing near the cough mixtures in one hour, however provisional things were.

He walked off, back to the troopie emblazoned with the ocean-like desert. He was one of those men with a high, rounded bottom so his tight jeans stretched flauntingly across it, and his wide chest and shoulders sat upright and strong on his hips. He didn't look back at any of us. I wondered how he could bear not to peek, to see our admiration.

In the supermarket, I worked it out: I could leave, for that man clearly wasn't my Ian; or I could make the best of a bad situation until Collin Collins turned up – and hope that he would come. Then I thought of E.E. Albert, and the warm feeling crept over me; I was in thrall to that feeling. I must keep her thinking I was an interesting person.

Meanwhile I was pulling goods down from shelves unthinkingly. Then I rebuked myself. I must be prepared for whatever happened, I must not daydream, and at the moment that meant I must put all my attention into my choice of oil, pasta, spices and vegetables.

He was suddenly beside me, eyes flashing angrily.

'They're all outside waiting for you.'

'You said an hour! It's only –' I consulted my watch, 'fifteen minutes!'

'I told you, here, everything's provisional.'

He grabbed my cart and pushed it through the aisle in a speedy, muscular way as if he was in a wheelbarrow race and determined to win. With his eyes on my shopping, I selected healthy toothpaste, unperfumed soap and whole-grain cereal self-consciously and then ran to catch up with him. In case he was the boy of a quarter of a century ago, I wanted his approval.

'They're eating dinner,' he said, amused at my contrition. 'I've parked out the front and bought them Kentucky Fried Chicken.'

When he held up a bottle of balsamic vinegar, I tried to judge his expression. Should I want it, or not? We might as well be children again. Does he want me to throw this fish that's too small back into the river? Though of course, he wasn't Ian.

'Yes,' I said, though I could have just as easily said no.

'How long is our journey out there?' I asked, walking fast but always behind him. Would I always be stumbling behind him?

'We drive up the highway, and turn left,' he threw at me over his shoulder. 'Back towards where you've flown from. The tar's fast, the rest is slow. There's been rain and the roads are bad.'

'So how long?'

'Seven hours if we're lucky.'

He made time to greet acquaintances, looking down during conversations, and I wondered if the looking down was a deliberate mannerism, or if he was shy. There was a sweetness about the way he looked down and then his eyes came looping up to rest on mine for a little, then further beyond my shoulder. The Ian of my memory was never shy.

Or was he?

Perception's a strange thing.

'You've done a unique job,' I heard him say twice, but to different people, one near the meat section, another far away near the vegetables.

I hoped they'd done different jobs.

He came across another acquaintance, a dark-haired, open-faced woman with a Spanish accent, a marvellous artist he told me as he introduced us. She greeted me politely but turned away to say to him in an intense voice: 'Eduardo is leaving me in a few days. Will you come in to his farewell lunch?'

'Of course.' He took her hand. 'You poor thing. Are you all right?'

She tipped her head in a pleading way.

'I'll get through it if my friends help me.'

He pressed her arm. 'Whatever's happening out there, this time I'll definitely come in.'

He was introducing me – the linguist from the university who doesn't speak the language, isn't that funny! – and I was shaking hands with her, belittled by his description but trying for a confident air. Then words dried in my mouth.

I was staring at his hand on her arm, his fingers so long and slender, even his fingernails that seemed the fingernails of a woman, just as Ian's used to. His pointing finger was scarred.

*

You save my boat, against the huge waves my slow-sliding river has suddenly become, but your hand catches in my rope, your hand is suddenly not a hand at all but a red mess of blood, you're squealing in pain and your hand's a red pool.

*

'You had an accident?' I asked. 'Your finger?'

They both looked startled. He examined his hand.

'I had a rollover in a troopie, happened on our treacherous road, but I only needed stitches.'

We were all gazing at Ian's finger.

'You were lucky,' I said lamely.

'Yes,' he said.

I held onto the handle of the shopping trolley for support.

He disappeared when I waited in the checkout queue, but I made sure I was standing outside near the display of cough mixtures, still within his hour.

He drove up exactly on time with a troop carrier full of black people sitting sideways on the seats in the back, and two in the cabin with him, and medical equipment in boxes strapped to the top along with boxes of food – and there was my suitcase and my workbag. I worried that the people in the troopie would be like him, all expecting a linguist to speak Djemiranga, and then there was a new worry – what was I going to say to them on the seven-hour trip across the desert?

But at least I'd be able to listen to the sounds of their language.

Adrian – I had to start thinking of him as Adrian – jumped out of the troopie cabin and came towards me.

'Where are the girls?' he demanded.

'What girls?'

He groaned. 'Haven't you been with them?'

'No.'

I looked up and down the street, but it was empty.

'Have they been here, and gone?' he asked.

'I don't know,' I said, ashamed that all I'd been concentrating on was him. For years, it was him I'd been concentrating on.

He sighed, because I'd failed to be useful again, and strode around to the back of the troopie, flinging open the door.

'You'd better get in.'

I peered into the gloom, into an unexpected smell of cooking smoke and fat and fried chicken. He pushed my box of food in between people's legs. There was a lot of wriggling to make space for me. Once I was in, we were as tightly crammed as the books in E.E. Albert's bookcase. No one greeted me. I expected Adrian to introduce me, but no one spoke, neither him, nor the passengers. One of the women smiled at me, but everyone else looked down. They didn't seem to notice me. Next to me was a mother with a runny-nosed child on her lap. And so I made my next mistake. I assumed it would be embarrassing for her to have a child with an unwiped nose in front of all these people, looking just like the pictures of Aborigines on TV of people sitting in the dirt, with never a chair in sight, and children with unwiped noses. I fossicked in my handbag for a clean tissue. But when I held it out, she didn't seem to notice. Perhaps, I thought, she didn't approve of tissues, perhaps she used cloth handkerchiefs, much more environmentally sound – but I couldn't help her there, I didn't have a cloth handkerchief – and perhaps she didn't even know what a tissue was – so in the air, I dabbed the tissue under two imaginary little nostrils. Still no response. All the adult faces were impassive, their eyes downcast. Only the eyes of the children followed me, large, brown and somewhat alarmed. Only then did I notice that all the little children had streaming noses. I poked the tissue up my sleeve as if that was what I'd intended all along, despite my ridiculous sketches in the air, and glanced up to see Adrian in the mirror, laughing at me. I looked away, feeling chastened, but bewildered.

He'll be thinking, the linguist from the city, she knows nothing! Later he was to work into a conversation that his doctors said that the mob seldom have colds, and suspected that the practice of not wiping babies' noses was useful.

Adrian drove around the town looking for the young women, so I got to see Alice Springs again and again, its glinting rows of shop windows like those in any other small city, its diesel-stained bus interchange with tired white people holding plastic bags bulging with sticks of celery and toilet rolls, its cafés with scatterings of always white coffee-drinkers under canvas umbrellas that attempted to look like Paris. I realised that we kept returning to the window with its display of cough mixtures.

By then darkness was settling in and the streetlights were glowing, casting shadows on places that before had been laid out for the sun's inspection and now were becoming secret, turning in on themselves, becoming sinister.

'We go?' he asked all the passengers, gesturing north. A few replied in English, 'Yes!' but the other replies were in Djemiranga. The English 'yeses' became louder.

Shouldn't we wait for the girls? I wanted to say, but I didn't want to make another mistake.

We drove out of town, and within five minutes we'd passed a petrol station with a large sign warning that it was the last before the desert. The streetlights petered out, and the vast stretch of sand and the night took over. Everyone gazed out the windows, and I wondered whatever they could be seeing. Sometimes they pointed out dark shapes to each other but it all just looked like undifferentiated scrub to me. The moon was full and speeding beside us, quite low, just clearing the tips of the scrub. There were half a dozen children on board, all plump and complacent, and none of them crying. I was to wonder at how calm they were, again and again.

And then we must've left the tar, for we were driving on a dirt road across the desert. I thought of it not as theirs, but as E.E. Albert's desert, for it was her book which first made me imagine that dry, dry land. Somewhere on that first journey there was a bump, and a cry went up from all the people on board as the drench of headlights picked up a kangaroo bounding away, its backbone a row of small white knuckles. I wondered if the words I heard meant 'Chase it!' for suddenly Adrian turned the troopie around to search the road, but the animal was bounding off into the endless darkness.

'Let's get it!' he shouted, and we lurched off the road, up a bank, and raced over what seemed to be an endless plain, mowing down thin young saplings that dared to rear up in the white glare from the headlights and dashing over humps of long grasses and bumping over hillocks, with the red ground leaping up to meet us and falling away under our speed, and the women around me in the back of the troopie bumping in their seats and trying to shield their children's heads from hitting the roof, and the men in the front shouting excitedly and gesticulating directions. I wished I could get out my recorder, but it was on the roof.

'We've lost him,' Adrian called out and slowed down and did a sharp U-turn to a murmur of disappointment. Something in our load loosened its ties and toppled in the speed of the turn and spilled out on the plain. Adrian braked and leaped out, but not like any other person might: he held onto either side of the door frame, bundled his legs up beneath him and, all balled up, jumped out, suddenly a schoolboy dive-bombing his mates in a council swimming pool on a steaming summer's day. He hit the hard ground with a thud which didn't seem to deter him, and bounded off.

In the glow of the headlights, I realised it was my workbag that had fallen, and panic grabbed me. My photos were in it, my photos that my last-minute reading said I should bring with me, so I could prompt conversation with people, so I could say, 'Look, this is my country.' So that they would talk about theirs and, hopefully, that would lead me to the singer. But the photos were of the river, and if this man was the Ian of my childhood, that was his country too – he could so easily recognise the photos of the river, our river!

But if he noticed, he didn't pause, and just pushed my papers and books back into the bag and zippered it up.

I must take more care, I must stop being careless, I told myself as I had a thousand times.

He swung up the ladder to secure my bag on the roof, and coming down he broke the quietness inside the troopie by calling out through a window: 'Five more hours, Kate, and Daniel will have made us a nice hot dinner.'

'Thanks,' I said, damp with relief, and moved by his concern for me. I promised myself as soon as we arrived, I'd hide those photos inside one of the books I'd brought – he'd never open them. I hadn't for months! And only show them to people when he was far away.

I didn't think then about what a maverick he'd become, charging off over the desert like that in an official car that no doubt came with all sorts of regulations about its use. All I thought about then was the promise of a nice hot dinner, and his melodious voice. I fell asleep, and dreamed the dream I was always dreaming.

You're bounding down the jetty, Diana's jetty.

'Look, something's on your line,' you're calling to me. Your voice is breaking as if you've got a cold, but that can't be right, you're never sick. Your silver eyes have the river light in them, the river just before the storm, just before the wild winds come and then rain explodes on our roof.

I look away from you and there's my river floating blue and silver beneath the jetty, just as it always does.

'You're daydreaming again! Go on, you've caught something, pull the line up.' You speak condescendingly because I'm younger than you, the years gape irretrievably between us. 'Don't you know anything? You're old enough to know when to pull up the line. Here, give it to me –'

But I don't hand it over. Instead, I'm fossicking for words for my deepest dread.

'Is Diana sick and not telling?' I ask.

There's no one else to ask. Only you.

You stay where you are, your arm in the air above me. It's as if the question has paralysed you. You don't reach over for my line. Time goes by. Fish jump around us. The line tugs and slackens. The river eagle swoops and skims on the mirror of the bay and brakes with a thrust of its body and a swish. Ducks sail by like toy boats.

'Pull up the fish,' you say at last.

'Why was she screaming last night?' I ask again. 'She did it last time I stayed as well. Did you hear?'

And I imitate her: 'Oh oh oh oh oh.'

'Shut up! They'll hear!'

'What's wrong with them hearing?' I cry. 'Is she going to die?'

Your voice is flat, you're staring at the river.

'They were –'

In your heated pause I suddenly know the answer, you're going to say the forbidden word, the forbidden thought, I can't bear what you're going to say, even the noise of the word as it comes out of your mouth. *Fucking.*

I can't bear it that you say it. Not you. It's a word that mustn't be spoken between us, a feeling that mustn't be noticed.

Before your face has turned towards me, I've thrown down the fishing reel and, despite my new pink shorts and striped t-shirt from Diana, I've dived into the river. I sink through green swirls lit by shafts of gold sunshine to the soft grey bottom of the river, my river, to the tiny fish and crabs, to the busy fish traffic that hurtles towards me and around me, as if I'm just a boulder in the way, and then my body shoots itself up to the surface and I don't look around until I'm halfway over the river and heading for the deep channel where the sharks swim. Only then do I pause mid-stroke. I look around. You're holding my reel. A silver fish is thrashing on my hook. You dislodge it, throw it back, and stalk down the jetty, away from me, always away from me, away, away.

Chapter 4

I woke up, still mouthing the word. *Fucking.* Perhaps I'd been saying it aloud. I often thought I'd been saying it on the mornings at home when I woke from dreams but there, it didn't matter. Now, three mothers in the troopie turned together towards me and smiled at me. I made my dry lips smile back.

Just as Ian – I must remember to call him Adrian (so many mistakes could betray my true identity) – had told me, there'd been rain recently in the desert, and in the headlights, the puddles on the red road reared up into the windscreen like an upside down drench of blood. The headlights picked out cattle, not kangaroos, not any more, and they moved reluctantly and sleepily at the sound of our horn. They were elegant, unhurried creatures, road-coloured, their exact outlines only clear when they moved aside and stood framed by the black bush.

At last a little township lit up the sky with orange neon, and I hoped we'd stop for a drink or chocolate or hot chips but there was to be no stopping. No one spoke to me, or to anyone else. I needn't have worried about how to make conversation. Another uncomfortable, cramped two hours and suddenly there was gravel spitting under the tyres, a windmill's silver blades glinting in the moonlight and there glowed a town with tarred streets and rows of houses and ordinary streetlights. I was so astonished I cried out: 'Where are we?' and dark sleepy faces turned to gaze at me. Someone said a word I couldn't catch, which I later realised was the way they pronounced Gadaburumili, nothing like the Anglicised way E.E Albert had pronounced it, which caused me some disquiet, but then she never claimed to speak Djemiranga, or any other language, she was a specialist only in Aboriginal affixes. Ian – no, Adrian – pulled up at an unexpectedly suburban house, bigger than the others, and said he'd bring in my bags when he'd delivered everyone, but for now, I was to go inside.

'My little bag?' I asked fearfully, but he nodded no, he wasn't going to hold up everyone while I fussed, he'd bring them both in at the same time.

My legs could barely straighten after the journey and, stumbling, I walked through a rusted gate, across a front yard of sand with no path, over a wide cement verandah, through an open front door, past a laundry and bathroom and down a hall that could be in a suburban house anywhere. Then the hall turned a corner and I was in a large open room crowded with two sofas that sagged so much they were like self-supporting blankets, several plastic fawn kitchen chairs, a large TV set, a music player, piles of videos and DVDs and a slow-combustion stove that must've seldom been lit because its top was piled with a jumble of car parts, and somebody had playfully put a stopped clock inside it amongst the hills of grey ashes. There were large, clear spaces of carpet with bundles of things in the corners, as if someone had begun tidying up but had lost heart and just shoved everything sideways. I saw a paddling pool, inflated but slowly caving in and empty of water, and inside it, jeans crumpled the way they were when the wearer stepped out of them – the leg holes upright like wells – and a pile of newly washed sheets dumped beside them. In another corner there was an ironing board that mustn't have been used recently for ironing because it was covered with a mess of old newspapers, paperclips spilling out of boxes, pens, rubber bands, pegs, car keys and a brown apple core. Over it all wafted the hot, salty, welcoming smell of roasting meat.

I didn't see a man sitting on a kitchen stool until he stood and moved towards me, hand outstretched.

'Oh – sorry – I didn't notice –'

'Have a good trip? It's long, isn't it!'

I had no words for the trip, except that it'd seemed endless.

'Do you know who I am?' I asked stupidly.

'You're Kate! I've been holding off dinner for you! Do you know who I am?' he asked.

He was short, with a large mop of wavy blond hair, a ruddy face with thick shiny black eyebrows so feathery they seemed sketched on with charcoal, and a wistful way of looking at me slowly and appraisingly before his large generous lips became a quiet, friendly smile: the slight delay made me feel as if he was examining me and approving of what he saw.

'A stockman?' I guessed.

He let go of my hand and laughed, in disappointment, I sensed, at my answer. I found I didn't want to disappoint this slow smiler; but this was not the man my heart had waited for all those years. I had to quash the profligate flirt in me.

'No, I just help Adrian,' he said. 'I'm Daniel.'

He laughed, and I was rescued from flirting by that laugh, a strange creaking sound uttered without amusement, that became by degrees an uncertain teenage boy's laugh rising like a question, though he must have been in his forties. A creaking-door laugh with a rise which made me uncertain – should I laugh as well? Confounded, I waited.

Then neither of us could think of a thing to say.

'What work brings you here?' he asked at last. His lips were so thick, they seemed to get in the way of his words.

'I'm looking for an old woman who knows an ancient song that only women are allowed to hear.'

'How ancient?' he asked, perhaps just to make conversation.

'From the Dreaming.'

He was immediately interested. When his smile broadened, his face was full of light.

'That's old!' he said. 'I used to look up hymns when I took my mother to church –' there was a note of sadness here, and I wondered if it was about the loss of the church, or of his mother, 'and I used to think Martin Luther's hymns were old. Then I found out there's a song from ancient Syria that dates from 5000 years ago. But a song from the Dreaming! That could be when they first settled here – you'd know all this of course,' he added politely, 'but archaeological evidence puts that at about 50,000 years ago –'

He saw my astonishment, and added, 'Or it could be when the watertable dried up and they left for a thousand years or so – that's more than 5000 years ago, going on current evidence – before the time of the Ancient Egyptians, and the evidence of course might change. Your song's probably from the more recent time, but it might be from the first occupation, which would be astounding. About the time when humans first used language, and danced, and did art. Either way, that's an old song.'

He laughed again. Creak. Creak.

I suddenly realised what he was saying.

'You mean – I might be looking for the oldest song in the world?'

'The oldest surviving song! That's quite a quest!' he said admiringly.

'It is, isn't it!' I said, feeling important in his eyes, as I hadn't in Adrian's. I glowed in that feeling. We beamed at each other, warmth bouncing between us. It came to me that I could understand the way he thought, that he was far more sympathetic to me than Adrian. I became annoyingly attracted to him, because in all this lonely desert it was him, not Adrian, who valued my quest.

The attraction forced me to admit: 'My university's not interested in its antiquity. Just its grammar.'

He nodded with understanding.

'Universities are like that,' he said, one end of his mouth turning down. It felt as if we were sharing a confidence about the absurdity of the world in general, and universities in particular. 'I did geology at university. What a disaster!'

His voice altered, and I could tell he was speaking from his heart.

'I drifted out to the Northern Territory with a mining company – after university it seemed a good idea – and then I got to hate the company and what it was doing to the land but I didn't know where to turn – and, to cut a long story short – at last I ended up here.'

'You probably know the singer,' I said.

I was immediately comfortable with him, as if I'd known him for years, with his feathery eyebrows and his full lips that seemed assessing and thoughtful, the way they bloomed and crinkled with his thoughts.

'I've never heard anything about this ancient song,' he said. 'Well – I wouldn't, would I, being only a man! But Adrian would know.'

'He must,' I said. 'He invited me. Well, Collins invited me, but Adrian signed the letter.'

'Adrian plays things close to his chest,' he said and looked away, embarrassed. I felt that something about the turn the conversation had taken was awkward for him. I didn't want to make him awkward with me.

'Would you like to see your room?' he asked, to change the subject.

He led me to a stark room with barely an object in it except a mattress on a double bed, a little stool, a table and chair and a big cupboard with a lower door and an upper section. There was a large window that seemed to face on to a street, judging by spots of light showing through the slats in a Venetian blind.

'I'll be able to sit here and work,' I said, more for something to say than any clear idea of just how I was going to go about my work.

'I'm very proud you're staying with us,' he said shyly.

When I looked surprised he said: 'Whites come out here with all sorts of silly projects, but they never honour the people's antiquity. Even if that's not exactly the university's aim.'

Now it was my turn to be shy. But all I said was: 'There's a lot of cupboard space for one person.'

Daniel nodded, but pointed to the upper cabinet.

'Don't open that door. Adrian's stuffed it full of papers,' he said. 'He's a bit of a hoarder. If they tumbled out, they could kill you. We wouldn't want your important mission to end up like that!'

I liked him saying we, as if he had a stake in it.

'What papers? Newspapers?' I asked.

'He cleaned up the place, and for once cleared his desk in the clinic – I think it was to impress you.'

We both laughed. I was relieved at his creaking-door laugh. I couldn't get a crush on someone with a laugh like that.

'I thought he'd sorted things out at last,' he continued. 'Then when I was looking for a report, he confessed he'd taken everything holus-bolus, wads of paper, and jammed it all up there.'

He mimed someone staggering under the weight of a toppling tower of paper and throwing it into a cupboard.

'Just like this!' Creak. Creak.

This time, I could laugh uproariously with him. There were almost tears in my eyes, to find I was so easy with him after the hours of tension with Adrian. I was revelling in his admiration of my mission. And he was comical, it was true. He repeated the action again, and we both doubled up in laughter. Then he stopped laughing.

'I'm not criticising him,' he added quickly, his charcoal eyebrows becoming a worried line wriggling across his forehead. 'He's my good friend. I wouldn't be here if he hadn't invited me when I left the mining company. It's just that the desert affects people in unexpected ways.'

He smiled in a self-deprecating way, his lips turned down.

'I'm sure it's doing funny things to me.'

As we walked back out into the corridor, Daniel pointed out his room. It was the only other bedroom.

I found myself staring at a messy room with a large, unmade double bed with red and navy blue sheets cascading onto the floor in what seemed to me a seductively masculine way. Out of the force of habit, I glanced at him, but there was nothing that suggested he was gauging me as a possible bedmate. However, I said, 'But there aren't any more rooms! Where does Adrian sleep?'

'Outside,' he answered.

He pointed out the window to a mattress on the sand, with white sheets glaring in the moonlight.

'You don't have enough room for me in this house! Why don't you put me up somewhere else?' I asked.

'There are only two other clinic houses, both full – well, not really, but Adrian didn't want you to share with his staff,' he said. He paused awkwardly again. 'To be explicit, there is a third house, but Adrian won't let anyone stay there. He wants everyone to know that it's empty because the government won't fund us a second doctor.'

'So in the meantime he makes do with a mattress on the ground.'

'He thinks the locals love him for it.'

'And do they?'

Adrian appeared at the door with my bag, my workbag slung on his shoulder.

'What's for dinner, Daniel?'

'There's trouble,' said Daniel. There was a crease of worry between his eyes, which I then saw were dark brown, almost black to match his eyebrows. 'But at least we have a roast in the oven.'

I heard Daniel tell him that the two girls left behind were nieces of a very powerful woman though she wasn't of these parts. They had rung ahead of us complaining to her that we'd left them behind. Graeme, a newly arrived great-grandson of Boney, one of the elders, had told Daniel that on behalf of the traditional owners of the settlement, Adrian was to be sacked.

Daniel reported all this rapidly.

'But no outsider speaks for everyone,' said Adrian quickly.

'He felt he could,' answered Daniel. 'No one contradicted him.'

'These bullies, they're always coming in from the cities and disrupting,' Adrian said to me. 'The people are so gentle, they're entirely vulnerable to bullying.'

'It won't be the first time,' agreed Daniel. 'But this bloke really means business.'

'But Skeleton likes me – he trusts me – he's told me, "Adrian, you're a good man".'

'His grandson's claiming you abandoned the girls,' said Daniel.

There was a pause.

'They weren't wearing watches,' I remembered. Both men glanced at me and looked away, as if I'd said something irrelevant.

'Where are the girls now?' asked Adrian. He hadn't put down my workbag. 'Silly girls. Scared of getting into trouble, so no doubt they lied. But everyone knew we arrived back late because we waited for them. Are they safe?'

Daniel said they were staying in town.

'Sleep now and we'll drive in at first light and bring them back,' Adrian told him. 'The mob always waits at my friend's,' he added, turning to me. 'The girls will be safe there.'

'What about the sacking?' asked Daniel.

Adrian said nothing, but turned to me again.

'Hotheads are always sacking,' he said.

'Graeme *is* an important relative,' Daniel reminded him, deferentially, but with such warning in his voice, it delicately brought into question Adrian's belief in how far Skeleton's love might go. Adrian breathed, stared at Daniel, then decided to ignore him.

'Is this hothead a medicine man?' I asked, wanting to be helpful again.

Both he and Daniel turned to gaze at me.

'Is he?' Daniel asked Adrian.

'The hothead – he might want these people to abandon your health clinic and go back to their traditional ways of health –' I began, but I wound down because of the angry silver flash of Adrian's eyes. The air conditioner seemed to change to a new note so that it sounded like an old-fashioned train hoot. But I was in the desert hundreds of kilometres from a train.

'Do they even believe in our medicine?' I asked.

I turned to Daniel for help. His beautiful eyebrows were in jagged lines. He laughed uncertainly. Creak. Creak.

'It's true that they don't seem to believe in the germ theory,' said Daniel to Adrian, as if he was pacifying him, so I realised that there'd been an ongoing argument about this.

'You'd need a microscope to believe in germs,' I said. 'It'd seem a fairy story otherwise, I suppose. Tiny creatures –'

Adrian interrupted. 'You're missing the point. They need our Western medicine. They're prone to terrible sicknesses, and our medicine works. He'd have sacked me not because of a belief about traditional medicine but because he wants the ambulance to go hunting.'

Daniel told him that people had been coming in to the clinic very anxious about what would happen. That seemed to cheer Adrian up.

'They'll soon see what's going to happen!' he said.

He turned to me.

'You have a nice warm bath and I'll make up your bed,' he said generously.

His ricocheting between sweetness and anger confused me, and I feared I'd be more appeasing than ever.

Ian was never like that – was he?

'You'd be tired too,' I said politely.

'We're used to it. We do the trip twice a week or more,' he said.

In the corner of my room, I didn't notice before that Adrian had left on the little stool a clean folded towel that smelled of sunshine, just like Diana used to do when I visited, even though she would've known that my mother had sent me to report on her, on her and my father. It crunched my heart, that little folded towel on a stool. He must be Ian, carrying that part of Diana with him all his life.

'To make you feel at home,' she'd say, not knowing my home, nor my mother. She'd never even met my mother until that fateful day. My father had always successfully kept them apart.

That little touch of Diana took me to the bathroom. I put my hand out to turn on the taps and found that they were partly eaten away by what seemed to be a white powder, the calcium from bore water. But in the welcoming stream of hot water, I realised I couldn't decide that he was my Ian because of a folded towel.

After dinner, Daniel began to clear the plates. I jumped up too. Daniel seemed to do housework as if he'd been born to it, so that

I could imagine him at university meticulously scrubbing bench tops down after he'd analysed ore samples. Something, not only about the height, but also the swagger of Adrian seemed too big for the kitchen. I'll please him by being like Snow White when she goes to live with the Seven Dwarves and helps keep house, I thought.

'I'll pop the dishes in the dishwasher,' I said.

'Dishwasher?' Adrian shrieked, and even Daniel laughed. Creak. Creak.

I blushed. Obviously these two bachelors didn't approve of such indulgent city appliances out here in the desert. But I couldn't stop myself from blundering on: 'Of course, it'd be hard to get a repair man to come all this way – what do the people do out here when their appliances break down?'

'Why don't you take her to see the settlement?' Daniel suggested to Adrian, searching in the silence for the sink plug, his face hidden.

'Now? It's so late!' I said.

I didn't want to disappoint them, but I longed to be in bed, where I couldn't make more mistakes.

'It's too hot to walk in the day,' Adrian said. 'Anyway, there mightn't be many more opportunities.'

'Will I go and get my phone?' I asked. 'For out there?'

'There's no coverage,' said Daniel. When he saw my horror, he added consolingly: 'Sometimes the landlines work.'

I heard Adrian groan derisively as his heavy boots stamped out the front door, but I lingered in Daniel's kind presence. In this shifting world, I needed kindness.

'So we all rely on landlines?'

'They,' this with the smallest indication of his head to his right, 'can't afford a landline. Only the whites.'

He flashed me a wry smile as the hot water tumbled into the sink.

'So don't get lost.'

Adrian headed away from the lit streets, walked between houses that he pointed out belonged to the clinic and the schoolteachers, and strode out ahead of me into the desert, a man busy with his worries.

In my exhaustion I didn't notice which way we were walking, and though I remembered I should carry a bottle of water, I didn't like to interrupt his momentum to run back for one.

We were in a flattened landscape, with only small rises, and I made out a huddle of hills, far off on the horizon. I ran to catch up to him.

A prickly bush burred against my bare ankles.

'What's that?' I asked.

'What?' he said, and to my surprise he stopped, pulled a torch out of his pocket and bent down to examine it, crouching, totally absorbed. I suddenly became paralysed with self-consciousness, now that the man I'd thought of day and night for decades was here, beside me, attending to me, or at least bending to examine a plant for me. I didn't know whether to crouch like him or to stay upright. Squatting would bring our heads close together, and that might seem too intimate. Besides, I was fighting back tears which I didn't want him to see. After all my yearning, I had him to myself, here we were together in a vast desert. There was no Diana, no father, no mother to distract. There was only him and me. I had never felt so attended to, not by anyone. No one, in my whole life, had stopped the momentum of theirs, just for me.

I must do nothing wrong.

And now there was another, more disturbing matter. I had a problem inside my chest. My heart seemed to take on a life of its own; it seemed to lift from its normal place and move across my chest like a boat loosing itself from its anchorage and fleeing on a running tide towards the ocean. My heart had never behaved like this before. Then it seemed to float back, to its resting place.

71

As I dithered between bending and standing, my heart took off again; my boat-heart flew again across the lake of my chest.

I half-bent, I half-straightened. I dithered, as my father had dithered all his life, except when he'd made the fateful decision to die in my mother's arms, not in Diana's. Finally, I bent – just at the moment when he straightened. There was a loud crack. We both reeled. We'd bumped heads.

'Idiot!' he yelled.

'Sorry,' I said, as the pain eased, and glad that the night hid my blushing.

He was clutching his head.

'Sorry,' I said again. In his pain, he'd dropped the plant as well as the torch and now he had to scrabble in the dust. I didn't dare join him, for fear we'd crack heads again. He finally found the plant and the torch and held the plant out to me like a bouquet, red soil clinging to its roots. His voice had recovered.

'When you come across plants like this, give them a wide berth.'

I was almost panting. He turned and began walking. Again, I ran a little to catch up with him. After a while, we were walking in step. I changed feet, but I wanted our walking never to stop, though I couldn't think of a thing to say.

I tried to reason with myself. The heart does not take flight across the body. It's tethered firmly like a boat to a jetty, even a boat in a strong wind, by muscles, bones, tissue. All that had happened was a visitation of my usual lust. I'd already taken too much notice of lust. And as for him, he probably gave that intense concentration to everything; probably he peeled an orange in the same engrossed way so that as he moved the knife, the whole world fell away from his awareness, and all he saw was the steel cutting into the orange skin.

I trudged behind him, my feet unsure. After the rattling of the troopie for hours I wanted the peace of the desert but now he insisted on talking about the stars, telling me their Djemiranga names, but they sounded like odd English words, and I suspected he was mispronouncing them – even making them up.

'Which direction are we heading?' He wheeled around to quiz me. I found one of my feet sinking on uneven ground. 'City people never know. You have to be able to work it out, in case you're by yourself.'

'I wouldn't dream of going by myself into the desert –' I began, but he was pointing to the sky, telling me how to find the South Pole by drawing a line from the centre of the Southern Cross to a rock fifty metres away. Straight afterwards, he tested me.

'So, which way are we heading?'

My eyes clawed at the sky. I wanted to pass any test he set.

'I don't want you to get lost,' he explained, and it came out of his mouth with such sweetness that my heart fluttered dangerously again.

I found his previous explanation tucked away in my tired brain.

'You draw a straight line down to earth from the Southern Cross,' I recalled. 'I'm to drop my eyes on a vertical to that rock over there,' I said.

But no, that was wrong, he told me I should've advanced the vertical from a point between those two stars, and that would mean south was that way, or perhaps it was north.

'You'd get lost in the ocean,' he said warningly, as if at this moment I was just setting out to go to sea.

'I come from a city.' I told him that lie.

Remember how we never steer the boats on our river by north and south? When we take our boats out at night, only in summer is there enough light in the evenings to see to steer by. In autumn, winter and spring we steer not by north and south, and not by the stars, for ambient city lights drown them out, but by the shapes of the mountains against the sky. Diana shows us that, remember, when I am only six or seven, and you are thirteen or so. Diana shows us that this mountain is like a camel's back, that one like breasts and, I secretly think, like her eager breasts, not the drooping, woebegone breasts of my own mother. So when I feel my way through the water in my boat, I don't need eyes, it's like feeling my own body under the sheets, as I sometimes do deep in the night when waking from a dream, yes, here's my heart, yes, here's my thigh. Because of Diana, our river is my body.

We walked on. I was careful not to step in time with him, in case it prompted more heart flutters. I mulled over his sacking, worrying that it might have implications for my mission.

'What's an elder doing with a name like Skeleton?' I asked. 'Isn't that disrespectful, to call him by a nickname?'

'It's not his real name,' said Adrian. 'Here, people belong to a skin group and have at least one bush name, and that's private, so whites would never know it, and if they do, they mustn't pass on the knowledge or the spirits will punish them.'

I wanted to ask more, but I was distracted by the colourless glow from the township that beamed on everything with utter indifference, from the thin boughs of spindly, straggly gums to the scrub scarcely higher than our knees. It drenched us with no colour and took all colours from us, so that I had to ask him the colour of the ground we were trudging on.

'Red,' he said.

'We could be walking on icing sugar,' I said.

'That's true,' he laughed. Sometimes he loved being the explainer, though sometimes he hated it, and when was I ever going to predict it? At least he seemed to have forgiven me for the head bump. His arm brushed mine, almost a caress. But of course he wouldn't feel it like that; he had no knowledge of who I was, I was just a stranger, an academic here to do a job he didn't particularly respect, it seemed.

But the landscape broke into my confusion: it at least was without contradictions. I turned on my heel in a circle, and right around me, stretching in every direction into the almost-hills, was the flat desert.

I observed to him that without mountains, everything was in silhouette. I didn't have words to tell him that my mind was holding back from this landscape, arguing against it as if the landscape was a person, someone with preposterous ideas I couldn't accept. For a start, it ought not to be so flat. There was just him and me and this flat land, this unending fierce sky. Only the sky could diminish us, and as yet it held only two stars. We were skyscrapers in that supine land. There was nothing to measure our thoughts against, except each other. That seemed enough for us to lose all perspective, to imagine that our thoughts were what really mattered in the universe. That could be dangerous.

'When the mob visit the Top End, they don't like it because of the trees. "There's no sky," they say,' he told me.

I exclaimed as he wanted me to. I saw in the no-colour light that his eyes were more expressive than they'd been in his young face, if that young face had been indeed his. Even the skin around his eyes now rose to talk, pouching when he was excited, and then the lower eyelids drooped.

'The mob believes there are still people out in the desert who haven't come in,' he said as we walked on.

'And are there?'

'Who'd know? Perhaps they just want it to be so. Perhaps they want them to be there.'

'Do the people resent us?' I asked. 'I mean us whites.'

He nodded. He probably expected resentment when he'd first come out.

'They're a compassionate mob. The pastoralists here didn't massacre their relatives, just –' he laughed, 'took their land and their livelihood. The kangaroos, lizards, snakes, bush turkeys – everything they lived off. They were allowed to keep their traditions because they didn't interfere with anyone's money-making, more or less, and that seems crucial to them – though the traditions are changing. When I first came to the desert, they did ceremonies all the time. Every time a plane flew in, for instance. Not any more.'

'That's why –' I interrupted, about to remind him of my mission.

But he didn't wait. 'That's why, because of the loss of their hunting grounds, they expect us to hold them.'

My other foot sank in the red icing sugar.

'Hold?'

'Look after them. The way they hold their land.'

I felt the enormity of this statement.

'You mean, hold them with government money?'

He seemed to think this was a question so obvious it didn't need answering, and walked on, though I had no idea if we'd turned a circle and were heading home.

'You've never felt a need to learn their language?' I asked.

'I don't need to,' he said. 'We understand each other's body language.'

'But there might be subtleties you'd be missing.'

Why was I arguing with him? Was I just arguing against the fluttering of my heart? Or was it some deeper mistrust?

'I miss nothing.'

We seemed to slide down a fierce slope, unexpected in all the flatness, but I took little notice because I wanted to assert myself against his certainty.

'For example, there might be women's ceremonies you don't know about,' I said, falling and righting myself and falling again. 'There's a lot of places away from men's eyes. A lot of desert.'

'Women don't have ceremonies here,' he said. 'They don't rate.'

There was such a gust of fury in his last sentence that I was lost for words. I stumbled over what seemed to be a kangaroo carcass with its heart ripped out. All that was left was a cave of a chest. I skirted around it.

But now I'd recovered enough to reason.

'Wouldn't women's ceremonies be hidden from white men? As this "Poor Thing" song seems to have been?'

He didn't deign to answer. But I made myself walk again in unison with him. After all, the quest was at stake.

'Can you point out the old singer to me tomorrow? The "Poor Thing" singer?'

Unexpectedly, a deeper darkness seemed to be creeping over the sky, a shadow shaped like a giant cloud. I'd thought the land couldn't get any darker. So I was unaware that he'd moved away from me until I heard him call: 'Come over here. Feel this.'

I followed his voice, and he, whose eyes seemed better than mine, picked up my hand as gently as if I was a child, and put it on what seemed to be wood tightly bound with cloth. Then his mood seemed to change.

'Your wrist!' he said, running his finger across my wrist bone, bared by my lifted arm. His voice seemed higher, almost a shriek.

'What about my wrist?'

'Your wrist bone – your ulna.' He jabbed my wrist, painfully. 'It's unusually prominent,' he said.

I felt condemned.

'People can't help their bones,' I said.

I tried to pull my hand away, but he kept hold of it and made me feel up and down the wood with its cloth wrapping. It was frayed and stiff with weathering on the top, but soft underneath.

'Stop!' I demanded.

But he kept on, again and again.

'Stop it!' I repeated, suddenly afraid of him.

He threw my hand down.

'It's just one of their old magic things,' he said. 'From last year's ceremonies.'

'I shouldn't have touched it! You shouldn't have made me touch it.'

'You deserve to be haunted by bad spirits.'

'What?' I cried.

His voice had become aggressive.

'What are you talking about?' I demanded. 'It could still be full of magic.'

'Still? You believe in their magic?' he said contemptuously. 'An intellectual like you?'

'What I believe isn't the point.' I made myself say: 'We should have respect. You should have respect.'

'You think I don't?' Then he said, quietly, with the blackness of night in his voice: 'Then I'll let you find your own way home.'

Chapter 5

And he was gone. Just like that. I heard the crunching of his feet, and afterwards, nothing.

At first I felt only relief, that his voice had stopped, and with it my constant questioning: Is it Ian? Does he look like him? Is that gesture familiar? What about that wrinkle down his forehead? That lift of his eyebrow? Am I sure? Why aren't I sure?

I stood, swaying with fear. I had no hope of following him in this inky blackness. Newspaper stories came to me, headlines:

WOMAN LEAVES CAR AND FACES HELL

NEW CHUM DIES OF THIRST NEAR HOME

All the warnings I saw on billboards on the highway out of Alice Springs:

Don't leave your car.

Don't leave the road.

Take water with you always.

It hadn't occurred to me that he'd abandon me. Abandon! The very word struck into my soul. He abandoned me with such ease, just as he did all those years ago. Though it wasn't me he abandoned then, but his mother. Ever since I'd met him in Alice Springs I'd feared he'd reject me because of my lack of learning, my clumsiness. It hadn't occurred to me he'd reject me because my bone stuck out too much.

But now I had to cope with being alone in the desert at night. This desert wasn't ordinary, accommodating earth to be trampled carelessly underfoot. Humans would only ever be a tiny part of this desert's life and like a river in a running tide, it must be approached with a knowledge of its ways.

I made useless promises. I would never come without water again. I would never forget to take my bearings again. I would never assume a companion wouldn't abandon me. All that, I promised God, E.E. Albert, and me.

Then the stillness settled down around me, the way I was used to it doing on the river, so that it seemed a living thing, as if not only must I listen to it, but it had stopped to listen to me – or perhaps it was my thoughts that had stopped whirling. I became purely a sensate being and realised that before this, my thoughts had been in the way.

I'd had long training in this. My river had trained me. So I stopped thinking, as I did on the river, so I could sense beyond my body. At first it seemed there were no sounds, nothing at all, and then I heard a bird nearby, not in the air but on the ground, a heavy bird, I heard the skidding of its wings as it landed, its weight pushing into the sand. So it wasn't a monster, and probably only a local bird, perhaps a bush turkey. Then I heard a quiet slithering, which stopped, so either the creature had gone or was holding its ground, wondering what sort of creature I was. I jumped because there was a sound like an old man clearing his throat, and then came the quiet, repetitive sound of leaves being pulled off a tree and munched in a business-like fashion. It was a serious muncher. I knew that noise from the river – it was only a kangaroo. I sneezed, startling it; it bounded away. Silence settled again until I made out what'd been there all along – the soft whistle of wind lifting sand and carrying it off, to layer it on ripple after ripple of sand, layers and layers of sand, kilometres of sand, a desert of sand lifting softly and settling into new ripples. And it was this sound, the quiet ocean of sand building itself all around me as it had done long before the first humans – Daniel would know how long – that finally calmed me.

Weariness overcame me. I sat, casting my hands around and behind me, and finding no prickles, or any antagonistic thing that might bite or sting, I lay down on the red sand, which was cooling after the heat of the day. The black sky domed over me, deep, unending, inscrutable, but benign. Though it shed no light, it held no terrors.

Perhaps I drowsed.

*

There's one other problem that tugs at my heart. I have strained my memory a thousand times, replaying the way Diana with her fixed grimace pulls alongside our jetty, leaning over to hold the bollard while my clumsy mother steps on board, pausing while the boat wobbles.

I've searched that moment so many times, wondering where you are and what you know. I remember that just as Diana gets under way, the motor coughs and cuts out and she has to start it again, but between the stopping and the starting is the sort of silvery stillness that settles over a river with the ripples spreading out in circles, broken only by the sudden scudding of a pelican artlessly creating a shining wake, or the rainbow leap of a fish plopping back into its own ripples. And you? At that moment, if you are on the rocking dawn train, heading to the airport and then on the plane flying you like a bird back to where you'd come from, back maybe to here, to Gadaburumili – what knowledge do you carry in your heart on that journey? Do you know, do you even suspect that your mother intends to kill mine? If it was the other way around, whatever my disgust, I would warn you. I wouldn't want my childhood playmate to face that terrible grief, that terrible abandonment. Why don't you come to me and tell me?

*

With my head on the cold desert sand, I made out a sound that seemed to come from deep inside the earth. I jumped up, panicking again. I wheeled around. I must find the house; I must find light and people. Perhaps the settlement was hidden behind a rock. I had no idea. I couldn't even see my arm, let alone my watch.

The vibration came closer and closer. Sounds travelled a long way here, as they did on the river. I walked, counting my steps, just a little way forward, six steps, then six steps back, six steps to the left, six steps back, a curious, blind dance. If I was walking through the bush near my river, there'd be vines and rabbit holes and snake holes and hillocks, but this flat country seemed as even as a cricket pitch. I comforted myself with this discovery: it was safer than home for walking in the dead of night. This made me braver: twelve steps forward, twelve back, twelve right, twelve left, and all the time, still no light; but the vibration came closer, closer. It was the crunching of footsteps. Human footsteps. That was when I realised that my worst threat in the desert was a fellow being.

I cried out.

'Going to stay out all night?' Adrian's voice asked. 'I thought you might need some water.'

I couldn't see what he was holding out to me, but I stretched out my hand to feel a glass bottle that sloshed. I seized it and gulped the water down, even though I wasn't thirsty. But he might abandon me again.

'You haven't thanked me,' he said when I handed the bottle back. 'Aren't you going to thank me? I put off going to bed to rescue you.'

'Thank you?' I tried not to shout. 'Do you treat all visitors like this?'

'I don't want visitors! This isn't a theme park for tourists.'

'I'm not a tourist, I'm here to record an old woman. And you invited me!'

'You're here to help your career. Everyone comes here to help their career.'

I was so angry, I was almost lost for words, but I managed: 'Who in hell are you to know it won't help them? In the future, if they've lost their language, how do you know they won't say to us: "With all your technology, why didn't you help us record our ancient language?"'

'But in the short term, you'll write it up in some journal; the – what's it called – the ancient verb – is that it? The ancient verb I've discovered.'

I took a breath, surprised at how anger had given me sudden clarity.

'My research isn't just for people's careers. It's about –' I searched in my heart for a feeling, the feeling that first attracted me to E.E. Albert's world '– it's about amazement.'

At least he repeated it, though doubting it.

'Amazement?'

Now I had to justify it, I was incoherent. I knew in my heart I was saying something sensible, but putting words on this feeling took time.

'We're so resourceful,' I managed at last. 'Humans.'

We were walking fast. I saw to my annoyance that again I'd fallen in step with him across the red icing sugar, which gave way beneath my feet with a crinkling sound. Then he seemed higher up than me, and I realised he was climbing a bank. I scrambled after him, and then through a thicket of scrub.

'You weren't lost,' he said. 'You forgot – we'd gone down into a creek bed. Why didn't you see the light? – oh, you aren't tall enough.' He laughed, answering his own question to prove he was innocent, that being lost was entirely my fault, being short was entirely my fault, he could never be blamed. 'Only a hundred metres from home,' he added, for now we were drowned in ordinary streetlight. It was the closest he could come to an apology.

I said nothing. I was determined not to even bid him goodnight, but at the front door, he turned to me, and said, his voice raised a notch, as if he was arguing in his head: 'This is the most intellectually challenging thing that's happening in Australia and I want to stay here. Nothing or nobody is going to stop me. I'm not going to be sacked.'

I blurted angrily: 'When are you going to point out the singer to me so I can go, and stop annoying you?'

'All in good time,' he said. 'We both need sleep.'

I knew in the pit of my stomach that his good time wasn't going to be my good time. Nevertheless, I fell asleep thinking of his freckled, slender hands soothing the sheets, wrestling the lower fitted one with its tight elastic band, tucking in the top one. I slept long hours. It's very comforting to have a bed made for you, no matter how confused you are, how exasperating the bed maker is, no matter who he is. For the first time in years, I was curiously at peace.

Twice I woke when there were knocks on the door. I heard Djemiranga, and I thought from the intonation that they were asking questions, if questions had a rising intonation in their language, as they did in mine.

'I looked for them for two hours,' Adrian answered each time, always in English. I imagined he was talking to different groups, assuming he knew what they'd been asking about. His voice was as soft, as reassuring as his bedsheets. There seemed to be many tones to his voice, all harmonising with each other, like his personality, which seemed to be many things at once. I didn't remember that about my Ian. As his visitors talked, I wondered that he hadn't asked someone to translate for him. That didn't seem to be his way. He was trusting to his body language, to his conviction that he knew their body language, his trust that they loved him, and that love would carry him through.

The third time I woke to hear three dogs barking. Then it seemed as if there were six dogs, then a dozen, and then a whole choir of dogs trying to harmonise, some sopranos hitting high notes, some deep basses, so it was a growling and a howling, a chorus that dwindled to become a train roaring into a city station. There was an odd yelp, as if one of the dogs had expected a second verse and launched into it and found itself alone, then a call from a human voice, something thrown, more yelps, then the desert took over, the desert of whirring insects, of small creatures hunting each other, of creatures living and dying, and of wind lifting and layering sand, of sand drifting and covering us all, until our concerns, our sadnesses and fears and triumphs and disasters and secrets had become desert too.

I turned over to sleep again. In the morning, there was no sound except the wind skidding a plastic bucket across the verandah, and under that, a curious swishing sound. I lifted a slat of the Venetian blinds and looked out. In front of me was a street of red dust, lined with identical suburban houses with walls dreary with smears and handprints. The houses were all dilapidated, with rusting gutters that often lurched down the walls, and broken windows boarded up with cardboard, and front doors with grubby remnants of paint, most of which had peeled off. Some houses had been painted with different colours, here scarlet, here pink, here lemon-yellow, but in their fading hues that early enthusiasm now seemed like pathos. Everywhere were gates rusted off their hinges, some lying on the ground, and rusting metal gate posts joined to wire-netting fences, sometimes slumped under a vine I could only assume was growing wild, since there were no flowers or lawns or vegetables or hanging plants or anything that would suggest cultivation. These people were not farmers, they were nomads, I reminded myself, still with their travelling embedded in their language, yet they'd been contained in this village as if they were poverty-stricken suburban whites. Torn paper and plastic rubbish had blown everywhere, on the roads, on the verges, but ending up against the fences and caught captive there, like children imprisoned inside a playpen and trying to break out of it, as if the very rubbish was willing itself to push through the spaces made by the wire netting so it could escape out into the desert beyond. In the front yards were broken-down cars propped up on blocks, and scattered plastic toys no longer glowing with shop-bought colours but tired and scratched, becoming the colour of the dust itself, and old flour tins hoisting timber boards that seemed to serve as tables. Often there'd be a bedraggled sofa with faded torn fabric and broken springs bulging underneath. Every front yard had an open fire, some still smoking, ringed around by blackened stones. But there was no one around. Breakfast had been cooked and eaten, and the families had disappeared. Even the leaves of the tree outside my window hung listlessly, moving backwards and forwards like shuffling feet. My eye searched for freshness, newness, but there was none. At that moment, as if the irony had been timed just for me, a muttering TV set in a scruffy front yard flashed to a shot of a cream-suited, cravated, handsome, beaming reporter with blond blow-dried hair holding a microphone to his mouth like a rock singer as he marvelled at the glowing splendour of a Hollywood film-star's mansion.

I fell back on the bed, and lay with my hand over my eyes. I groaned at my foolishness. Till that moment I'd only thought of two things: finding the Ian of my childhood, and heroically rescuing E.E. Albert's reputation, tarnished by championing me, so I would become once more an interesting person in her estimation. For a moment I let myself pretend that there was a town over the distant almost-hills I'd glimpsed last night – with rows of bright shops and cafés and piped music and theatres and bars and hotels – all of which, as we drove out of Alice Springs, I'd left cheerfully behind.

The trouble was, I'd given little thought to the mechanics of finding the old lady, let alone getting her trust and recording her song, and I hadn't for a single moment considered what it might be like to spend a month here in this desolate, decrepit mimicry of a white suburb, hundreds of bumpy kilometres from a white town.

I must've lain there for half an hour, half-asleep in despair. I was roused by a shout from the street, and prised apart a slat of the dusty Venetian blinds again. A few bare-footed black children pushed a stroller, laughing and shouting. I made myself copy the shouting but in a whisper. Though the stroller was heading away from me, I could see the long black legs of a teenager sticking like scissors out one side. So that was what the laughter had been about. Even the shouts sounded dusty.

I had to get up. The sooner I found the old lady and recorded her, the sooner I could leave. I made a timetable: I could surely do that within a day and then somehow beg a ride back to Alice Springs in the first car going, however rusted it was.

As I passed the washing machine, it switched its cycle – so that was the swishing sound – and I peeked in. There was a lone blue linen shirt swirling in a vast tub full of water, like a dead fish.

I went back to my room and dressed. Adrian had put in a hanging rack and many hangers. I dithered but in the end I unpacked only three skirts, and then stopped. My work would be over soon. I might not even need to stay the night.

I reminded myself: one step at a time. First, have breakfast. I'd get nowhere sitting in the house worrying. Go out to somewhere busy, I said to myself, and look for an old, sick woman.

It came to me that E.E. Albert might be impressed if I recorded more than the ancient song, if I recorded the language as it was currently spoken, to compare it to the song.

Such an interesting mind, she'd say. Even the thought of that made me flush with a warm glow.

I took out my recorder and put in a new battery, and then I remembered the photos in my workbag that had almost given me away, and I hid them under my mattress.

In the kitchen I boiled the kettle and riffled through my food box, which Daniel or Adrian must have brought in from the troopie, and made tea, my favourite tea, Earl Grey, and sat at the kitchen bench, like a woman alone in her house in an ordinary suburb. The familiarity of these rituals comforted me. One step at a time. I looked in my box and decided to keep everything inside it, rather than finding storage places. Now I'd accomplished getting here, I could see the most time-consuming job was over. I poured out my cereal, pulled the plug on my UHT milk, and ate, getting more confident by the minute. Next to me was a cardboard box, and on top of many papers was a faxed letter, signed with ornate swirls.

I remembered when Ian spent hours practising a signature that hid his name, to make himself seem enigmatic. I could only sign in my ordinary stilted handwriting, always with at least one letter crossed out, always with a blotch of ink, no matter how hard I concentrated.

'You write like you want to look obedient,' he'd say. Even then, he'd been a rebel and I'd been an appeaser.

I leaned over to read the faxed letter, its terseness palpable: *Thank you for your comments re the second doctor, which again contradict mine. By the way, practitioner is spelt with a second 't', not an 's'. It takes but a few seconds to check one's spelling, and would be a courtesy. My advice to the Board remains unchanged.*

I wondered if he had other enemies, besides hotheads.

Gloomily, I picked up a framed photo of the local children at a sports carnival, laughing and jubilantly holding their fingers in a victory sign. Their optimism seeped into me. Desert schools, I'd heard, were always in need of helpers. I'd go to the school and offer to help out in the classroom, and befriend the children. Schools often have photos pinned up of families, of grandmothers and great-grandmothers. I'd find a way to point out the pictures and ask them about their grandmothers, and great-grandmothers. 'Who has a great-grandmother who sings the "Poor Thing" song?' I'd ask.

I thought: I'll keep a journal, to show E.E. Albert how focused I've been.

Someone had thrown down several biros amongst the mess on the ironing board. I reached for one and opened my notebook. I'd begin with the date – even, given how short a time I'd stay here, the hour. But on the first digit, the biro spurted a last drop of blue ink and dried up. I picked out another biro from the pile. It'd dried up too, and so had the next one, and the next one. I went back to my room and found my own biro in my workbag, and determinedly returned to the journal, but my pen had dried up as well. I wrote the date over and over, and my intention for the present moment, though afterwards there was just a crankily ploughed furrow in the page.

Day 1: Today the children will lead me to the singer.

It was as if I hadn't written it. Only the full-stop after 'singer' was visible.

It was almost ten o'clock, way past school starting time. So I gave up on the journal, grabbed my recorder and my hat and shut the door behind me. The heat had an insatiable feel. I worried briefly that I must be careful not to offend Adrian, who would probably say I should wait for him to introduce me to the settlement, but he'd appreciate the urgency, anyone would. No one who didn't belong here should be expected to live here.

No one seemed to be on the streets, though I passed some toddlers playing under a bedsheet, and I comforted myself that they were for all the world like white children playing at cubby houses. I walked past the derelict houses I'd seen through my window, and stepped over a rubble of corrugated iron and posts lying in what had been once a front yard, and wondered if local people just ripped down houses out of bad temper, or drunken boredom, perhaps. I thought that I'd do the same after a while in this heat and squalor, especially without a café or a job to escape to for a while. I saw ahead a crowd of women sitting in a circle in the shade in their yard, with children lolling against them, and other men and women, shabbily but colourfully dressed in crumpled, dusty op shop remnants, standing at the darkened doorway of a small, surely one-room corrugated hut in such a familiar way that I decided it was the home of everyone in the yard. Their poverty was so stark that I suddenly felt shame, that I shouldn't be there, that I had no right to be there, only the right of a scholar to investigate the world – but does a scholar have that right everywhere? And anyway, I was hardly a scholar. I thought of calling out to them – in English? Would they speak English? What would I say? Ask for the old lady? Of course I couldn't. Apologise? And for what?

But then I heard wild barking, and wheeled around to discover a rabble of dogs roaring towards me – probably the pack of last night – circling me; snarling, barking, half-starved, sick dogs without any fur, pink dogs with their ribs jutting out from their sides. A terrier, hungrier and madder than the rest, jumped on top of the others and rode them like a circus dog on horses prancing around a ring – so with it on top, they were a growling, shaking pyramid. I screamed for help. The women in the yard crowded at their fence and yelled, but the dogs ignored them.

'Just stick your arms high up and the dogs will think you're tall,' a voice shouted behind me.

There was a man, a white man, running towards me, one of my kind, a chestnut waist-length pony tail bumping behind him. He yelled at the dogs with both arms above his head, a notebook flapping as he ran. Everything about him was menacing.

'Get lost, you mangy bastards!' he roared. The dogs faltered, their eyes flicked to him, back to me: they were unconvinced. One of them leaped at him vengefully and I stepped back. The man lunged at it with the full length of his body, notebook flapping wildly, and suddenly the top circus-dog terrier was convinced, leaped off the backs of the others and ran away, almost sideways like a crab, and then the others ran away too, knocking over the littlest one, a black-haired puppy, so it had to right itself, rolling and finding its feet before it raced after the others, yelping in indignation because they'd left it behind.

'See what I mean?' he said. 'Are you a visitor or something?' He had bright blue eyes that glittered out of a taut, sun-reddened face.

'I'm just here to record the song of an old lady,' I began, but he interrupted me.

'I'm doing my best to help too,' he said. He was getting his breath back. 'But you can't help those who don't help themselves. It's taken me months to get the work this far.'

He waved his hand behind us. I turned to see three partly built besser block houses.

'Everyone blames me. The government blames me. The families here blame me. "When are we going to move in?" they ask. But the problem is that the government makes me use apprentices from here.'

Terror was still making me pant, but I was relieved to have someone to talk to.

'Apprentices!' I said. 'I suppose you'd have to teach them how to build.'

This seemed to make him angry.

'Building's beside the point!' he cried. 'I have to teach them how to count; I have to teach them numbers up to ten before they can use a tape measure! What city builder has to do that? I have to teach them English words for –' he cast around for examples, 'hammer, ladder, tape measure – everything. On top of that, they have no work ethic so I have to teach them to turn up.'

His blue eyes settled on me, suddenly squinting with fear.

'Are you from the government?' he asked. 'A bureaucrat?'

'I'm here to record –' I began.

'I'm not saying they're stupid,' he said quickly. 'I'd never say that, I tell everyone that they're clever but in their own way. Their kinship system, of course, you'd have to be Einstein to understand it. And that corrugated iron I saw you inspecting – they don't rip down houses out of spite – when someone's died, they think that the dead's angry spirits will haunt them. Though they're going to have a hard time pulling down my houses! What I'm trying to say is – don't put me down as racist.'

Because he seemed to know a lot, I asked him: 'Do you know an old woman who's dying? It's her I've come to record.'

But he was backing away from me.

'Got to get on with the job,' he said. 'By the way, have you reported to the elder?'

'I was invited here,' I said. 'I don't need to – do I?'

'You haven't? You'd better go and introduce yourself,' he said. 'He says who can stay and who can't.'

'I didn't know that,' I said.

'Just round the corner. The purple house.'

Purple. A regal colour. It was right that the elder should have a purple house.

'I'll go right now,' I said.

'You'd better.'

I began walking up the street again and then there was a honking behind me. It was Adrian, again in a pale blue linen shirt. I kept walking. He pulled alongside.

'Where do you think you're going?' he demanded.

'To do my job,' I said. I kept walking.

'I asked where you think you're going.'

'Have you told the elder that I'm here?' I asked.

'They're not interested in white business,' he said. 'Imagine trying to explain your important mission!'

I ignored that barb.

'The builder said it's necessary. Don't worry. I'll go and introduce myself.'

'You can't just barge into an elder's house! Things are more delicate, especially now with my sacking.'

But he could see I was determined to stride off.

'It's not a good time for me to take you,' he said. 'There's a lot of discussion going on.'

'I don't need taking,' I said.

He hesitated. I started walking again, so he had to drive beside me.

He must've suddenly decided that I could be politically useful to him. Because of his energy, everything about him seemed spontaneous, impulsive, but also, underneath it all, calculating. He must use people for his own ends, I thought, he must use Daniel, perhaps, he must use me. I knew that he thought like that, I knew it in my bones – but how did I know? How could I be so certain? Then I remembered my mother used me to spy. My father used me to show Diana he was a family man, not just a – my heart crunched – her lover. Admit it. Her lover. But Diana – Diana loved me. Adored me. I was the daughter she really wanted, when all she had was a son. She was the one who didn't use any of us, didn't use me.

'Hop in. Now,' ordered Adrian.

I slowed down. I reasoned that it would probably be easier to be introduced than going to the purple house alone and explaining myself, explaining about the song, and – worst of all – explaining about the travel affix. So I got in. He drove off in the usual cloud of dust, but in the opposite direction.

'The builder said that street,' I said, pointing.

'I'm taking you somewhere to explain.'

'Explain what?' My heart lurched.

But all he said was: 'You've got to behave. You're making a mess of things. You're being uncouth.'

'Uncouth?'

'Stop talking. Just listen.'

So I listened. Skeleton, he explained, had been a stockman in his youth.

'So he had some English and he was used to white ways, more or less. But he's eighty and very traditional. When I first came, if he wanted to speak to me, he'd linger at my gate until I invited him inside. He expects that old-fashioned sort of behaviour.'

He interrupted himself.

'What's that for?' he asked of the recorder I was holding.

'My job.'

'They'll think it's surveillance.'

'I'll ask Skeleton's permission, of course. I'd like to record the sounds of what he says. If he's traditional, he might use traditional ways of saying things that could be useful for me.'

'You'll record no one till I give you the go-ahead! The mob hates being studied.'

'How do you know?' I demanded.

'I've been here twenty years, remember.' He pulled up.

'Where are we?'

It was as if we were in an above-ground car park in a shopping mall. At least a thousand empty cars waited, more or less in rows, for their drivers.

'No one comes here.'

As I gazed I realised that no one would come here because all the cars were rusted away, mere shells of chassis, with smashed windscreens, doors flung open, engines dragged out. Wheels and vinyl seats lay on the red dust, along with a litter of abandoned car doors.

'Why don't they get repaired?'

'Like you realised about the dishwashers.' He began to giggle, and then stopped. 'What mechanic's going to come out here? And who could afford the bills?'

I smelled smoke: a pile of rubbish was on fire in a vast pit to the side of us. On top of it was a cardboard carton, licked with flames, and sticking out of it was the corpse of a dog, its ears upright, the jaw flung back in a terrible grimace.

I cried out and lunged out of the troopie. Adrian grabbed me.

'You're so sentimental,' he said. 'Families can't afford these dogs. They're better off in the fire than starving to death.'

'What happened to it?'

'I killed it before it killed me!'

'Feeding it would've been better.'

'I'd rather feed the mob.'

When I saw the sense of that, he added: 'I've killed more dogs than I've patted.' It was a boast, not a confession.

'How can you wish death on anything!'

He looked away.

On the other side of the car graveyard there were several huge concrete tubs, like big washing tubs, and a huge metal structure that could once have been a shed.

'Melancholy, isn't it?' he said, pleased to change the subject.

Mould was already blackening the tubs, and weeds plotted to take them over. Little hills of red sand had blown against their sides and settled there. Grey birds swooped above us, whirring as they perched on the walls, heads tipped to watch for worms.

He told me that it was the wreckage of a white's multi-million dollar plan to cure kangaroo hides for overseas markets.

'A job-creation scheme,' he said.

A crow flapped onto the wall, keeping its distance from the other birds, cawing at us to keep our distance too.

Adrian had fallen silent, so I knew I was supposed to respond. 'What went wrong?'

'White people's vision,' he said. 'City types. Not theirs. They hunt kangaroos to feed their families, not so they can send skins off to countries they've never been to.'

He checked the rear-vision mirror and hurried on.

'We're here because a man mustn't be alone with a woman he's not married to. I needed to stop you before you race off making things even harder for me. For a start, the mob here don't say hello.'

I nodded as if I knew that, though I didn't.

'Or goodbye.'

'So that was why no one greeted me in the troopie –'

'They don't make eye contact. Whites stare at them, they say. They find it rude. Uncouth. They have a word for uncouth.'

'What's the word?'

He ignored the question. 'Just glance up between sentences, and only once,' he said. 'Like this.'

He hung his head but rolled his eyes skywards. It gave him a furtive look and despite myself, I burst out laughing. 'You look like a burglar!' I laughed.

But then I knew why he downcast his eyes. He was attempting to copy them. To make them love him, as Daniel had said.

He didn't laugh.

'And no handshakes. And don't say thank you or please because they don't. No small talk. Behave well, or he might tell you to leave. After all, you're of no use to them.'

'So this elder really is their ruler!' I said.

'They're not like Native Americans. They're not hierarchical. Don't you know anything?'

He started the troopie, and headed towards the purple house.

Chapter 6

E.E. Albert imagined a meeting like this, and I'd read about it so often I could recite it:

In the man's eyes I'd see his childhood in this scorching, inhospitable desert that he and his ancestors knew as home for perhaps 50,000 years: I'd see his youth as he learned its ways, assessing the seasons that in the city we barely notice; I'd see reflected in his eyes this red life-giving earth with its fat snakes and fleshy bush turkeys and fruit trees, its hidden waterholes, its honey and meat hidden deep in the trunks and roots of trees; I'd see the lean seasons when there were no lizards and snakes, when fruit died on the boughs, when waterholes dried up; I'd see in his face his years of considering and assessing the men of his tribe, their loyalty and bravery, I'd see the signs of someone who has absorbed secret and esoteric knowledge that explained and ritualised his world, the like of which a white man used to cities couldn't know or dream of, I'd see how he had endured, even welcomed, ritualised pain to learn it; I'd see a lifetime of a ruler who's had to find in himself fortitude and compassion and patience and endless bravery, decades of trying to persuade it into the men around him, and women too.

We pulled up a short distance away from the house, which wasn't purple at all, more a grubby mauve. Otherwise it was identical to all the other houses, a glass window broken and boarded by a bit of wood, the guttering sagging, a downpipe broken off, children's handprints on the walls, and all ringed with rubbish that had blown against its cyclone-wire fence.

'This one?' I asked.

Adrian didn't bother to nod.

This wasn't the dwelling place of a ruler of the desert.

'Don't be uncouth this time,' muttered Adrian.

I repeated to myself the rules: no eye contact, no greetings, no handshake, and no small talk. I dared to glance up for a second. There was a black man in a cowboy shirt, sitting in a chair on his sunny but dusty front verandah. Although we were approaching his court, Adrian couldn't repress himself. He dive-bombed himself out of the troopie, but paused ostentatiously at the gate; I imagined he was trying to pause like the young Skeleton used to do. I cast down my eyes and began walking, examining minutely the grains of red dirt in the yard all made into sunlit mounds and shadowy valleys by the trampling of many bare-footed visitors, as if all I'd come for was to examine red dirt. The gate's hinges were off and it wouldn't open, but Adrian unhesitatingly squeezed instead through a narrow gap in the fence as if that was the most natural way to approach a ruler, and I followed. Three dogs scrambled into my limited view, better fed than the ones who tried to attack me, their backs sleek and furred. They didn't bark, but they escorted me towards the verandah, two behind and one leading, as if they've been trained to do this. It was a short yard but it seemed a long walk.

I was doing this for E.E. Albert. No eye contact, no greetings, no handshake. But I couldn't help peeking again to see that the elder had risen courteously out of his chair at my approach. I stopped short of his verandah, in case going further would be considered uncouth.

For the hundredth time in the last twenty-four hours, I wished I'd been E.E. Albert's best student, not her worst.

'This is Kate, the city woman I told you about, who's come to work with Collin Collins,' Adrian's voice was saying beyond my downcast eyes. 'She's learning language but she can't speak it yet.'

I felt like a short child with the adults talking above me. I kept saying to myself: *no eye contact, no greetings, no handshake.* I saw black bare feet near mine. Then a black, outstretched hand came into my limited field of vision. What should I do? I could do nothing else than reach out and shake it, though this was prohibited, but I made my eyes see only his hand.

He kept shaking my hand. Shaking and shaking. There comes a moment in a long handshake when your gaze simply has to travel up the hand of the person you're shaking, up his forearm, up his elbow, up his shoulder, onto his face.

In front of me was an old but erect man, slender, tall and powerful, with square, broad shoulders and a handsome, chiselled face. In that moment I remembered the photos in E.E. Albert's book, which I'd come later to realise were well-known photos of statuesque, slender Aboriginal men and women, the women often standing with a shield horizontal on their heads, the men often standing on a rock, surveying the distance, with one foot propped on the knee of the other leg.

My brain was hammering: *Wait till I tell her about this!* In his eyes, I'd tell her, I saw his magnificence, his charisma, his patience, his bravery.

But that wasn't true: all I saw was a reflection of me, puny and sweating, and behind me a yard of rippling dust, with rubbish blown against a wire fence. I downcast my eyes.

Then he spoke in English. 'You are learning language.'

I almost jumped at his voice. It wasn't a question. There was no rising inflection.

'Welcome to my country,' he said.

I looked up again, astonished.

His eyes gripped mine.

I decided, despite Adrian, to gaze back.

He had the sort of gaze, I'd tell her, that makes you feel you have to pass a moral test. In that way, I'd be able to truthfully corroborate her fantasy – I wanted so much to corroborate it.

I felt muted, inarticulate, how I wished I could pass his test, how I wished I knew some of his language.

'Thank you,' was all that I found to say, smiling back.

Then I found something else to say: 'Your land is beautiful.'

I blushed that I'd uttered small talk, Adrian would be embarrassed and appalled, but Skeleton kept gazing and smiling. And then there came a further shock.

'Thank you,' he returned.

Adrian's feet were crunching on the ground, perhaps in irritation. Ordinariness came back to me.

'Goodbye,' I said to the elder, as I wasn't supposed to.

'Goodbye,' he said, as he wasn't supposed to.

Then I cast down my eyes, turned, and walked back across his red and furrowed yard, so overwrought I was almost sleepwalking. I wondered if he could tell from my body how deeply I'd fallen under his spell. E.E. Albert had been right, after all. He would've seen many people fall under his spell, male and female, white and black.

I squeezed through the gap in the fence. His dogs, padding beside me to escort me out, paused, and returned to their master.

'Adrian!' His voice suddenly interrupted my reverie.

Adrian, who'd led me out of the yard, swivelled, immediately all attention.

'Too much rubbish in my yard.'

Adrian looked around at the rubbish as if he hadn't noticed it before.

'That Bruce is lazy as well as cheeky! He doesn't do his job. He's no good! I'll get his truck and drive round and personally pick it up.'

I allowed myself to glance at Skeleton. I saw him struggling with intractable English, probably his fourth or fifth language.

'No. Too much rubbish footprints!'

Adrian was surprised into examining the ground, which was indeed pock-marked with footprints.

'I can't tell who's been in my yard,' explained Skeleton.

Adrian didn't miss a beat.

'I'll find you a rake. I'll rake it myself,' Adrian called to him.

I followed Adrian to the troopie and opened my door, dreading a lecture about my disobedience. Adrian got into the driver's seat silently. Only when the vinyl of the seats was burning into the backs of our legs did he speak.

'He was showing that he knows white culture. From his stockman days. You did well,' he said. 'You played it by ear, and did well.'

In my relief, I realised how little I knew Adrian.

But I was hugely pleased because of his praise. I was reasoning: if I jump through all the hurdles as well as that, I'll be out of here in no time.

'So I'm allowed to stay?'

'Only if I'm here. Skeleton and the mob here assume you're my wife. A man is responsible for what his wife does.'

I turned in alarm.

'Your wife! Why would they think I'm your wife?'

'Because you're in my company. It's the only way a woman is here. That's what women here do. Be wives.'

This roused me to fury.

'I don't think you'd know all about women here. Or what everyone single person here thinks,' I cried.

'All you know is what you've read in books,' he said.

He didn't know what a taunt that was.

A cloud was coming over my mind, like a cloud starting to blot out the stars in a night sky. It was covering my relief. It carried with it, in the way a coming storm stirs loose leaves in its path, a deep suspicion.

'When you wrote to the university and asked for a woman to come, did you know she'd be staying in your house?' I asked. 'As if she was your wife?'

He gunned the motor into action.

'Introducing you has been a big concession to you. Now I must devote time to saving my own skin.'

He was pulling up outside the house. I refused to get out. He reached over and pushed open my door. He said:

'Of course you had to stay in my house. Housing for whites is limited. Now, get out, please.'

I obeyed.

'Don't leave the house,' he shouted after me.

I made another cup of tea. I sat down at the kitchen table, I caught sight of my journal. Now the indentation of the dried-up biro was like a child's secret message with only the dot at the end of the sentence showing: Today the children will lead me to the singer. I thought: if he's sacked, it might be very difficult for me to come back. I must at least try to find the old lady right away. That's my job. I must be able to say, At least I tried to find her. I couldn't tell E.E. Albert that I couldn't look for her for fear I'd displease my host.

I had to stop appeasing everyone. I had to stop appeasing him.

So I left the house for the second time that day, trying not to be timid, but nevertheless looking to right and left in case he was nearby – and I walked in the heat up the red road which was again empty of people except for the builder who was too busy hammering inside one of his houses to notice me, and past the dogs who were too busy quarrelling with each other, and past the rows of derelict houses – and I turned a corner and there was the hubbub of the community shop Adrian had mentioned, with family groups waiting quietly in the hot sun to go inside. No one noticed me or even looked around. Maybe all white people looked alike to them – just another pale face, another set of staring eyes. Or perhaps they were accomplished at taking information in without staring, I thought.

I peered inside the shop. It was a large space, with a checkout and cash register in the centre, and clothes, plastic furniture, toys, DVDs and TV sets for sale, as well as rows of tinned food and giant fridges full of drinks. But there were only a dozen people inside, while outside in the heat people waited, their arms limply at their sides unless they were holding children. I thought of the poverty-stricken houses I'd walked past and wondered if they didn't have enough money to buy anything, I had some dollars in my pocket – should I go over and smilingly distribute them? Or would that incur Adrian's wrath? Or perhaps they weren't Westernised enough to know to go inside? I paused. Should I help out, should I stand at the shop doorway and wave them inside like a policeman? I rather fancied myself as a Person Who Knows About Shops.

But for the first time, a little voice inside me cautioned, and reminded me of my mistakes so far, and I turned and walked on, downcasting my eyes. I rounded another fenced corner and, in my near-blinded state, almost fell over the hills and folds of what seemed to be a grey bulky blanket dropped on the ground – but the blanket let out a startled bray. It was a donkey sleeping in the sun. A donkey! Why was a donkey in the middle of the desert? Donkeys belong in farms! European farms! It clattered off towards the shop, moving like an elegant woman in high heels and a tight skirt hurrying for a bus. Then, suddenly, I was at a school gate, a dusty schoolyard with three separate wooden buildings in an ocean of red earth, and far off in a corner, two or three children were perched high up in a tree like goannas. I paused, a little shy of walking over to them, but that was exactly what a scholar must do, she must go to the people. But before I could become a scholar, a red-cheeked, balding white man in his thirties but already with a vast beer belly bouncing above tight blue jeans emerged from one of the wooden school-houses and crossed a shady verandah carrying a large, oddly shaped bundle, which he held away from his chest. Behind him strode a woman in black shorts, a black shirt and pink-blonde hair in a crew cut.

They both noticed me.

'See, one has come,' I heard the woman say to him. 'After all.'

She seemed to be reassuring him.

'You're early,' he called to me in a jolly way. 'You can help scrape the hairs off.'

I walked across the playground. Behind them was a door opening on to what seemed to be a staff room with computers and gleaming musical instruments.

I put my hand out to shake the man's hand – he had to shuffle his burden into his other arm – and then the woman's. I told them my name.

'Craig Harmond,' he said. 'Headmaster.'

He didn't introduce the woman, but she told me she was Beth Simmons, and – with a shy glance at him – the head teacher.

I explained I was a linguist.

'That's OK,' the man said cheerfully, as if I'd admitted to a wrongdoing that he would generously overlook. 'Glad you accepted the invitation.'

Scraping off hairs was woman's work, they told me, but the women hadn't turned up.

'Wouldn't you know it?' said Beth. She seemed to be addressing us both, but I wasn't sure what I was supposed to know. I felt I had to explain myself more fully.

'I've come to work with Collins,' I said. 'You'd know him, of course.'

'Collins the Bible-basher?' Craig laughed.

Beth laughed with him, and their laughter seemed to last for many seconds. I felt anxious for the man who was to be my saviour. I had to stand up for him in the midst of what seemed to be disregard for the only white here who'd learned Djemiranga.

'I know he's a missionary but that was why he lived here ten years and worked out their language,' I said. 'He's a linguist of international renown. Apparently he found a manuscript dating back to 1840 out in the desert and –'

'Worked out this language? Hah!' said Craig. His laughter made his stomach bounce up and down, and his cheeks ballooned until they almost covered his eyes.

'You speak it?' I asked, delighted.

'Anyone could,' said Beth, glancing at him, as if she constantly checked what she said with him. 'It's just – what – a few hundred words?'

He nodded. 'That'd be overestimating it.'

I struggled with disappointment. She had a thin, sharp nose and her hair leaped vertically out of her scalp in a crew cut that would be severe too if it were not for the way she'd dyed it baby pink with blonde highlights. Its tips curled forward, catching the light, rebellious in their prettiness.

Again, drifts of a scarcely heeded lecture were coming back to me. Odd, that something that meant nothing to me a few months ago had become imperative.

'One of the famous early linguists, Stanner, complained it was "just too hard". Thousands of words. Ten thousand, at least,' I told her. 'Almost rococo in its difficulty.'

'That's my point,' Craig said. 'Highly evolved languages simplify themselves.'

Beth however was exclaiming in surprise, this time not bothering to look at the headmaster, but gazing at me. Suddenly, ignoring him and hoping I could talk to the part of her that prompted her to stand in front of a bathroom mirror dyeing her hair pink, I managed to add more, extemporising a bit though with uncertainty, because if either of them had questioned me, they'd find that I knew little more than them.

'Some verbs have hundreds of variations of their own. For example, to kill or to hit – their word sounds like just one word to us – but one of the first researchers tracked down sixty-seven variations of the word, which I suppose they'd need, being hunter-gatherers – to kill or hit when you're walking forward, when you're walking backwards, when you're walking on a slope or on the flat, when you're walking towards home or away from home –'

Craig had heard enough and made an impatient noise that came out as a snort, and even Beth looked uneasily back at the classroom as if she'd suddenly remembered something more pressing than attending to a list of sixty-seven words. So I changed tack and said instead: 'I was wondering if you'd like me to come and help out with the children here.'

'We don't have children here,' said Craig while Beth gave a nervous giggle. 'So that won't be necessary.' I glanced up at his lips, and saw them thin with bitterness. So I had to come clean.

'I'm actually looking for an old lady who sings an ancient song. It's called the "Poor Thing" song. I wondered if you'd be able to help me.'

'Poor Thing!' said the woman, softening, giving me her attention again, and I noticed her blue eyes – so blue it was as if they held the sky, with lashes long enough to tangle at the corners. Her upper lip lifted like a child's hair bow. She had one of those odd, bony faces that could become beautiful, so that you watched it in suspense, waiting for the next instalment of beauty. 'Who's the poor thing?'

'It's a secret woman's song, so maybe the poor thing could be a woman,' I said. I was extemporising even more now, but Beth's pink curls were somehow prompting the words out of me. Our eyes met.

'She'd probably been given a hard time,' said Beth.

'It's more likely to be about a poor wombat,' snorted Craig. He put his bald head close to mine, confidingly, as if we were old friends. I smelled his aftershave, so recently applied it stung my eyes.

'I wouldn't say this to everyone, but since you've deigned to come to my public relations barbecue – not like the rest of the whites, you can't count on anyone's loyalty here – this is the most degraded people on earth.'

I took a step backwards.

'And I'd know,' he said. 'I've been out here two years.'

Beth nodded. 'He has,' she said.

'I came out because I'm an idealist. An educational idealist. I was shocked at the state of these people and I wanted to lift the IQ points of their children. You'd know, you're an educated person – South-East Asians have an average IQ of 103. Caucasians – you and me – have an average IQ of 100. But these people, they have an IQ of a mere 65.' He bent his head to me again, with another blast of aftershave. 'Not many people will tell you that.'

Beth had been told it many times.

'I wanted to save them too,' said Beth warmly to me. 'Even as a kid. I'm sure –' this, glancing at him, 'we both wanted to help.'

She nodded for him. He just looked at his watch.

'I remember an old Indigenous man came to our school on Multiculture Day and told us about what he called the old days, and the old people,' she said to him as much as to me, though he'd clearly heard this before. Now in her enthusiasm, despite him, her blue eyes seemed to be throwing reflections of blueness down her cheeks, like blue pathways on a pink and rolling landscape. 'They used to be able to do strange and marvellous things, like Indian gurus, because they'd trained their minds.'

'The old people were different, we all know that,' Craig said. 'It's what they've evolved to.'

'They apparently could raise the temperatures of their bodies on cold nights –'

'Probably by lying near their dogs,' he said, but he seemed to be laughing fondly at her so she continued.

'And they could travel across the desert at astounding speeds, so it seemed they could fly.'

We both gazed at her. She was trying to persuade him of her vision, trying to ease him out of his disappointment, using my presence to restore his sense of purpose, and for a moment I thought she might succeed.

'This old man described a life so different from our humdrum one that afterwards, I'd hang around in the bush – in those days everyone in the suburbs had bush in their backyards – and I'd draw pictures on the rocks, hoping that one day a lost tribe would see my pictures and come and find me. And I'd run away with them!'

She tried laughing into his eyes.

'Like running away with the circus?' he suggested.

She was dashed.

'That was then,' he said, wanting to indulge her. 'But now, they have the lowest IQ in the universe.'

She had one more try.

'Don't you think,' she added, almost beseechingly, 'we'd look bad in any IQ test they devised?'

She turned to me for corroboration.

'Their kinship system,' I began, remembering the builder and before him, lecture notes I'd taken down uncomprehendingly in what seemed a century ago – but I couldn't go on because I knew no more.

Craig saw me flounder.

'We owe it to them to lead them out of darkness,' he said.

We were interrupted by a shout. One of the boys had fallen out of the tree and was lying on his back in the dust. Beth gasped. I started to run towards the fallen boy. At exactly the same time, a beeper sounded and a red light flashed on Craig's belt. He cried out in alarm.

'Hell, it's feeding time. I promised to go to her.' He caught my arm. 'Here, make yourself useful, take these to the barbecue,' he said, thrusting his burden into my arms. To Beth, he said, 'You check the boy. I put hours into a requisition to have that tree cut down – too late, wouldn't you know it!'

Then the beeper sounded again and he was no longer an authority figure but a desperate man, breaking into a wild run towards the teachers' houses, his stick legs under his large belly flailing, one foot turning out sideways in a limp brought on by anxiety, his shirt coming untucked from his jeans and flying out behind. Beth, on the other hand, broke into a neat, athletic run towards the boys.

I looked down at what he'd thrust at me and found I was holding half a dozen stiff animal tails. Kangaroo tails, said the shop labels. They were black and hairy, frozen, with Glad Wrap around each. At least they didn't smell.

'Where's the barbecue?' I yelped to Beth's back.

'Follow the smoke!' She didn't pause in her stride.

Behind me was the roaring of a car motor and a clanking of hooves. I wheeled to see that the donkey was trotting across the schoolyard with the pack of bald dogs that had menaced me now running and jumping at its throat, open-mouthed, teeth bared, but the donkey, head held high, hooves elegantly lifted, refused to seem menaced by this lowly mob, as if to trot ahead of them across a schoolyard was its considered choice. Behind this cavalcade was the newly washed troopie of last night's journey. Adrian screeched to a dust-clouded halt near me.

He was shouting so angrily, he forgot to wind down the window and I couldn't lip-read. At last Daniel in the passenger seat leaned across and cranked the window down.

'I've been looking everywhere for you,' Adrian yelled.

'There's an injured child – a boy fell out of the tree – could you tell your doctor?'

'Not now I'm sacked,' he said.

Daniel and a young man in a white coat both strained to see through the windscreen to see the boy. There was a woman in a nurse's uniform in the back. I appealed to Daniel.

'Is anyone here a doctor?'

'The clinic's on strike,' Adrian said.

Daniel didn't meet my eyes. He just looked straight ahead, trying, I saw, to do what he was supposed to do.

'But the boy might be injured! He might be dead!' I said.

'They know how to fall. They're always falling,' said Adrian.

'Help him!'

The young man in the white coat said something to Adrian, who gunned the troopie into life so I had barely a chance to jump back. He roared across the playground towards the boy, scattering dust, dogs and the donkey, who had at last deigned to bray. Adrian screeched to a halt and called to the boy by name. The boy stood up, laughing at the fuss he'd created. Adrian did a wheelie around him, so that the braying donkey and the dogs chasing all had to leap backwards out of the way, the dogs falling over each other, and he drove back through his own dust towards me, with the animals, all either barking or braying, racing behind.

'Let's go,' he yelled to me, yanking up his handbrake.

'But I've just started work,' I shouted, against the din.

'We're going back to town,' he said. 'My staff are leaving with me. One out, all out – that's it, isn't it?' he called to his passengers, who either stared or nodded. 'And you're my responsibility, until Collins turns up, so get in.'

'But I've got to scrape hairs off kangaroo tails,' I said.

'For him? For Craig?' said Adrian. 'He's got it wrong. The mob don't scrape them off. They burn them off. Of course he wouldn't do it their way. Throw the tails to the dogs. Here, let me –'

He was reaching out to grab the tails. I swung them out of his reach.

Just then two Aboriginal women came through the school gate, heading towards the back of the school, where I now saw smoke drifting.

'Those must be the women who've come to cook,' I said to him, relieved, and ran after them.

'Excuse me, excuse me,' I called.

I sounded absurdly European, and they didn't turn around.

'Could you wait?' I called.

They kept walking as if they hadn't heard me, and it came to me that English was just a noise to them, as Djemiranga was to me. Behind me, Adrian honked the horn which started up a fresh crescendo of braying from the donkey and barking from the dogs.

I ran in front of the women, and held out the tails. Surprised, they stopped, and smiled.

One said a word. I copied it.

They both corrected my pronunciation.

I mimicked what they'd said.

The first woman added something else, something more than just a word. It might've even been a sentence.

I repeated what she'd said after her, though I didn't know what I was saying.

She laughed approvingly and they both nodded. I was blushing and laughing with my success.

I'd mimicked what seemed to be a whole sentence! My first sentence! And embedded somewhere in it, it could be that I'd just uttered, without knowing it, the travel affix that the Dean and E.E. Albert were so interested in!

But there was no chance to celebrate because Adrian had driven up in another choking cloud of dust, which all three of us had to wipe off our faces. I was doubled-up in a fit of coughing and, as I recovered, the women carefully prised the kangaroo tails away from me before I dropped them in the dust for the dogs to eat, just as Adrian wanted.

'Get in,' he said.

The women walked away again.

I called out goodbye to them in English to try to lengthen the moment. They didn't turn around. I stood staring after them, bereft.

'Get in,' Adrian ordered.

'I can't leave,' I cried out. 'I've just had a success!'

'In the back,' Adrian repeated. 'We've got to get out of this place.'

But I had to share the moment with that man who was once my soul-mate, perhaps. The Ian of old would've cared, surely, he would've cared.

'We had a conversation, well, almost. I mimicked them and they smiled –'

I was gabbling in my excitement.

'I said, get in.'

The white woman in the back threw open the door for me.

'I won't go! I'm staying!'

I turned, walked away.

Adrian pushed open his door, dive-bombed himself out of the troopie and ran in front of me.

'If you hold out any hope of doing your work, any hope of returning, you'll come with me!' he shouted.

'No,' I shouted.

'Yes,' he shouted.

We glared at each other.

'Stop making this scene,' he hissed, 'in front of my employees.'

'I have every right to stay,' I shouted.

'You're nothing here without me. Get in,' he shouted.

The woman in the back leaned out the window.

'I'm Gillian,' she said, speaking kindly as if I was a demented patient. 'I remember when a patient taught me the word for "pain". I repeated it after her, and wrote it down on a bit of paper and tried it out on the next patient. He understood me! It was a life-changing moment.'

I looked between Adrian and the nurse – his insistence, her kindness.

She had a way of opening her mouth into a rectangular shape like the opening of a letterbox. It opened before she spoke. It made her seem utterly without guile.

Her kindness dissolved me. I capitulated. I stumbled into the troopie and subsided on the seat.

'Life-changing!' I said.

'It made me feel I could belong.'

'What was it?' I asked. 'Their word?'

She looked abashed.

'I lost the bit of paper,' she said.

Adrian gunned the engine and I held my head in my hands.

'We've got to stick together to show them,' said Gillian.

'Show them what?' My voice was croaking.

'That they shouldn't sack Adrian. One out, all out,' said Gillian. 'We've got to show them our work principles.'

'Do you think they'll be impressed?' I asked.

She paused.

'Dunno,' she said. And smiled. 'It's our only hope, isn't it? Being perfect models of the way whites should do things.'

'Hope of what?' I asked.

'Dunno,' she said again, and this time I shared her smile.

I lolled back against the metal frame of the troopie. We pulled up at the house. Adrian leaped out and ushered his staff to sit on the verandah. Daniel sat with them, not meeting my eyes. Adrian bustled towards the kitchen to make them a cup of tea before the long trip into town.

'Pack up your things. Have you had anything to eat?' he asked me.

I stood in the corridor, refusing. 'I came to do a job.'

He ignored me. 'Hurry up. Don't you understand? They're doing this for me.'

I went to the bedroom and sat on the bed rebelliously. My old appeasing self struggled with my new resolution. I stood and pulled down the three skirts I'd hung up and the hangers clanked disconsolately. How would I go about doing my work? The only people left here I could talk to were the builder and Craig and Beth, and they made my heart sink. But I should at least try. I left my bag inside my room, and went back to the kitchen, where Adrian was jiggling teabags in the cups.

I tried another tack.

'Why don't you just stay here, in the house?'

'The best thing to do when you're sacked is to leave. There was to be a change of staff at the clinic today anyway, and I've told the new staff to wait in Alice Springs.'

'Shouldn't you stay and stand up for yourself? Not skulk off?'

'I've been sacked twenty times in twenty years,' he said.

'And always reinstated?'

He got milk out of the fridge and set it on a tray with the cups.

'It's better they experience life without a clinic, rather than listen to arguments,' he said. 'These are practical people. What really happened will stand up for me. The mob are fair. I'm sure I'll be reinstated within twenty-four hours.'

'But what'll they do without a doctor?'

'The hothead will have to run the clinic on his own. He'll find it's not all about grabbing power and going hunting. Someone might get really sick.' He saw my shocked face and added: 'In an emergency he can ring the Flying Doctor Service.'

As he spoke, the phone rang. He picked it up.

'We're leaving now. I'll bring you back. The roads are worse than ever, the trip's slow. I asked my friend to make you some lunch. She's got cable. Put on the TV.'

There was a pause.

'Don't cry. It'll be fine.'

His voice was sweet with kindness. He put the phone back in its holder.

'That was Meagan. They're at the house of my friend.'

'Who's Meagan?'

'One of the silly girls I've been sacked over,' he said. 'Get your bag.'

He was so sure I'd follow him, he turned and walked away through the laundry, heading to the verandah.

'Just tell me who the old singer is. I could run over to her house and record her while you're having your tea. Then I can get out of your hair and fly home.'

He laughed. He didn't look back.

Chapter 7

On the long trip into Alice Springs, Adrian took first turn to drive. Daniel sat beside him, sleeping. Gillian and I sat in the back with the young doctor and a black woman with her baby who Adrian needed to take to a specialist in town, despite his strike.

At the shop we'd sped past last night, we stopped for petrol. The young doctor leaped out, nimble and long-legged in cheerful Hawaiian beach shorts under his white coat, and called to Adrian: 'Interest you in some hot chips?'

Adrian woke up Daniel. 'Hot chips?' he asked.

Daniel nodded, and fell right back to sleep.

Adrian went inside the shop with the doctor. When they came out, laughing and talking like conspirators, both with hot chips in white paper bags, and a third bag for Daniel, the young doctor noticed me wide awake. He offered me a chip through the window.

'Want to see my new painting?' he asked. He didn't wait for me to nod before he reached under the front seat, his hair behind a girl's headband falling on his cheeks, and drew out a furled canvas, which he unrolled.

It had a startling simplicity and beauty – great round whorls of colour which, he said, showed secret dreaming tracks.

'Have you chosen the spot in your house where you'll hang it?' I asked.

'I'll hang it in my gallery,' he said. 'Cool, isn't it!'

He was pleased with my surprise.

'I'm starting up a gallery in Perth with my girlfriend. We've collected four thousand paintings for it,' he said. 'Ready to go. You should get some if you go back out there. Don't pay Alice Springs prices. Undercut the market. Take them a primed canvas and some paints. I paid $500, enough to keep the artist and her family for a couple of weeks. Bargain basement. This one should sell for about $5000.'

Out of the corner of my eye I caught sight of Adrian listening to the conversation. With a chip between his fingers he was gesticulating to me, pretending to slit his throat with the chip, his wind-up sign. But I wasn't going to appease. I turned my back on his gesticulation.

'That's a bit of a gulf,' I said to the doctor. 'With what you paid her.'

He didn't seem to mind.

'Oh, money means different things to us than it does to them,' he told me breezily.

He saw my reaction, and added: 'They're happy with very little, don't you know? You'll see. She was happy. Besides, she was grateful for my doctoring. Saved her kid.'

'But the painting might've kept her and her family for a year,' I argued.

Adrian had no choice but to speak, his mouth full of potato.

'Doctoring's what you're paid to do,' he told the doctor. 'That's carpetbagging.'

'But they love me!' cried the doctor. 'They give me paintings out of love! They wouldn't sack *me*!'

Adrian and the doctor glared at each other. Adrian wordlessly climbed in the back and the doctor climbed into the driver's seat alongside Daniel, and sped down the dusty road so fast we hit our heads on the ceiling at potholes.

Adrian's silver eyes were flashing as he sat across from me. He hissed under the noise of the motor, 'You put me in a spot where I had to reprimand him. After what he's doing for me!'

'But you've let him get away with it 3999 times!' I said.

'His paintings aren't all from Gadaburumili,' he said. 'Anyway, the territory's crawling with carpetbaggers. Stamp out one, a hundred more scramble over him to take their place. And by the way, how long have you been here?'

I slumped in my seat.

Adrian dozed on the seat opposite me. Sometimes he opened his eyes, checked out the window, and fell back to sleep. He must've been dreaming happily because when he woke, his mood had changed and he put out his arms to hold the baby.

'Want a baby?' he asked teasingly after a while, holding out the child to me.

I quelled my resentment and took the little boy clumsily, but when I rubbed his back, my fingers glided with astonishment over the fine, smooth, moist skin. His mother had the same smooth finely knitted skin. The baby cried as I held him. He hadn't cried with Adrian. My own eyes filled with tears again.

'Don't worry,' Adrian said, his voice so conciliatory, it almost melted my bones. 'It will all go on, just the way it was.'

In that sweetness, I felt the thump of capitulation again. I tried to resist it.

'Nothing does,' I said. 'Nothing goes back to where it was.'

'Toilet stop.'

Adrian's voice woke me up out of a deep dream in which I was falling off the sandstone escarpment that reared behind our house on the river, falling past dark trees, golden sandstone ledges, down, down, down. I woke to a clench in my heart.

People were clambering out of the troopie, men off to one side of the road, the mother and baby off to the other, disappearing beyond the fringe of scrub. I stood on the heat of the road. I squinted at the sky, so stunned with heat its blueness had faded. I found myself walking beside Gillian.

'I really felt for you back there,' she said.

'Thanks.' We walked in companionable silence. I was relieved by her friendliness. Perhaps she could help me in my quest, I thought. As we walked I blew my nose, but my tissue came away red with blood.

'That happens to me every time I come out,' she said. 'It's the dry heat, such an assault on the body.'

'But not for them?' I asked.

'They're used to it. They probably suffer when they come south but in a different way. Watch out for those,' she added, making a clear half-circle around some spiky spinifex. 'Looks like it won't hurt but it's nasty. Like men.'

We both laughed. I was smelling the red dust, the heat on it, the heat on that vast red, rippling ocean.

'Out here it's so dry that the wild horses, when they come into the settlement, learn to turn the taps on with their noses.' She noticed the incredulity of my smile. 'It's true! I've seen them myself.'

'What do you think will happen out there to the clinic?' I asked.

'I'm leaving, thank goodness,' she said, heading towards two red boulders. 'It's not my problem. I work in six-week stints. Most of us do. Six weeks on, six weeks off. Though whether I'll have a job to come back to in six weeks' time remains to be seen.'

She told me her home was in Port Augusta.

'Is leaving home for six weeks hard for you?' I asked.

'It's perfect for my love life,' she said. 'Last time I went home, Mr Right moved in to live with me. He's absolutely perfect. Except for his kids. I don't like his kids. It's good to get away from them. I'm going behind this bush,' she added. 'Why don't you use that one over there?'

I walked around the bush, to make sure I couldn't be seen from the road.

'There'll be no traffic for a couple of hundred kilometres,' she laughed. 'On these dead straight roads, you hear the hum of a car ten kilometres away. Not used to this, are you? City Girl, that's what they call you, I heard them. They call you City Girl.'

'You can speak their language, after all?' I asked excitedly.

'No, they say it in English. They don't speak much English, but they've learned that. City Girl! Fondly, I have to say.'

I was reassured by her warmth.

'You think they like me? Already? They don't know me!'

'It's probably because they're pleased Adrian has his girlfriend here.'

'I'm not his girlfriend!' I protested from behind my bush, my trousers down at my ankles.

She came out from behind her bush zippering up her jeans. She was elegantly slender.

'I'm sorry, I thought you were.'

'Did he give that impression?'

'I just assumed, I'm sorry. I didn't think you were Daniel's. Lovely guy, but he's totally under Adrian's thumb.'

'Adrian's his dear friend,' I protested, pulling up my trousers.

She laughed. 'Don't worry, he'll break out one of these days.'

She let the sentence fall away.

'I'm neither's. I've come to work,' I said. 'I'm a linguist. I'm here to record the song of a dying old woman.'

'Who's that?' she asked in surprise.

'That's the trouble, I don't know,' I said. 'But in the clinic,' I added quickly, 'you'd know who's dying.'

'No one's dying,' she said. 'A lot of people are sick but we're doing well by them. Adrian hasn't told you who it is? – Don't!'

I'd been charmed by the emerald green pincushion plants, as I thought of them, that tapered into feathery mauve grasses riffling in the wind like hair. Even in that midday sun they seemed moonlit, and I fondled them. Now I pulled away in pain, and saw that the emerald cushion was another manifestation of the spinifex spikes both Gillian and Adrian had pointed out earlier.

'I warned you!'

'Nothing here is what it seems,' I said.

'Why hasn't he told you who it is?' she asked.

I spread my hands. 'He said to wait till the time's right. I'm worried how long that's going to be. In fact –' I wound down, changed course, 'could someone show me through the clinic's records? Could you?'

'You'd have to look through the records of hundreds of people,' she said. 'And of course we don't classify people under how sick they are. You can't just type in "s" for sick or "d" for dying, you know. And the records are confidential. I'd get into trouble helping you. That's if I ever go out there again. You might have noticed I'm not a favourite. It's strange he hasn't helped you –'

The rest of her sentence was drowned in a hurry-up honk from Adrian.

'He does get bees in his bonnet,' she said. 'I should know – I'm one of them.' She laughed in a friendly way. 'Maybe you are too.'

'What's he got against you?'

'I told him something once. I shouldn't have – my mother would've turned over in her grave. Made him go funny – I don't know why. Jealousy maybe. That's the thing about the desert – you get so lonely, you blurt. And you? What's he got against you?'

But we were nearing the road and when Adrian saw we were talking, his face darkened. I was beginning to know that look well. I feared that he'd read my body language and suspect my new plan. He ushered Gillian into the front seat to sit next to him now that he was the driver. The doctor and Daniel were to sit in the back with me and the Aboriginal woman.

'Your job is to keep me awake,' Adrian told her. 'Not to gossip.'

I dozed again.

When I woke, we were a hundred kilometres out of Alice Springs. Here hills erupted without foothills, without warning, like a monster in my head, like something I was trying to forget that was refusing to be forgotten.

I dozed again – and woke to an explosion. The troopie swerved, Adrian steered across the sandy ridge of the road, mounted a sandbank, pushed over low-lying scrub and pulled up just before we hit a tree.

'It's a blow-out,' he called amiably. But his mood changed as he burst open the back doors and remembered me. It was as if the driving had soothed him till then. He searched under my feet for the toolbox and a jack.

'You fix this up,' he demanded of Gillian.

'I don't know how,' she said.

'You should learn. It might happen next time when you're driving alone.'

'I'm going home,' she said sulkily. 'And none of us might be coming back.'

But he insisted. She jacked up the troopie, under Adrian's impatient instructions.

I stood nearby as she handed me the nuts, trying to get a chance to continue our chat, but Adrian stood his ground. 'You've always depended on a man to do this, haven't you?' And when she'd finished, he told her to take the old wheel to the back of the troopie. She lifted it up.

'Roll it,' he barked at her. 'It's not a basket of wet washing.'

'Of course,' she said, blushing a little, a little ashamed to be treated like this by the boss in front of everyone. Adrian stood in my way as I went to climb back into the troopie.

'Don't make her your best friend,' he hissed. 'I'm sacking her.'

Nevertheless he handed her into the back of the troopie, an old-fashioned, courtly gesture meant to charm her. As he did, he spoke quietly to her. She nodded in agreement. Her eyes seemed attached to him, clinging to him. I knew how bewildered she felt. In the last day, I'd seen how quickly he could change. He touched her arm kindly, like a parent who'd roused on a child for its own good, then wanted to restore peace.

'It's your turn for a rest,' I heard him say. 'But rest, don't chat.'

It was an order, not a piece of advice. He slammed the door. Through the dust-encrusted back window, I watched him stride away. Red streaks had stained his blue shirt in a jagged pattern.

I had to leave this place. I didn't need to find out who he was. I didn't need this puppeteer; I didn't want to be one of his marionettes. It was just a matter of getting on a plane, flying home, admitting to E.E. Albert I was a failure.

Inside, Gillian arranged a jacket against the wall of the troopie and lolled her head, shutting her eyes against the enquiry in mine, against his humiliation of her.

The voice in my head started again, insistently. I'd explain to E.E. Albert that nothing was as it was said to be, that the assignment was made impossible by this man, that he who should've paved my way was making obstacles. It wasn't my fault I'd failed, I'd say. It was impossible. Impossible. But the road sang under us. *You're a failure. A failure.*

I fell asleep alongside Gillian.

*

I call it the Bay of Shadows from the moment my family first gaze at the decrepit row of houses on the banks of a river as brown and thick as old stew. It must've been raining for days, and I don't yet know that rain turns the water from silver to sludge. I shiver, and wonder if it's always chilly here.

There's a high aloof cliff beetling over the houses, punishing us for being what we are, squatters, making sure we're cut off from the sun.

My father says, 'What about that one?' His voice is hearty, although I've already begun to notice he uses that tone to get his way. He hearties us into what we don't want.

I look along the row, one house after another, one little more than a stone chimney, and one with all its window-glass broken and curtains lacy with age and a rain tank so rusty there's reddish water pooling on the cement stand, buzzing with mosquitoes. One house has a wooden staircase coming adrift from the wall, leaning out dizzily into sheer blue air. One's propped on foundations of bits of broken tiles and fibro, all so awry that the edifice seems to float. There'd be no escaping down the river when the tide is low because all the houses have front yards that are fields of mud, grey and thick with the twisted, sulking roots of mangrove trees, and popping like farts with the burrowings of tiny crabs whose eyes glint pleadingly up at me when I take a stick to explore their holes.

I turn to follow my father's pointing finger, hoping against hope that he isn't pointing at the dampest, saddest, muddiest, smallest, most decrepit, most shadowy one.

He is.

'Perhaps it's best to pick the worst,' my mother says. She's what everyone calls a soft touch. It makes me cranky. 'Then the owner's less likely to turn up.'

'The tide will come in soon,' my father says. 'You'll see.' And he's right. The tide slides across the mudflats in silver mirrors, and we hear no more from the crab families for a while.

'Will it stay up?' I hope.

'No, but it will always return,' my father says. 'The good things are worth waiting for – eh?'

He ruffles my hair, as if he means me. My father has charm. He's a ne'er-do-well, that was what my grandmother, my mother's mother, called him on her deathbed when I wasn't supposed to hear. He believes, if only he didn't have us to look after, he would've been an artist bound for great things. He could've lived in Paris or Vienna or London, the cultural centres of the universe, where his talent would've been appreciated. As it is, the one painting he's sold was bought by Diana. When she heard he couldn't pay the rent on our city house, she said: 'Bring your wife and the child to the Bay, just round the corner from me. There are deserted houses there needing a bit of love and care. Like I do.'

My father, who no doubt believed he too needed a bit of love and care, tells me that last sentence much later, when he thinks I'm old enough. He never tells it to my mother.

*

When I woke in the troopie, Adrian was beside me, touching my hand gently. I was back at the river, my river silvered by sunshine.

*

My gentle mother, red-faced, yells at my father as he comes in the door one Saturday morning, back from a week of working at your mother's.

'You and this Diana! You have nothing in common! What do you talk about?'

My father says, with triumph in his voice: 'Nothing.'

My mother, blanching, turns sobbing into the spare room she calls her bedroom.

'They don't need to talk,' I hear her sob again and again, to my bewilderment. It takes me years to work out what she means.

My father stalks out to our jetty to check the crab pots I'd put out, the way Diana has taught me.

It's true that not an earnest thought seems to pass between them, though they chatter constantly, Diana's earrings dancing with every wobble of her double chin. Her hands tumble in the air for emphasis, and twinkle like wineglasses held aloft, for she wears rings on every red-nailed finger. My father's eyes follow her twinkling fingers like a hungry dog when you move a biscuit through the air in front of its nose. Her voice finishes off his sentences, and his voice finishes off hers, as if they're singing a duet, though, as my mother would say, with only nonsensical words like *fal-de-lal* and *fol-di-didio-loh*. I'm ten before I realise that if their thoughts lie side by side without speech, so too must their bodies in the darkened, frightening, silent spaces of her house.

You know that I spend my visiting nights on your red dusty sofa, out on your verandah amongst the twittering, humming night world. You don't know that I never dare go through the dark house to the toilet to pee in case I hear what I shouldn't. I'm terrified I'll wet the bed. I'm guilty about knowing what everyone pretends I don't know; but worst of all, I'm guilty about being my mother's spy.

*

His touch on my arm was disarmingly intimate, now that his anger had passed.

'You're talking in your dream,' he was saying.

I opened my eyes, icy with fear that I'd given myself away.

'What did I say?'

'Nothing interesting.' His silver eyes laughed at me. 'You sleep sweetly, like a child,' he said.

Out the window of the troopie was a suburban street without red dust and dilapidated houses, just tall buildings and gleaming shops and a cement footpath, the busy supermarket, and new cars without rust dashing by.

'Why wouldn't you point out the old singer?' I asked.

He ignored me. 'We're in Alice,' he said. 'I've taken my staff to the best hotel. They'll stay overnight before they fly out. The new staff are already here waiting on my orders. If we go back to the settlement –' he emphasised 'if', 'Daniel will take them in the second troopie. Right now, I'm off to my friend's to stay. You can wait in a hotel the clinic has an arrangement with. It's pleasant enough –'

'I won't,' I said.

'It's clean,' he said. 'No swimming pool, that's its only problem.'

'I won't stay,' I said.

'You know someone here? You can make your own arrangements? Or –' he laughed, 'do you fancy a park bench?'

'I'll fly home,' I said.

'There's no need,' he said. 'The sacking is just a hiccup –'

'Your sacking isn't my problem,' I said. 'My problem is you. You're making my job impossible.'

He paused. 'We see your job differently, you and I.'

He inflamed me with rage.

'How you see my job,' I said, 'is immaterial. I've been sent to record a dying old lady and you won't even tell me who she is!'

He said, evenly, reasonably, in his sweetest voice: 'I've watched, over the past twenty years, many academics study my mob.'

'*Your* mob! You own them?'

'I hate the way academics breeze in, get the bit of information they need for their careers, leave and never come back. That's not what my mob want – they want whites to be like family, to return. Yet whites notice nothing but their own little patch. They say their information's going to a good cause, but it's only a good cause for them, never for my mob. And yes, they're my mob because I'm one of the few who protects them and stays with them, without any benefit.'

'You get a wage!'

He ignored me.

'My way, you won't be able to do that. You'll have to get to know them. Oh, I'm ready to give you any advice, I'm always helpful, I can't be faulted on that –' He paused. 'But I'm not going to let one more academic exploit them. I'm afraid my new policy starts with you.'

'So when will I know them enough?'

'It'll be clear to both of us.'

'I'm not going to have you hold my university to ransom.'

'You can stay, or not. Up to you.' He got out of the troopie, but with my bags.

'Leave them in here,' I said.

'You can't stay in the troopie. I have to take it in for a service. Your bags will be in the hotel lobby. You can order a taxi to the airport from there, or you can stay.'

He shut the door behind him. I watched him go into the hotel lobby, no doubt making arrangements for me. I sat in the troopie. I listened to the ticking of the hot engine as it slowly cooled. I felt myself to be the child that was always inside me, the child that never grew beyond that silver river, beyond the day he left. Sometimes, many times in the past decades, I'd admitted I was no older than that child.

After a while he emerged empty-handed, heading back to the troopie. I got out. I walked past him in silence and into the lobby.

I'll ring E.E. Albert and ask her what to do.

That thought gave me enough determination to take my bags to my room. Unexpectedly, I sobbed with relief when I locked the door behind me, unzipped my toiletries bag and set up in the tiny bathroom my toothbrush, toothpaste and nailbrush, in the very order they'd been in at home, snapped on the TV news, and hung two pairs of trousers up in a wardrobe so flimsy that the hangers rattled. I shut the door, and reopened it to make sure that I hadn't sent the trousers sprawling to the floor.

Then I fell onto the cool comfortable bed without washing or changing out of my dusty clothes. Sometimes a mattress seems to caress you, to allow you to confide in it all your wearisome weight and exhaustion. So it was with that bed.

In the night, when I woke on the cool hotel sheets, I switched on the bedside lamp and dialled reception, to be put through to E.E. Albert's voicemail. I imagined her voice. I cleared my throat. I dithered.

I hung up. I rang back. I planned to say: You must stop thinking I'm interesting. I can't live up to it.

I couldn't say it.

Then I worried myself to sleep that her voicemail had magically recorded my thoughts.

*

My mother and I always expect the owner of our house to show up in the Bay of Shadows, to claim his house.

At first I try to persuade my mother to always let me put out an extra plate at mealtimes in case he should suddenly appear. My imagination is fed from a framed sepia photo found in a bottom drawer amongst dust and rusting paperclips. He doesn't look like the sort of man who'd take kindly to finding a family using up all the spaces in his house. He has a sharp face that demands attention and his fist is clenched tight over his large stomach, as if he's about to throw a punch, but in his other hand he holds a miner's cap between his first finger and thumb, as delicately as a woman would. He's standing with a group of Aboriginal people, all smiling. We can tell where the photo was taken by what he's written on it. My mother has never heard of the place.

My mother says that in fact you could interpret his face as a worried one, and that in his clenched fist is maybe a fishing line, too fine for the camera to pick up.

'All we can do for a while,' she says, one day when I'm worrying about being a squatter, 'is to look after his house, for everyone knows that a house likes to be lived in.'

Not that the house seems to agree. It sulks damply all winter and bakes all summer, it creaks through the black nights and ticks through the hot days, as if it's an animal trying to throw us off its back, and all the while, mists lick through the gaps in the fibro walls with a prying tongue.

As the years pass and the owner doesn't return, my mother takes to wondering aloud if he met an untimely end, perhaps in the house itself.

'It does have that sort of feeling,' my mother says, 'as if we're sharing the house with a ghost.' She's fighting depression, and often takes to her bed.

It's a relief for me to be invited to leave our Bay of Shadows and go around the corner to stay at Diana's house, even as my mother's spy, to leave the reminder that we're squatters.

Under what he's written there's a cross, which I worry is a sign of death, until my mother explains it's a kiss.

Greetings from Gadaburumili, he's written across the photo. *Wish you were here.*

Some time later, perhaps months, perhaps a year or two, I find it's missing from the drawer. I try other drawers. It's nowhere to be seen. I ask my mother.

'Ask your father,' she says.

When I ask him, his mouth sets in a thin line. I think: he's thrown it away, because he doesn't want the reminder that we're squatters either.

There are so many mysteries in childhood, so much waiting for time to solve them.

In the hotel room, I slept beyond breakfast; I woke feeling porous and insubstantial. But when I stood under the shower, real dust from my body pooled in red-edged irregular circles at the bottom of the white tub, and refused to leave until I put in the plug and ran water, then flushed it out again. The red dust had made rusty spots on my clothes, so I put them into a washing machine in the hotel laundry, but when I hung them on chairs in my room, the stains stayed. I picked desert prickles from the insides of my sneakers.

I went to lunch and chose a seat by the window. Next to me was a table of American tourists and a guide with an Australian accent, long curly red hair and deeply lashed eyes.

'Why won't the black people talk about themselves?' the American women were asking her as I examined the menu. 'We asked about their ceremonies but they won't say a word.'

'Perhaps they don't speak English,' the guide replied.

'But we heard them swearing.'

'They might be shy.'

'They didn't seem shy when they were swearing.'

'They mightn't think it's any business of whites,' said the guide. She was keeping her voice professionally even.

'But don't they want us to buy their paintings?'

Beside the guide sat a very handsome teenage boy with smouldering black eyes and glowing copper skin, but something about the length of his face was European.

'It takes a while to get their trust,' said the guide. 'I taught for a whole term on a community before I was given a skin name. That's where Billy –' she indicated the teenage boy, 'came from.'

I could see the eyes of one of the women tourists darting between the guide and the boy, the question trembling on her lipsticked lips: A term as a settlement schoolteacher and you got pregnant?

But politeness demanded she swallow it, so she tucked it away and licked her lips shut.

'It only took a term?' she said instead, and when everyone looked at her, she added: 'To get a skin name?'

A bored, listless-eyed waiter came over to wipe an already gleaming glass so that he could stand and watch out the window. I watched with him. I glimpsed Daniel walking up the street carrying boxes. Daniel! It came to me that, away from the settlement, I might have a chance to persuade him to help me – after all, he believed in my quest. I remembered again his rush of empathy, his admiration. Why didn't I think before of cornering him? But by the time I'd got to the door, he'd disappeared.

The waiter followed me.

'Madam? This man is important to you? You want me to run after him?'

'No.'

I sat back down and ordered a meal and a glass of wine, as if it could clear my reasoning and tell me what to do, and some time during that clear cold wine there was a familiar laugh on the street and I looked up to see both Daniel and Adrian walking up the road again, in the same direction, carrying more boxes. They were deep in conversation, Adrian talking, Daniel nodding. Daniel was far shorter than Adrian. My height. His thick mop of wavy hair gleamed in the sun. I must stop fancying him. He was a nodder, as Adrian wasn't. It was Adrian I'd come to understand.

I thought: if I fell under Adrian's influence, he'd make me into a nodder, too. I'd be just like Daniel.

I caught a glimpse of my face in the windowpane. It was a shock, my black hair, my olive skin. It came to me that my disguise mightn't work for him. Perhaps that might explain his antagonism. But in the window, I scarcely recognised myself.

I tried to weigh it up. He was bossy, and that might fit, because Ian had been rebellious. But someone who'd worked in remote places with no whites to answer to, that might lead to bossiness in itself. He was self-centred, and Ian must've been, to leave Diana like that, but many people were self-centred. He had a scarred index finger on his left hand, and so did Ian – didn't he? Was it on the left hand or the right?

I ordered another glass of cold clear wine and by its end I worked out that Adrian had calculated that if he brought a white woman to his house, he'd be more loved by the community – and their love seemed to be what he cared about most. When the old lady fell sick and he heard that Collins needed a female linguist, he'd have seen his chance.

By the end of the next wine I'd decided that there was no dying old lady, there was no 'Poor Thing' song, and there was no Collin Collins. I had to correct that when I recalled, over a black coffee brought by the waiter who seemed to be smiling more sweetly at me, that Collin Collins was an international linguist known to E.E. Albert, although of course not to me. Next, I suspected that Daniel and Adrian were lovers, and they needed a cover, who was me.

By the second coffee, when the waiter smoothed my tablecloth with broad brown hands and put two foil-wrapped chocolates by my serviette, I was sure that Ian had known that Diana was going to kill my mother, and hadn't cared. He wanted us all dead.

As I left, the waiter offered me a comfortable seat in a sofa near the window. I could read the newspaper till he finished his shift.

'Then I could show you the sights,' he said.

'No thanks,' I said.

I went back to my room, lay on the bed fully dressed again and fell into a deep sleep.

When the phone rang next morning, I was so deep in a dream that I expected Diana's voice, she who used to explain everything about the river and its habits – everything except about herself and my father. Did she ever consider what Ian and I would make of the two of them?

I reached my arm out for a clock, knocking over a glass of water. The phone stopped ringing. I wept for the loss of her, as I had many times. As if it heard me, the phone started ringing again.

'You haven't left,' came Adrian's voice.

'I don't make decisions fast,' I said.

'I'm going back to the settlement this morning,' he said. 'The mob have visited me. We're in discussion. Are you coming?'

'I'll decide over breakfast,' I said.

He rang off.

I packed, ready to fly back to the city, ready to drive back to the desert. I was in the breakfast room ordering toast and coffee when he walked in, and all over again I was sure he was my Ian, just walking into his mother's kitchen, swaggering because he's caught a big mullet, and Diana is squealing with pride.

He sat at my table without greeting me and ordered from the waiter – who seemed to have forgotten me as his possible date of last night – a breakfast of ham, eggs – soft – avocado and mushrooms. 'No toast, no coffee but two pineapple juices,' he said. 'It's good for the system,' he told me.

'I don't need any,' I said.

'They're both for me,' he said.

I played with the sugar bowl.

'Is the problem solved? Your sacking?' I asked, trying to sound convivial.

'Why do you think that?' he asked.

'You're returning,' I said.

'The two girls are still here. I must take them back. But I predict I'll be reinstated within twenty-four hours.'

He'd already said that over twenty-four hours ago. But I said, 'Have the people had their meeting?'

He sighed. I knew from his sigh that he was going to launch into another exasperated explanation.

'This mob doesn't have meetings, like whites do,' he said. 'Whites find that strange, but they think whites are strange, always calling meetings which generate disagreement. They don't like disagreement. They don't disagree with each other. What they really say behind closed doors, who knows? But they don't like speaking out, or being singled out. They call it shaming. We translate their word as shy, but the word means much more than our idea of being shy.'

He sat back, proud of his linguistic knowledge.

'What's the word?'

'Words are mere details. I'm a big-picture man.'

'The devil's in the detail,' I said.

'Stop interrupting me! That's why they don't like democracy. It's not just their problems with the word. Democracy makes families argue, and what they care about is family. Consensus is necessary for family harmony. It amuses and irritates them that white people are always having meetings. Whites are always talking, they say. Talking, talking. All the experts have written about that, Lieberman, Folds – who have you read?'

'E.E. Albert,' I said quickly.

I became preoccupied choosing a jam for my toast from a little wire rack at the table: blackberry, marmalade or bush tomato.

'What's bush tomato?'

'A jam from native tomatoes,' he said. 'Whites make it. They try to make my mob pick them, and for a while they do, but when they hand over a few kilos, they won't go back to pick more. Whites say they've got no work ethic. But they have their own work.'

'What work?'

'Their lives. Their cultural obligations, relatives, ritualistic connections, rituals, and ceremonies. Doing our sort of work would make already complicated lives impossible. Very hard, for instance, to serve in a shop when a customer comes in who ritualistically you must avoid, or who you must share everything with.'

He was concentrating on eating mushrooms with his fingers. It came to me that he didn't talk to explore ideas, he already believed utterly in his ideas. He didn't talk to think aloud, but instead, to shine. Under my attention, he was shining, showing me how much he knew about his mob.

I didn't shine.

We ate in silence. He ate sloppily, tearing off pieces of ham with his fingers and dipping them in the yolks of his eggs as if the yolks were tiny bowls of sauce. When he put his elbows on the table, egg dribbled down, streaking his pale blue sleeves with yellow.

*

Don't you remember, how could you forget – Diana is a stickler for table manners – elbows off the table, don't stick your elbows out like chicken wings, lay the knife and fork down side by side to show when you've eaten enough, don't speak till your mouth is empty. I, who often eat alone, relish the rules. When my father first takes me with him to Diana's house, she laughs at the way I eat.

'She's like a savage, a sweet little savage!' she tells my father laughingly while fluffing my hair. 'Doesn't her mother teach her how to be a woman?'

There's a look that passes between them in the silence that's like lightning sizzling across a blackened sky.

With your manners, you couldn't be Diana's son.

*

'I've forgotten city manners,' he said, interrupting my thoughts, aware of my eyes on him. He was proud of that. He'd laid aside his own culture, or much of it, to be part of the culture of his new family, hoping to be a valued son.

'I assume that you went to the supermarket for anything that needs topping up?' he said. 'That's if you're going back out with me?'

'I don't need anything – that's if I'm going out with you,' I said.

'Have you checked plane times?' he asked.

'I'll just go down to the airport and wait,' I said.

'You'll have to take a sleeping bag. There's only one flight a day and you've missed it,' he said triumphantly.

Then it was I who disobeyed all the rules that Diana had so painstakingly instilled. I put my elbows on the table as if they were heavy baggage I could no longer bear to hold and, wrinkling the white damask tablecloth, I rested my head in my hands.

E.E. Albert, if I'd been a better student, would I have made the right decision? I thought.

I grimly decided to stay in the hotel one more night, and fly back to the city on tomorrow's plane. I no longer wanted to find out if this man was my Ian. If he was, he'd transformed into someone I didn't like. If he wasn't, I'd live out my life in the knowledge he was lost. At least I tried, I said, though that gave me little comfort.

And the recording of the song? I was doing that solely for E.E. Albert – and, of course, for the Dean. Then I thought of the realisation Daniel had led me to, that it might be the oldest surviving song in the world. That frightened me. It seemed too much to live up to. I wasn't the sort of person who'd know what to do with something as important as that.

There was a knock on the door of my hotel room. I knew it was Adrian. When it suited him, he could knock on a door the way he touched people's arms, almost a caress, a respectful stroking of the wood.

'I could show you something wonderful if you come back,' he said through the door.

I sat up.

'The old lady?' I asked. 'That's all I want to see. That's what I came for.'

'My river.'

'Your river?'

'My river,' he repeated.

'That dried-up river?' I demanded. 'That's not a river! That's a joke of a river!'

I was sounding petulant, a child angry that a river wasn't flowing.

'My river is pink,' he said.

I opened the door.

'Why do you think I'd be interested in a pink river?'

'You're a coastal type. I'll show you, as long as the rain holds off. Want me to carry your bag?'

'To the singer?'

'Soon. I want to help you,' he said in his sweetest, most melodious tones.

And so I capitulated. Because of the promise of a pink river, I followed him out to the troopie. But this time, I carried my own bags.

Part Two

Chapter 8

'I'll sit in the back,' I said when we reached the troopie.

But that would mean the girls would be obliged to sit next to Adrian, and sitting beside a man wasn't right, even if it was a man they knew.

So I did what he wanted and climbed into the front seat and we drove through the suburbs of Alice Springs, which I valued more now, the neat houses and neat backyards, no shadowy overgrown places, no places for the errant heart to wrestle with its secrets. No places for the errant heart at all.

Adrian talked to me as if nothing untoward had happened in the last few minutes, as if I hadn't done an about-face. He said that Daniel would wait in Alice to collect the new clinic staff. Whereas he, Adrian, would return to the settlement immediately with the girls, their saviour.

Did he spend all his time scheming?

We stopped at a little house in a quiet side street.

'The house of my friend,' he said, and as I hung back shyly, he added, 'Come in.'

The girls were sitting in a dim lounge room lit by the flickerings of a TV set, nursing their babies and drinking cups of tea. I greeted them, and they turned their solemn black eyes on me, and then looked modestly down.

'Ready?' he asked them in his kindest voice.

They nodded, stood up, gathered their blankets and bags and filed into the back of the troopie.

'They don't do small talk,' Adrian reminded me.

I swung around to check on them. Some impulse inside me was stronger now.

'They're not putting on their seatbelts,' I told him.

His silver eyes bulged with resentment.

'Whites are always demanding these things. You just don't think it through,' he said. 'Some of the mob have to travel in the troopie with skin groups they're not supposed to be with, so they need to face whatever way they like, and seatbelts don't let them do that.'

'But you have been in a rollover –'

He sighed.

'OK, they're the same skin –'

He asked the girls to belt up, and they complied.

But I ruined any sense of victory by crying out: 'The shop!'

'What about the shop?' he asked, starting the engine.

'Skin's why they wait outside the shop!' I said.

'Don't chatter any more,' he replied snakily. 'I need the trip to figure out the right thing to say back at the settlement.'

'And the pink river?' I asked.

'In the fullness of time,' he said.

'Like telling me which is the old dying lady?' I asked.

We drove for hours in silence. In the back, the girls dozed, and I dozed too. The satellite phone attached to the dashboard jolted me into wakefulness.

'I didn't think that thing worked,' said Adrian. 'Pick it up.'

Through the static I made out Daniel's voice, asking me to pass on to Adrian the news that the new nurse hadn't arrived.

'Bugger. We'll have to ask Gillian to come back –' Adrian began, then he glanced at me, Gillian's confidante. 'Tell Daniel to hold on.' He braked in such a cloud of dust that it enveloped us and plumed in front of us like smoke. He pushed open the door into the smoke, strode out into it and turned his back on me. I wound the window down quietly.

'Say I'll give her one more chance! No more mutinies! … Blast and damn Jesus Christ,' I heard him mutter as he climbed back into the cabin.

As if it heard him, there was a clap of thunder and a flash of lightning that lit up at least a quarter of the huge dome of sky and zigzagged in a quivering but uncompromising white line to the earth.

'How awful to be where it landed,' I said.

'Nobody's out there for hundreds of kilometres,' he said. 'Only cows. And the odd roo.'

Then the rain came. It'd been ahead of us for hours, grey clouds dribbling down a white-grey sky. Now in the headlights the rain blew directly towards us, so that it seemed it wasn't raining on the entire breadth of the road, but directly in front of our lights, just for us. I broke our silence by saying that to him and he turned off the lights, to show me how foolish I was, again. The whole desert was lost in rain; rain swooping so densely that there was no mulga, no rocks, no sand, no earth and no sky. No us, no desert. We were all one.

I was comforted by rain, as I always had been. Rain is kindness to a troubled heart. Rain says you can put it off for a while, this problem, this thing you don't want to do, and nobody will condemn you. They'll say: 'Oh, of course you couldn't do it: it was raining!' The rain seemed to ease him too.

'I'll show you very soon, but some other time,' he said suddenly.

'What?'

'The pink river.'

'You read my thoughts,' I said.

'I often do. You're very transparent.'

'What else have you divined about me?' I tried to sound casual.

He glanced at me, and changed the subject.

'When I drive with them, they're looking out the windows all the time. You don't.'

'What's to look at?'

'Everything. It's their home. How many trees are fruiting together and how far they are from the road and from home and whether they're worth spending expensive petrol driving to, and where bush turkeys might be hanging out.'

'Like going past the shops in town?'

'Not to mention birds,' he continued, ignoring me. 'To them, birds aren't just ornamental, they're useful. There's one that tells them if strangers are approaching, because strangers used to be lethal. There used to be a lot of violence between groups, before whites came.'

'How do you know?'

'I read, you know. Accounts of nineteenth-century men digging up fractured skulls, pre-whites. It wasn't all sweetness and light out here.'

'Whose accounts?'

He shrugged. He seemed about to say something else but he had to steer up and along an embankment because the road had deteriorated into crevices and rocks.

'The roads haven't been graded for a while,' he said as an understatement. 'Only the mob uses them. And a handful of whites. Why would a government spend money on grading?'

I laughed with him ingratiatingly because of his pink river.

'Did you grow up in the Territory?' I asked him.

He steered around a pothole.

'Look!' he said. It'd stopped raining, or perhaps we had driven out of it. A line of brown camels slinked by, heads high, majestic in their gait, as measured as if they were a trained dance troupe.

'They were brought out here by Afghans before the roads went in,' he told me. 'Now they've gone feral, tens of thousands of them.'

He slowed down to let me watch.

'Their necks strain forward like figure-heads on the prows of old-fashioned boats,' I said, then I wished I hadn't spoken. Keeping silent about boats and rivers was harder than I'd thought.

He didn't react, he just reached down to the little shelf in the door beside him, pulled up a bottle of Coke and took a sip, without offering me any. I'd watched him often do these prevaricating things to play for time, pour himself a drink, yawn, stretch, to organise his thoughts, perhaps his lies.

'And you – where did you come from?' he countered instead, speeding up now that the camels had veered away from the road.

I knew when I agreed to come here that I'd have to make up a plausible story, but I'd continually put off thinking about it. I'd never been forthcoming about my childhood, not to my short-lived husband, nor to my shorter-lived lovers. I never wanted to tell them about Diana, or even about how after the funerals I stayed with my father while he slipped deeper into dementia and death.

Now that the moment was on me, it was too late to make up anything; besides, his energy seemed to demand utter spontaneity. I found a way to half tell the truth.

'I've spent a lot of time in Sydney. The inner city.'

I described the house I'd glimpsed on E.E. Albert's desk, E.E. Albert's house. I made it mine, and that gave me a comforting glow. I described tall buildings and apartment blocks with noisy cement staircases and walls emblazoned with graffiti. I added cats.

But as I talked, I was thinking about the river.

* * *

It makes us seem important, our river. Living near it is like living in the muddy forecourt of a great monarch, waiting for his visit. For whenever we're doing the dullest things – collecting kindling, hoeing the vegetable plots, pumping the water to the top tank for the gravity feed, setting the fishing lines, checking the crab pots, cleaning out the droppings of the possums and the leaf litter from the gutters – there is the river, shining silver again, sliding majestically into the sea, sliding majestically back to the mountains.

It isn't till I hide in the city that I discover how puny I am, how mired it seems I will always be in low, muddy tides.

Adrian nodded as I talked about the city. He wasn't interested in things that didn't directly concern him, so I thought I'd succeeded in distracting him.

'You're wondering how I came to be out here?' he asked. I almost jumped, I was so startled, and I was glad that his silver gaze was on the road. He wasn't noticing me, I believed.

'I came here when I first left the city –'

I couldn't wait. I blurted, 'Why Gadaburumili?'

He paused. 'Why not?'

'The desert's very big.'

'I was offered work in a settlement not far from here, that's why. I did council stuff – the sort Bruce is paid to administer. Organising rubbish collections, helping with welfare payments. Sometimes I fixed houses – I'd rather work with my hands, or with people. Not this desk stuff.' He flashed a rueful smile at me.

'What happened?'

'I fell foul of Bruce's equivalent.'

'Who was he?'

'Why do you want to know? Just an old bloke topping up his super. Usual story. The desert's full of incompetent CEOs. The good ones are legendary.'

He steered around a ravine in the road.

'So I ended up at another settlement where the hunting grounds had been ruined by cattle, and the old knowledge was dying out and the mob was starving. They live such short lives. In that settlement, my best friend – he was my age and I watched him die a long, slow, horrible death –' his voice broke. 'He was robbed of forty, fifty years of life.'

He struggled with his voice, and raised his hand to brush away tears that were sheeting his face. When his hand went back on the steering wheel, I put mine over his for a moment.

'So I began a store there. I bought a truck and drove out with dried goods – salt, sugar, flour, tea – the usual. I wanted to save them from starvation because I knew this culture was unique.'

'But wouldn't a store have changed the unique culture? Isn't food and how you get it part of culture?'

His anger was always sudden, like a blow I wasn't expecting.

'You think they should've starved instead? For the amusement of whites like you? We whites don't live like we lived fifty years ago.'

He put a layer of certainty over what was uncertain; it clung to all his thoughts, that certainty, like the powdering of red dust flying in the open window and already beginning to cling to the hairs on my arm.

'You want to see them as they used to be, so you can be fascinated, so they please your Western sense of history? You say, if only they were still exotic!'

I blushed, because indeed I had been wishing that.

'But they *are* exotic, despite the changes and adaptations in their ways. It's just you haven't got the eyes to see. I'm forcing you to develop those eyes.'

Then all the books I hadn't read stood upright and condemned me. He paused for me to contradict him further, but I said nothing.

'By then I'd become legendary – people still come up to me in Alice Springs and point me out to their children. The Gadaburumili people asked me to help them with their clinic. I knew this was what I'd been born to do. I wanted to stop the deaths, the illnesses, the wasted lives. I wanted to show that it could be done. And the settlement was dry, so I knew I stood a good chance. A chance to save them!'

He glanced at me.

'Do you understand me now?'

I nodded.

'Did you come out here alone?' I asked.

'Are you enquiring about my love life?' he asked with a wry smile.

'Yes,' I admitted. My heart gave an annoying bump. I hoped he couldn't see how my shirt fluttered.

'Thought so!' he said, pleased at his intuition. 'You see – you are transparent. There was a woman at the previous place but it didn't work out. My fault, I suppose. I was still getting over my childhood. In my childhood –' he took a breath and paused.

'Things happened.'

I cried out then, but I was saved by a sudden squall of rain boring holes into the dust of the road, making wild wind-blown zigzags on the windscreen, intersected by others, cancelled by the wipers, and instantly making new zigzags. I had to resign myself to waiting to find out who he was. Whether, under the surface, he was who he seemed to be. The silence between us deepened but was crammed with thoughts. I hoped we were communing. The red road we were climbing was so furrowed with tyre tracks, it was like a child's finger painting with red paint. I told him this. He nodded.

'Was there a lot of sadness in your family?' I asked after ten kilometres or so of silence, just the hammering of the rain that had begun again, and the swishing of the tyres.

He glanced at me in relief that I'd given him this way out.

'That's one way to put it, a lot of sadness.'

Parts of his face smiled independently of each other. The years seemed to have taught his muscles different contradictory lessons, and it was as if each set of muscles had to negotiate with the others. As if his eyes had learned different lessons from his cheeks and each had learned different lessons from his lips and from his forehead. So all of them, eyes, cheeks, lips, and forehead had to negotiate with each other and join in his smile one at a time, in their own time. It made me wait to see if his entire face lit up.

'It was important to get away from it, up here,' he said.

There was another pause.

He said confidingly, 'It hasn't followed me. I hope it won't.'

I tried not to swallow loudly.

Then suddenly the troopie veered into the soft embankment on the road edge, narrowly missing the spindly trees, and to my surprise Adrian wasn't struggling against the troopie's veering, he was steering with it.

'Don't worry.'

He put his arm out in front of me to stop my body falling forward. The troopie surged across the road and limped, then he got it under control, and braked.

He grinned, pleased with himself.

I whirled around to check on the girls and their babies.

'A good thing that they were wearing seatbelts,' I said. 'They've slept through it.'

He ignored me.

'That's how to handle a troopie!' he said instead. 'Did you see how I did it? A lot of tourists don't know how to drive on these roads. You wouldn't have known how. There are a lot of rollovers.'

He got out of the troopie and looked at the front wheel, the rain instantly flattening his grey hair to his skull, his curls to his forehead, his pale blue shirt to his chest. I stopped crowing about the seatbelt, moved to capitulation by his muscular chest.

'It's another blowout. Can you get up on top of the roof and throw me down the spare wheel while I take this one off?'

I was scared of heights but I wasn't going to be humiliated the way he'd humiliated Gillian. I braced myself and climbed nimbly up the troopie's ladder, and though the wet roof dented under my weight, I planted my feet carefully and somehow I didn't slip. I threw down the tyre, careful not to hit him with it, and climbed down, holding my breath that I didn't ruin it all by falling off the ladder.

Adrian was bent over the wheel, undoing nuts. Still trembling, I hid it by fossicking for an old dirty blanket under one of the jacked-up troopie's seats – folded probably by dependable Daniel – and held it over us both as an umbrella. He glanced up at me, smiling, preoccupied.

'You don't have a clue what you're doing, do you?'

Now my pride tumbled, but I was immersed in holding the blanket.

'As a linguist,' he pursued.

'It's my first time in the field,' I mumbled.

'You know what I think?' He didn't wait for my answer. 'I think you've only come out here to impress someone –' he was too busy to notice my blush, 'some tutor or lecturer. I don't think you care about what happens to the mob or their language. You're a compassionate, sweet-natured person but you're overruled by someone else's agenda. That's why I've got no hesitation in changing that.'

His face was engrossed with the nuts he was tightening. He handed me the wrench without glancing at me. I thought: I could kill him with this.

'There's no point hitting me,' he said. 'You need me.'

You are always flagrantly abrasive and tactless. There are boys at school whose older brothers have promised to avenge them by killing you. My father promises the same, but secretly, gnashing his teeth only in front of me.

I'm always white-hot in your defence.

'He's honest,' I say. 'He says what he thinks.'

'Who cares what a whippet like him thinks,' my father says.

'Diana,' I say.

Even her name brings a deep colour to my father's cheeks.

'Ah, Diana,' he says.

*

Now I looked down at the greasy rag I was holding for him.

'You like having us in your power,' I said to Adrian.

'That's true,' he said.

We got back in the troopie just as the rain stopped. We opened the windows to dry off. Then I slept, and woke as we were coming into the settlement. It was midnight. All the lights were out, but the sleeping houses were watched by a giant, benign but very distant moon.

I was sleepily walking into the house when he suddenly said: 'They've given you a bush name already. They don't normally do that so fast.'

He seemed pleased with me, and with himself.

'What is it?'

'Ngadju. It's a bird they love, that leads them to water. I don't know why they'd call you that.'

I clapped my hand over my mouth: I suddenly remembered that he shouldn't have told me, he'd explained that. But all I said was: 'How do you know?'

'You were walking towards them and I heard them say "Ngadju!" and I've often heard them call a bird that. A little, insignificant grey one.'

'You hear what they say, after all!'

'They're my life.'

We were in the kitchen. He opened the fridge door, bending, finding the pineapple juice.

He turned his head towards me.

'You got it because they love me, of course.'

He made a face over the juice. 'Funny – this seems off. It's probably the fridge.' He shut the door and poured the juice down the sink.

'We'll deal with that in the morning.'

Chapter 9

'You'd better come to the funeral,' he called through the bedroom door in the morning. 'If you don't, the mob might think you're hiding.'

I was instantly wide awake.

'Is my old lady dead? You've kept me from her and now it's too late!' I threw open the door. 'You realise what you're responsible for? This game you play –'

'It isn't *her* funeral,' he said gently.

I crumpled with relief, then remembered what he'd just said. 'Hiding?'

'When someone dies here, someone else is to blame.'

'A white person blamed? I could be blamed?'

Daniel was in the hall. He'd just arrived back from Alice, grubby, sweaty, slouching in exhaustion. Nevertheless, he summoned himself to defend me.

'Don't frighten her.'

'Mind your own business,' Adrian snapped at him. It was the first time I'd seen him unpleasant to Daniel.

'It's hard enough being out here,' said Daniel, 'without being scared.'

'What's hard about it?' Adrian snorted, but he relented enough to say, 'Everyone's expected to be there.'

'Everyone? My old lady? She'll sing?'

'Remember? She can't sing her traditional song in front of men. Even you know that. That's why you're here – isn't it?'

He went away.

'It's true that everyone will be there,' said Daniel quietly to me. He went into the bathroom, and then I heard a yelp.

'There's no hot water! I bet it's bloody Bruce again.'

'How can the CEO have used up our hot water?' I called, but he couldn't hear me.

Daniel came out in a towel. Water was still running down his tanned chest. He looked both strong and vulnerable. I was always moved by the vulnerability of men. Suddenly, my bowels seemed to squeeze together.

'I hope you had a shower last night,' he said to me. 'There's no electricity.'

'The water wasn't hot,' I remembered.

Just then Adrian returned. He'd been to the clinic.

'The generator's broken down. I'm off to see what I can do.' He glanced at Daniel's near-nakedness, and strode out of the house.

'I won't be able to have breakfast!' said Daniel.

'I'll go out and make a fire in the yard for a cuppa for you,' I said to Daniel. 'Maybe fry some eggs and bacon.'

'I'll get dressed and make a damper for us,' he offered, cheering up. 'The local ladies taught me how.'

He headed towards his bedroom, and then doubled back.

'No, I should make the batter first. It's better if it's had a chance to sit.' He grinned. 'That bit about sitting is from my mum.' Creak. Creak. He laughed his unoiled creaking-door laugh.

'I'll stay and learn how to do it,' I said.

But it was really because of his bared and vulnerable chest that I sat on a kitchen stool to watch him as he mixed the batter.

'No egg to stick it together?' I asked.

'They don't,' he said. He grinned at me, enjoying himself. 'I suppose eggs would've been luxuries. It's all in the mixing.'

Creak. Creak.

He threw in a sprinkle of salt.

I'd often sat in Diana's kitchen watching her mix a batter, her beating action controlled by her powerful wrist. But he put his whole forearm into it, his upper arm muscles flexing.

'This is a show of strength,' I laughed.

'I was hoping you'd notice,' he laughed.

Suddenly Adrian was between us.

'I hoped you'd follow me,' he said to Daniel.

Daniel kept beating the mixture.

'Got to keep the momentum going,' he said.

'I need help figuring out how to start the generator,' said Adrian, a little nettled.

'What's wrong with using a key?' asked Daniel, still not giving Adrian his full attention.

'Bruce has gone off to Alice with the key.'

'There's no spare?' Daniel was then putting his entire body into the beating, bending from his waist.

'That's lost.'

'Isn't anyone else trained to do the power?' I asked Adrian.

'There's Russell, a black man, Bruce's assistant, but he's in Alice too,' explained Daniel.

'They're friends, gone off for a holiday together?' I asked.

Adrian leaned on the working board, groaning. 'You and the crazy things you come out with! Do you ever think before you speak?'

He prised himself up and draped his arm around my shoulders. It was quite a considerable weight, the weight of him.

'Russell's been gone a month,' he explained in a comically slow voice as if he was speaking to a simpleton. 'Doing whatever the mob does in Alice. Bruce has gone in for the weekend, doing whatever whites do to paint the town red.'

Daniel was pulling the fork out of the bowl to test the thickness of the batter mixture. He was satisfied, and offered us both a lick of the fork. Adrian refused it but I accepted, my eyes downcast.

'Watch Bruce put the blame on Russell,' Daniel said.

'What do you mean?' I asked.

Adrian groaned, but Daniel didn't mind explaining.

'Bruce should've been checking that generator once a day. That means about thirty checks he's missed since Russell left.'

He tested the batter with another fork.

'It's done.'

'Are you going to come and help me?' It was more a demand from Adrian to Daniel than a request.

'I'm having a well-earned bit of R and R,' said Daniel to him. 'Showing off my cooking skills.'

'Medications could go off in the clinic,' said Adrian, his face glowering.

'I suppose the damper's ready for a well-earned rest too,' said Daniel. Creak. Creak, he laughed.

'Put your shirt on first!' said Adrian, and slammed his way out of the house.

'I didn't know there was a dress-code here,' Daniel called after him, knowing he couldn't be heard. But he went, head lowered guiltily, into his room and came out buttoning, on a shirt.

'I'll set a fire before I go,' he said. 'The way the mob does. Just twigs and dead spinifex. It's probably its resin that does the trick.'

He laid down half a dozen twigs and a ball of spinifex which happened to be blowing about in the road, and lit a match.

'Faster than the stove,' he grinned.

I watched him, surprised at how economical the technique was. In my fires at the river, I'd have used a lot more wood.

He returned half an hour later, just as the fire had died down to its ashes, and he put the damper straight in on top of them, without a baking tin.

'Adrian's got the generator going. I've never asked him, but he must've had a good father – a real jack-of-all-trades,' he said.

I couldn't tell Daniel that the jack-of-all-trades was my father.

By mid-morning, Adrian had fixed the generator enough for
half the settlement to get power for two hours and the rest of
the settlement to get power for another two hours, more or less.
Daniel, hailing the grease-stained Adrian as a hero, offered him a
chunk of the warm damper, once he'd brushed off the ash, or most
of it. I pretended not to notice that some ash seemed cooked in.

'Wouldn't touch stuff like damper,' said Adrian.

'What's wrong with it?' demanded Daniel.

'Got my figure to watch,' said Adrian.

I almost said that dampers hadn't hurt Daniel's figure, but I
stopped myself in time.

I followed him and Daniel quietly out into the hot street to
the funeral. We'd all had cold showers, and we were dressed in
white shirts, he and Adrian in black trousers, me in a black skirt.

I had my recorder in my pocket.

'The funeral,' Adrian threw over his shoulder, 'is for an old
lady who had a heart attack doing what she loved the most.
She went hunting despite the doctors warning her about a weak
heart.'

We walked on in silence.

'Going by the funerals, death seems to have a different
meaning to the mob than to us. You don't have to be solemn like
in our funerals,' said Adrian. I saw that his white shirt ballooned
around his belly in a holiday way.

'What happened when you got back here?' I asked.

'A group of elders was waiting for me. I said that there'd be
no clinic without clinic staff, and no one would work without
me because I'm the manager. Dora came forward and said "You
must come back!" Everyone laughed, and so it was agreed.'

I wanted to say that there had been a meeting after all, but I
held my tongue.

'Who's Dora?' I asked. 'Was she running this non-meeting?'

'Dora's very powerful,' said Adrian, sighing because he had to explain. 'She's married to Skeleton's brother, Boney, who's on daily medication.'

'So she'd believe in white medicine,' I said.

'Not exactly,' he said. 'They look at our diagrams and nod and say, OK that's how the woman died. But Collins said they ask the bigger question.'

'Which is?'

'Why she died.'

I walked struggling in the heat and new confusion.

'Were they relieved you'd got the power back on?' I asked his back.

He told me that it didn't affect many people.

'If they don't keep up to date with their bills, Bruce turns their power off anyway,' Daniel told me. 'A lot of people have no power.'

He glanced back at my startled reaction, and went on, 'They make do by cooking outside, as you know, and going to bed when it gets dark. There aren't many TVs, and no one reads.'

'And hot water?'

'Some have no water – let alone hot.'

But Adrian hushed me because we were turning a corner into an empty space between the besser block houses, and the noise of a crowd was upon us. On the outskirts was a ring of parked cars with children bobbing inside, eating snacks out of silver packets. Inside the ring were rows of people sitting on the ground, men on one side, women on the other under a bough shelter, with four forked boughs supporting a roof where mulga branches had been thrown, lacy with leaves already dead in the sun. There were many rows of old women, and I lost heart. I'd never find her by chance.

'They've all been doing sorry business,' Adrian said. 'In the clinic, they came in to smoke away the bad spirits, with white paint smeared on their faces.'

I saw a group of white people across from where I stood with Adrian and Daniel – Craig, Beth and Dudley, who Adrian whispered was a teacher living and working at one of the outstations. Daniel waved to the new clinic staff. Amongst them, to my relief, was Gillian, chatting to an elegant stranger in a white coat – so she must be the new doctor. I smiled across at Gillian when Adrian wasn't looking. She grinned back, and stood behind another nurse, an older, short woman in a white uniform. Gillian gesticulated behind her, like a lit-up pointing hand in a shop window: 'Crazy prices'. The nurse looked around, and Gillian quickly rearranged her face and explained something to her – probably that a grub had been crawling in her hair, from the way the nurse combed her fingers through it.

A four-wheel drive arrived, a coffin on top loaded with a festivity of green roses, purple daffodils and yellow hydrangeas.

'How did they dye flowers those colours?' I whispered to Daniel.

'Plastic,' he whispered back, and Adrian shushed us.

A young but authoritative man, perhaps a preacher, stood up in front of the crowd.

'That's Graeme, the man who tried to sack me,' whispered Adrian.

I'd imagined a mean-looking man, but Graeme was large and strong and good-looking. He spoke in Djemiranga – he had to shout because the microphone wouldn't work without electricity – and I surreptitiously turned my recorder on. Then the chief mourners, all women, clasped each other in a circle and sang in Djemiranga to the tune of 'All to Jesus I Surrender'.

'Collins translated this,' Adrian whispered to me.

'Is my old lady one of the singers?' I whispered back.

He didn't reply.

Graeme started speaking in English and I turned the recorder off. His sermon drifted in the heat like dust, the familiar English words of salvation, the cross, Jesus. Young boys riding around the outskirts of the crowd on bicycles listened intently, their front wheels wobbling. Children played quietly, and a mother bared her breast to suckle her chubby, naked baby. The donkey ambled behind everyone, its lips stretched amiably, peering into the parked cars, but bumping its nose on the glass as the children inside rapidly wound up the windows. At last it saw a car without any windows and its amble hastened to a trot. The singers began another hymn, again in Djemiranga, and I switched the recorder on just as the donkey was poking its head into the car, showing the children inside its long yellow teeth. The oldest child bravely pushed at its protruding, obstinate nose, hoping by this means to propel the entire baggy fawn body of the donkey backwards out of the car as if it was a rigid stick, but the donkey wouldn't step backwards. Instead, its head concertinaed into its neck and it let out a whole raft of cries and snorts, high-pitched, descending. The children yelled and the donkey brayed again. Another child reached over and pushed open the car's back door and banged it on the donkey again and again, puffing red dust out of its ragged hide but still the donkey didn't move and its brays were making the hymn's second verse incoherent while the congregation craned to watch. There was a guffaw behind me from the white builder I met – how many days ago? three days ago? – with his waist-length ponytail. Then a tall black man strode across the dust and thwacked the donkey's ragged carpet rump, and at last it gave up and backed away.

When the service ended and the people got in cars to drive out to the burial ground, I walked back to the house. Adrian accompanied me until the turn-off to the clinic.

'Was the old lady there? My old lady?'

'Everyone was there.'

'How can you do this to them?' I demanded. 'Ruin this chance for their language to be preserved?'

'Only city whites think that sort of thing is important,' he said.

'Collins thought it was.'

'Not enough to stay to help you.'

He walked away.

That afternoon, in my room, I tried to make sense of my recordings by using Toolbox to parse the language, as E.E. Albert told me to do, one syllable arduously after another, unsure what syllables belonged to what word.

Daniel passed by my open door just as I'd turned up the recording to full volume, putting my ear to the speaker.

'Getting anywhere?' he asked sympathetically.

'No!' I shouted over it. Because he kept standing there, I re-played to him the phrase I'd been listening to over and over again, then I turned it off. 'This word seems to have five syllables but there might be another one in there somewhere,' I mused.

He came further into the room and lingered. Encouraged, I turned the recording back on and inched forward.

'You brought me luck!' I cried. 'Hear that? It's a conjunction! I've found a conjunction! Don't know which, but it's a conjunction, for sure!'

'You mean, like "and" or "but"?' he asked, trying to enter into my triumph.

'Maybe I was beginning already to doubt it!'

'You'd need to add to or contradict ideas, wouldn't you?' he reasoned. 'What a milestone! When you find a few things, will you teach me?' he added. 'I've always wanted to learn Djemiranga.'

'You have? That's music to my ears,' I said, smiling up at him.

'I'll bring you a cuppa, spur you on,' he said. But Adrian called him, and he hurried away, the tea forgotten.

It was two hours before I'd figured out the grammar of one short phrase though I didn't have a clue about its meaning. I was relieved when the battery ran out.

I began filling in my journal with the little I'd achieved. *There seems to be no definite article*, I wrote. Without the air conditioning, the heat made me sleepy. I fell asleep over my work.

*

'Do you remember when I got this scar?' you ask.

You're standing near my red sofa, my bed for sleepovers at Diana's house. You've switched on my bed lamp. I move over for you, you get in, and I'm delighted to have the strip of warmth that's you beside me. You snuggle under my blankets.

'There are seagulls cawing,' I say happily, knowing I will always remember this moment, whenever I hear seagulls.

But you explain that the scar isn't on your finger, it's on your thigh, on the inside. You pull down the sheets to show, but arrange them modestly around your crotch. You're like an angel with a wisp of genital-covering cloth on one of the frescoes my father longed to live near, and there's the scar.

In the circle of gold from the lamp, the scar's embedded into your skin, the same shape as the scar on your slender finger.

'Touch it, it doesn't hurt,' you say.

I watch my dream finger, my touching finger, my hand with purple veins almost breaking through the skin-like slats of water-rotted timber floating just underwater.

Then I panic, and I forget about your scar in my panic.

'They're not my hands, I don't have hands like that,' I say. 'Those hands are an old person's hands.'

I say it aloud. My voice breaks through the surface of my dream.

*

I woke to a commotion outside in the front yard. A group of people had gathered at our gate, a family of women and children holding long thick sticks, and Daniel listened to them, his head bent deferentially. It came to me that he deferred out of a deeply felt acknowledgement of others.

Just then Adrian drove up.

Even though my errant body leaned towards Daniel, I could've just got on with my work. But once Adrian arrived, I simply had to go out into the yard. It was impossible to be apart from him, he'd magnetised all my thoughts for years, since my childhood. I'd never been much more than a mere splinter of lead waiting to cling to him.

'Jimmy Thatcher's out of jail,' I heard Daniel tell him.

Adrian dive-bombed out of the troopie, all pale blue shirt and energy. 'Out of jail!' he shouted.

He left the car door open in his agitation, though the donkey was munching grass in the gutter nearby. It ambled over to the troopie cabin and gazed in, sniffing hopefully.

'Thatcher told them at the jail he had to visit Dora's family for cultural reasons and the authorities believed him,' said Daniel.

I heard the family murmuring in Djemiranga, and fleetingly considered running in for my recorder, but this wasn't the moment to be a linguist. It never seemed to be.

'He's three hours' drive away,' said Daniel. 'But –' he indicated the sticks, 'Dora's made a nulla nulla for everyone.'

One of the children proudly held up a stick for Adrian's inspection, a heavy piece of a bough from a tree, white because it had been so newly carved, with a long point at one end, like a giant sharpened pencil.

'That means business,' said Adrian appreciatively to Dora. He showed it to me for my admiration.

'But can you use it?' I asked him.

Adrian trod on my toe.

'An impressive weapon,' I said.

'Dora, come and sleep at our house,' he said. 'Thatcher won't look for you here.'

'I'll bring Boney and Susan and Wendy,' Dora said.

'Of course,' Adrian said. 'Bring the family. I'll drive you back to your house so you can pick up your blankets.'

Inside, Daniel told me that two years ago Thatcher had been jailed for drunkenly stabbing Boney in the ribs near his heart for an old, imagined slight. Now he'd been let out on parole, pleading family business, and rumour said he was heading towards the settlement. Dora had good reason to suspect the family business was a plan to kidnap one of their daughters, a very beautiful young girl who'd caught his eye.

'Some of these judges are so eager to do the right thing, they lose their common sense,' Daniel said, and this was a criticism so unusual to him and his good nature, I guessed he was repeating Adrian's beliefs.

In my room, I sat down on the bed and got ready to record. At last I'd be able to do my job. I wasn't permitted to go to the community but the community was coming to me, and Adrian couldn't object. I might be able to record them all through the afternoon. The front door opened and I started in excitement, but then I heard it slam. Daniel's door closings were gentle and tentative, but Adrian's slams were adamant, especially in the middle of the night. He seemed to have no respect for the slumber of the household. I didn't remember him as a door slammer. Diana would never have allowed it.

Now he came into my room abruptly, filling my room, holding the nulla nulla.

'Where's Dora? Are they following you?' I asked.

'They'll come in their own good time. We owe it to them,' Adrian said. Then he added, 'I want you to make Dora welcome.

I'm courting her friendship. She could be very useful to me. Come and help tidy up.'

He told me that Boney had worked with his brothers as a stockman on this land when it first became a pastoral lease, and Dora had worked as a maid in the homestead.

'Dora's nulla nulla – do you know how to use it?'

'Of course,' he said. 'I've been in the bush twenty years.'

'I don't,' I said.

He laughed at me.

'Shouldn't we tell the police?'

'They're four hours' drive away,' said Adrian. 'Between their station and here, there are many more urgent problems.'

He lifted the nulla nulla and hit the air with it as if it was a cricket bat.

'Isn't this a gesture of trust in me!' he said. He lifted it upright above his head with both hands. 'It'll be good for keeping the dogs off. They'll think I'm even taller than I am.' He saw the recording gear. 'Don't use that today,' he said. 'Don't turn their distress to your advantage.'

The rhythm of housework eased us all in to a new familiarity. Daniel was asked to come over from the clinic and help. We tidied up the living room to make space for the family to sleep. Daniel found a place for all the objects that'd been pushed into the corners. The collapsing paddle pool we gave to passing children, who yelped with glee as they ran away with it. The photographs were bundled into a cupboard in the living room. We dragged mattresses out from the storage cage on the verandah, and made them up with the sheets from the clean washing that still lay crumpled on the floor. I folded the extra sheets.

'Where will I put these?'

Adrian waved his hand in the direction of a cupboard next to the washing machine.

'The linen cupboard of course.'

I laughed when I opened it because it was full of tools.

'On the shelf – can't you see?' he said, glancing over at me.

I stood perplexed, wondering where he meant. He took the folded sheets out of my hand.

'There,' he said. He'd balanced the sheets on a pile of new copper bath taps. He touched my elbow.

'Most things are easy, you know.' He took his hand away. We both downcast our eyes.

There was a knock on the door, more of a banging really. I opened it. There was a swarm of dusty little boys with uplifted faces, huge brown eyes and skins slightly darker than their eyes.

'Met, met, met!' they shouted together.

Adrian came to the door.

'None!' he shouted and ran at them, chasing them in a joking way so that they escaped, yelling with laughter. He closed the gate and returned.

'Who's met what?' I asked.

'Meat,' he said. 'They're hungry.'

I felt abashed.

'We should've given them some,' I cried.

'Have you noticed the prices at the shop? They're selling half a lettuce and a tomato for ten dollars,' Daniel said.

'Can't you complain about that?' I asked them.

'I do! But there's not only whites on the shop board, but blacks, city blacks, Westernised blacks who need the money, or say the settlement needs the money. And who am I? Just a white do-gooder,' said Adrian.

I went back to tidying the ironing board, finding places for pins, needles, paperclips. Adrian stopped me as I took the troopie keys to hang them up in the kitchen on a hook.

'Don't tidy them away,' he commanded.

I dropped them clanging into the sink.

'Why not?'

'We're always using them.'

'Isn't it better,' I asked, 'that they always be on the hook?'

Without a word he picked them up and put them on the hook.

'Just don't get carried away,' he said, smiling at me with some fondness. He added, jokingly, 'Never know when we'll need the troopie to run away.'

Daniel looked proudly at the cleared spaces.

'I'll vacuum now,' he said.

'You can't. No electricity!' Adrian and I chorused together, and laughed at our synchronicity, and high-fived each other.

In the evening when we had our turn of electricity, I charged my batteries. Adrian was at work with a needle and thread and scissors, cutting front pockets off a new set of matching blue shirts he'd bought in town.

'Such a contrivance,' he said. 'Stitching useless pockets on shirts.'

'Where are you going to put your money and credit cards and keys now?' I asked.

'Don't need them out here.'

'But you mightn't always have this job,' I said.

Daniel had been immersed in reading a scrap of old newspaper that he'd brought in from the floor of the troopie. It was covered in dirty footprints, which he brushed away to peer at the print. But when I uttered the words, they both looked up at me.

'Rescue is on its way?' Daniel laughed, to lighten my gaffe.

Creak. Creak. His unoiled-door laugh.

'I mean, one day you're sure to live in a city again,' I said. 'One day. A long way off.'

'After all, like it or not, we're whites,' Daniel said.

To my disappointment, Dora and her family hadn't arrived by dinner. About ten o'clock I gave up waiting and went to bed, secretly worried that Adrian would knock on my door and demand that I give up my own bed, saying, *We owe it to them.* I'd come to love the silence of the night in my room with the stars twinkling like Christmas lights would be in the city by now. I looked out the window and saw his bed in the front yard. He'd moved it almost out into the road, so he'd be better at keeping a watch out for Thatcher. Above him, dry desert lightning speared the black sky like nulla nullas.

I woke up excited, but the family still wasn't there in the morning. Without power, I built an economical little fire in the yard, the way Daniel had shown me, and boiled the billy.

'What's happened to our visitors?' I asked when Adrian came back from the clinic.

He shrugged theatrically. 'Things take their own time here, I told you that,' he said. 'Go to the shop and get them food. Eggs, bacon, white bread.'

I was pleased at that. It was customary for famous linguists to pay their informants with cigarettes. I'd much rather pay them with food.

'Shouldn't I get them healthy food? Vegetables. Low-fat meat.'

'They don't eat our vegetables.'

'I can make vegetables taste good,' I said.

'Remember? We're holding the mob.'

I was about to argue that providing healthy food was part of looking after, but I decided not to argue for once. I walked quickly in the heat down the dusty street to buy the bacon and eggs and bread for our visitors, and reeled at the prices, as high as I'd been told. But because I felt adventurous, I bought fillets of kangaroo meat. Again, though there were just a few people inside the shop, whole families waited outside. I was pleased that I now understood this, at least a little. On the way home I passed the builder. He was ringed around with children, holding out a large document. I imagined he was showing them a house plan. He saw me.

'I was sacked today,' he called. 'I'm off home.'

So that's what it was, he was showing the children a map of Australia.

'The call came from the government,' he said as I came near. 'They claim I haven't taught my apprentices properly. But I'm a builder, not a teacher.'

'I'm sorry,' I said.

'I can't wait to get out,' he said.

He turned back to the boys, and straightened out the map again.

'That's my country,' he explained, pointing out New South Wales. 'You know where that is?' he asked the nearest boy, who shook his head no.

'None of you know where New South Wales is?' he demanded of another boy.

The second boy shook his head no, his eyes downcast. The others ahead of him in the circle looked down the street, or studied the dirt road.

'They might know it as a Djemiranga name,' I said. 'They'd have relatives there. Maybe what matters is whose country it is.'

'You need to know our names. You need to know what matters to us,' the builder told them.

His gaze moved from one downcast child to the next in the circle. No one spoke.

'See, if you don't get your education, you're good for nothing,' he said. He looked around at me. 'Isn't that right?'

I had to take sides.

'It depends what you think's important,' I said.

There was a pause. The builder glared at me. He'd done a thankless job, in relentless heat, he'd been humiliated by his sacking, and now a white woman had betrayed him in front of a ring of little boys. He folded up his map and used it as if it was a stick, pointing at me, condemning me, almost as menacing as he'd been to the dogs.

'Our world is taking over theirs,' he yelled at me. 'And you've forgotten that in – what – half a week?'

The children's eyes followed me as I walked away. It was a relief to get inside the house and shut the door. All was quiet. I put the shopping away and went to my bedroom, sat on the bed and took out my equipment with a pang. I was only a linguist, here to record an old lady's song. Surely I would find her that afternoon. Or, if I didn't find her that day, I'd beg Gillian for help.

I heard the front door open and shut and went out to find Daniel examining documents at the kitchen table with a worried air. He seemed to be doing a lot of that lately.

'Something up?'

He pushed his wavy hair out of his eyes.

'We might be closed down,' he said. 'The whole thing. The clinic.'

'Closed down! The health clinic? But you can't close a health clinic!' I said.

'Adrian hasn't done the monthly report again,' he said.

'Why not?'

Daniel did a shrug that was a pale copy of Adrian's.

'He says there are more important things than making some little clerk happy.'

At that moment, the door opened and slammed adamantly. Daniel went back to his documents and I busied myself washing-up.

Dora's family still hadn't arrived by dinnertime. I decided to cook the kangaroo, and leave some for them if they turned up. Out the kitchen window I saw Gillian walking up the road after her shift, slowly, with a little backpack. I wondered why she needed to carry it when she lived three houses away from the clinic. I ran out to the verandah and hailed her.

'Like a cuppa?' I called.

'I'm in a hurry,' she began, but she leaned on the gate as if she was happy to stay a few minutes.

'Who were you pointing out at the funeral?' I asked.

'Sister,' she said. 'She's an old hand here, as she'll tell you before she says hello. If any white knows your old singer, besides Adrian, it'll be her. I'll arrange something so you can meet her – but be sure to get on the right side of her. And stay on it!'

I held her hand, and thanked her. She was about to go.

'How do you cook kangaroo?' I asked.

'You're eating kangaroo?' she asked.

'Shouldn't we?' I asked. 'I was going to cook it for Dora's family.'

She sighed, looked up and down the road for inspiration, and then said softly: 'I used to.' It seemed an admission she didn't want someone to hear. But she stirred herself.

'Here, they seem to dig a trough in the ground, burn a fire inside, then lay the kangaroo on the hot coals, so it's like an oven. Sometimes they put a sheet of corrugated iron on top. Don't know what they used instead of iron in the old days. But I don't suppose you'd be up to doing that.'

I recited her alternative recipe:

Put oil in a pan and heat it, then drop in the kangaroo and sear it for a few minutes, flip it over and sear it on the other side. Then turn down the heat and sprinkle soy sauce or tamari over it, cover, and cook gently for a few minutes. Take it off the heat while the meat is still pink inside, and let it rest.

'The builder had a point,' I said to Adrian and Daniel as we ate the seared kangaroo and mashed potatoes and all the fresh vegetables I could find in the shop. The electricity had come on just at the right moment. We ate without Dora's family, who still hadn't turned up.

'He shouldn't have had to build all the houses alone. He should've been given trained assistants, who could buddy up with his local apprentices,' I said.

'He can't have allowed for that in his quote. He would've tried to undercut everyone, to get the job,' said Adrian. 'That's the trouble with new chums.'

He ate quickly, like someone who'd grown up in a hungry family of half a dozen brothers, but I knew there'd been no brothers in his house. It was hard for him to wait until everyone was served, and he was often wiping his plate clean with a slice of bread before Daniel and I had started eating.

Now he clattered down his knife and fork and jumped up to get pineapple juice from the cupboard. He tipped up the tin and drank straight from it before he noticed our eyes on him.

'Sorry,' he said, wiping his hand against his mouth. 'Anyone want some?'

'Not now,' laughed Daniel meaningfully, creaking with laughter again, but Adrian noticed nothing.

All afternoon he'd been arranging for patients to go to town, which person could drive because their licence was current, and what to do about petrol because the clinic owed the shop money and the shop was the only place to buy petrol; the lack of cash was the fault of the accountant in town who was overworked and should be sacked except that he knew the entirety of the clinic's financial history. In the end Adrian calculated how far the troopie could go on the petrol it had, and organised that his friend in town would fill a jerry can with petrol, get in a taxi with that and a thick novel, and wait at the given point for the ailing troopie.

Against these important arrangements, table manners counted as nothing.

'Don't worry about that builder,' said Adrian as he left the table. 'A bad workman always blames his tools.'

Now I'm back at our river, remembering how my father, the handyman, waits for the high tide and heads off in our boat down the river to your mother. He stands in the stern and steers our little boat with a nudge of his knees, while the boat's prow rears up like an eager dog sniffing the way, and around him the light falls, dazed.

'It's taking him a long time to fix up her house,' my mother says behind me on the step. She never seems these days to change out of her grey chenille dressing gown. She's come to watch me untie the last rope for him. In my memory, her voice has a peculiar ring to it that makes me turn around, away from the light into which my father's disappearing. I'm not reporting enough, I'm letting her down, that's what her voice says.

'There's a lot wrong with her house,' I lie. 'Worse than ours.'

She goes inside and takes up her post on our old sofa, which has broken belts underneath which Dad will fix up one day, he says.

I'm marooned with the wrong parent. I'd much rather be visiting the glowing Diana. But I'm sorry for my mother, so I tell lies about Diana's weatherboards falling off the side of the house, a collapsing ceiling, and windows that won't open. 'And Dad's slow because he has to do things the long way round. He hasn't got modern tools. Only what's in their old toolshed.'

'A bad workman blames his tools,' my mother says.

'Haven't you heard that?' asked Adrian. 'It's an old saying. I thought you linguists knew everything about language.'

He looked pleased with himself.

'I might dig a vegetable garden and get seedlings next trip to town,' said Daniel. 'We could have fresh vegetables every day, to go with Kate's cooking.'

'I'll be gone soon,' I said.

'I've always meant to have a vegetable garden,' he smiled. 'You'll be the inspiration to get started.'

Creak. Creak.

I was getting fond of his laugh. I laughed too.

That night he lit a fire to burn off the weeds, which, he said, had spread from the nearby pastoralist's lease.

'See,' he said. 'I've already got the shape of a garden. When you're back in the city, you can think of us eating the vegetables you inspired.'

Chapter 10

In the morning I was woken by a phone call ringing through the house, so it must've been our turn for electricity. Gillian asked if I'd like to go for a walk with her. I made my eyes focus on my watch hand. It was only six o'clock.

'I'll go and have a coffee to wake up,' I said, not wanting to get up, but wanting to be friendly.

'No time,' she said. 'We've got to walk before the sun comes up. Bring your hat in case we're late.'

'Late?'

'It's too hot out in the sun by seven.'

Adrian had had breakfast and was gone, I could tell by the breadcrumbs and smears of butter on the bench, and the troopie keys missing from the hook. So that was why she'd felt free to ring me.

'Adrian's already hard at work,' I told Gillian when she appeared.

'He's like that every morning when patients have to go into town,' she said. 'Haven't you noticed? He was up at five knocking on everyone's doors. No one has clocks on the wall or watches, so they need his knock. They come out of their houses immediately and silently, like sleepy ghosts, wrapped in their blankets and with their children, and sit in the troopie.'

'They're silent because they're sick?'

'They don't do small talk, Adrian says,' she said.

'Of course.'

I seemed to be a very slow learner.

We walked off the road and through the space between the clinic houses. She pointed out the second doctor's house, a little set apart from the others.

'It's a shame you can't stay there,' she said. 'It has the best view. Of the desert, of course.'

'I could pretend it was the sea.'

Indeed, all around us the red desert looked like the sea in its serenely wrinkled expansiveness.

'Do you remember in primary school we learned that the old explorers hoped for a great inland sea?' said Gillian, as if she was reading my thoughts. 'I often wonder if they were going on reports about here when it floods. The salt lakes look like sea.'

I looked back at our footprints on the ripples of sand, like a wake on a river. Gillian carved a line in the sand with the side of her shoe. It was like making a wound in the earth's skin. Under it was even redder soil.

'All the time,' she said, 'the great inland sea was hiding from them, just a few metres underground.'

*

Not only do I believe that our stay in the Bay of Shadows is temporary, but our stay in Australia. My father speaks with such yearning about Europe and its frescoes, I believe we'll be leaving any day now, before the owner comes back. We'll take Diana, of course, and you, and we'll all live together happily near a fresco of richly robed figures with pale bodies and solemn faces too lofty for mundane worries. Here my daydream fades a little around the edges, like an old fresco, since I know we'll have to live in a real house with sofas and basins and taps, and arguments between my mother and yours, but it'll be lit by the blues and crimsons and purples and golds of a fresco, or at least, by the idea of a fresco.

'When are we leaving?' I ask my mother several times over the years.

'We've got nowhere else to go,' my mother says.

Geography's the only subject at school that interests me, and only the geography of Europe. I want to be of use in our new life and so I memorise every river in Europe in alphabetical order. I never learn the rivers of my own country.

One day, I mention our imminent departure to Diana.

'It won't be for a while,' she says.

'How long?' I ask.

'Maybe his lifetime,' says Diana.

I pick at the new paint on the door he's done recently, where a hardened dribble wanders.

'People dream,' says Diana. 'So why don't you fill in the time learning useful things? Like when the next running tide is. They're the dangerous ones.'

*

Gillian was changing the subject. 'So Adrian invited you here?'

'Collins did. The letter was from Collins, but with Adrian's signature.'

'He loves Collins. He'd do anything for him. Everyone loves Collins.' She paused. 'Except his enemies.'

'Who are his enemies?'

'Bruce and Craig. They think he despises his own culture.'

Then, in amongst the paddymelons like small pumpkins, the squashed soft drink bottles and lolly wrappers and empty tins of Tom Piper stew and the clumps of blue-grey dung from the donkey and the low bushes too sparse to be scrub, often drying to a little spray of tufts clotted with red sand, Gillian found a pair of baby's trousers. They had once been white, but now they were red.

'Out here everything turns to red dust. Only the little buttons are still white,' said Gillian. 'Like little moons that won't set.'

She told me that the local people didn't seem to view rubbish like we did. She'd seen old thongs recycled as bats for children's balls, and old tins used as cups – just like in their old, nomadic days, she said, when everything could be recycled.

I found a car battery, by now only vertical layers of silver lace dusted with red, like a Lilliputian building with many floors and high windows. She found two little high-heeled play shoes in pink plastic, one on its side, as if the wearer had just thrown it off.

'They're branded "Life",' Gillian pointed out. 'Like a message, though I can't work out what the message is,' she laughed. 'We'd better go back,' she added. 'Sun's getting high.'

The morning was becoming stripes of colour – brown in the leaf litter on the ground, mauve in the soil, green in the mulga. After the rain there were clumps of mushrooms, grey, no bigger than the nail of my little finger, with petals suspended on long slender stalks. Worms had made wriggling paths, like the meanderings of city drunks, but the movement was always onward. In that light, even the indentation of their paths raised a shadow.

She said suddenly: 'I come from round here.'

'From the desert?'

'No. Further south.' She mentioned a town near the state border. 'I mean, my people do. I mean –' she was walking fast, as if she wanted to run away from the thought, get it over, get back to ordinary life, 'my mother was told on her deathbed that her great-great –' she counted it on her fingers and added one more, 'great-grandmother was Aboriginal. Four generations ago. Mum died in shame! Because of that, I didn't tell anyone. But one day Dora said, "We know you." They can always tell. They can recite generations of families. I said nothing, I just laughed. Then last time I was here, I told Adrian. That's why he's mad at me.'

'Because –?'

'I suppose he fears that they'll accept me more than him. But I don't think it counts. So long ago.'

'You're lucky,' I said.

'Lucky?' She stopped in surprise, and pushed her hat back to gaze at me, though sun streamed into her eyes. 'I wish you'd told my mum that!'

'I'd love to belong.'

She put her arm lightly around my waist.

'Do you –' I began to say, her arm warm around me while we were walking. I changed the direction of the question. 'I find myself, despite my outrage, my fury, my exasperation, capitulating to Adrian. Do you know what I mean?'

She laughed. 'He's my boss. But I know what you mean.'

On the way home the sun was so high we had to tip our hats to shade our faces. We cut through the schoolyard and I stood on a pile of bricks and peeped in the school windows.

I found I was looking at a library.

'It's such a mess,' I told her. She didn't want to dawdle.

'I've got to go home, and get ready for work,' she said. Her faded green t-shirt was stained with perspiration from her neck to her waist, with circles where her bra had absorbed the damp. She lifted her arms and smelled under them.

'Need a shower. It'll probably be a cold one. But come to the clinic at lunchtime. Adrian and Dr Lydia are off visiting a pastoralist and Daniel and Sister are at the outstations, so we'll have the run of the clinic. You can look through the records. Come in with a casserole just before the break.'

'Why a casserole?'

'So you look like my mate, just bringing me lunch.'

I ran up to the shop – only the shop had electricity all the time now – and over a fire I made a stew that smelled of hope. Then the electricity came back on.

When I arrived, the clinic was empty of people and Gillian had her feet crossed on a desk.

'That's them over there,' she said.

In front of us were four battered grey filing cabinets, one with a tuft of yellowed paper sticking out of a drawer. They were divided into boys and girls, men and women.

'Aren't the records computerised?' I asked.

'You're in the desert,' she laughed. 'We've never had time to do that. We've only got computer records of people who've come in to see us since we've had this computer. Otherwise, past patients are in the paper files.'

'That means only a fraction of the settlement is on computer?'

She looked at my face. 'I think we'd better eat.' She got up to find plates and forks, which she rinsed. 'Never know how carelessly the washing up's been done,' she said.

'If the files were made so long ago, could the boys now be men and the girls women?'

She nodded. She waved towards the cabinets with the paper files.

'You might as well tackle the difficult part first,' she said.

I opened the women's paper files, typed by an old-fashioned typewriter.

'Are they arranged in order of age?'

'No. Usually people don't know their age. They don't count time the way we do. Even the month – it's just said that they were born on January first, and someone takes a stab at the year.'

'In order of names?'

'That's hard too. When you think about it, all our systems are arranged for our culture, not theirs.'

She explained that everyone had skin names that were inherited since the Dreaming and connected each person in ritualistic and ceremonial ways to someone else, to their ancestors, to the places they were responsible for, and to the stories and songs about them. I'd heard about this in E.E. Albert's lectures, in what now seemed a different lifetime.

'We put them under their English first names. It's all we know. They do have English surnames, but it's often all the one surname.'

'Addresses?'

'Ever seen a street name here?'

'What age would be old here?' I asked. 'Fiftyish?'

'Forty,' she said.

'So how do I find forty-something women?'

She looked nonplussed. 'Could be anywhere.'

'So you can't ask questions of these files?'

'No.'

'Hasn't anyone tried to? Like, what diseases are the most common? What do people die of? What age do they die? Don't government surveys ask that?'

'The way we keep records makes research impossible. Your research, for instance. Most desert clinics I've worked in, they've only got these paper records.'

After half an hour of sifting through the papers, I'd found six women born forty or so years ago.

'Where would the other women be?' I asked.

I read out their names and she listened to them, munching thoughtfully.

'Do you think, if she's dying, her relatives would've brought her in, so she'd be on the new records, the computer records?' I asked.

She reached over and helped herself to more meaty pieces from the casserole.

'Try them.'

'Can I ask questions of this system?'

'No,' she said. 'It isn't that sort of software. Clinics in the Territory don't usually have that sort of software.'

'Aren't they supposed to?'

'No, we're supposed to have this useless sort.'

We sat back and gazed at each other, damp with heat and frustration.

'Her family mightn't believe in Western medicine,' offered Gillian.

'But they believed enough in Western stuff to want us to record her.'

'That's different. They'd appreciate what a recording of a song can do – the grandkids can listen to it, all that sort of thing. Whites are sometimes considered a bank. They might've asked because the family, whoever they are, doesn't have a recorder that works. Kids might have trashed it. Technology here gets dust in it and grinds to a halt. Worse, I'm told, than water. Anything could've happened.'

She pushed her plate aside and helped me search through the computer records, looking by gender and age. But there was no sign of an older woman who was very sick.

We heard a troopie's brakes crunch outside at the front of the clinic.

'Out!' said Gillian. She jumped up, ran to the back door and yanked it open. I grabbed my now-empty casserole bowl.

'Thanks for the lunch,' she said loudly. 'You're a good mate. Set me up nicely for the afternoon.' Then she whispered: 'If she doesn't believe in Western medicine, she mightn't believe in anything Western. So she might be living out bush. Or on one of the outstations.'

Chapter 11

By six o'clock the family still hadn't arrived, but Gillian had invited us all to her home for coffee. She had the little two-bedroom house. The other house of five bedrooms was crammed with the older nurse, the doctor and Nick, a male nurse who'd brought his wife and two children to the settlement, all because, she confided, Adrian didn't want her to infect his staff with her rebellious ideas.

'Come just for half an hour or so, to meet someone,' she'd said.

'We're meeting someone!' enthused Daniel. He went to his room and came out buttoning on a shirt with a paisley pattern. 'I hope she's pretty.'

In the candlelight he seemed more vulnerable than ever.

'Where have you been keeping that shirt?' I asked. He laughed back shyly.

'It's a special occasion.'

'How do you know it's a she?' Adrian asked, eyeing him and sensing our attraction, for that's what it was, sexual attraction. But I'd given up that old life.

Adrian found a clean shirt in the pile of washing on the floor, found the iron, dusted it down, took a new collection of biros off the newly cleared ironing board, and only when he was plugging the iron cord into the power point, did he remember that an iron needed electricity.

We'd watched him, bemused, because we were accustomed to him commanding the world; it was as if he could make the electricity obey him. Now we shared a glance, silently knowing this about each other.

'Dampen it down and put it on. It'll dry less crushed,' Daniel advised him.

We admired the effect together.

'It'll be like having your own personal air conditioner,' I said.

Daniel creaked about that.

'It might seem like we're in the desert but I'm off to a café in Newtown,' he said. 'I'm going to order the cheese cake. Double serving. With cream. Might shout you both.'

Just then, the lights burst back on.

'Damn timing,' Adrian swore.

A second later, the phone startled us by ringing. Gillian asked to speak to me.

'Could you come over now?' she asked. 'Just you?'

Then she whispered: 'Can anyone hear me?'

I walked to my bedroom with the phone.

'Not now,' I said.

'I organised this for you. She's coming. Sister. She'll know, if anyone besides Adrian does. But be careful. Watch your words.'

I stood outside her door and I heard an odd noise, a crackle, a momentary impress of a small weight on the floor, another crackle, almost a sneeze.

'Wait a second,' called Gillian. 'I've got to be careful.'

The door swung open just wide enough for me to squeeze through. Unlike our house, when her house was constructed, the builders faced it the right way around so the lounge room was the first room you went into, not the laundry, so you didn't have to call out greetings against the swishing of the washing machine. It made her house seem sophisticated.

'What's up?' I asked. Then I saw it.

As if we were in the khaki scrub of the desert, a tiny joey bounced in graceful arcs across her blue nylon carpet.

Gillian laughed at my astonished face.

'Some children were teasing it, so I bought it off them for twenty dollars,' she said. 'But I'm frightened I won't be able to keep it alive. I need you to help me feed it.'

'Tell me how to help,' I said.

It bounded to her and she held it still and sat on the sofa with it on her knee, wrapping it up like a baby in a blue plasticised blanket from the clinic designed for incontinent old people. The joey peeped above the folds, its eyes too large for its face, its head jerking as if it was trying to catch flies.

'Pass my backpack,' she said, indicating where she'd dropped it beside the sofa. She'd brought tins of milk from the clinic for the joey, and a syringe. So that was the weight I'd seen her carrying up the road.

'I shouldn't have asked you how to cook a kangaroo,' I said apologetically.

'How could you know?' she said.

We both tried to squeeze a drop of the milk into the joey's tiny mouth, with me holding the dropper, and Gillian holding the joey. But the joey's mouth clamped shut, and the syrup ran down its body. In the struggle, we leaned into each other. I slipped my hand between Gillian's arms, right under the jutting of her breasts. As a child I used to lean into Diana like that, when she taught me how to sort out weeds from plants, her soft body supporting me. I wondered if women in older times used to touch each other unapologetically and easily like that, discovering a comfort in holding a sick child or caring for old people, probably in the laying out of the dead, getting babies to take the nipple, even feeding a joey. I was aware of how aloof from other women I'd become in my circumscribed city life. Even that very day out my window I'd glimpsed the undulating bodies of a family of women exhausted by the heat and lying together in the afternoon shade on a verandah, and my heart had strained with loneliness; I've always lived as if I'm rehearsing the solitude of death.

'I tried to save a joey last year,' said Gillian, interrupting my thoughts. 'But I put it on an electric blanket one cold night and overheated it. I don't want to be responsible for another death.'

The joey at last chanced to open its mouth and, chuckling, we slipped in some milk, then more. It shut its mouth and bounded away, up on the sofa, pausing to nibble crumbs it found under the cushions.

'My Weet-Bix,' said Gillian. 'I must've dropped them there while I watched TV. We should put it to sleep now,' she added.

So we bundled it into a cardboard box, its legs at odd angles like sticks.

I laughed. 'The boys have dressed up for a pretty stranger!'

Gillian got out cups and a packet of biscuits for her visitors just as there was a knock on the door that made the joey's legs jerk in the air, but the blanket settled and was still. The door was pushed open, and slammed, and Sister stood there, gazing at us both.

'Have you heard the news?'

We both jumped up in alarm.

'What's happened now?'

She was a large bottle-shaped woman though her unlined face showed she was only in her early thirties at most. Everything about her was authoritative; her huge breasts commanded the room. She wore a white uniform so plastic I had the feeling that it'd been wiped clean of all sorts of human suffering, drip-dried overnight in the shower and put on the next morning, ready to face more pain. She made few concessions to femininity except that she wore on her pocket a little green badge with gold writing saying 'Sister'. I wondered whether the locals who could read English imagined she was claiming to be one of the family.

Gillian introduced me.

'You haven't been in a community before?' Sister said. It wasn't a question but a statement.

'Does it show?' I asked laughingly.

'Yes,' she said, without laughing.

Just then Adrian, Daniel and the new doctor, Dr Lydia, all crunched across the front yard at the same time.

Dr Lydia had arrived at the settlement in the troopie with Sister, and it was her first time. She was dressed expensively, as if she hadn't left the city. There was something private-boarding-school about her. Her hair was swept back into a bun like a cameo portrait of a well-born English lady. She had candle-wax skin so pure its subdued sheen was like creamy velvet. A silver necklace tangled nonchalantly in the string of the workaday stethoscope she wore around her neck despite being off-duty, and insisted on transforming it into jewellery. We all gazed at her beauty when we thought no one was watching.

'Nick's on his way,' Daniel said. He and Dr Lydia stood at the door waiting. Nick and his little wife from Singapore were coming up the road, he in a brown turban, she in a white silky dress and white high heels that sank with each step into the red dust, so her progress was slow and he had to wait for her to catch up.

'Come and sit down,' said Gillian.

Everyone did, except Sister, who continued to stand, despite the friendly way Gillian patted the sofa cushions.

'You should all know that men's business is going on and women mustn't wander around the desert or they'll get attacked,' she announced as soon as Nick had arrived and his wife was arranging her flared white dress on the grimy sofa. I nodded to them both, not daring to greet them while Sister held the floor. Nick translated what Sister had said to his wife, who cried out, holding her hands up to her carefully curled hair in alarm.

'But the men here are so gentle. They wouldn't hurt a fly!' said Gillian.

Sister snorted. 'How many times have you been out here?' she said to Gillian; it wasn't a question.

'They are not so gentle to each other,' Nick said. Although he was contradicting Gillian, he inclined his brown-turbaned head towards her in a polite way. 'A grog-runner brought in alcohol last night, remember, and Dr Lydia stitched up three split heads.'

'Well, they wouldn't hurt a white fly,' Gillian added.

It was clear that to Sister most of what Nick said wasn't worth listening to, and absolutely none of what Gillian said.

'No more walks for you for a while,' she told Gillian. 'That's an order.'

'Tell your wife, no walks,' she added to Nick.

'I already have,' said Nick. In English he said to his wife, to please Sister: 'No walks.'

Her eyes held on to his, questioning why he was talking in English to her, but accepting that he had an important reason.

'I've just told her she must keep the children indoors,' he informed Sister. They had brought out their little Singaporean-raised son and daughter to the settlement.

'We don't need punishment, as well as everything else we have to deal with,' Sister said, sighing heroically. I caught Adrian's eye, but he diplomatically kept silent.

'The clinic has lost hundreds of thousands of dollars worth of vaccines because of the blackouts,' she added for my benefit. But she'd been mollified by Nick's obedience, and sat down. There was something almost comical about her youth and yet her middle-aged manner. She even sat down like an older person, as if she was expecting insurrection from her joints.

'But what would the men have against us?' asked Gillian.

'Believe me, such stories are a method of controlling women. These people have a very different culture and you have to understand that,' Sister told Gillian. 'They don't follow our ways.'

Gillian poured tea into cups. 'I need my walks,' she said defiantly.

We all sipped our tea loudly.

'Who gave this warning to the clinic?' Daniel asked. 'It wasn't Anna, was it? Because I heard her giggling with her sisters this morning.' Daniel didn't want to offend Sister, but he was obliged to suggest, 'It might be just Anna's idea of a prank.'

He turned to me and explained that Anna was a twelve-year-old girl from a difficult family. I nodded because I'd already noticed Anna. All the other young girls, including her sisters, were enchantingly pretty, with turned-up noses and full cheeks under eyes leaping with laughter, but Anna had a pitifully plain face, and a heavy, ambling body.

Sister exuded resentment like a puffing kettle at Daniel's contradiction but she couldn't object because Daniel wasn't a newcomer.

'The girl might think it's funny to scare white women,' said Dr Lydia.

'I must repeat this warning to all of you,' said Sister. 'You wouldn't know this yet, Doctor, but what we're up against in this culture is extreme misogyny. In all the stories I've ever been told, in all their myths from the old times, the women are always punished.'

I turned my cup in its circle on the saucer, not wanting to catch her eye in case she sensed my disbelief. Everyone else looked into their cups as well.

Only Dr Lydia spoke up in her well-groomed voice.

'The stories might not be a celebration of misogyny, but a warning to women to behave.'

I was remembering being a child in a shouting schoolyard, staying cowed and silent while another child was bullied by a fat, older girl. But Dr Lydia had never been cowed by anyone, not yet. She met Sister's eyes without flinching, her deeply set dark eyes gazing into Sister's little fat-sandwiched ones, gauging her. In their small surgery the two women must have been contending with each other every minute of their shifts, and then they went home to a crammed clinic house.

Sister sighed. 'It's living in the bush that's the great teacher,' she said. 'Practical knowledge. Not book knowledge.'

We all gulped tea.

Adrian stood, anxious to change the subject before more tension erupted that he'd have to waste time calming down tomorrow, and even more anxious to have the approving eyes of the beautiful Lydia on him.

'City people think that the men's ceremonies are only for men,' he said. 'But the women are significant in them. The mothers – isn't this beautiful? –' we were all watching him in relief, 'the mothers farewell their sons by pushing them forward with their breasts. Like this.'

He strode around the lounge room, thrusting his chest forward, pushing imaginary boys. When no one reacted, he did another circle.

Dr Lydia and I spoke at once.

'Have you no reverence?' she chided him. 'You were privileged, surely, to witness it.'

'How do you know this?' I asked. 'Without their language, are you sure it's what you think it is?'

I saw everyone glance uneasily between us.

'Adrian's been here quite a while,' said Sister. 'Even longer than me. I came out bush as soon as I graduated,' she added, perhaps for my benefit. 'He's notched up his time. He certainly shows reverence, but amongst friends, he's allowed to relax the rules.' She was flirting with his rebelliousness.

'Time could deepen misunderstanding.' It was out before I could stop it.

The corners of Gillian's mouth turned down in warning, but too late.

'Exactly,' Dr Lydia said, smiling at me. 'I'm sure as a linguist – I heard you're a student of that profession – you'd have read a thousand times about fieldwork gone wrong. Prejudices becoming as firmly set as cement.'

'You looked more like a pigeon than a mother,' said Nick to Adrian, easing the tension, and the laughter was louder than he expected, so he beamed, and his wife caressed his arm proudly.

It was Daniel's turn to try to change the subject.

'When is she arriving?' asked Daniel. 'The stranger we're to meet? Before we lose the electricity?'

'She's already here,' said Gillian, and jumped up to carry the joey's box to the table for us all to see.

Everyone crowded around, glad to marvel at the joey, blinking but on its back with its stick legs in the air, though everyone had seen many joeys before.

Dr Lydia excused herself because she had to go to the outstations tomorrow, and we moved towards the door.

Adrian said: 'Gillian, can I have a word?'

'Of course,' she said.

I heard their murmur, and guiltily worried that he'd discovered that Gillian had helped me, but Daniel pushed me out to the verandah.

'It must be difficult in the clinic,' I murmured.

'I'm expecting a murder any minute,' he murmured back.

'No sign of a psychopath,' I said loudly, looking out at the streetlights, and then out to the rest of the settlement shrouded in darkness. 'Dora's safe for another night, maybe.'

Daniel turned his back on the house and walked to the gate. I followed his tall figure.

'It's not true about the attack?' I asked.

'We make the mob in our own image,' he answered.

A battered car, without a windscreen, passed. The front seat was full of children who hailed us excitedly, standing on the front passenger seat and almost toppling out.

'They should be in bed,' I said.

'This is the desert,' Daniel reminded me gently, and waved back. I decided to do the same.

'Can you keep a secret?' he asked.

'Yes,' I said.

'From next week no one in the clinic will be paid,' he said quietly. 'The little office clerks are withholding our funds. Adrian hasn't put in the reports on time for months. That's the news he's breaking to Gillian.'

'How late were they?' I asked.

'None are done,' he said.

'Can you do them?'

'He never lets me. He says they're historical records, and he writes essays instead of ticking boxes like he's supposed to. Of course, there's never time to finish the essays.'

'Will you all be kept on?' I asked.

'It depends when Adrian chooses to finish them. And then he got Sister up in arms. The men refuse to have health checks but he's bringing them in with bribes. Sister says the authorities will catch him and we'll all go for a row!'

'Bribing!'

'With meat pies. And tomato sauce. Sister says it isn't ethical!'

'And is it?'

He waved to another passing car.

'As long as he doesn't get caught.'

Adrian came out of the house cheerfully.

'Let's get bedded down before the lights go out.'

I was relieved at how cheerful he sounded.

'When we were at a pastoralist's today,' he said as we crunched across the road, 'his wife was complaining how much housework she had to do. I told her I know women who'd work for her. But she said she wouldn't employ blacks. She said, "The lubras are filthy and the gins leave the gates open." Her language was so mid-twentieth century!'

He took my arm playfully.

'Did you like that, linguist?'

'It's appalling!'

'I meant I named the era when people used "lubra" and "gin".'

*

I think of you at the end of the jetty, your shirt too short for your growing body. Your shirts can never keep up with your growth, we can never keep up with you, you're so upright, slender, alone, defiant, self-righteous.

I shade my eyes from the sun, anxious on the grass of your mother's lawn, the lawn she insists on growing though it's next to the crackling mudflats.

You're about to dive in the river.

'Don't,' I plead. You've told me there was a shark circling the jetty that afternoon.

Your face is tight. You dive in.

I sit on the rocks and wait for you to surface. You know I'm waiting. You'll stay under as long as you can, to frighten me, hoping you'll frighten us all, hoping you'll have an effect on us, hoping we'll change the way you want us to change, waiting for the high tide for my father to take me home. Hoping I'll never be sent around to spy on your mother and my father again, there'll be no need because your mother will give him up.

*

As we opened the front door, I heard the gate creaking behind us.

'You look exhausted,' said Daniel kindly to me. 'You have first bathroom.'

I'd just squeezed toothpaste on my brush when there was a knock on our door. The bathroom was close to the front door, so I put my brush down on the sink and found I was ushering Dora and Boney in.

'Sit down, sit down,' I said. I looked out into the blackness they'd come from, but I saw nothing up and down the street, just houses sleeping under the streetlights.

Inside, they were both already sitting on the sofa.

'You'd probably like to go to bed,' I said. 'There are your mattresses and clean sheets. Will I make you a cup of tea?'

'Kate, we had no dinner,' Dora said.

I was tired and thinking slowly. 'Because you had no electricity?'

Adrian bustled into the kitchen in an overcoat that served as a dressing gown, and gave me a scorching look.

'Why aren't we looking after them?'

'We ate all the kangaroo,' I remembered.

'We've got bacon and eggs and toast. And electricity for about twenty minutes. Hurry up.'

He turned on the TV for them. They sat on the broken sofa. He came into the kitchen and watched me cook.

'I'm hurrying,' I said. I turned away, angry with my sleepiness.

'The bacon's burning,' he pointed out, rescuing it.

They were hungry and came to the table as soon as I slid the eggs onto the plates.

'What are we going to drink?' asked Dora mopping up the last scrape of egg with her toast. She didn't look at me as she said it, so in my sleepy state I took it as a philosophical question about humanity and its thirst. I worked out slowly that it was part of their politeness, not to ask me directly.

'I forgot,' I said. 'Forgive me.'

So I made mugs of tea and served it. Adrian disappeared.

'Where's the milk?' Dora asked into the room. 'Where's the sugar?'

This time I knew immediately it wasn't a philosophical question. Daniel and I didn't take milk or sugar in tea. It took me a while to find a packet of sugar in the pantry, and a packet of UHT milk.

As I forced my eyes to stay open, I saw that Boney lifted his mug with perfectly shaped fingers, his silky skin burnished to almost purple black. Against the ordinary laminex table, his arm was moulded perfectly like a Greek god's, the way a young white gum bough seemed moulded to perfection against a blue sky. From somewhere, perhaps his stockman days, he'd learned to keep his little finger aloft, though he pushed aside the small bread and butter plate as a contrivance he didn't need, and buttered his toast on the tabletop.

'Tea,' he said, indicating his cup, which was by then drained. I watched him struggle with memory, and then add: 'Please.'

I was moved by his struggle, and made another pot.

'Get my blanket from the verandah,' said Dora to the room.

I went outside into the stillness. Dora's blanket was bundled up where she left it when she came in, perhaps out of politeness.

When I brought it in, she said to the room: 'Mend my blouse.'

She held up her strong arm to show a rip in her blouse, the threads almost plaintive, barely covering her smooth black skin. I paused, struggling with myself. I reasoned: she might have no thread or needle in her house. I always had to search for needle and thread in my own house. Besides, no one might ever have taught her to sew. But I also thought: no one's going to order me to mend clothes.

'In the morning,' I said. 'We're due to lose our light,' I added, trying to make my refusal more amiable. 'And you'll need another blouse to wear while I do it. Otherwise my needle might scratch you.'

She said nothing.

I pointed to the corner, to change the subject.

'Pillows?' I offered.

But no one responded. Perhaps the word was unfamiliar. Perhaps they didn't use them.

'Good night,' I said, hopefully. I went to the bathroom to finish brushing my teeth. In the heat of the night, the toothpaste on the bristles was already dried up.

Next morning, I heard the troopie roaring outside, and saw the figures of patients waiting. I quickly dressed and found Adrian eating cereal in the kitchen. He told me today was the farewell lunch in Alice Springs for the lover of his artist friend. I felt bereft; I quickly turned aside, as tears sprang into my eyes. 'What about me?' I wanted to say. Through the window I saw Daniel raking the ashes in the vegetable garden, making black stripes in the red soil.

'If you get me a bucket of water,' Daniel said when I went out, 'your garden will be just about ready. Ask Adrian to bring some dynamic lifter out from Alice.'

'I'll ask him nothing,' I said.

Daniel was preoccupied digging a ditch around the perimeter of the planned garden. I was to fill it in with the water. Soon he was standing on an island, which shrank as the sides caved in. I laughed, forgetting my worries.

'You'll have to jump to safety!' I laughed.

He dug a little more, then, as his island shrank even more, he leaped, hands held above his head like a star.

'Tonight your garden will be ready for planting,' he said.

He told me he had to go to one of the outstations today. Patients were waiting. Adrian, ready to leave, was watching us, hands on his hips. With Daniel nearby, I felt braver.

'What about the psychopath?' I burst out.

'My friend needs me,' Adrian said. 'Besides,' he added cheerfully, 'he won't attack a white.'

'There's no knowing what a psychopath will do! I might just be an innocent bystander.'

'You've got the nulla nulla. It's beside the front door.'

'She's no match for a psychopath, even with a nulla nulla,' said Daniel. His charcoal-sketched eyebrows were raised at Adrian. 'I don't think she should be left alone,' he dared to say.

But Adrian laughed, strode out the yard, gunned the motor and disappeared.

'Gillian's at home if you need her,' said Daniel. 'She's got today off.' He drove off in the other troopie.

Dora had left the house, but I'd scarcely put the kettle on when she returned and plopped down on the sofa. She put a bulging plastic bag on the floor.

'Make me tea.'

'I'm just about to make a pot,' I said, determined to be a better hostess than last night.

I busied myself in the kitchen – luckily we had electricity – but popped my head around the kitchen door.

'Teach me how to talk your way,' I said.

'What you want?'

'I'll record you talking,' I said. I ran to my bedroom and brought back my recorder. She eyed it.

'I need money for my family,' she said.

'Of course,' I said. 'I'll pay you twenty dollars an hour.'

I was thrilled and proud. At last I felt like a linguist. I'd be able to tell E.E. Albert, I'd be able to say I paid for the language, just like the fieldworkers of old I'd read about (I hadn't, I'd only heard of them in one of her lectures).

But she was looking out the window, which I then saw was hung with red dust and the redder nests of wasps. Cobwebs in the corners of the glass were red hammocks for brown insects. Around the windows there was red dust on each row of besser blocks.

She kept staring out the window, as if at something she'd never seen before. A warm breeze lifted the dust on the road outside and jangled the gum leaves. A group of women walked by, their arms around each other in a lacework of conviviality. I guessed that the silence meant something – perhaps that I should offer more money. I offered thirty dollars and, when she still stared out the window, forty dollars.

'All right,' she said.

With her I learned the words for colours by showing her things of various hues, and discovered to my surprise that there were only four: red, white, green and black – no blues, no yellows, no pinks, let alone turquoise and purple. She taught me the word for home, which literally meant camp – so that when she said 'Go home' in Djemiranga she was actually saying 'Go back to camp'. I was charmed by that discovery; she didn't return my smile. We began on the names of relatives – grandfather, grandmother, auntie, uncle. This was much more complicated than I'd anticipated. It depended on whose auntie, whose grandparent, which bloodline or no bloodline. Even the word for the simple English 'we' seemed to have thirty variations, depending on who was speaking and who was included. Then I was astounded to find that there was no word for 'or'.

'How do you weigh up arguments without an "or"?' I blurted. She looked down.

I wished I'd bitten my tongue.

'Do you know any songs?' I asked to change the subject, or rather, to bring it nearer to my pressing concern. 'Women's songs?'

'Of course,' she said.

She was about to burst into song.

'Wait a minute,' I said. I started the recorder again. She sang for several minutes. I was elated, thinking: Look at me, E.E. Albert; I know how to do this, after all! I've got it! I can go home now!

'This must be a very old song,' I said.

'Yes,' she said.

'From your great-great-great-grandmother?'

She looked down again. Perhaps I was embarrassing her.

'Maybe from the Dreaming? Is it the "Poor Thing" song?'

'No,' she said.

I was a little deflated.

'I'm looking for a woman who sings the "Poor Thing" song,' I said.

She looked down again, and then glanced up at me.

'I go to the shop for food for my family now with the money,' she said.

'Of course,' I said, getting up. Perhaps I didn't know how to do this at all.

As she left, I noticed the bulging plastic bag was still slumped where she left it.

I hurried after her.

'Do you need this?' I asked.

'My washing,' she said. 'Do my washing. Hang it out.'

Her family's clothes seemed too intimate to touch. But we had electricity for the moment, and a machine, which she probably didn't have, so I had to do it, and do it now. I couldn't put it off while I dithered. I carried the bag to the laundry and, holding on to the plastic, dumped the bagful in the tub. I put in detergent and switched on the machine.

But my mind was whirling. I went over to Gillian's house and asked her to make me a cup of tea.

'What's wrong?' she asked.

I slumped on her sofa like the plastic bag of dirty washing. I noticed how calm the room was.

'Where's the joey?' I asked.

'Adrian took it into town to a wildlife refuge. At least that was what he said he'd do. For all I know, he might let it out into the bush. He's a law unto himself. You'd have noticed.'

She poured hot water into the mugs.

'I've got problems with my perfect man,' she said.

We both sipped our tea miserably. I was too anxious to enquire about her problems, and told her what had just happened to me.

'I don't know what to do,' I wailed. 'I've got to make up for 200 years of massacres, murders, rapes, genocide, slavery, humiliation, contempt. The destruction of a culture. Two hundred years of white bastardry.'

'That's a tall order,' said Gillian.

'From the moment our boats arrived in this country, we tried to wipe them off the face of the earth. I've got to be different.'

Her letterbox mouth opened to confide in me.

'She bosses me, too, even in the clinic. I keep hoping Sister won't notice that I'm doing exactly what Dora says!'

'I should look after her. I should be thrilled to make her food. I should be thrilled to mend her blouse. I should be thrilled to hang out her washing. I should do everything she asks, and more,' I said.

'But people don't respect you if they can order you around,' said Gillian.

'But these people? Do we know them? How do they really think, these people who have thirty words for "we"?'

'I wish I'd been taught the language of my great-great-great-great-grandmother,' Gillian mused. 'Then we'd understand –' she waved her hands in the air, 'all this.'

'I have to knuckle under,' I said. 'For the sake of our race, and hers.'

'Why don't you come over and stay in my spare room?' suggested Gillian.

'I'll go right now and get my things!' I said.

'I'll walk you over,' she said.

As we crossed the street, she added: 'Do you think she mightn't mean to order you – do you think it only *sounds* like an order? You're the linguist and all, but once when I complained about Dora's bossing, Collins said that to them it doesn't seem rude.'

Her words had a ring of truth, that awful sense of truth when you see beneath the surface to how complicated and contradictory the world is. She was right: I was a linguist, and Collins was my leader. It probably was a language misunderstanding. I stopped in the middle of the road, bowed.

'But all languages have polite ways of asking for something – last night she was so polite, it was bewildering. Today, she only had to think: what's the polite way to say this? But politeness might mean something different for us than for them, this mightn't be about politeness at all …' I wound down. 'Maybe I should try again,' I said.

I stopped just outside my gate.

'I'll stay and protect them. How am I going to feel if this psychopath hurts them?'

'How are you going to feel if he hurts you?' Gillian asked.

'If I'm hurt, that's the price a white has to pay,' I said grandly.

'You're not going to be much of a protector with that nulla nulla. Can you even lift it?' She paused while I nodded no. 'Just give them the run of the house. The house is what will protect them.'

As I went inside, I heard that the washing machine had finished, or perhaps the electricity had cut out. Dora was at the kitchen door, her shopping in the stiff, large brown paper bags that the shop provided. I was just about to tell her that I'd start cooking dinner right away when she said: 'Hang out my washing.'

Gillian stuck her finger in my back again, a reminding jab. Because of that finger, I couldn't let myself down, not in front of Gillian. I pointed in the direction of the front yard.

'Dora, the line's out there.' Then I told her that I was going to stay with Gillian. 'But please use the house as much as you like.'

I held out my key.

'Please lock up when you leave and when you stay through the night, and even in the day. So you're safe.'

Dora accepted the key silently. I couldn't tell if she was angry or surprised. Then we turned and left.

'You did right,' said Gillian as we crossed the road again.

'But I let everyone down!'

I'd barely unpacked my bag in Gillian's spare room when there was a knock on the door. I heard Dora asking for me. She was there with her granddaughter, Wendy. She held out my door key.

'You lock up,' she said. Gillian, still at the doorway with me, jabbed me again in the back.

I swallowed.

My mind was a tumble of memories; of my mother, of Diana, of the river. Of you. Of my grief at Diana's death, my grief at my mother's. Of my anger at them all. I'm a little child again on the river, wanting to sail down the silver river away from my father's sexual passion, from Diana's sexual passion, from my mother's despair, from the terrible curse and threat of sex.

I didn't know what to do, how to think about Dora, how to think about anything. Nothing in the city, nothing in the paltry life I'd led, nothing in what I'd read, in all the movies I'd seen, nothing in my grief about you, nothing, nothing had prepared me to know what to do. Then words came.

'Wendy,' I said, turning to her granddaughter, 'would you mind going back to my house and locking up for your grandma?'

Chapter 12

I woke to morning light through the curtains, and remembered that I was in Gillian's house. I stretched out my legs under the sheet.

Someone, probably Adrian, for he seemed to keep close control on all matters except paperwork, had chosen for that room old-fashioned chintz curtains with swirls of pink and yellow roses in full bloom, gathered like the long skirt of a giantess onto the waist of a curtain rod and falling in folds to the carpet. It was a strange choice for a man in the middle of the desert to make, I thought dreamily, and suddenly I was wide awake, remembering Diana's chintz curtains in her sunroom looking out to the river.

Diana's curtains were exactly that pattern, full-blown pink and gold roses, falling in ripples down the length of her windows, hiding the river until she threw them apart to show how gleaming with light the river was, the way I imagined that she unveiled her own voluptuous amber body to delight my father. The curtains brought back that memory of shame I'd had as a child, standing on one leg, visiting with my father, hoping to be offered lemonade, believing I shouldn't look even at her curtains because they, like her skirt and blouse, hinted at her beauty.

I didn't want to be caught gazing, especially by you, I was painfully self-conscious that you'd imagine I was dreaming of being like Diana, dreaming of you touching my slippery body, which I was. The day of my twelfth birthday when Diana had baked me a cake and insisted I blow out my candles, it had become unbearable to walk into your house with an easy smile, to walk into the living room past you without trembling, to look at you all for the flames that leaped up in my body. I thought my lust – I had no word for it then, except evil – had been visited on me because I'd watched my father and Diana too closely, because I half-knew far more about sex than I should, while I knew nothing at all. For a month after blowing out those candles, I refused to visit, preferring to endure being away from you, for I feared everyone – my father, Diana, but most of all you – sensing the heat of those flames inside me. No one spoke then of how passionately a young girl burns.

My only comfort through that month when I said no to Diana's repeated invitations, was that one day you and I would grow up and be together, lie together, in our own little house, our own tumbled bed, the sheets hot with our love. I'd be like Diana, oh, I'd learned from her a thousand lessons in flirtation and seduction, and you'd be like my father was to her. I was scarcely able to sleep for imagining what we'd do through the long river nights.

I only saw you once more before you left.

And I'm still dreaming of you, Ian, touching my breasts, holding their weight in your hands, weighing them. My Ian. I'm twelve years old and waiting for us to grow up.

Now as I gazed at the chintz curtains, I told myself they were only a pattern printed on a fabric, like any other, and Diana was long gone, my father was gone, my mother was gone, and their lust and sadness were ashes in the grey ground.

But Adrian had chosen them. Adrian chose his mother's curtains. He must be my Ian.

That's why it took me more than a little while to notice the sound. It'd been on the edge of my consciousness, a noise that didn't seem to come from inside Gillian's house, for her house had that listening silence that constantly lived-in houses have when you're in them but all alone, as if they were patiently waiting for their real residents to come back to argue and sing and cook and sleep and make love. Gillian must've left already, either on a defiant morning walk despite the warning about punishment, or she'd been called to emergency duty at the clinic. The noise was growing, it was like a muttering, restless audience in a large theatre, with people coming in and greeting some and pushing past others to find their seats. Slowly I registered that it was coming from outside, from the dusty red street beyond the small front yard with its cyclone fencing festooned like all the others with old newspapers and ice-cream wrappings. Then I saw shadows move along the curtains, the shadows of many people, both big and small, moving between the swellings and troughs of Diana's chintz, their bodies distending through the fabric's swelling hills of swirling roses and shrinking its valleys, and people's noses extending and dwindling. Someone's hand pointed a direction, became ghostly in its length like one of the magic spirits, then suddenly short, just an ordinary human hand again.

In your reckoning, on your jetty, perhaps I am only a stick figure, as insubstantial as the shifting shadows in the curtains. You wouldn't even remember me.

I lifted the hem of the curtain, so it made a v shape against the glass. The air was full of red dust, as if there'd been a dust storm but there was no sound of wind, and on the nearby trees, leaves pointed towards the ground, disconsolate in the sun. The dust wasn't from a movement of air, but from the tramping of many bare feet. I could see through the red mist to as far as the street corner beyond the clinic, where the street turned and did a dogleg towards the airstrip. All along its length were men, women and children, families holding hands, old people as thin as sticks, occasionally a group of young men with American-style back-to-front baseball caps like they saw on the occasional TV sets in their backyards, young girls linking arms, all quietly heading towards the airstrip.

They might be going to a ceremony, I thought. There might be singing. The women might leave the men and go somewhere hidden. I might find my old dying singer at last.

I pulled on clothes and threw open the front door. No one stopped to look at me, but opposite, at my house, a black man stood in the doorway. It was Boney. He wasn't moving, just holding the door open and gazing after the throng. I remembered my recorder, and went back to grab it.

At the clinic, Gillian ran past, scarcely noticing me. Behind her strode Nick in his brown turban, his loose trouser legs rippling. I heard Sister in the emergency room.

'Let me talk to them. I'll show them what's what.'

Dr Lydia's cultured tones argued: 'I don't think you ought –'

But she was drowned by Sister's rising voice, obviously shouting at someone on the phone.

'We'll make a formal complaint about yous if you don't come, we'll personally see yous all sacked.'

The phone slammed down.

Then I heard Dr Lydia say: 'Go home and make a cup of tea. It might be half an hour before the plane. You fly with him.'

I was wondering, in amazement, if the atmosphere in the clinic had become so inflamed that Dr Lydia had taken to telling Sister to go home and make a cup of tea. I dared to peep. No – I was wrong. There was a family of four or five people, heads bowed, resolute, refusing.

'You get results if you know their language,' Sister told her, with a smile of superiority in her voice.

Then she shouted, unadorned by any sentence, let alone any grammar, the phrase in Djemiranga: 'Go home.'

She pronounced it as if they were English words that she'd picked up somewhere, not the way people said it, so perhaps to them they didn't seem Djemiranga words at all, just another strange, indecipherable English sound that white people made. Dora, in her little lesson, had explained that the phrase literally meant: *Go back to camp.* Sister wouldn't like to know she'd said that, it would lower the standards she'd like them to have.

But Sister's order had no effect.

'Half an hour,' I heard her add. I could imagine her lifting her plump freckled arm and showing them her watch, a large Sisterly one with fluorescent green numerals. But Gillian had told me that no one had a clock on the wall or wore a watch – surely Sister knew that?

'Gotta match words with action,' said Sister to Dr Lydia, and, so saying, I heard a shuffling.

'No – no – really – you shouldn't –' I heard Dr Lydia, over the noises.

'Get out of the way, useless,' said Sister to Dr Lydia.

She opened the street door and pushed the family out, actually bringing up her substantial bulk against the nearest woman – who I now saw was Dawnie, Skeleton's pretty wife – so she had to move in the direction Sister wanted, and her daughter and sisters had to move with her or fall over, rather like the way Diana taught me to move errant chickens or ducklings back to their nesting mother.

'This is unseemly!' Dr Lydia called out.

'Gets results!' Sister countered, rather breathlessly, and she blocked the doorway to stop them coming back in. Out the window, I saw the family bowed, defeated, walking away. I felt ashamed of her.

'What's happening?' I asked Gillian when she dashed by.

'Skeleton's had trouble with his heart. It might be his last day,' she whispered to me, and then ran for the clanging phone, but Dr Lydia had grabbed it first.

I heard her say, 'You're helping us, then.' She put down the phone. Then, presumably to Sister, but with ice in her voice: 'Congratulations.'

And Sister's: 'It's all in the way you handle people.'

Then Dr Lydia's voice to Gillian: 'Nurse, the Flying Service is diverting. They're on their way. Hurry with those towels. Nurse Nick, you drive Skeleton out to the airstrip, but pick up his wife and family first. Then come back for us.'

Gillian hurried with the towels, and Nick ran for the troopie, which had been parked outside his house, adjoining the clinic. The troopie's door banged and he roared off after Skeleton's wife.

I decided now wasn't the time to look for the singer.

Almost immediately the troopie was roaring back into the clinic driveway, and Nick jumped out and ran inside. Dawnie was in the back, along with her sister and daughter. But, to my surprise, Nick's children were in the cabin, jumping on the passenger seat and sliding down its back as if it was a slippery dip. The boy's buttoned up shirt and long trousers stretched taut and threatened to pop its buttons as he slid, and the girl's full gathered skirt ballooned behind her like a bride's veil.

They saw me and clutched at the open windowpane.

'We're going to see the doctor's little plane,' the girl called out to me.

I went over to them, putting my fingers on my lips.

'You'd better stay here with me,' I said. 'What's going on is very serious. People are very sad.'

'No,' said the boy, grabbing onto the door handle and holding onto it, so I couldn't have opened it without a struggle. 'We haven't been out of the house for days and this is fun!'

'You must be silent then,' I said, my finger on my lips. 'The man who's going off on the plane is very sick. He's the leader here. He's –' I wanted to make an impression on the child, 'he's like the king here. Everyone is worried.'

The boy was not impressed.

'But we've only seen big jets,' he said. 'We want to see a little plane.'

'A little plane, a little plane,' sang his sister, tobogganing down the seat again. 'We've only seen big jets.'

Behind me was the screech of the trolley, with Sister and Gillian wheeling it out and Dr Lydia hovering uselessly. Skeleton was by then only a long thin shape raising a checked hospital blanket into a long narrow mound. His face was covered with an oxygen mask.

The children saw my anxiety and slid down to hide on the cabin floor as Sister bustled to the back of the troopie with the trolley and loaded it. Nick ran around to the driver's seat, slammed the door and roared off. I joined Gillian as she watched them leave.

'He's been a grand old man,' she said. 'Everyone's gone to farewell him. Everyone's in grief.'

'I hope Nick's kids stay quiet,' I said.

'Nick's kids?' asked Gillian, looking around. 'Where are they?'

I told her.

'Why didn't I see them?' she asked.

'They hid when you came out.'

'Sister will be furious with Nick,' said Gillian. 'She's such a stickler for the rules. But if Skeleton survives, it'll be due to her. She made that plane divert. No one gets the better of Sister.'

She turned away.

'I'd better go and clean up before they get back, or I'll have her wrath on me as well.'

I decided to sit on one of the benches outside the clinic. There was always something to watch in this landscape. In the morning sun an ant crossing a sandy track was less visible than its long-legged shadow. Even the tiny pebbles had long legs. And later that day, the afternoon sun would change the shape of the distant hills, the way shadows carved other shadows out of the hills with the sunset, so the hills became a different shape. Light ruled this landscape and its shapes.

I heard the plane before I saw it, a silver bird against the searing blue, tiny body and all wings, whining its half-circle overhead and then falling into no sound as it came in to land out of my sight. Then the desert took over, insinuating itself, making everything belong to it, the way the desert could, the rubbish, the houses, the abandoned hide-curing sheds, the trees, the boulders, the people, in a way that city people who rule their landscape would never know. Out here everything always became red silence; the bench I was sitting on with its sun-hardened blobs of spilt food, my recorder still in my hands, me, anyone who sat here – we all surrendered to the desert's insistence, so it could do whatever it liked with us.

So deeply immersed was I in gazing at the light that I scarcely registered a dark figure emerging from my house, carrying something by his side. The dust from people's feet hung still in the air like red mist on that breathless day, so he was almost level with the clinic before I made out that it was Boney, striding with the nulla nulla that had rested beside my front door.

I wondered why Boney hadn't gone to the airstrip to farewell his brother, but I forgot that as I noticed how purposefully he held the nulla nulla. He was still an athletic man despite his age; he was upright, muscular, slender like his brother Skeleton, like all the older men there, the men who'd had desert childhoods away from white people's shops. From a distance, he could still be taken for a young man living in the bush. Though I knew that in his youth he'd hunted big animals with a gun, I imagined that a nulla nulla would have always been in reach to finish off a kill.

He stopped abruptly in front of the clinic, on the incongruously emerald patch of grass that one of the Aboriginal women, Mandy, hosed so often it'd become like a square of green carpet on a red floor. He was gazing down the road towards the airstrip, the nulla nulla across his body, and there was something about the tension in his stance that alarmed me. He was in mourning, yet his stance seemed angry, not sad. I wanted to distract him, though from what, I wasn't sure. I wanted to make the morning ordinary, I was always doing that as a child, cheering up my dressing-gowned mother as my father puttered his boat away from her, heading towards the amber Diana.

I fossicked in my mind for something to call out to him.

How are you managing in my house? I could call. Or, Have you found enough food in the fridge? Or, Have you heard from Adrian? People there were always asking the whereabouts of Adrian. But calling out to Boney seemed like impertinence, something only a crass white woman would do, something too domestic and familiar when our only connection was that I'd cooked him bacon and eggs. I couldn't even ask after his health in a language with no small talk. Besides, it wasn't the moment for white people's chatter. He might not even remember who I was. Perhaps white women all looked the same to him. I considered going inside the clinic and asking Gillian's opinion, but I stayed sitting on the wooden slatted bench, gagged as usual by indecision, irresolute and frightened, though of what I wasn't sure.

People were beginning to drift back down the street, in twos and threes and sometimes in larger groups, still subdued, filing into their houses. There were a few glances in Boney's direction, at that strong old man unexpectedly holding a nulla nulla, but no one waved to him or called to him and he didn't acknowledge anyone's presence. It must have been very different for him once,

I mused, when he and Skeleton were young, when they were both the leaders. I wondered what twists and turns of life had caused him to be standing on Mandy's square of toy grass while the whole settlement silently farewelled their elder, his brother.

A man opposite the clinic came out to make a cooking fire in a front yard, glanced at him and, bent-headed, went back inside. Someone came to a doorway to strum on a guitar, then fell silent, and a group of young men looked over at Boney, but talked quietly to each other near the uplifted bonnet of a battered car. One of them slipped into the driver's seat and tried the ignition. The noise startled the air. The man quickly turned the motor off as if he'd shouted in a church. Boney still stood unwavering with his nulla nulla as if he was waiting, every muscle tensed, upon the stray movements of an unaware animal.

Then the troopie turned the corner, brown-turbaned Nick driving with his children still in the front cabin, in sight now but sitting quietly. He pulled up and Dr Lydia pushed open the back door to get out, I could just see her well-shod foot as she was about to step down, when Boney moved at last, running now. He ran around to the driver's door, shouting, wielding his nulla nulla from waist height like a cricketer with a bat, but this wasn't play, the bat was menacing. His face was that of a hunter. He yanked open Nick's door.

'I kill you, I kill you,' he shouted in English.

Nick didn't get out. He yelled: 'Don't you touch my kids.' He lunged across the children, to the passenger door on the side away from Boney, grabbed the screaming children as if they were already lifeless dolls, threw open the door and pushed them out onto the roadside, shouting to them in Hindi. The children tumbled into the dust, the boy righted himself and without looking back at his frantic father still in the car, grabbed his sister's hand and they both raced up the street, screaming for their mother, the girl's dress flying, the boy's heels almost kicking his little bottom. Nick followed them out, on their side, the side away from Boney. He was then facing Boney, the cabin between them. Nick's hands were in the air to show that he wasn't prepared to fight.

'I kill you,' shouted Boney.

Dr Lydia stood on the road, helpless, silenced, her face a picture of elegant horror. Then Sister, out of the troopie and standing in the road, arms folded, boomed: 'Boney!'

But Boney, stalking with his nulla nulla halfway around the back of the troopie towards the retreating Nick, ignored her.

'He's a nurse, Boney,' roared Sister. 'You will not kill one of my nurses.'

'Our nurses,' corrected Dr Lydia in her cool, quiet voice.

'Get inside!' Sister exploded in her direction, and Dr Lydia obeyed instantly, gratefully.

But Sister, despite her uniform and her little brooch that claimed kinship, was just a white woman after all, and Boney continued his menacing walk towards Nick, who backed away, arms still raised above his head, stepping closer and closer towards where I sat, unmoving. Although I was behind Nick I could see the strain of his body. Sweat was pouring down his back, staining his shirt. We heard his children screaming in the arms of his wife, as she watched helplessly from the road outside her house.

'You are not going to kill him,' roared Sister.

Boney, still stalking his prey, paused long enough to shout again, not to Sister but to Nick: 'I kill you.'

He continued to stalk his prey and Nick continued to retreat.

Sister boomed: 'That nurse looked after your brother.'

Unheeding, he advanced on Nick.

'I kill you,' he shouted at Nick.

'If you kill him, he can't nurse you any more,' shouted Sister.

Boney's steps paused, just momentarily, and his head jerked over his shoulder to the silly fat woman.

'I kill him,' shouted Boney that time to her, but also to the desert, to the silence. 'I not kill him dead.'

Understanding came to me. I jumped up, though no one noticed my sudden movement, and edged closer to Sister.

'He doesn't mean it,' I shouted.

No one noticed a shout from another silly white woman.

Nick, on the other hand, hadn't glanced at Sister, hadn't slowed down, and suddenly he had gained the door of the clinic, which was swung open by Gillian, who'd been inside watching every moment. Boney hadn't calculated on this. Nick ducked inside, and Gillian banged the door shut after him and locked it.

Boney paused.

Sister registered Nick's escape and turned back to Boney.

'You should be ashamed,' she roared.

Boney's powerful body almost collapsed, after all that he'd demanded of it, after all the bravado of a young man. He leaned on his nulla nulla as if it was a walking stick, panting, remembering that after all, he was an old man.

'You shame,' he cried. 'You white shame. You shame! Shame to you!'

'Me?' Sister's voice squeaked, but she forced it into a roar again. 'I'm the Sister here. I say what goes on here. I diverted the plane to save your brother. I saved your brother!'

'You shame,' cried Boney, recovering a little in his anguish, now struggling to stand erect and upright.

'What have I got to be ashamed of?' shouted Sister.

'You take kids, say bye bye to my brother. Here!'

He banged the troopie door with his nulla nulla.

'Kids. Kids *here*.'

The insistence was unmistakable. He was banging the cabin seat through the still-open door. *'Here.'*

Sister, despite her years in the bush, foolishly imagined that Boney's rage was something like hers. Or perhaps it was because she'd spent years making people in her own image. She breathed out, she beamed that, despite it all, this black man had noticed her white rules, had respected them.

'Yes, it was wrong. Absolutely wrong. Nick broke the rules,' she said still loudly but in conciliatory tones, so that everyone could hear. 'Kids aren't allowed to ride in the troopie when it's an ambulance, you'd know that and you're right. No kids in the ambulance. I'd already reprimanded him and I'll do it again. No kids in the ambulance.'

'No,' shouted Boney.

He struggled with the impossible white language, with these uncomprehending white people.

'Skeleton my brother. We elders –' he pointed to the sky, surely to the plane now winging its way to the hospital. 'My brother and me, elders. My brother, dead. You take kids to plane *here* –' He banged the door again. 'You don't take me.'

It was as if the air was stilled. As if the whole community bowed its head at the way he'd been shamed. He was spent. He turned, and limped up the red street to my house, past the group of young men who'd been watching respectfully, past the dogs, past the open doors. Everyone looked down, no one peeped out, and no one watched his retreating back as he stumbled with the nulla nulla. Not even the dogs called to each other. Even the desert was in awe of him.

But Sister was not one to be gripped by awe. She banged loudly on the locked clinic door.

'Nick! Come out this second and park this troopie where it's supposed to be!' She yelled. 'Right now. Come out!'

I found my legs shaking and went back to sit on the bench.

After a pause it was Gillian who emerged, not Nick. She didn't look at me, and she didn't look at Sister. She walked past us both, intent only on re-parking a troopie that was in the wrong spot. She didn't acknowledge Sister and, for once, Sister decided not to notice.

I went back to Gillian's house, and, thankful we had electricity, made lunch carefully, roasting chicken legs from the shop, and steaming frozen spinach. But when Gillian came home, she merely toyed with the food.

She turned on the TV, although there were only talk shows.

'Sister's demanded Adrian come back from town,' she said. 'Not that it affects you.'

We looked at the TV because it was easier than talking.

Sister knocked on the door.

'Adrian's granted us a plane into Alice Springs. We'll leave mid-afternoon, so we get to Alice in the light.' She saw me listening. 'This is how you teach these people. Leave them, let them think about it. I've contacted Adrian and he agrees.'

'Can we stay at a hotel with a swimming pool?' asked Gillian.

'Of course. Pack your bikini.' She paused, then startled us both by adding, 'I might pack mine.' It was very easy to forget she was our age.

'But what if there's an accident here?' asked Gillian.

Sister was roused to anger.

'People have to learn not to be violent. Nick could've been killed!'

'No clinic because of one man?' I asked.

'There are many men here. You saw them standing around. Not one of them moved to defend Nick. So we're showing them. It's solidarity.'

'They mightn't have read their Karl Marx,' I dared.

I was rewarded with a quick but wry smile from Gillian behind Sister's back.

'Their what?'

Why was I such a coward in front of this woman? When I

argued with her, my voice clotted, even my brain almost clotted in terror.

I said, trying desperately not to sound as if I learned it in my one week's reading: 'Boney said "kill" and then said he didn't mean "kill dead". There are lots of words for "hit".'

She was so large and trenchant and vehement. But I struggled on, my voice thick with daring.

'What I'm trying to say is, if English isn't your first language, maybe your fourth or fifth, which you only use on official occasions, and you've been lying in wait for a psychopath, while your brother, the elder of the community, is dying, maybe in all that turmoil, you'd get your English confused. They've got sixty-seven words –'

'What's confusing about threatening murder?' she shouted.

'I'm saying that maybe he was only threatening to hit Nick. And he got his English mixed.'

She was one to recover fast.

'He was going to *hit* Nick? He was going to hit one of my staff? So you're telling me that my staff have to put up with being hit? I haven't time for this nonsense.' She sniffed. 'Go back to your books.'

She turned away.

'Gillian, come back to the clinic and help close it down.'

I told Gillian I'd drive them all to the airstrip. If I didn't, Sister would've had to ask a local person to bring the troopie back, but she wasn't talking to the locals, so she reluctantly agreed. Gillian told me that with an averted face. She didn't want to be in trouble for being my friend.

I picked Sister up at the clinic, and then, because by now she also wasn't talking to me, she told Gillian to direct me back to her house. I was surprised, because Sister wasn't the sort to leave something behind. I pulled up at her gate. She went inside and emerged leading a young white teenager I hadn't glimpsed before, who followed her to the back of the troopie and clambered inside. The girl greeted no one, though everyone greeted her as if she was a much younger child, and was eager to be helpful stacking her many bags along the seats – a computer bag and four backpacks in various sizes and shades of pink, all labelled. Until that moment, I imagined that Sister had no family.

Daniel, sitting beside me in the cabin, didn't meet my eyes. Dr Lydia gazed out at the desert. Sister held a sole prim backpack on her lap, as did everyone else.

Gillian had forgotten to follow Sister's instruction to bring the airstrip gate keys, so despite the frigid atmosphere, the barbed-wire fence around the airstrip made us work together pulling the lower and upper wires apart for each other in a diamond shape. Nick's children ran around, delighted at the game. Sister declined to let me part the barbed wire for her.

'Gillian?' she ordered.

But she couldn't persuade her daughter to step through the diamond shape. She was forced to explain, though not looking at anyone in particular: 'She doesn't trust diamond shapes.'

So we all pulled up the wire more or less in a rectangular shape, and then Nick's wife thought to step through herself, turned and held out her dainty hands for the girl's. The girl glanced up at the kind face gravely, deciding whether to trust it or not, despite the shape of the wire being so recently a diamond. Everything about the girl was grave, her face raw and shiny with scrubbing, her hair squeezed tightly into a ponytail so not a strand would disobey. For a second I imagined Sister at her age. Then the girl made her decision to trust the barbed wire, and stepped through. She looked down again at the ground, every second in our company a torture, clutching, white-knuckled, the brightest pink computer bag. We all picked up her other bags.

The airstrip was a long stretch of tarmac hedged on either side by tall weeds. There was no building, just a box to hold the flares that lit up the strip at night. Two black women with babies strolled down from the settlement to watch the plane come in. A toddler swung a gecko by its golden tail. His mother laughed, proud in front of everybody that he'd caught his first animal. Sister turned her back ostentatiously.

'What if Thatcher chooses tonight to come?' I whispered to Gillian as they lined up to get weighed, on ordinary household scales, to check that the plane could hold them all. As I spoke, Sister stepped on the scales, sending the indicator whizzing all around its clock face.

'A wonder it didn't break,' murmured Dr Lydia.

Then it was the turn of Sister's daughter. She'd been hanging back, letting everyone else go before her. She obviously didn't trust scales either, gazing at them wide-eyed as if the machine was a living thing. Her mother pleaded, the pilot explained uselessly that his regulations said he wasn't to fly until everyone was weighed, but again it was Nick's wife who made a game of it, taking the girl's hand and standing beside her on the scales. They almost toppled, and everyone laughed, including the girl, her face suddenly beautiful. Because they were both so tiny, somehow they both fitted. The pilot did a quick calculation – he had already weighed Nick's wife – and the moment passed.

'She knows how to manage her,' Dr Lydia whispered to me, as Sister supervised the pilot, to his irritation, about weighing the bags. 'She's a specialist in autism.'

'She was working out here?' I asked, surprised.

Dr Lydia nodded.

'Being a wife,' she said, pulling her mouth downwards.

The pilot paused at the girl's multitude of pink bags.

'Sorry,' said Sister.

The pilot sighed. 'We'll manage,' he said.

'Keep staying in my house if you like,' Gillian whispered. She resisted kissing me goodbye. 'Just a handshake,' she mouthed.

'Or stay in mine,' said Dr Lydia, not whispering. 'And keep the lights down. You'll be safe from the madman if no one's quite sure whether you've gone off with us.' She took me aside. 'Warn Adrian he's got enemies in high places,' she whispered. 'I have no love for him but – forgive me – I can see you do.'

I flushed, even more so when she touched my hand gently.

'Are you coming back?' I whispered.

'Into this hornet's nest?' she answered, without whispering.

Sister decided against noticing and became preoccupied in taking her daughter's hand and coaxing her into the plane. Nick's wife took her other hand.

'The plane's our friend – remember?' I heard Sister tell her daughter.

Her voice had a new tone – a mixture of gentleness, sadness, pleading and embarrassment, almost as if she was a child and feeling the grown-ups would blame her for something she'd done, or omitted to do. For the first time, I felt she could almost be my sister.

Chapter 13

I examined all the clinic houses. There was a certain satisfaction in weighing up the merits of each house; how soft the beds were, how effective the air conditioning was when the electricity worked, what bottles of sauce were in the fridges. At last, feeling defiant, I chose the forbidden house, the unused second doctor's house. I discovered it was already set up with bedding and kitchen utensils. I was relieved it didn't have chintz curtains. I sat in the living room with the blinds down and only a torch musing over what I'd seen. At the end of the porch there were slats of lattice, and, when I peeped out the door, people in the dusty road seemed between the slats like puppets, for the slats disjointed their normally graceful movements.

About midnight, I heard a noise. I checked the wind's shadows in the yard past the mulberry tree drooping with fruit. But it wasn't the wind; a pale shirt gleamed almost blue amongst the waist-high grass of the front garden, then a figure moved to the porch. I gasped. But there was a knock. It was Adrian. I opened the door. He kissed my cheek.

'I'm sorry this all blew up,' he said.

'If you would only tell me which old woman I'm here to record, I could get out of here,' I said.

There was a pause, he said nothing, he didn't react. A muscle in his sunburnt neck twitched. I wondered if he could hear the twitching of my heart, since it felt as if a wind was blowing across it, like the wind across the desert out the back door, standing everything to attention, letting it fall, rounding it up again.

'I had to go into town,' he said. 'After all, you're not my staff. You've only just come here, of your own free will, sent by your university. And I didn't really believe the psychopath would risk coming out. I always thought Dora was worrying unnecessarily. I didn't think he'd dare. And I thought, maybe you'd learn something, living with Dora.'

I dared to ask, now that the desert wind had blown against my heart: 'You always know what's going to happen?'

He ignored that.

'Come back home,' he said.

His voice could still infuse my heart with irresistible yearning. He was Diana's son and she'd enchanted us all – except my mother.

But I tried to resist.

'Just show me the singer,' I said.

He left.

For the next two days I worked inside the second doctor's house, trying to make sense of the sentences I'd recorded – grammatical sense, at least. By now I'd become convinced that finding my singer depended on my work, not on Adrian's help. I found myself staring out the window abstractedly, the one that looked into the street, and it was Daniel who I hoped would return from town. The psychopath didn't arrive, and all was quiet except in my nightmares. I couldn't remember them afterwards, except that the spaces of the empty house seemed to ring with my cries. At dawn on the third morning, I heard a troopie's engine switched on, then off. I peered out. I knew that Dora's family needed to go to town for a doctor so Adrian was probably taking them in and bringing back the new change of medical staff, and Daniel. The fear of the psychopath must be over.

I imagined Adrian ripping open a packet of Tim Tams in the lonely kitchen, unscrewing a large bottle of Coke so he'd stay awake on that long red road. I thought of that long red road, his fast driving, his regular blow-outs, his rollover. If he was taken to hospital, I thought, I'd lose any chance of finding out who he was.

I packed my nightie and my few clothes into a bag. I walked down towards Adrian's house. Outside the gate, a troopie was parked, now with the engine running. I checked inside to see if it was scattered with roast chicken wrappings and empty plastic drink bottles, the sure sign that someone had just driven back from town. But it was clean, so someone must be setting out. As I came through the gate, a figure emerged from the shadows on our verandah, just outside our front door, a blanket piled beside her, as if she was about to travel. The figure turned away as she saw me, as if she'd been merely examining the clothesline in the front yard. But there was nothing to examine, only the droop of the empty line, and beyond that, the cyclone fence with its ruffle of rubbish.

It was Dora.

We hadn't seen each other since she'd visited me at Gillian's, and now she was between me and my front door. I halted. Something about her seemed too intense, imminent and brooding for me to pass by with an English 'excuse me'. But my background, unlike hers, was full of small talk, crafted especially to ease over jagged situations. I'd observed that, for these people, to turn away was often a sign of discreetly absenting oneself from a situation or conversation, but I was still too European. I couldn't mimic another culture, I couldn't mimic their subtle ways. I simply couldn't sidle past her. Small talk jolted out of me.

'Off to town?' I came up with. The words, perhaps the English silliness of them, acted like a lasso, and brought her to me, forcing her presence.

In the grey light, there was no flash of her eyes. She was looking down, examining the cement on the verandah. She seemed unable, at that moment, to move out of her culture

223

and return the small talk, although I'd seen her at other times remember how to be again the young lubra, as she'd have been called in her youth, surrounded by English small talk in the vast kitchens and shadowy corridors and richly furnished rooms of a pastoralist's house as she swept and cleaned. When I'd watched her speak in English, I'd had the impression that her whole being was twisted, even dwarfed in the banal murmurings of a foreign culture. It was probably why her English was reluctant, though competent.

We both paused. But then she reached out a forefinger to touch my arm. She'd never touched me before. From her fine velvety finger, it was almost a caress.

I looked down at my arm, astounded to see her finger lingering on my skinny wrist.

'Kate.' She paused. 'I sorry for what I done.'

Tears started in my eyes. I buckled with shame that I'd resented being bossed by someone in need, shamed that I'd resented someone who'd been coerced into servitude by my people, whose kin had been massacred by mine, a long time ago but still by my people, someone whose pain about that was incomprehensible to me. My shame became a sob, and tears flooded my face.

'Adrian said you don't know the Aboriginal people, what we do.'

I was jolted by the simple grandeur of her words. I had no words in return, just tears, just my body. I was only, irretrievably and exclusively, a European, though I'd unthinkingly expected her to be European like me, to be adept in what it means to be one. In that moment I disgraced myself. I stepped close to her, as close as I'd ever been with Diana, in fact, I forgot all about Diana. I threw my arms around her, my bag and all.

She flinched slightly in surprise. After the tiniest pause, her arms came around me to hug me back.

'He's right. I don't know anything, Dora,' I managed to say into her blouse.

When we drew apart, I remembered enough to downcast my eyes. I gazed at the verandah, then almost the colour of the desert around us, glowing dusty red in the dawn.

At that moment, Adrian came out the front door. He pretended not to see us, though he had to skirt around us in a wide circle, ducking his head under the droop of the clothesline.

I found something else to say to her.

'Would you like me to sew up your blouse?'

It was a successful diversion.

'It's back at –' her head was thrown in the direction of her house.

'Any time,' I said, in the hope that something would continue between us; I wanted her friendship, but I already knew that it was a hopeless wish. Gillian had told me Collins explained there was no word for friendship in Djemiranga. 'Who needs friends when you have hundreds of relatives!' she'd said, and there'd been yearning in her voice. She'd added, however, there seemed to be a word for life-lasting friendship, but that it was only for birds.

'Dora – you did a great job on the house,' Adrian suddenly called over his shoulder. He was at the gate.

She nodded. 'Took a while,' she called to him.

'The house?' I asked them both.

'Took a while,' she said again.

'What do you mean?' I asked.

But she'd scooped up her blanket and was walking her straight-backed, dignified barefooted walk out to the troopie.

I went into our kitchen. I'd never seen it so clean. All the washing-up had been freshly done, the plates and cups were gleaming and even the inside of the teapot had been scrubbed and was draining on a tea towel. The spills and spots on the cupboard doors and the stove had vanished, so everything looked new. The kitchen lino was swept and freshly mopped. The cobwebs that used to be tiny hammocks of red dust at the corners of the windows were there no longer. The wasp nests of red dust, like tiny edifices, were gone. The windows sparkled. In the living room, the carpets were swept, that windswept look that was the tell-tale sign of a stiff straw broom, not a vacuum cleaner. The armchairs were arranged conversationally, with no abandoned open books or out-of-date newspapers. The bathroom glowed clean and sweet-smelling. The beds were all made, the rooms tidied, the windows half-opened to let in the desert air.

I ran out the door to say something, something European, I didn't know what, something like thank you, but the street was empty of everything except new sunlight. I could just hear the engine of the troopie labouring over the hillocks of the shortcut in the direction of town.

For the next twenty-four hours, I worked on my recordings, puzzling over them, charging my computer and battery in the times when I had electricity. It rained, so outside fires were impossible, and I cooked meals when the stove worked and ate biscuits when it didn't. For a break, I hung around the shop and listened to the people. I was beginning, or thought I was beginning, to hear pauses between words so that I no longer seemed to be listening to an unbroken stream of sound. I thought I recognised a word every now and then – one word out of hundreds, and always only at a sentence's end.

'A politician is coming to the settlement,' Adrian told me over breakfast when he returned, bringing back Daniel, Gillian, Sister and Sister's daughter, but not Nick, who'd taken stress leave, or Dr Lydia, who'd resigned, much to Sister's jubilation.

'Stuck-up idiot,' she said. 'I knew when I first clapped eyes on her she wouldn't last.'

Gillian and Sister would work double shifts to make up for having no doctor.

'We need hands-on people out here. Not bookworms,' she'd said, not quite looking at me. Coming out, they'd struggled for ten hours over almost impassable roads, which by now hadn't been graded for months. While they'd been doing all that, I'd parsed two sentences.

'A politician! An election must be coming up,' laughed Daniel. Creak. Creak. I was pleased to hear his laughter again. Suddenly I knew I'd missed it inordinately. He'd just come in to the kitchen from his cold morning shower. His mop of hair was still dripping in spikes. His charcoal eyebrows were awry.

I'd boiled the billy on a small fire I'd made in the yard.

'Tea?' I asked, and it still seemed a small triumph to be able to offer hot tea from my cooking fire.

'How do you know about the politician?' I asked. We seldom heard news from the outside world. Everyone was usually too exhausted after a day's work to turn on the TV when the electricity happened to be on. There were no newspapers in the shop, because only the few whites here would read them. The outside world had fallen away.

'Craig stopped me in the street, boasting about how hard he'd worked on his submission,' said Adrian. As usual he refused my tea, gulping glasses of water instead, since we could no longer keep his beloved pineapple juice because once he'd opened it, it needed the fridge.

'Careful of Craig,' said Daniel. 'He's great mates with Bruce. Bruce is always going to Craig's house.'

'That's not friendliness. That's flirting,' said Adrian.

'Flirting? The CEO is flirting with Craig?' I asked, sipping my tea, enjoying gossip after my solitude.

'With his wife,' said Daniel. He'd had to raise his voice above Adrian's snorts.

'Craig doesn't let her out,' said Daniel. 'Would your fire be good for bacon and eggs?'

I fried us all bacon and eggs in the iron camping pan in the front yard. Now that I often cooked on an open fire, I'd copied the local ways, just a ring of stones for the fireplace and to rest the pan on when it was hot. Adrian had refused to let us copy them on chilly nights, however, when small fires burned on a piece of corrugated iron on the cement porches of their houses all over the settlement. After the families had drifted away for the evening to the warmed room behind, the dogs inherited the fire, sitting upright and alert, straight-backed, their eyes on it like sleepy but well-behaved children.

'What will people do with this politician?' I asked Adrian as we ate. 'Will people want to meet him – or her?'

'Whites will,' said Daniel.

'Probably not your old lady,' Adrian said, guessing what was on my mind. 'Though in the old days, you're right, there'd have been a big turnout. A ceremony. People will come for the barbecue, but they'll take their meat home – you'll see. Eating in a big group, that's not how they do things here.'

'Skin issues?' I guessed, rather proudly because I knew more than when I came. He didn't bother to nod.

'Are we going to ask this politician for something?' Daniel politely changed the subject. 'Everyone will bring their agendas. We should. Don't you want to raise again the issue of a plane for patients? Especially with those roads?'

Daniel often looked exhausted after the frequent trips to Alice, though Adrian never did.

'Craig won't give me a chance, he'll hog him,' said Adrian. 'He'll say he can't educate the kids because he's got no money. And Bruce will blame the mess-up with the power on having no money for a second assistant.'

But he agreed to try.

The yard in front of the council building thronged with people. There was the hot salty smell of cooking meat in the air from the giant barbecue out the back, bought especially for occasions like this, despite the locals' non-attendance. I'd come to suspect more and more that public things were done in the settlement only in the white way, not in the Aboriginal way, as if the whites didn't know, or didn't care. The politician had arrived in a plane; because of the rain the roads were more treacherous than ever. His pilot was sitting in a white plastic chair nursing a cup of tea while he waited to fly the politician to the next settlement. Bruce was shaking his hand and introducing him to Skeleton, who'd unexpectedly returned, now so thin he seemed almost to float. I'd been expecting Bruce to be an old man, but he was about the same age as Craig, thin and still handsome, with an exuberant head of prematurely white frizzy hair. He'd brought back from town a most unlikely dog which he carried under one arm, a well-fed, perfectly groomed fluffy toy dog, a Bedlington terrier adorned with little white curls all over its fat body, a canine copy of its master.

Craig, in tight jeans, was proudly brandishing a thick document.

'I've given the kids the day off school,' he told me without irony. 'I've got an appointment to tell our leaders why education doesn't work here.'

'Why doesn't it?' I asked.

He looked at me in surprise.

'Because I've got no money,' he said.

I'd seen Dora and the other women in the crowd, excused myself and headed towards them. They didn't greet me, but I smiled, looked down and sat in the dust quietly surveying the scene. After a while, Dora spoke.

'Lot of people.'

'A lot!' I agreed. So I felt included.

The women seemed excited as they spoke with each other. Something was in the air. Once more I wished I could understand what they were saying, but at least I could make out their word for 'not'. Each of them at one point said 'not' to Dora, though what they were refusing, I had no idea.

The politician emerged, accompanied by Bruce still carrying the toy dog, to a smattering of white applause, but black silence. I saw Craig edging near him. Daniel and Adrian arrived just as the politician began a speech about his government and its achievements.

The women around me examined the ground.

At the speech's end, men thronged around him. He talked to them, but after a while I was astonished to see that he was heading towards us. Craig stood in his path and handed his document over. But the politician wasn't to be deflected. He kept advancing, and the men fell away. My surprise at that was taken over by a further surprise – another couple of words popped into my understanding: after hours of uncomprehending listening, I could suddenly make out the women around me saying, 'You ask.' 'Not.' 'You ask.'

The politician was amongst us, holding Craig's document behind his back.

'Greetings, ladies,' he said. 'I've come to confide in you. The real purpose for me in flying here is to talk to you.'

He was in his early thirties but his hair was already starting to retreat towards the back of his head, as if it planned to abandon him. Nevertheless, he had deep-set eyes, a practised, winning smile, knife-edge ironed trousers and a shirt so white it almost hurt my eyes.

'I had other pressing matters, it's true, but closest to my heart –' He spoke softly, as if he was sharing a secret, 'I believe in talking to the grandmothers. That's where the soul of a community is. You'd all be grandmothers, right?'

Dora nodded politely, but the others gazed at the ground, unmoved, perhaps overwhelmed by the important government man talking to them, or simply uncomprehending.

'I loved my grandmother. She got me where I am today,' he smiled. 'I owe it all to her.'

I heard again, 'You ask,' muttered in Djemiranga by the women around me. The politician didn't notice, but anyway, since he didn't speak Djemiranga, he'd just hear it as extraneous noise.

'I didn't want to go to school – like any child.' He was confiding in us about this, his peccadillo that he'd triumphed over. 'But my grandmother cared about my future. I'd be in my little uniform, my little white shirt and little navy shorts I was always growing out of –' He smiled winningly again. These grandmothers, they'd be vexed with the problem of boys constantly growing out of their new clothes, especially since they lived so inconveniently far from the shops of Alice.

'She'd wash them every weekend –' His smiled wavered at the lack of response. 'She always washed my uniform on Saturday so it'd drip dry on the line bright and beautiful, and on Sunday night she'd get out the iron –' He faltered, suddenly aware that no one in his audience seemed to have ironed their dresses today, but he had to go on, 'And get to work on it.'

He decided to solve the problem by miming ironing, twisting his body to and fro in a most unlikely mimicry that suggested it wasn't he who'd ironed his knife-edged trousers.

'So I'd look clean and neat.' He stopped the mime, which hadn't really accomplished anything. 'But I'd be playing with my train set –'

Faced with twenty or so ladies gazing at the dust, he again wavered. Then it came to him how to win our attention, and he was down on his knees in the dust, a six-year-old boy shoving a train around a track. He smiled up at us. A second before he did, I hoped he wasn't going to do a train toot. But he did.

'Toot-toot, toot-toot!'

He got back on his feet, a little sheepish but pleased with himself, for this surely was what a politician must do to reach out to the people. He dusted his hands and the knees of his previously immaculate suit, but red dusty patches adamantly refused to budge – his wife would be explaining proudly to the dry-cleaner that her husband knew how to get down amongst the voters.

'I'd be hoping she'd be too busy to notice a little child. But she was never too busy. She'd tap the big clock on the wall –' Despite his concern about his suit, he beamed his most engaging smile. 'And she'd point out to me that it was ten to nine.'

The ladies merely gazed at the dust.

'Ten to nine,' the politician repeated, a little louder this time.

He was rewarded by the ladies lifting their heads a little, perhaps hoping his speech was finishing.

'She'd say: "Off to school with you!"'

But he seemed to have lost them again; their heads bowed. He had to try harder; any audience could be won, he obviously believed, if you really tried. He put on a grandmotherly voice, found a high note but it became a squeak:

'Off to school! Put down your train and go.'

Perhaps he was rewarded; the ladies muttered again. Against the previous stolidity, this was a promising noise. He went back to his normal speaking voice.

'If I didn't obey her, she'd go to the kitchen jug where all the big utensils were kept – the egg lifter –' here, the egg lifter slid under an imaginary fried egg, 'the potato masher –' the masher crushed boiled potatoes that resisted so fiercely, he had to smash them, almost unbalancing, but he regained composure, 'and the big wooden spoon.' The big wooden spoon stirred a steaming pot full of nutritious, grandmotherly stew on a stove.

'"I'll give you a paddywhack if you don't move," she'd say. Often I didn't move, hoping that this day I'd be allowed to stay home.'

I heard muttering again amongst the women. I made out again, 'You.'

'So she'd take the big wooden spoon out –' He paused again and I was astonished to see that his eyes were wet with tears. He was moved by his own memories, he was genuinely back in his grandmother's kitchen, or perhaps the grandmother he wished he'd had, or at least he so desperately wanted us to believe he had. But he was baffled that the women had resumed gazing at the dust.

'And you know what she'd do? She'd paddywhack me out the door with the wooden spoon.'

He repeated himself, the tears then running down his face.

'Paddywhack me off to school!'

I heard more muttering, and suddenly I made out an English word. It stood out. 'Grader.'

But I dismissed it. I must've made a mistake.

'And look where I am now!' said the politician. 'All because of my darling grandmother!'

He dashed the tears away. His beautiful, deeply set eyes moved along the row so that every one of us was included in his gaze.

'Because of my grandmother.'

There was a deep silence from the audience. Craig came over and hovered hopefully. White-haired, handsome Bruce and his white toy dog followed, the dog trotting obediently. Surely these old women didn't deserve such extended attention. It warmed my heart that Adrian and Daniel kept their distance, leaning against the wall of the council building. The politician glanced behind him, perhaps sensing the approach of Bruce and Craig out of the corner of his eye, and flapped his hand to them behind his back, hoping the ladies couldn't see him. *Go away, go away,* his hand said. *I've nearly got them. They're tough, but I'm nearly there.*

Craig and Bruce backed respectfully away. Even the toy dog walked backwards.

This speech of his must become a turning point in the disastrous state of education in the Northern Territory. He would make his audience appreciate his conviction, feel his passion, act on it. His audience would from then on be inspired to iron their grandchildren's clothes before school on Monday, be inspired to check the time on their clock on the wall, would reach out for their wooden spoons, be inspired to paddywhack children off to school. From that moment, the lives of Aboriginal children would improve, and Western education would succeed at last.

But the ladies sat, heads down, gazing at the dust.

'Don't you agree?' he asked them at last. He'd been the darling of ladies' lunches and ladies' afternoon teas, many of whom had opened their purses to his party because of his engaging smile.

Again I heard the muttered 'grader'. I could only think that there must be a word in Djemiranga like it. The politician, listening for any reaction at all, heard the word too.

'You saying that it could be greater?' he asked, a little desperately. 'Your effort? Your involvement?'

I thought I make out in Djemiranga: 'He's stopping. You.'

'It could indeed be greater! If grandmothers get more involved, that'll change the lives of our children! The futures of our children depend on grandmothers!'

But no one spoke.

'Tell me, so I can leave here with my heart high – tell me that from now on you'll be like my grandmother!'

So Dora spoke.

'Can we have a grader?'

Chapter 14

The next day, I worked on my recordings. Between the understanding of Djemiranga's grammar that Toolbox was giving me, and my fieldwork, as E.E. Albert would call it, I was beginning to guess at the meanings of words even when they occurred in the middle of sentences. *Eat, sleep, sit, drink, sing, cook, come.* Yesterday as a child pointed to chocolates at the shop, I'd made out *there, here.* I repeated the recordings again and again to correct my pronunciation. I wrote a column of the words I could decipher so far and was proud that the column stretched all the way down the page.

Gillian rang, startling me. I hadn't thought the electricity was on. I wanted to tell her how many words I'd discovered, but her voice was like a wounded bird dragging its wings along the ground.

'He broke it off,' she said.

'Your man?'

'His kids told him they don't like me.'

'I'm sorry,' I said. 'But you didn't like them.'

'They're spoiled brats!'

'Want a cuppa?' I asked.

There was a pause.

'I've been thinking about your song,' she said.

'You've worked out who's the singer?' I cried.

'About what's going to happen when you take it back,' she said. 'Men will hear it. Whites won't care!'

'Some would – I could ask if it could be protected –' I began.

'I know I sound like Adrian, but maybe you shouldn't give it to the university. Maybe you shouldn't even record it. Maybe it's a natural thing, the song dying out. Maybe change is natural. I mean, if the next generation doesn't want to learn it, maybe they have their reasons.'

'But – you're connected with these people!'

'That's why I'm saying this.'

'But I've promised it to my supervisor. I owe it to her. Protocols are in place. I'm sure she'll look after it.'

'Are you sure you're sure?'

My voice, my mind faltered. I thought of the darkness in Dean's face, his bloodless knuckles on E.E. Albert's door, his disapproval of our laughter, of how she smiled at him too much. I thought of how I'd been invisible to him.

If I'd been invisible to him, what else was?

I imagined the demands of a life of competitive research, the requirements at conferences to say something no one had said before, the pressure for constant publication of articles with new findings. I thought of E.E. Albert and the photos on her desk, and I thought of the compromises that loneliness and fear create.

'Can you be sure?' Gillian was asking. 'What's she going to use it for? Won't they want to publish it? Won't they write articles about it?'

Assertions about the integrity of human nature dried on my tongue, as if they were trudging wearily across a dry desert. The world of E.E. Albert and the university and my studies was beginning to feel like a dream I was waking up from.

'I'd be burning my bridges,' I said sadly.

'We'd better have that cuppa,' she said.

We sipped our cuppa that evening, sitting in the dark of her verandah, the side that looked out into the desert, with just a candle to light our thoughts.

'I don't know what to do,' I said.

'I don't, either,' she said.

Coming home in the dark, I almost tripped over several trays of seedlings, newly unloaded from the troopie.

'Our vegetable garden!' I cried joyfully.

Some were spinach and capsicum and mint, but there were tiny flowers as well. Daniel, in the candlelit living room, told me that Mandy, grower of the little carpet of green outside the clinic, wanted to start a garden. Mandy came to the clinic every day to sweep and clean, and to hose her square of grass. She was the only black person to work at the clinic. Adrian didn't want to employ Aboriginal health workers.

'I've been asked to, by white office clerks, but they don't know what they're talking about,' he'd said.

'It'd please them. Consolidate your position,' I'd said, while Daniel, sitting at the table, nodded quietly.

'My position is hard, dedicated work.'

'It'd please everyone.'

'Not the mob here and they're my bosses.'

'How can you know what everyone here thinks?'

He'd showed me a charter entitled *Aboriginal Workers' Rights.* The last rule was that a nurse wasn't obliged to help someone of the wrong skin.

'What if there's a car accident?' I'd asked. 'What if it's life-threatening?'

'Exactly my point,' he'd said.

'They're compassionate people,' I'd argued. 'Surely it only means they're not compelled to do something routine, like giving someone of the wrong skin a needle. They'd rescue someone suffering, whoever they are.'

'You'd know, of course.'

* * *

The lights in the living room leaped on, and Adrian left to check something at the clinic.

I sat alone outside on the plastic chairs, watching the night.

'Mandy asked for pink and purple flowers,' said Daniel, coming out to the verandah. His black feathery charcoal eyebrows were arched, his sweet face lit up with the thought of happy colours. 'Pink and purple. "Pretty flowers," she said.'

He was following Adrian to the clinic, just in case he was needed.

'I'll help her,' I said, but I was thinking, perhaps Mandy would tell me who the singer was.

Just before midnight I woke to hear shouts and the sound of running feet. I wrapped a sheet around me and went out to the living room, where Adrian stood in his makeshift dressing gown, holding a lit candle, his head tipped on one side, listening.

'Another grog-runner,' he said. 'I suspect I know who she is.'

'A woman!' I gasped.

'There might be violence. I'm worried now we're without a doctor. The injuries might be beyond Sister and Gillian.'

He put down the candle, went to the sink to get a drink of water, and offered me one.

'What about the Flying Service?' I asked, sipping in unison with him.

'The landing strip's got overgrown with all the rain we've had. I went out there yesterday for the mail plane. I should've hacked back the weeds then I suppose – even the flares to light the runway are hard to find – but it's an all-day job and I hadn't time.'

'Who normally does it?'

'Bruce.'

I'd learned to sigh at the mention of his name.

'I reminded him, and he said if the pilot wanted it done, he could cut the weeds himself!'

'But he'd have to land first!'

'Landing's OK during the day. It's seeing the flares at night, that's the problem.' He put down his glass on the sink. 'I think I'd better go and fix it up. Don't want a death on my conscience.' He headed towards the bathroom with his candle, where, since he still had no bedroom with a wardrobe, he'd taken to keeping a pile of clothes on the floor.

'You're going to cut grass at this hour?'

'At least clear the flares. By the headlights.' He was pulling on clothes with the bathroom door open. 'I heard Wendy, Dora's granddaughter, walking by a few minutes ago,' he continued, planning aloud. 'She's always sober, and she was with two strapping young fellows. Might ask their help. Want to come?'

This last was flung over his shoulder as he strode, now fully dressed, to the door.

'Yes,' I said.

'Take the candle to get dressed. Blow it out afterwards – don't want a fire to add to our troubles. And bring torches,' he said.

'And Daniel?' I asked.

'Let him sleep.'

By the time I'd dressed, he'd returned in the troopie with three young people all laughing and horsing around with giant clippers.

I joined them in the back, trying to make out what the young people were saying, for many sounds were familiar, but my tired mind protested. We drove through deserted and dark streets. At the airstrip, Adrian discovered that the fuel for the flares was low. He swore about Bruce, but drove off for more fuel, while the young people and I, holding torches, scoured through the long weeds for hidden flares. Because the sky was black with further rain and our torches were weak, we found them at first by tripping over them and banging our shins, though after a while we could predict their whereabouts within the range of a metre or two, because someone – I hoped Bruce – had spaced them evenly apart. Then we worked in pairs, one holding the torch while the other hacked down a circle of weeds around each flare. I worked with Wendy, and longed to find some Djemiranga to exchange with her, but she had little English and all I could muster was 'bravo'.

But at least I learned to shout 'Here's one!' in Djemiranga, because we said it about sixty times.

I knew that for the rest of my life I'd never utter those words without recalling this night: the glancing torchlight, Wendy's laughter, the vast sky arching over us black with rain, and the soft, rich Djemiranga syllables.

When Adrian returned in the troopie with fuel, he too said, 'Bravo.' He squeezed my hand as I climbed into the cabin.

'Thank you,' he said, to us all, but he seemed especially to smile at me. We drove the young people to Dora's house, then went home. He leaned over and opened my passenger door.

'I couldn't speak Djemiranga!' I said in frustration. 'All I could understand was when one of the boys said "I'm tired".'

I repeated it to him, enjoying the sensation of it in my mouth.

'Body language,' he said, his face near mine. 'That's what counts.'

His closeness became a kiss on my lips, but a dry kiss, that of a brother to a sister.

'Go to bed,' he said, as if once again I was the little girl from round the corner.

'Aren't you coming in?' I asked, for he hadn't turned off the engine.

'I'll do the rounds of the streets,' he said. 'Checking for casualties, like a matron.'

I was asleep long before he came back.

* * *

In the morning, we planted the vegetable seedlings in Daniel's new garden. But as I walked past the clinic, I saw that its front yard had been dug up as well, and fenced off to keep the donkey out. Mandy was already planting her pink and purple flowers, and Adrian had come out of his office to pass them to her one by one.

'Any casualties last night?' I asked.

'Nothing, thank God,' he said. His face seemed to glow just for me. He saw me watching Mandy.

'Come over and help,' he said. He assumed I knew about gardening because I was a white woman – or did he remember Diana teaching me how to garden?

I thought, I'll find out who the singer is today. I'll wait till Mandy and I are both busy and then I'll ask the question. Then I can leave.

Mandy and I crouched together, our knees out like frogs, to press the seedlings into the rust-coloured, warm, gritty earth. Adrian, satisfied, went back inside the clinic.

'Pretty flowers,' she said from time to time.

I found myself repeating it.

'Pretty flowers.'

Calmed by the rhythm of the work, I let peace wash over and take me away from my thoughts. At first it came because I was intent on being helpful, but slowly, I found myself not wanting to chat. Occasionally I said, 'What about here?' and dug a hole with my fingers. And again 'Here?'

I thought, I'll ask her about the singer by the end of the next row. Then I put off asking to the next row, and the next.

We were coming to the last tray of seedlings, and still I hadn't asked her.

We stood up, wiping the red dirt off our hands and onto our skirts. I found the hose coiled up inside a shed full of office

241

furniture, screwed it on to the tap at a tank, brought it to her, and went back to turn on the tap.

We stood watching the sparkling arc of water.

Suddenly Mandy confided: 'So boring, at the camp.'

She was telling me that home was boring! I was astounded, but I was learning not to say unnecessary things. I just nodded.

'Gardening is fun,' I said.

'It's fun,' she repeated.

I felt I was beginning to understand consensus.

One of her grandchildren called her, and my chance to ask was over. I should've been angry with myself that I hadn't popped the question, but I was curiously satisfied.

I stood gazing at our work. Adrian came out and joined me.

'You're learning,' he said, beaming again.

'I'm learning gardening?' I was about to refute that, but it would mean mentioning Diana.

'I've been eavesdropping,' he said. 'You're learning silent communing. They have a lot that feels like conversation. Certain silences and glances, certain patterns of breathing. The word sounds like *jirriku*. Very big here, *jirriku*.'

'You're speaking Djemiranga!' I exclaimed, and repeated it after him.

At dawn the next morning, Adrian left the settlement again with a troopie full of patients. His lips from the kiss the other night still seemed imprinted on mine.

I was getting used to his frequent absences. On the washing machine lid, two of his pale blue shirts waited for him. He bought them six at a time, always blue linen, amply cut so they billowed luxuriously when he tucked them into tight jeans. 'They wear out,' I'd heard him tell Gillian, 'always within weeks of each other – figure that!' Then when he'd go to town, he'd buy another six. On the machine lid they were dust streaked, vulnerable, childish, like cowering animals. From the jagged streaks on the back of one shirt, it seemed he'd stretched out under a broken-down troopie on the road. From the back of another shirt, I saw he'd leaned against a burnt tree, a moment memorialised in a diamond of black soot. I threw a load of my own dusty clothes into the water. I hesitated, then picked up his shirts to throw them in as well. But I stood fingering them, to touch him. Here were his skin cells powdering my hands. Here was the grime from his sunburnt, muscular neck. Even the tufted weave of the shirts smelled of his life, of cooking smoke and oil, the smell of a troopie, of him. Two unwrapped squares of chocolate, grit covered, distorted the shape of a pocket he hadn't scissored off. I took them out, and popped them both in my mouth at once, grit and all. Then I feared he'd divine what I'd done, and he'd think I was in love with him.

Perhaps I was. I could fill a room, a street, a whole settlement with thoughts of him. But between us was an ancient grief.

'I don't know what to do,' I told Daniel a few days later. 'I've been here nearly three weeks and I still haven't found my singer.' We were walking in the evening when he came back from the clinic. Daniel and I seemed to be moving in a silence that came with us, in a hush that began in our minds and spread beyond us. We stopped at a grey-leafed bush which had suddenly sprouted lime green leaves, a colour so unlikely it was as if a child had chosen the wrong crayon for colouring in.

'Why don't you insist on Adrian helping you?' he asked.

It came to me that Daniel seemed more relaxed when Adrian was in town. Perhaps, I thought, he felt torn between Adrian and me.

'How? As Gillian says, he's a law unto himself.'

'I've been thinking about your bedroom.'

He laughed uncertainly. Creak. Creak.

'My bedroom?' I laughed with him. I couldn't think why I'd found his laughter strange at first.

'The cupboard I warned you not to open. We're missing a whole lot of paperwork. Medicare claims. It'd give us a lot of money, and the clinic needs it. And you know what I'm thinking? Remember I told you that just before you came, I saw him stuffing papers up there?'

'Why would he do that?'

'So he didn't have to think about them. I wonder what happened to him,' he groaned.

'Happened? Has something happened to him?' I asked. I was surprised at how high my voice was with worry.

'In his childhood,' said Daniel. 'Something must've gone really wrong.'

We passed a white gum tree. I touched its bark and white powder like talcum came off on my hands. The tree was like a woman in a slender white evening dress. Where the boughs joined on to the trunk there were creases, like ripples of satin.

'Look,' I said to Daniel. I stood like the tree.

He laughed. Creak. Creak.

'Make me a neat martini,' I joked.

'Even miming trees is funny here,' he said.

I brushed his hand accidentally as he swung it by his side. I would've liked to have caught and held it, to have asked what went wrong for him in his childhood, that gave him such a wistful air. How little I knew about him, how little I'd ever known about anyone. I wondered if all the whites who came to the desert hoped that the desert would be kind to us, that it would in some way heal us.

We wandered in the sort of silence that's almost love. I pointed out to him a festoon in the russet soil of turquoise weed and, hidden in a crevice from the sun, a tiny yellow flower.

'Most flowers out here are yellow or purple,' he said. 'I wonder why.'

I wondered if he missed the rigours of science, now that he was engulfed in Adrian's chaos. I didn't know how to ask him, not yet. There seemed so much I wanted to ask him.

He pointed out a bush that whirred by my legs.

'It looks like wild lavender,' he said. He bent and pulled at its leaves. 'It smells like lavender. Here –' He shared the leaves with me, holding them up to my nose. 'Do you think it *is* lavender?'

We both stroked the leaves in a sort of wonder. Green budgerigars in a flock flew by so unexpectedly they seemed like a sudden clotting of the air, and so low, Daniel almost had to duck.

'I don't know,' I said softly. 'Perhaps.'

He threw the leaves away. It was like throwing the moment away, resolutely. He'd made a decision, I dimly thought, about me, about our connection, probably to do with his loyalty to Adrian. But I had no idea if he felt any attraction to me, except that his hand returned to his side when it could so easily have strayed to mine. He moved in respectful silence with Adrian and with me, a man, it seemed, without ambition for himself. It felt ennobling to be with him. I became less anxious, less self-engrossed, less fixed on the past. Some people are ennobling, and I hoped, that in being near him, he could ennoble me.

The budgerigars lifted away up into the sky, all the while crying or perhaps singing, in a swoop of green bellies.

Daniel mentioned he had to be up early, to go back to one of the outstations. He had to help a visiting dentist, and take Tillie, an old person, to respite care in Alice Springs.

'How can you help a dentist?' I asked. 'Pass him the drill? Give injections?'

'I just talk people into having their teeth fixed,' he laughed.

'Aren't they eager to have them fixed?'

'Does anyone ever want to go to the dentist?' he asked.

'There aren't appointments booked?' I asked.

'I told them last week, I tried to book them – not times of course, just "after breakfast", "before lunch" – but who knows when lunch is, or breakfast, or if a meal is going to happen?'

I walked on, musing on how difficult it was to stop thinking in a city way.

'Could she be out there, my old lady?' I asked.

He said hesitantly: 'They're very traditional there because they still hunt. They haven't a shop to buy food.' Then he took a quick breath, and looked away.

'What's wrong?' I asked.

'Nothing,' he said.

'Can I come?' I asked. 'I could help you find patients.'

'No,' he said. 'Please don't ask me to go against Adrian.'

We walked into the deepening darkness.

'Adrian doesn't want you there,' he said at last. 'He told me that specifically. He doesn't want them studied.'

'I'm here because he invited me,' I said.

'I know,' he said.

He deflected to something that was for him an easier subject.

'Have you done something to offend him?'

'*I* offend him,' I answered. 'Gillian tells me she does too.'

Every day I examined my disguise. The blonde roots of my hair weren't showing through yet, my eyebrows were still black, my skin was only slightly less bronzed, and I was careful to wear my spectacles every day.

He laughed fondly.

'Gillian's a mischief-maker – in the nicest way, of course.'

Walking behind Daniel, I found a bird's nest, flattened by its fall but still intact. I carried it home two-fingered, fearing lice. It seemed like an artwork, with its lacing and twining and weaving. It brought to me a sense of the extraordinary; like a creature on the moon might feel when it came across signs of humans.

'My girlfriend says she's coming out the weekend after next.'

Loss hit me like a thud.

'Your girlfriend?'

'I hope you'll still be here. She lives in Alice Springs. Sometimes I see her when I go in.'

'Sometimes?'

It was ridiculous, this sense of loss. I'd come all this way, this journey after all these years to find Adrian, and now I wanted to monopolise any stray man who happened to share his house?

'She's an artist. She wants me to leave here – but I can't.'

So this is why he'd held back with me – and I'd thought he'd been attracted to me but was loyal to Adrian! How vain, how self-engrossed I'd been!

'That's hard,' I managed to say.

As we crossed the road to home, the streetlights were already on.

'We've got electricity for a while,' I said, deliberately steadying my voice despite my shock that seemed to be exploding along my veins.

'Bruce confided in me he doesn't know how to fix it,' said Daniel.

I managed a laugh. 'You make even Bruce trust you?'

'He's lonely. It's said three sorts of whites come out here – the mad, the mercenaries and the missionaries.'

'Which are you?' I teased, to cover my sadness.

'Look – a scorpion,' was all he said.

It plodded over the road with heavy feet. I told Daniel it had the determined fury of a headmistress in heavy shoes marching down a school corridor to catch a girl who'd rolled down her socks to show off her ankles.

'You were a girl like that, weren't you?' said Daniel a little wistfully.

'Was your girlfriend?'

He laughed, a little embarrassed.

'No – or at least, I don't think so.'

I was pleased that he wasn't sure.

'What's her name?'

'Anastasia.'

I burst out: 'She must be beautiful with a name like Anastasia.'

'Very,' he said, in a voice no warmer than usual. 'Waist-length blonde hair, fair-skinned.'

I wanted to childishly blurt: But I'm like that too! But she probably had curling golden locks, a sculptured, symmetrical face with eyes blue as the sea, eyelashes like stars, full lips that demanded to be kissed, a slender build with long glamorous legs and full breasts – did she have full breasts? I'd begun to lose faith in the ability of large breasts to guarantee love. Perhaps I wasn't sure about her breasts.

'And her painting?'

'She's good – she paints traditional landscapes. Her hero's Turner – she does wild, marvellous skies, with the sort of clouds you could walk in to find lands that no one's ever known.' I could tell from a dreamy note in his voice that at that moment he was with Anastasia, considering the way she saw skies. 'She feels very unfashionable, she can't compete against all the concentration on Aboriginal art here. She wants to leave the Territory, go south.'

We always took our shoes off at the door.

'Let's make dinner right now before we lose the electricity,' I said.

'I'm a misfit, probably,' he said as he chopped vegetables and I browned kangaroo steaks I'd bought frozen from the shop. 'That's what's wrong.'

I hoped he was thinking about what was wrong with Anastasia, but I didn't dare ask more.

We had dinner out on the verandah – al fresco, we joked.

We hadn't settled anything about me going with him to the outstation. In the early days, I would've pushed it, but something about this place had taught me to let things take their own course. The sky seemed huge, portentous, dark and steely with rain – a Turner sky, I almost said.

'What would you do down south?' I asked instead, unable to leave the question alone.

He shrugged. 'I've reinvented myself before.'

'But you had to. This time would be because someone wished it of you.'

As we lounged back afterwards with glasses of tonic water which we pretended were laced with gin, he said: 'Adrian thinks he's indispensable.'

'He's bombastic,' I cried.

'The trouble is, with his energy, his anarchy, his self-absorption, his determination to get the job done whatever it takes – he might be right. He might be indispensable.'

He stood and collected our empty glasses.

'I can't go behind his back about the outstation. He's done too much for me, giving me a job out here. I'm sorry.'

I made myself cast down my eyes to examine the laborious progress of an ant across the floorboards, stumbling over red dirt caught in the cracks.

I washed up, while he had first turn at the bathroom, by candlelight now. He came out, brushing his teeth, his mouth foaming with toothpaste, the candle on the floor lengthening his face.

'After the outstation, I have to come back here before I go into Alice.' I wanted to ask if he was seeing Anastasia when he was in Alice, but he was continuing: 'You *could* come out with me, if you keep it a secret, and I could drop you off back here.'

'I swear.'

He turned.

I called out through the shut door: 'But what would I do out there?'

'Help me,' he called back.

I couldn't help myself from crying into my pillow, like a spoilt child. Every shy smile, every generous gesture of his flitted through my mind. He'd not only been my advocate to Adrian, but to myself. He was the one who'd said: 'I'm proud you're staying with us.' He was the one who'd pointed out that I was searching for the oldest surviving song.

Though I'd come here for Adrian, the desert had revealed what an anchoring love might be – from a man in love with a beauty called Anastasia.

Part Three

Chapter 15

In the morning, I heard him shower. I stumbled out into the hall.

'You're coming?' he asked.

I nodded. He seemed crestfallen.

'I was hoping you'd sleep in. Promise me,' he said, 'promise not to ask about the singer.'

I promised again. He seemed to reconcile himself to my presence quickly.

'Pack food,' he said. 'I told you how traditional it is. There aren't many houses. People went there a while back for a funeral and never returned home, even though it has no shop. They live like they did in the old days – almost.'

'Why do they love it?'

'It's their ancestral country. That's what matters.'

Daniel drove carefully, far slower than Adrian would've done. With his air of wistful playfulness, there was something toy-like about the troopie, as if it wasn't an ordinary four-wheel drive, more like a huge billycart.

'Can I drive? Just for a while?'

'It's not insured for you to drive.'

'Even Adrian said that.'

'I'm relieved to hear it!'

I laughed. Daniel glanced at me, and smiled.

'I agree, that's a surprise,' he allowed himself to say about his friend.

That day, something happened to my way of seeing things, perhaps because of Daniel, perhaps because I feared my days with him were coming to an end. As we drove down the orange-red road, red as home-grown tomatoes on the vine, all around us was the waiting, the stillness. It was a country that invited drifts of the imagination, I thought, as Daniel steered into a pastoralist's land to dodge a pond stretching from one side of the road to the other. The lower branches of the mulga looked manicured, I thought, as if eagles had swarmed over them and, hanging upside down, had bitten off each branch as a hairdresser might chop hair, even perching afterwards on a nearby tree to check that each group of branches now made its own neat semi-circle against the sky. Or perhaps a sky-borne herd of cattle had come along afterwards, neatening up the edges.

'When I first came here I wanted hills,' I told Daniel.

'Hills are easy places for the soul to hide,' said Daniel.

'Soul?' I looked at him in surprise.

'Remember I told you I used to take my mum to church?' He drove back onto the road. 'I'm trained in science but the desert changes you,' he said softly. 'It's like in physics – you can't both observe it and be in it at the same time. Out here, you lose your objectivity.'

'So we don't know we're going crazy?' I laughed. But he didn't.

'Do you know how the people see this country?' I asked.

'Not really. You'd need their language. And maybe you'd need to be born here. There are dangerous places where no one's allowed to look. If they're laughing and talking with you and aware of you, they'll say: "Don't look, Daniel!" with real terror in their voices. Then, at other times, I imagine they think whites are immune to the spirit dangers. Maybe to them we're still white ghosts in a way.'

He added, glancing out my window: 'There's a sacred track over there. It's part of a track where women danced.'

'When did they dance there? I'd like to see them dance

again,' I said. 'Adrian said that no women's ceremonies out here have survived. And I said: "how would he know?"'

He laughed. Creak. Creak. His laughter was so endearing. Had it changed? Had I?

'The dancing I'm talking about – that wasn't in this lifetime. In the Dreaming. The whole area was crisscrossed with tracks, song lines, and people had to know the songs and the dances to cross safely into the territory of other tribes. Singing the right song was like a passport, like getting immunity. The dancing women's track goes a long way. I've heard of it going hundreds of kilometres.'

'How do you know about this dancing track?'

'It's on a map in a book Adrian owns. Didn't he show you?'

When I shook my head, he said: 'He won't do his job properly, and he stops you from doing yours.'

I thought, Daniel is my true friend. But all I said was: 'I've been thinking I might open that cupboard. Just, you know, absent-mindedly.'

He almost pulled the brake on, so great was his anguish.

'I shouldn't have told you! He's my best friend! I don't want to shame him!'

'Wouldn't it help the clinic if Adrian cashed in those Medicare receipts?' I puzzled.

'Of course!' said Daniel. 'The clinic would get the money. But Sister would insist it go on medical equipment, and Adrian would insist on the second doctor –'

'So the cupboard in my room is the too-hard basket!'

We both laughed in exasperation and guilty relief. Creak. Creak.

He drove on.

'It'd be easy, if you were in Greece, to be conscious of the ancient times – Aristotle and Archimedes and Plato – but out here, what with all that's going on, I keep forgetting there's such antiquity – apart from the rocks, of course. You know that Gondwanaland, including here, is one of the oldest continents.'

He paused, then added: 'Other continents broke off from Gondwanaland. That's why there are some of the most ancient rocks on earth here. And, see over there –' he pointed to a group of broken rocks glowing golden in the sun, 'people quarried stone for thousands of years.'

'What for?' I asked.

'Grinding stones,' he said. 'It was taken far and wide. Everyone wanted their grinding stone to come from here – it had spiritual power, they thought.'

At the outstation, Daniel was told that the old person he was taking into respite was asleep. He was to come back later.

'Is she an old lady?' I asked, suddenly excited. 'Could she be my old lady?'

His face tightened.

'You promised.'

He told me to wait in the troopie and he disappeared. I gazed around at the settlement. There were four besser block houses, each with a tumble of children's worn toys in their front yards, alongside the remnants of cooking fires. Fifty metres away was a long edifice I imagined to be a rubbish pile. The dentist had a shiny, well-kept caravan. A camel leaned against it, slowly munching, everything about its musculature slack. Its coat hung in tendrils from its belly, its sides were as flat as a book's covers, its hump a bony cushion.

Daniel came over to me.

'I have to clean up the room the doctors use when they visit. Someone's been sleeping in it and it's filthy. But there aren't enough patients for the dentist – he has to meet his government quota. Would you help round some patients up? Something must be distracting everyone.'

'Won't the dentist tell Adrian I was here?'

'He'll just assume you're some nurse from the clinic,' said Daniel. 'Act like Gillian.'

The caravan was divided into a tiny waiting room, with three women sitting on chairs, and a tiny surgery. I walked in just as the dentist's nurse farewelled a family. The children rushed past me but paused long enough to jubilantly hold up new toothbrushes and new tubes of toothpaste for me to admire, their young mothers giggling behind their hands. Then the children dashed out and swung on the handrails above the caravan steps, yelping with joy. Even a tiny toddler clambered up the steps to swing upside down, holding onto the rail with bent knees like her older brothers and sisters. I started forward, but she held herself ably, the red dust earth two of her body lengths below.

'Be careful,' I gasped.

The nurse laughed at my reaction. She was dark-haired, with olive skin, red cheeks and a broad Italian–Australian accent.

'They're natural athletes,' she told me. 'Toothache?' she asked one of the three women waiting, but the English word meant nothing and the woman shrugged.

'Come with me,' the nurse said kindly, and taking her hand, led her gently in to the dentist. 'Here's your next patient,' she said to someone I couldn't see. Her sisters followed her to watch.

'I hope he doesn't scare them off with the drill,' the nurse confided in me. 'Could you block the steps? To prevent her sisters running away before he checks them as well?'

But a few minutes later, all three sisters emerged.

'Beautiful teeth,' said the nurse to me as they went. 'Like last time. They hunt animals and gather berries. But you'd know that.' She assumed the women didn't speak any English and perhaps she was right.

'Could you go and find us more patients?' she asked me, but when she saw my bewilderment, she pointed across a clearing towards the edifice I'd noticed before.

'Will anyone be there?' I asked, fighting shyness at the thought of meeting strangers.

'You don't normally come out here, you clinic mob?' she asked.

'Not me,' I said, blushing. 'Just Daniel and a doctor.'

'It's a big humpy,' she laughed. 'It's home to about twenty people. Surely there's someone there with a toothache.'

I walked across reluctantly to what I then discerned wasn't a rubbish heap at all, but a collection of the pretty bough shelters they often built in the area in an emergency – for the funeral when I first returned here, for example. And, when a car broke down, I'd often seen mothers get an axe out of the boot and chop down four young forked saplings and erect a shelter within minutes for the children to play under. But these were covered more formally, with carpets and the usual colourful nylon blankets, and on the top were clothes and cooking pots with blackened bottoms and bins that once stored shop-bought flour and sugar, all out of the reach of dogs and children. As I stood at the entrance to the edifice, I found I was gazing into a long meandering room of about head height that seemed to change both its direction and width every few metres, so that I was in fact looking at many rooms, perhaps family sections, shadowy but not dark. Even from where I stood I could feel cool air because the humpy faced away from the sun and towards any breeze. The red dirt floors were so neatly swept I could see the furrows of a stick broom. More collections of rags, perhaps clothes, hung on ropes inside. Everything was orderly, as orderly as anything I ever saw on board a boat on the river. But what took my breath away was that in every room, women, and occasionally a man, sat cross-legged on the swept floors painting colourful pictures on large canvases.

The nearest woman looked up at me.

'Teeth,' I said, pointing to my own, smiling. 'Dentist. Teeth doctor. In caravan,' I added, pointing.

A few other women looked up, smiled, but looked down and continued painting, utterly absorbed.

I went back to the caravan and reported to the nurse.

'We came on the wrong day,' she said. 'I just heard that there's a famous artist due. He's coming to collect his paintings.'

She mentioned the name.

'*His* paintings?'

'Why not?' She laughed. 'It's what happened in the Renaissance in my country. He's like Michelangelo and Rossetti. They had studios of assistants, too. These women paint in his style and name. He'll come out and check and collect the paintings, probably just like those famous artists did.'

At a loss, I went and sat in the shade at benches erected for people to wait for a turn at the one public phone booth. Two women walked up. One put her money in the slot and dialled a number on the phone. Her friend sat with her back to me, but threw over her shoulder: 'You a doctor?'

I was surprised to hear English.

'No.'

'A teacher?'

'No.'

'Where's your country?'

'Sydney.'

Her body edged a little more to face me, so I felt I could question her.

'You grew up here?'

'Near here. Only my kids grew up here.'

'It's good here,' I said. I was learning not to say that the country was beautiful. It didn't seem to be what was said. Country was your homeland, almost like your body, or it was dangerous, or it was good. No one seemed to call it beautiful, or be astonished at its colours or its flowers.

She smiled at me. She was very pretty, surely not any older than me, with round cheeks and long hair covered elegantly in a veil, though when I looked more closely, I saw that the veil had been a boy's white singlet.

Minutes passed. We looked together at red dust, the stunted trees, leaves, and the dentist's van. I didn't know what she saw, but her quietness made me wait.

Something did happen. She laughed fondly.

'The camel,' she said.

'It's crazy?' I asked, because of her laugh.

'It wants to eat bread,' she said.

We were being quite chatty, though not by white standards.

In between our sentences, she traced a shape in the dust on the bench beside her with a graceful finger. The shape was a rectangle. She drew a diagonal that could be a plant, because her fingers feathered out in curving shapes towards each corner of the rectangle. I was astonished at the symmetry of the design, but she wasn't satisfied, she rubbed it out, and began again in more dust on the bench, trying the same pattern but from another side, with less leaves this time. She rubbed that one out, and then she did a third, and a fourth. It came to me, judging by the beauty of the drawings, that I might be sitting beside a serious artist, perhaps even a famous one. But I knew not to ask her name. She sat gazing at her last picture, satisfied, and then she looked up at me as if she'd forgotten her surroundings in her musings, and was surprised to see me there. Something about her slow-focusing brought the question out of me.

'Is there,' my voice said, 'an old lady who sings the old songs? There's a special song. Whites call it the "Poor Thing" song. It's only for women. From the Dreaming.'

She looked away. A crow landed and called plaintively. We both looked at it. It was as if she hadn't heard. Whatever had been between us, I felt I'd destroyed. She looked at her etching, at the sky, at the bench, at the crow, at her friend on the phone. She rubbed out her latest etching, deciding it displeased her after all.

I was ashamed of myself. I'd betrayed Daniel. If it got back to Adrian, Daniel's job could be jeopardised. I'd failed myself, I'd failed him. He wouldn't want me as his friend any more. I put my head in my hands. Why had I spoken, why, why couldn't I hold my tongue? When was I going to learn that lesson?

Adrian, I decided, was right in another thing: I didn't understand Aboriginal people. I was full of city needs, like the sacked builder, demanding that everything move at my pace, everything follow my values.

In my shame, I became aware of the voice on the phone.

'2500,' I heard in English, in single digits, and then the rest of the sentence was in Djemiranga. She mustn't be talking to a white person, because the only English was the digits – I knew the lack of numbers in Aboriginal languages – and she must've been talking money. She seemed excited, as if she was negotiating in hope. Then, a little less excitedly, I heard, '2000.' Then, despondently, '1800,' then, sadly, '1600.'

She put down the phone.

'1200,' she murmured to her friend, the artist beside me. They walked slowly away together towards the big humpy, their shoulders rubbing against each other in a consoling way. I wished every time I was disappointed, I could walk away from it with such a friend, rubbing shoulders. I wished I had a friend now, who I could tell my conflicts to, my betrayals. I could of course talk to Gillian, but I couldn't even begin to explain my past.

Suddenly Daniel was by my side.

'We're to pick some people up, and I've got to go and get Tillie,' he told me. 'But I mustn't carry her, being a bloke. Can you help?'

We drove to her front yard. Tillie was lying on a bare mattress and her daughter, herself a middle-aged woman, crouched by her side. Her daughter gestured that I should take her mother's legs, while she held her mother under the arms. But the old lady sagged in the middle, a dead weight. It felt as if we could break her in two. Her sons stood by the fence, impassively watching, arms crossed. Daniel stood with them. I wanted to ask for their help, but suspected that would break a cultural code. Like Daniel, probably they were not allowed to help. The old lady stirred on her bare mattress, turned her head and groaned. Her sons spoke to each other, and went away so I thought they were abandoning her – but then they were back with a tabletop that was really a door, and they handed it to Daniel, who handed it to me. By lifting her first to one side and then the other, her daughter and I slid the door under her mattress, and then we could lift her, door, mattress and all, into the troopie, and lie her on its floor. For a second it flitted through my mind that Tillie could be my old lady, but in Daniel's presence, I didn't dare think further.

We drove off, with my feet near the old lady's head. Then, down another dusty street, we saw people waiting at a doorway out of the sun. A young girl came forward carrying a baby. An older woman followed with blankets. The girl climbed in the cabin, and held her baby close while she turned her head towards her young husband, not looking at him, but acknowledging him by the turn of her head. He'd blonded the hair above his ears but the bleach had fought with his black hair and compromised on orange. He assessed whether there was space for him, swung himself in against her, and they both sat gazing at their baby asleep in her pretty, rounded arms. I thought, again irreverently, that their gaze was so devoted, they were almost like Mary and Joseph contemplating their child.

It came to me that in comparison to their love I tried to live on only a mite of emotion, like someone going through the world with eyes half-closed. It seemed I'd lacked not only the opportunity, but the courage to live fully.

The young woman's mother was at the back of the troopie, struggling with its high steps. From inside, I held out my hand to help but she didn't seem to notice. She turned her back to me, laid her chest down on the floor and kicked the air until she could wriggle her way in, just like a swimmer trying to get out of the pool at the town baths. Then a little child of about three clambered in after her and sat beside her cross-legged, watching me solemnly, despite my smiles.

I heard the ringing of Daniel's satellite phone. He climbed out, listened, then ran back to the troopie.

'Quick, I've got to get you home,' he said, turning to me. 'You know why!'

I slammed the back door. We roared towards the gate that led to the road, a gate that looked as if it was seldom shut by the way weeds had grown up around the fence posts. A crowd of women were milling there. A four-wheel drive had pulled up.

Daniel groaned.

'We don't need a traffic jam now!'

A town-dressed black man was talking to the crowd. People straggled over the road to listen, some of them holding rolled-up canvases.

'Paintings,' the woman in the back informed me in unexpected English.

The artist I'd sat with near the telephone booth was on the outside of the circle as we pulled up. She leaned towards my window, waving me to open it, smiling warmly, as if I'd ruined nothing. I tried to open the window but it was stuck.

'Please wait while I get this thing open!' I called to Daniel.

'Sorry,' said Daniel. 'But I'll lose my job.'

The crowd cleared for him, and he roared through the gate. In the rear-vision mirror, the woman was still gesticulating.

She could've had an answer to my question, I wanted to say, the question I'd promised not to ask.

It was almost lunchtime as we turned into the main street of the settlement. Suddenly, Daniel braked.

'He's beaten us back,' he said, his voice a little higher than usual.

Down the road, a dusty troopie was parked outside our house. The doors were wide open; the way Adrian always left a troopie except when he was in town. It was as if he was always poised for flight, here in the settlement he wanted to save.

'I'll be in trouble. Quick, get out and walk home slowly,' said Daniel and I noticed how his lower lip crinkled when he was worried. 'No, that's no good, he'll guess you've been out there with me. I know. Go down to the school. So you're coming from a different direction. Do something that'll take an hour or so before you come home.'

I clambered out.

'What will I do there? I haven't got my recorder –'

The woman in the back threw out my hat.

'You're always resourceful,' said Daniel. He thought to give me an encouraging grin and started up the troopie.

Chapter 16

I trudged down the street in the sun. I'd offer to tidy up the library that had looked so messy through the window. Doing that should take me an hour or so, and then I could innocently saunter home.

The schoolyard was, as usual, just furrows of sand to show that only the wind had been there – no children playing and shouting, no dogs, not even the donkey. No dark, curly heads to be seen through the windows. An Aboriginal woman sat alone on a bench under the shade of the tree, surprising me because people here seldom sat alone. I nodded to her, but she didn't nod back, in fact, she was so deep in her thoughts that I wasn't even sure she'd seen me. I thought of sitting beside her companionably, but instead I took the easier course and wandered shyly over to the staff room.

Craig came straight to the door, almost as if he'd been waiting.

'I just popped in to see if I could be of use,' I started to say. 'Is there anything that needs doing? The library –?'

Craig shook his head.

'You've come just in time to listen to my letter to the Department.'

'I looked in the library window and saw –'

But he wasn't interested in what I'd seen; he led me into the room, to his desk which seemed, democratically, as modest as the two other desks in the room, clearly the desks of ordinary teachers – Beth, and Dudley from the outstation, who I'd glimpsed at the funeral.

'I'll read it to you,' he said. 'I've had it with these people shaming me.' He sat down at once at his computer and began scrolling to the start, while I gazed at a framed photo of an improbably beautiful Asian teenager. But he roused himself, remembered to be gallant and reached over for another chair.

'Sit down if you like.'

We were in for a long reading, I saw. He pulled over his cup, brimming with hot coffee with a white powdery scum on the top. I wondered if the powder was dust, or from the bore water.

A voice came from a corner in the shadows. I hadn't noticed Beth.

'It's terrible, what they're doing to him,' she said, coming over. 'You'd never know it was our Rejoice in Literature Day, would you? Fancy that – not coming to school on Rejoice in Literature Day.' Her look towards him was full of tenderness, and the pink curls on her head strained towards him.

'They're breaking his heart!' she added.

As when I first met them, Craig and Beth had a way of sweeping me into their preoccupations, as if I was a member of the family who'd just come back after popping out to the local shop for milk. I found myself wondering whether she was in love with him.

She added, looking out to the schoolyard: 'That's Libby, my useless assistant teacher. She's meant to be helping me.'

'She seems in trouble,' I said, for the woman outside now seemed slumped on the seat.

'She is! She should be preparing my charts, covering my books and mounting my photos. She's paid to teach the kids to read in their own language,' she answered. 'Though why the government demands it, we don't know. The kids are here so seldom they have no hope of reading even in English!'

'You can't expect anything of these people,' Craig reminded her absent-mindedly as he used his spell-check on the letter. 'Not even common decency.'

And then, while he kept scrolling, he told me that one of the schoolgirls, only fourteen years old, was being raped regularly. He named the girl and boy and the outstation I'd just come from.

'They have a new baby? The boy has orange hair?' I asked.

He glanced up. 'That's them. Reprehensible, isn't it!'

'But the boy is her husband!' I cried. 'They were in the troopie!'

'You helped them?'

Beth glanced between us. Again, she seemed to draw strength from me.

'They do marry straight after puberty,' she told him, nodding enough for the two of them.

'But that's against universal standards! The whole world would condemn them,' he said. 'Remember the sports weekend?' He turned to me, the letter forgotten for a moment: 'People just threw their mattresses and blankets on the ground to sleep on later, and left them unattended while they went off to watch the football –'

'Wait till you hear the next horror,' Beth interjected.

'And Sabah, my little wife, couldn't believe her eyes – we saw the donkey standing on one of their mattresses nosing into a plastic bag of bread while it defecated – wait for it –'

'On someone's pillow,' they said together, a choir.

'Isn't it terrible, little Sabah being exposed to that!' said Beth to us both.

'It was Sabah's first drive around the community and she said it will be her last,' said Craig, while Beth nodded at the wisdom of that strategy.

'We're parents of two little children,' Craig decided to confide in me. 'One's twenty months old and the other's just four months, and they're both so smart! Already! Our baby can shake her rattle! And listen to it, wondering, "What's making the noise?" And our toddler can talk the leg off an iron pot! You know what he said the other day? He said, "Daddy, I lub you always!" Imagine knowing about *time* at twenty months! We've bred a couple of Einsteins!'

It was as if just speaking about his children opened a door into a different part of his being. His voice had deepened, his back had straightened, and even his belly had flattened somewhat. I could almost imagine him being a husband with some charm.

'I go back and help her out every lunchtime,' dropping his voice, though Beth knew it already and nodded sympathetically. 'She misses her mother, of course. I have to make up for her mother, imagine that! But we'll have to leave –' this to Beth. 'We can't raise our Einsteins in this filth, with these primitives.'

He looked back at me for corroboration, then at Beth. I had a sense they were turning a corner, and he was making it public right now, their farewell. I felt for her, thinking of my imminent loss of Daniel. But she couldn't allow a farewell. She spoke brightly.

'One more chance. You must give them one more chance. Let's try your new plan of driving around the houses before school and picking them up. I told you that I was happy to do the driving.' She looked at me. 'He wants so much to rescue them.'

'No,' he said flatly.

'No?' asked Beth.

He turned back to his computer.

'I can't do it to my children.'

It was as if Beth had been slapped. The vivacity went out of her face, like a light turned off. Her shoulders hunched. Her chest seemed to collapse inward. Then, as he found a patch of poor phrasing and pounded on his computer, she moved across the room to look out the door to the schoolyard, where the woman still slumped.

Clearly hoping Libby could hear her, she said loudly: 'It's English they've got to learn. Our language. Not theirs.' She turned to see the effect of this on him. But his muscles, unaware of her gaze, moved with his typing.

To us both, she added: 'I'm right, aren't I?' Then, even louder: 'It's one thing for them to retreat out here, as if they're the Amish. But it's another to hold their kids back!' Then she was yelling: 'They're part of the wider world and they shouldn't hold their kids back!'

I went up to Beth and put my arm around her shoulder. It was bony and unresponsive.

'Is she waiting for her child?'

'She's waiting for her husband. Quentin. What a name – where do they get these names from? Hasn't anyone told them no one's called Quentin nowadays?'

'Perhaps fashion doesn't –' I began desperately, for I was fearing that Libby could sink further into distress.

'He's as useless as his name but our bosses in their ivory towers have ordered us to employ him. Who got to them, to make such a mad, bureaucratic decision? He's uneducated so what's he good for? We told him to clean the toilets every day and you know who ends up doing it? Me! He doesn't go near the toilets! He's useless! Useless.' By then she was shouting so frenziedly that Libby looked around.

'Don't,' I begged.

But now she was yelling directly at Libby, while in the background Craig pounded his fury.

'There's no point waiting for your husband! He's not in the toilets!'

Ashamed to be standing near her, I walked towards the door.

'I came to tidy the library,' I said. On the verandah, I turned. 'How should I arrange the books?'

Beth, red-faced with fury, shrugged.

'We only use it as a place to send the kids for time out,' she said. 'None of them read. They wouldn't know what a book was.'

Pity made me try to distract her once more.

'I still haven't found my dying singer,' I said quietly.

It succeeded. She turned.

'Haven't you?' she asked. 'That must be hard for you.'

I said, keeping my eyes on the curling lengths of her hair, still almost fairy floss: 'Such a pity, not to be able to save the "Poor Thing" song from extinction. I was thinking –' I was rambling, but surely E.E. Albert would try to reach out to Beth if she were here, 'it's possible the poor thing of the song is a mother who's having a long vigil through the night as she watches her sick child die, or a woman unable to marry the man she loves.'

Beth, nodding, turned away, secret tears in her eyes.

'Perhaps she found her love too late,' she murmured.

I spent the next hour rearranging books into the Dewey system I'd tried to learn before my life took this direction, and dusting the shelves with tissues from a box on a table. I put the rubbish – the lolly papers, the ice-cream sticks, and the empty drink bottles – into a cardboard box I'd found thrown on the verandah. It was very calming, the arranging of books, even in a desert where no one wanted them. I'd become a reader of stories when Ian left the river, and learned to love holding books, their rectangular compactness, their smell of dusty, ageing vivacity, the sense that in your hands you've got a flight to some better place where people like you are understood.

As I worked, memory surged over me, again and again.

My mother often complains that I don't chat enough. 'Open your mouth,' she says. 'Be company!' So I stand one-legged while she worries aloud about stains on Dad's shirts and whether it'd please him if she ironed the tablecloths, as Diana probably does – 'Does she?' she asks, but she doesn't want to hear the answer – 'That's why he goes to her, because she's a better woman than me, I'm the dreamy type, always was –' and I say 'Huh-huh,' waiting for the fall in her voice that means she's petering out, so I'll be able to go to my room and drag out from under my bed a story that has no cognisance of betrayal. A story that promises one day I'll live amongst people whose hearts aren't breaking in a way I can't mend.

In that neglected desert library, I still thought of the pages of an opened book as being like arms, ready to enfold me.

By the time I'd stood all the books upright and put them into a semblance of a system, I had a leftover pile of books that were too large to fit in the shelves. They weren't really books, I decided, resentful of their size, they were only home-made and clumsy, with bright plastic film over cardboard covers, and yellowing pages rippling with badly stuck down photos. They didn't fit into the system I'd created. I was annoyed at them as if they were petulant children – just someone's amateurish effort, not real books. I was wondering if anyone would notice if I hid them in the cardboard box and took them to the rubbish tip. In that desert library, who would know or care? The makers of the books were probably white and long gone. I picked them up to throw them away, but at the last second the top book slid on its shiny plastic out of my hands and onto the floor, flipping open. As I retrieved it, I stayed on my knees, surprised. Here was a photo of the track Gillian took on walks into the desert, here was the humpy at the outstation with its pile of black-bottomed cooking tins on the roof, here was the tree outside my window. Here were people squatting at fires, women holding little children, women gathering bush fruit, men coming home from a hunt with kangaroos proudly slung around their necks, like fur stoles. I sat down in an armchair that puffed red dust, and leafed through the pages. The text was entirely in Djemiranga, whose grammar was my daily struggle. I picked up another book, and another. I couldn't guess the plots of the stories but when I looked again at the covers, I saw that they said, both in English and in Djemiranga: *Stories of Our Dreaming 1*, *Stories of Our Dreaming 2*, and so on, right up to *Stories of Our Dreaming 10*. They all said, in both languages: '*As told by the storyteller, Quentin.*'

A chill came over me, there in that steamy library. I realised slowly and guiltily, that these books I'd been about to throw away were not the least important books there, but the most important. I'd been about to throw away what might be unique stories of that country, possibly stories of that tribe, possibly stories as old as the song I searched for. I'd planned to extinguish unique stories from a culture not my own. I'd been like a barbarian sacking the libraries of the ancient world.

I lay back in the chair, relieved that a book had flipped open as if it was a living thing, warding off my attack.

To make amends, I cleared most of a shelf of ordinary printed books, and displayed the home-made ones as the centrepiece. Perhaps in the distant future when a literate child found them, they'd relish anew their own people's ways.

And there it would've stopped, except that as I walked home, I passed Libby in her front yard, sitting with a group of women and children. They didn't seem to notice me, although I'd learned by then that the people were very observant, though they never even seemed to glance. They were able readers of body language, as Adrian said. Behind them was her dilapidated, three-walled, one-room tin house. The open side of the house faced discreetly away from the road, so that it was like a proscenium arch but there was only desert for an audience. In the front yard was the usual tabletop made from a door resting on empty flour tins, and mattresses lay on the cement porch, along with a sheet of corrugated iron heaped with ashes. There were mattresses spilling out on to the porch.

I'd been told by Adrian that the assistant teacher lived there with seventeen relatives.

'So her family should get one of the new houses the builder's made,' I'd said.

He'd immediately fixed me with one of his silver glares.

'The elders decide these things.'

Confused, I'd dropped my gaze, blushing because again I'd offended him.

'It's not for us to make them be like us, or at least like we ought to be. You people always want to make them like ideal whites, not like the whites you really are.'

He'd stood, screeching his chair across the floor, then stalked out and banged the door.

Daniel and I had taken to washing up together, our arms mirroring each other's in the simple repetitive movements, like dancers' arms, as we watched the warm night blacken the window panes. Daniel wiped while I washed, and his tea towel looped like a veil that could hide my shame after Adrian's barbs, or like a hammock that could gather me in, but it would be to cling figuratively with him – someone also at Adrian's mercy, I saw then, also floundering in the eddying currents of Adrian's convictions, passions and assumptions, that all who were near him must share them or be ridiculed. It seemed Daniel's fate, like mine, was to be enchanted by Adrian, but frustrated in that enchantment, and constantly threatened by rejection. I still didn't want to admit that the glowing Ian of my childhood had become this contemptuous derider, or worse, consider that he might have always been this way, and I clanked dishes noisily all the way down the dish rack.

'Adrian's got a lot on his mind,' Daniel had said, throwing the wet tea towel over the confusion of things that again were taking over the ironing board. 'Bruce almost ran him over today.'

And so, as always, we began the familiar process of reconciling ourselves with the disappointment of Adrian, so we'd remain enchanted.

'Bruce! Why?'

Daniel had sat down and leaned back on his chair, so that the front legs lifted alarmingly off the floor. 'Adrian told him off because of the power cuts. So, when Adrian was crossing the road from the clinic this morning, Bruce revved his car and headed straight for him. Adrian had to jump over a ditch to safety.'

I'd sat beside him, still holding the dish mop, my head close to his in case Adrian was on the verandah, so close I felt the heat of his body.

'Bruce wants to do him in?'

Daniel had lowered his voice.

'I caught Bruce snooping around, asking Mandy questions. Be careful what you say at the school. Bruce is always visiting Craig.'

'But Adrian has nothing to hide! He's just –' I wound down, 'an innocent with paperwork.'

He'd looked at me with one of his lop-sided smiles.

'Many people would be only too happy to get rid of him.'

For a moment, I'd felt a rebellious flash of sympathy for his enemies.

'He has enemies in high places,' I'd said, remembering Dr Lydia's words.

But now as I walked home from the school, I longed, as I had many times in the last weeks, to be alone in my room. I was so far from all that I was sure of, except that I'd never been sure of anything at all. Confusion and bewilderment, that was my home, my family.

They were all in the ground, those people I loved. There's only you and me who remember, and to you, the memories are as deeply buried as Diana, my mother and my father; deeper perhaps. I'd lived in the hope that one day patterns would become clear, for if there were patterns, there was meaning. But that has never happened. Why ever did I think that I could see that river more clearly in the desert? I should give up now, I thought, and leave, go back to the city, and wait quietly until I die.

Just as I neared home, something called to me, like a bird in my heart. I looked up at the biggest tree in the settlement, the one in the book, the one I could see from my window. I paused. The bird had made me pause, as if it knew about humans, as if it was a spirit, not an ordinary bird. Because of the bird, I turned. I walked back up the red dusty street, as if my feet were leading me, or the bird. I could go past Libby's house and pretend I was walking back to the shop, as if I've forgotten to buy something, if anyone was curious. But no one was, or at least, no one seemed to notice me. They were all looking up at the bird, which I couldn't see, and talking. Perhaps it was an important bird to them, one of their totems, one that foretold the future. My feet or the bird kept deciding for me. My feet, or the bird, veered me from my course towards the shop, my feet went over towards Libby's fence, though what I hoped to happen, what I was going to say, I didn't know. I stopped. I waited there for words to come, my eyes downcast. Or for her to come. After a while, I heard a soft swishing of her skirt, her feet padding the earth. She was coming over.

I looked up the road, not directly at her because I was learning, so slowly was I learning, to downcast my eyes. She stood near me. I didn't know if she was looking at me, but she was waiting.

'The school,' I said, and petered out. 'I went to the library,' I floundered. 'I saw books.'

She waited.

'Books made – about here.'

Her waiting made me blurt.

'The teacher is cheeky,' I said. I'd heard Adrian use the word 'cheeky', and the implications seemed immediately understood.

There was a long silence. She looked up the road with me, at the dust and the local children walking to the shop for ice-creams, and up to the tree where the bird called again.

'The headmaster is cheeky too,' I added.

After a long silence, I said: 'It's very bad for you, for the people, for you all, that they're cheeky.'

The bird flew away. People spilled out of the tiny house, like the mattresses had. But they didn't seem to be listening to us, they were just people watching a bird as it faded into the sky.

'In the library, the books of stories, the covers say: *As told by Quentin*. Your husband. They must be your husband's stories.'

I struggled to make it clear to myself.

'I didn't know that he's a storyteller. Perhaps the headmaster and the teacher, perhaps they don't know either. And perhaps whites don't know why that's important.'

There was another silence.

'Storyteller,' she repeated.

I was encouraged. At least she was joining in. That meant we might have a conversation. That's how conversations seemed to go here, with a lot of consensus, as Adrian had explained, a lot of repetition, and not the driving wind behind them that I was used to.

'However,' I said, carefully, 'Someone's written down the stories he told. In your language.'

'Not my husband's stories. They're the old stories,' she said. 'My husband was taught all the stories. The old men taught my husband.'

'They're dead then, these old men who taught him?'

'The old men are dead,' she said.

I tried: 'No one made up the stories?'

The question is met with silence. Perhaps it was an incomprehensible question.

'The stories are from the Dreaming?' I tried again.

'The stories are from the Dreaming.'

So then I knew that Quentin didn't make up the stories, in the way I was used to, with an author who's responsible for making up a story from scratch.

'Someone wrote down what your husband said,' I said.

'Collins wrote down the old stories that my husband tells,' she said.

'But they didn't really need to be written down, with your husband here to tell them. Why did Collins write them down?'

'White people,' she said.

She tried again to explain something she couldn't quite fathom.

'White people need books,' she said.

'But you have storytellers instead,' I said – and now I was reasoning it out to myself, 'to pass on the stories. And after your husband, one of the children whose life work it is, will pass them on. Storytellers, not books, are essential here.'

I felt exhausted with the realisation. I wished I could sit on the ground. But that might break the moment, and I mustn't do that.

'Because –' she cast around, looking back at the group, 'that's the only way the children know the stories.'

'Are any of the old stories translated into English?' I asked.

'No.' To her, the question seemed to be irrelevant. 'We all speak Djemiranga,' she said. It might not have occurred to her that whites couldn't read stories written down in Djemiranga, or even that whites might want to. Her people, after all, didn't send missionaries to us. They weren't interested in changing us, as we were in changing them. Till that moment I'd thought that was because they felt that we were the victors and they were unimportant. Now I wondered if the pretty tourist guide in Alice Springs had been right when she'd suggested that maybe Aboriginal people thought their stories were none of our business.

'There's a big mob of stories,' Libby offered suddenly.

A silence followed so long that the children stood up from the blanket and came over and leaned on her, looking up at me with huge solemn black eyes.

The children's presence seemed to bring more words out of her.

'Everyone listens to my husband's stories.'

She looked down at the children and gravely told them what she was saying, or at least that was what I thought she was doing. They seemed in their nodding to be as old as the old men now dead.

There are moments when you hear a whole chunk of the world sliding into place. I was almost dizzy with the sound.

'So,' I attempted to reason, 'the only way for the children to know these stories is by your husband telling them.'

She didn't need to agree, and we both knew it in the silence.

'And the stories tell people how to live? About what's important?'

'The stories tell them.'

'Your husband told these stories in Djemiranga because Djemiranga says things that English can't? That English has no words for?' I struggled with the admission, though it was something I already knew, that a white language didn't map on to theirs. But now I was realising the implications – why had it taken me so long? That a white language, my language, had a lack. 'That English has no ideas for?' I found to say.

There were times in the settlement when I could imagine that the very dust of that ancient land seemed to be listening, the dust full of bones of generations straining to hear, the bones of generations that have lived before us, the dust stained red with the living, the learning how to live, of tens of thousands of people over tens of thousands of years.

'So your children must learn English for when they go to the cities, but they also must hear your husband's stories in Djemiranga for living in their country?'

'The children must hear the stories to live,' she said.

'That's why the Education Department,' I added, 'the government, pays your husband to be a storyteller, not a toilet cleaner. Because someone in the government understood this, there was a boss in the government who understood how essential it is that your husband tell the stories.'

'Craig told him to clean toilets.'

'Instead?'

There was such a long silence then that the darkness seemed to enter us, and fall into our hearts. Her face was becoming harder to see. The children seemed to sense that something was over, or completed, and wandered back to the group. I was wondering if I should go, if I was being dismissed. Then suddenly she said: 'That Craig, and that cheeky teacher, they don't like black people. They hunt black people away.'

It was my turn to repeat. 'Hunt black people away from their school? From their stories?'

Someone called her, and she stepped towards the voice, but turned back to me to say: 'They hunt us away.'

Chapter 17

I walked home through the darkness.

I tucked myself into my bed, but I couldn't sleep. I got up and felt my way to the kitchen in the dark, for the power was off again. I found some old bread and gnawed it, anxiously listening out for the sound of a troopie. I didn't want to face Adrian and his certainty, and the questions that still tormented me. Today I'd been almost a barbarian, almost destroying unique knowledge. I was no better than cheeky Craig.

In bed I drowsed at last. There was the scrape of footsteps, many footsteps on the front verandah, and I heard voices speaking in English. Adrian's rather high-pitched voice rose above the scraping.

'They're eager to take you out bush and show you.'

I pulled the covers over my head. But a knock came on my door.

'Kate, Kate, are you in there?'

'I'm asleep,' I said.

'Please come out and look after our guests,' he asked.

All the lights were on, all through the house, so it must've been our turn for electricity.

I swung my legs out of bed, straightened my clothes and went out to the verandah in case a local family was there. I was blinking as I found a group of white people from Alice Springs. Two introduced themselves as nutritionists, two were power workers come to repair the generator and one, Vanessa, was an academic studying the way plants were used in the old days. They laughed as they explained that they'd all met on the road when one of the cars had lost its steering and mounted an embankment.

'Death traps, those roads!' chorused the nutritionists. Now they'd arrived and knocked on doors but no one had answered.

'The CEO was told we were coming,' said one, a power worker. 'Don't you whites talk to each other?'

'As little as possible,' Adrian answered cheerily.

'We heard your CEO knew fuck all about the generator,' said the power worker. 'It wasn't in his job description. When he did check it, he was only doing yous all a favour.'

'It never ceases to amaze me, why the locals put up with the hopeless whites,' said Vanessa. 'They're stoics.'

'They wait for the idiots to leave – and that always happens,' laughed the power worker. 'I reckon they're waiting for us all to get lost – just get back in our dinky little sailing boats and fuck off to where we came from!'

Everyone reacted, some in amusement, some in alarm.

'Have dinner with us,' Adrian said placatingly to someone, perhaps to all of them. 'But I must get to the clinic, see what's happening over there. Kate will cook – won't you?' he added to me.

'Should we bring our stuff in?' Vanessa asked me.

Behind them were their dust-emblazoned troopies.

'Perhaps leave it till you know where you'll sleep,' I said, becoming a hostess again. 'Would you all like a cup of tea?'

'We're longing to clean up,' said another.

'Of course, come in,' I said.

The kitchen was suddenly bright with chatter. As Adrian left, he turned on the washing machine.

'Can it wait?' I asked him in an aside. 'People will want to hear each other talk. And it's a bit inhospitable, doing housework when you're entertaining.'

'But I'm a very busy man and must use any downtime,' he argued. 'They'll appreciate that. They know how hard I work. They can open the lid and see it's my clothes, not yours.'

'They're not going to open the lid of their host's washing machine!'

By the time everyone had showered and changed into clean clothes, three chickens from the shop were roasting in the oven on a high setting, and I'd begun a salad and a dessert. The washing machine ground all through the dinner until the power cut out. Later I opened the lid and there was just one lonely blue shirt, drowning.

Vanessa, the academic, was excited. 'Tomorrow they're going to show me how they traditionally made flour out of bean pods. That's before a white man's shop with tins of white man's flour.'

'Damper's very popular here,' I said.

'Damper-making on an open fire is an ancient skill when you have to make the flour first from beans,' she said.

'*Make* the flour,' I repeated. I thought of their nomadic ways. 'Would this bean flour have been stored?'

She nodded.

'They made flour out of grass seeds as well as beans,' she said. 'We're just finding all this out. It's new knowledge for us.'

Adrian had returned for dinner, and everyone crowded around the table.

'Why are you here?' Vanessa suddenly turned to ask me.

I told her.

'But I can't find the singer,' I said. I was ashamed to admit it in front of an academic who seemed perfectly able to do her research, whereas I was so mired. I busied myself putting the chickens on the table, crisp and brown.

'Doesn't Adrian know who this woman is?'

'If he does, he's not telling,' I said, trying to make it sound like a joke.

Vanessa's eyes moved between us, gauging whether or not it was a joke. After all, he was her host. She decided it was funny, and laughed.

'Why don't you come out with us tomorrow? The grandmothers will tell you what's what, who's who.'

Just then, the chickens on the table oozed grease.

'I might stick to vegetables,' Adrian said with distaste. He helped himself to a plateful, though the others hadn't sat down.

'It's hard to approximate city food out here,' Vanessa said kindly. 'Even custard goes brown because of the dust.'

In the morning, Adrian stopped me just as I was heading towards the bathroom.

'There won't be a seat for you in the cars,' said Adrian.

'Vanessa asked me to come,' I said.

'I've donated the use of a clinic troopie and I don't want you taking a place that could be used by an Aboriginal woman.'

'Then I'll go in Vanessa's car,' I said.

'The places there are needed as well!' he said.

'You can't tell your guest who to put in her car,' I said.

He was unusually cranky, and I worried he'd found out about the outstation. I wanted to ask him if Daniel was staying another night in Alice, but now was not the time. Perhaps it would never be the time.

I needn't have argued with him about cars. We drove only two kilometres along bush tracks, four or five cars, with the donkey lolloping behind in a friendly way. Vanessa stopped when we saw bean trees, with their long hanging pods, like a child's yellow ribbons tied to the branches. But when the children ran to a fruit tree heavy with tiny purple currants, grabbing handfuls, it was decided to let them collect the fruit first, before the hard work began of making flour. The children scrabbled excitedly in the dust.

'But they're swallowing dirt,' I said to Vanessa.

A memory came to me of a picture postcard of Greek villagers shaking olives down from trees on to a blanket tied to the branches and another blanket waiting below on the ground.

'Have you got a picnic blanket in your boot?' I asked Vanessa.

When she nodded, I rummaged for it, then, asking the children to clear me a space, I laid it out.

This caused much discussion amongst the women. I thought: they're praising my Western ingenuity. This will start a new tradition. Perhaps they'll even name it after me: the Kate Method of Fruit Collecting.

The women called to Vanessa. I thought: they'll be telling her how useful it is to have me around. Perhaps they'll be asking if I could accompany them every trip, to contribute Western ideas.

Vanessa came over to me.

'Kate, the ladies don't want you to be hurt, but they're asking me if you could take your blanket away,' Vanessa said.

'Take it away?'

'Apparently the dust cleans the fruit.'

'Cleans it?'

'I didn't know either. As I told you, we're just starting to learn desert ways.'

As I sheepishly folded up the blanket, she explained to me about bush tomatoes. In the old days, they'd been stored and dried, and eaten as a staple food. But when whites processed and bottled them, people complained of gut-ache. She'd recently discovered that there's a toxin on the tomato skins that rolling in sand in the traditional way had removed.

'The sand might be removing toxins on the currants as well,' she said. 'But they'd love to use your blanket to harvest the beans.'

No one seemed to mind my mistake. They smiled when I handed over the folded blanket, and laughed and chatted as they pulled the pods off the trees in clutches, and threw them into the blanket.

I heard high-pitched, excited children's laughter. Adrian was coming towards us, the only man present, carrying a bin for scraps, and trailing a couple of kids who vied with each other for him to piggy-back them.

When he caught sight of me, he glowered. I blushed a little; he would've seen my latest mistake.

The donkey was ambling through the group. When a little girl picked up a stone to throw at it, Adrian grabbed her and carried her over his shoulder to his scraps bin, while she screamed and hooted.

'I'll put you in the bin if you throw rocks at the donkey.'

Her friends were doubling over with laughter, their white teeth flashing.

You deign to be my playmate that last day, as if you've changed your mind about me. We fish side by side and you don't criticise me; we row in your boat, one oar each, and when I hit your knuckles with my oar, you only laugh.

'Clumsy little one,' you say, but fondly.

We swim and for once you don't outdistance me, but backstroke with me, watching the eagle, willing it to come down and swoop above us, and we float on the tide, like big leaves. I keep waiting for you to get tired of me and leave, but when I flop on the bottom step of your jetty exhausted, you tell me to change steps. You are on the top step.

'You'll get washed away by the tide. Come up here.'

I look up. You are taking up most of your step.

'No room.'

You wriggle over to make room. When I don't move you add: 'It's less splintery up here.'

'No splinters down here.'

'You don't want to hurt your lovely body.'

My lovely body. My lovely body. I am glad to lie face-down on the step, to hide my blushing in the warm wet wood. You've mentioned what has become between us – another forbidden word. My body.

'Come on.'

I can't move, I don't dare, for what my body might tell you. You'd know, you've lived longer, a whole six years longer than me. Lovely. Body. Body. Lovely. The words ring out into the air, then circle me with shame and confusion. I think: inside lovely is the word love. Does that mean that you love me? Does that mean you dream of me, that you're waiting to be lovers one day with me? Does it count, what's inside a word? That love is inside lovely?

I am shivering with thought.

'I can keep you warm up here,' you call down.

My voice is muffled by the wood, by the slap of the river against the pylons.

'I'm hot.'

'Come on.'

Diana calls us for lunch.

'Hurry up!'

'Damn,' you say.

I leap up, nearly slipping because it's true, the tide is coming up, I run up the steps between us, I jump over you and keep running. Your footsteps are thudding behind me.

And now I reach for a memory of air rushing past me, of the silver ribbon of river and the long trunked trees suddenly hanging upside down from the sky, a firm grip around my waist, a boy's body much bigger than mine, almost a man's body. I remember a burst of joy at the sudden warmth of you, then terror, escalating terror. I reach for the memory of Diana's laughter that becomes a yell –

'Put her down, put her down!'

But her voice is receding, the boy's body is running and the scrub speeds past me, whipping against me, my legs, my arms, you're running and jolting me and my teeth crash against each other with the jolts, and my father's catching up with you, with us.

'Put her down. That's an order!'

'He's going to throw her in the river!'

I scream.

And suddenly my stomach empties itself all over my face, all over you, and I'm dropped thuddingly on the ground, and then there's blackness.

You're that boy. You're Ian.

I sat on the red sand, winded, as if he had dropped me for the second time. I tried to reason: I'd been lying to myself, telling myself that my main purpose in coming here was to find the song. That was not my main purpose at all. It never was. There are times when what's true creeps away, hunched down so you scarcely notice, and you live mired in the mud of lies. Oh, I could be self-righteously indignant that he wouldn't show me the old singer, but I'd been living a lie, and perhaps, on some level, he sensed it. Not only a spy, but a liar. I'd always been a spy.

I must break my silence, I must go to him and say – what would I say?

I came to find out what you knew.

I rehearsed the words so many times, they lost their abrasiveness, became reasonable. I came to find out what you knew, I came to find out what you knew.

A breeze tumbled over the stilled landscape. That was how the landscape often seemed, as if a vast force had clutched it, and it dared not move. This was a country so ancient, so withholding in its secrets, that a breeze seemed a dramatic, rebellious act.

They were simple, little words, I said to myself, sifting sand grains between my fingers.

I came to find out if you knew they'd die.

Somehow the very puniness of the words deluded me that they were weightless, innocent as clouds on a summer's day, innocent as red sand, innocent as the breeze now making the bean tree leaves clatter.

I stood. I would walk up to him and say the tiny, weightless words: I came to find out why you didn't warn me.

I was interrupted by cries and laughter from the women.

'Come, Kate,' they called. They wanted to include me, and were waiting till I joined them to watch. Perhaps, with the blanket, they saw that I'd only been trying to help, being a typical white, thinking that we always know best, even about what they'd been doing for tens of thousands of years.

Four women picked up the corners of the blanket and, walking towards the women on the opposite corner, made it into a package with the bean pods still inside. Then they put it on the ground and trampled on it, crushing the pods. With much merriment and many good-natured instructions to each other, they then unbundled the blanket and walked away from each other, holding it out again by its corners.

'Like an ancient dance,' Vanessa whispered to me.

Now the blanket became a trampoline. They tossed the blanket up and down so the broken pods leaped and fell like tiny beings, to the noisy joy of the children. The chaff blew away.

'Good wind today,' I heard them exclaim in Djemiranga, and tears came into my eyes, because at last those hours frowning over my recordings were paying off – occasionally.

Afterwards, in the hollow of the blanket lay only brown seeds.

Adrian stood nearby, holding a baby. I could've gone over to him, but I didn't want to interrupt him, or myself. And so, the moment passed. I didn't speak.

The harvesting and winnowing over, the women lit a fire to cook kangaroo tails, and they burnt the fur off it, rather than scraping it, just as Adrian had said. We sat on the ground for a barbecue, their style, with their relatives. Vanessa again called to me, and peered with me into the pile of seeds in the blanket. She pointed out that it'd take half a day to make what she calculated was half a kilo of bean flour – and the seeds were still not ground.

'No wonder they like shop-bought flour,' she said. 'You just pay money for it, without all that work! I wonder if that's why men needed more than one wife? Because the daily damper took so long?'

Then, eager to be part of the excitement, an idea came to me. I remembered Beth mentioning the visit of the old Aboriginal man to her childhood school.

'Why don't we invite the ladies to the school to show these skills to the children?' I suggested. 'Perhaps it's the very thing the school needs to entice the children back.'

And so it was agreed.

'Afterwards, I'm sure the ladies will help you find your singer,' Vanessa said.

And then, amongst the colour and noise and happiness, and my heart churning about Adrian, a group of little children called to me. 'Play planes with us.' It was the first time they had treated me with the ease they treated Adrian. So I dashed my tears away, and picked them up one by one, becoming the big person who turned their world upside down, but kindly. They watched me with eyes as pale and pearly against their black skin as seashells, and nestled their little hands trustingly into mine. On the drive back, they took turns to sit on my knee, and the ones too young to get a turn leaned against my seat from behind. At home, we found the electricity on, and I was able to make early dinner for everyone – the local favourite, mashed potatoes and bacon which I rushed to the shop for.

'Did you hear?' the white woman in the shop had said. 'They've fixed the electricity! We'll have dinner at home tonight!' She'd been cooking food in the shop every night.

As I cleared the plates, Vanessa told me that everyone knew about a precious old grinding stone by our water tank. It had belonged to Libby's great-grandmother and great-great-aunts. I blushed. I'd made another mistake. Because it was a large and unusually flat stone, I'd sat pots of herbs on it. 'I didn't know,' I said sheepishly, removing the herbs.

Vanessa explained that heavy grinding stones were always left by women in the same places on their route around their homeland, their walkabout, as whites called it. My front yard with its grinding stone was on the route Libby's ancestors walked. They'd time their arrival at the bean trees just at ripening season, they'd harvest and winnow the seeds, and they'd bring their cache to the grinding stone in what was now my yard to make flour. The stone had been in place as far back as anyone could remember.

'It's as if you've commandeered a family's kitchen appliance, inherited from mother to daughter for generations,' Vanessa said. 'For maybe 60,000 years.'

She laughed at my red face.

'It's OK,' she comforted me. 'They understand you don't know Aboriginal ways. Who would've guessed? It'd just have seemed like any old rock.'

'It's probably from here, with spiritual powers,' I said, telling her of my conversation with Daniel.

Vanessa looked at my herbs. 'The basil's doing really well,' she smiled.

I tried to make amends by carrying it to the ladies in the shade of the verandah, but it was too heavy to even shove.

'It's as if it's a fridge I'd commandeered,' I said.

She tried to lift it with me, but we collapsed on the ground.

'That's why they left it there,' she laughed.

The women laughed with us.

'Good little farm.' Dora laughed about my herbs, and Vanessa and I exchanged a glance.

There was such comfort in their smiles, their sympathy, their understanding. They sat cross-legged on the earth in the sun next to the grinding stone and, twisting a smaller stone into the big one, they took turns to grind the seeds. It was a long job, requiring all their strength, and the sun had gone down by the time there was a little hill of powder.

Vanessa had to write up the women's accounts of what they'd done. She estimated that they'd be finished by tomorrow after lunch.

'Ask if we can take the women elders to the school then,' she said.

As I got ready for bed that night, I was appalled that I hadn't spoken to Adrian honestly. The words I'd found to tell him were, after all, small, weightless pebbles.

I came to find out who you are.

But when I'd unbuttoned my shirt, I decided that the words were boulders that would sink my connection with him. When I took off my bra I was appalled I kept silent, when I took off my pants, I was relieved I'd kept silent. I lay in the air conditioning, the spy, the pretender, the liar. And then the images of the day filled my mind, the yellow ribbons of bean pods, the black smiling faces of the women, the red and endless desert, and I fell asleep, comforted.

The next morning, as I walked past Libby's house, the women and children were gathered as usual around the cooking fire, and one of the women was making a damper with shop-bought flour for breakfast, piling ashes on its top to cook it through. Libby was nowhere in sight, but I guessed she knew I was there, and I lingered with downcast eyes. Soon, sure enough, she emerged from the house and came over.

We stood slightly turned away from each other, facing the blue smoke, as if we were watching the damper.

I told her about the flour-making yesterday, though I was sure she already knew.

'After lunch, the ladies could come to the school to show the children who didn't come the old ways with bean pods,' I said. 'But would the children want that?'

'If the ladies come,' she said, 'the children will come.'

There was a pause and I waited silently, as I was learning to. Waiting always seemed to pay off.

'Craig will be cranky,' she said after a while.

'I'll get his permission,' I assured her.

'The cheeky teacher too?' she asked.

'Her permission too. But she'll love it!' I said. 'It will remind her of something wonderful that happened in her childhood – you'll see!'

She stared at the fire, then looked up at me.

'The ladies are elders,' she said. It was a warning.

'I know,' I said. 'The school will know they are elders, and honour them as elders.'

I said to myself: *Then the women will lead me to the singer.*

I passed the shop on the way to the school, with its usual crowd of people waiting outside. I was so glad I didn't give in to my impulse on that first day to encourage them to go inside. Perhaps I'd learned my lesson, perhaps I'd make no more mistakes, I thought. And when I go back to university, I'll no longer be the worst student.

But unexpectedly the thought of leaving here tore into me, almost punching a hole in me and filling it with sadness.

As usual, the playground was empty. I found Craig at his computer, checking a literacy table. Apparently the school had one of the lowest scores for literacy in the country. I looked over his shoulder. It seemed like the highest score was achieved by one child who could spell only one word – 'it'.

'I'm being blamed,' he groaned.

I told him that I'd invited the women to explain some traditions.

'The ladies are elders,' I said. 'We must honour them.'

'The kids won't honour them,' he said. 'You can see how many kids are here. It's useless to bring visitors to an empty school. Are you trying to shame us?'

'The school won't be empty after lunch,' I said. 'The kids will follow the elders.'

'You know how to bring the kids to school?' he asked in surprise.

'The elders do,' I said.

He put his head in his hands, then looked up at me, one eye almost shrouded by despair.

'I told you: the world's most degraded culture,' he said.

I found Beth talking to Kana, a newly arrived student teacher, a fresh-faced Japanese girl, and explained the plan. Unexpectedly, Beth pulled a face. 'It's not what school is for,' she said. 'The kids can't read and write. This isn't reading and writing, is it, this event?'

I tried to conjure up the softness I'd glimpsed in her face before.

'You inspired it, with your story of the old Aboriginal man at your school,' I said.

'Indigenous,' she corrected. 'You must get the word right or you'll insult people! At my school,' she continued, 'we'd learned to read and write. That old man's visit was just icing on the cake.'

'Craig said it's OK,' I said, to avoid her indignation.

'If Craig approves this nonsense, well, then it's OK, I suppose,' she said sulkily. 'He keeps changing the rules. I don't know how to keep up with him.'

She turned to Kana. 'It's your practice lesson after lunch,' she told Kana. 'Are you happy with this intrusion?'

Kana's black shining eyes were full of light.

'It's exciting. I'll learn so much.'

'It's not you who's supposed to be learning,' said Beth. 'It's them.' Her face had become a severe, jagged oval.

On the way home for lunch, Kana came part of the way with me so she could go to the shop, she told me. But as soon as we were out of sight of the school, she stopped.

'Will you show me the desert?' she asked, to my astonishment.

'Why, it's all around us,' I said.

'I grew up in Tokyo,' she said, as if that explained her request. 'This place is so strange.'

So I took her to the path where Daniel and I had walked a couple of days before I went to the outstation, the path photographed in the books I'd found. The desert quivered with heat like a vast animal.

'So empty, this desert,' she said. 'There's nothing out there.'

'For them, it's a pantry!' I said.

She looked at me, her almond eyes wide.

'And a cathedral. It's filled with the spirits of their ancestors. That rock might be an uncle, that tree might be a great-grandfather, it's filled with their relatives and their stories,' I added, and for the first time, I found it moving, to know this.

'Australia is not like Tokyo,' she said.

Daniel was at home, with the fridge door open. I felt a rush of relief that he was there, so that I could talk what I'd arranged over with him. He was making a bulging tomato and ham sandwich, with spinach leaves.

'That looks delicious,' I said.

He cut the sandwich in half and put my half on a plate.

'Olive paste?' he asked. In the supermarket in Alice Springs he fossicked for delicacies if he had to wait for patients to bring home. When I nodded, he lifted the tops of both our sandwiches and clumped the paste on.

I told him my forebodings about the school. 'Do you think I should take the ladies there?' I asked.

'It'd be good for the kids,' he said, manoeuvring an escaping young spinach leaf back into the sandwich.

'But I might be making another mistake,' I wailed.

'You can only try,' he said.

I left the house before Adrian came in, and dropped into Gillian's house. I told her not to make me a cup of tea.

'You have a rest,' I said. The clinic always closed briefly for lunch. 'But tell me what you think.'

'If it brings the kids to school, it's good,' she said. 'Do it.'

'But what if it turns sour?' I cried.

Chapter 18

In the desert, all time schedules were provisional, as Adrian had explained right at the start. Vanessa rang to tell me that the ladies would be half an hour late.

I rang Kana to tell her.

'Fine,' she said.

I was sitting under the tree in the schoolyard when Vanessa drove up with Rosa, Dawnie, Mary and Fanny. Craig stood at his door, watching. He didn't come over to greet the ladies, who didn't seem to notice, but just downcast their eyes.

Then, along the road came a clamour, and we all craned our necks to see its cause. We didn't have to wait long. In through the school gates, came a procession, perhaps two dozen children, older girls and boys carrying young ones, laughing and shouting at first, and then, at a look from Dawnie, silencing each other. Craig didn't notice them either. He still didn't notice when there was more noise in the street, and through the school gates burst a larger crowd of children, at least another dozen of them, the oldest about eighteen and the youngest about two, the teenagers piggy-backing toddlers. There were now about fifty of them all shouting and calling, then, when they saw Craig at his door, dropping into silence.

I feared he'd shout at them but he retreated. I knocked on the door of Kana's classroom. Through the windows I was astounded to see the room packed with little children. There were only a few chairs free.

'You're late.' Beth came to the door and spoke in a caustic, headmistressy voice of the sort I remembered from my schooldays, so that I felt ten years old, accused of making a mess. I was ashamed that the ladies would hear her unpleasant tone. Or the children, who by now must've numbered a hundred or so. 'You'll just have to wait. The pupils who came at the right time are listening to a story and can't be interrupted.'

'But I rang Kana and explained we'd be late,' I said. My voice had shrunk almost to a whisper.

'You'll still have to wait,' she said. 'And even then we can give you only half an hour.'

'May we sit inside? The women are hot and tired,' I said, struggling to regain my composure.

'You'll sit out there,' she ordered. Not only had the frivolity and prettiness gone from her hair, but she was hollow cheeked and shadowy under the eyes, as if she'd aged by decades within a few days. I wanted to find out what had happened between her and Craig, but now wasn't the time.

'And send that rabble home.'

She shut the door in my face.

I looked around at the women, and at the mass of children, who even now, were growing more numerous. Other children were still swarming through the gates. They stood quietly, copying the example of their elders. The women said nothing, but sat down as a group under the tree again. Vanessa pulled a face at me.

'I don't know how to apologise to them,' I said. She murmured agreement.

'The kids have come to school today. Must be because it's not hot,' said Mary, the oldest of the ladies. I could've hugged her for her diplomacy.

We sat, watching the afternoon shadows creep over the playground. The crowd of children waited in silence, some sitting on the ground, some standing on one leg then the other. I tried to keep at bay the premonition that something terrible was about to happen.

'Do you think we should leave?' I whispered to Vanessa.

'But the ladies were so pleased to be asked,' she said. 'And the children all want to hear what the ladies have to say.'

Half an hour went by. I was astonished at how demure the children were. A few younger ones went to climb the trees, but were called back by the older ones.

At last, Beth opened the door.

'You can come in now. Just the women. No one else.' Her voice was almost a growl. 'Kana is finishing her lesson. She wasn't to be interrupted. She was teaching reading.'

Kana was standing in front of the class and Libby was sitting up the back. Beth took a seat behind the teacher's desk out the front, and busied herself writing on little bits of paper. We all trooped down the back, with the children in the class turning around and smiling at us. Surely, I thought, Craig would be impressed by such attendance.

There was a subdued murmur outside, and I turned to see that the irrepressible children were crowding at every single window. The room was surrounded by verandahs on four sides, and every window framed children's faces: perhaps directed by the older ones amongst them, the littlest stood at the front, faces almost inside the room, and the tallest stood at the back, with other little ones perched high on their shoulders. They were all silent, waiting. Beth, with an exasperated sigh, marched loudly over to the windows and, one by one, slammed them shut, making the rows of children jump out of harm's reach. But they crowded back to breathe on the glass.

Inside the room, Beth turned to face us all.

'Continue your lesson,' she barked at Kana.

So Kana, voice trembling a little, in front of her huge audience, both inside and outside, went on with her lesson.

'Write down your name,' she told the children.

Not a child picked up a pen.

'Go on. Write it down. You can all write your names, surely.'

She was met with a profound stillness.

She glanced uneasily at the audience outside the glass windows, worrying how to exert authority, as she'd been taught in her city training. But no city training had prepared her for this. So she threw a look over to Beth, but Beth's head was bowed, writing.

'Well, talk to me then,' Kana found to say. She turned to one little boy. 'What's your name, your English name?' she asked him.

He turned to confer with his friends.

'Tony,' they told him, giggling. Kana thought they were laughing at her, but she was determined to be good-tempered.

'Don't play with me,' she said in a patient, kind voice. 'School is serious.'

'He's forgotten, miss,' said one of his friends.

'Forgotten his own name?'

'Not his name, miss. His English name.'

She paused, puzzled, but she had to carry on. Then came a further puzzle, when she asked if any of the children were related to each other.

'She's my mother,' one of the little girls told Kana, pointing to a little girl sitting beside her.

'Not mother,' said Kana again in her carefully kind voice. 'Another word. You know any other words for relatives? How about cousin? Cousin. She's your cousin.'

'No,' all the kids called. 'She's her mother.'

Kana wheeled around to Beth.

'Don't they know what the word "mother" means?'

Beth continued to bend her head to her writing.

'She's her mother, she's her mother,' the children were calling.

So Vanessa explained.

'It's a cultural relationship,' she said, from up the back of the room. 'By skin rules, this little girl must look after the other little girl always, as if she's her mother. Isn't that right, Libby?'

Libby looked away, embarrassed perhaps.

'I'm sorry,' said Kana to the child. 'I didn't understand.'

There seemed a hiatus. I waited for Beth to formally greet or at least introduce the ladies, but all she did was write.

So I spoke.

'I've brought Vanessa who studies plants and how they were used in the old days, and you all know Rosa, Dawnie, Mary and Fanny.'

I paused, wondering what was appropriate to do next. I didn't want to make the women feel uneasy, but I did want them to feel honoured, if only in a white way.

'Please welcome them.'

I began to clap and the little children joined in, enjoying themselves making such a noise, and getting carried away with giggles, and then the watchers at the windows broke their silence and applauded too, laughing and cheering and stamping. There was a ragged roar of applause. Inside the room, the little children had to be shushed. Slowly, the watchers outside subsided.

I didn't suggest the children in the room say hello, partly because that might make the ladies feel uneasy because saying hello was such a white convention. Besides, they might well have been in their company all morning. They might have just now eaten lunch together.

Kana asked Vanessa what she'd been doing with the ladies. But before Vanessa could open her mouth, Beth strode to the door, threw it open, and glared out at the children. By now, there would've been at least three hundred on the verandahs – perhaps all the children on the settlement.

'You're being too noisy. I will not be insulted like this,' she roared. 'This is meant to be a place of learning. You're trespassing in a place of education with intent to create a public nuisance.'

Some older boys at the back sniggered. 'Loser!' I heard one call, but he was hushed by the others.

'I thought we're supposed to be here,' another, more irrepressible boy called, and the young girls around him laughed.

That was enough for Beth.

'Get out,' she yelled. 'All of you. Or –' her voice rose to a shriek, 'I'll get the police.'

At the word 'police', everyone understood. There was a collective indrawn breath from the children both on the verandahs, and in the room. Two little girls cried out and, hand in hand, jumped out of their chairs and flew out of the room, almost knocking Beth over, yelling to their relatives in Djemiranga. I heard the colourful Djemiranga word for 'police', which I'd remembered because it described the metallic numbers on official shirts.

'Sit down,' Beth hurled at the little girls, pointing to the room with a long outstretched finger in case they misunderstood. They returned, their eyes out on stalks, one hiccupping in her sobs. The nearest watchers on the verandahs turned and walked off, then more children filed after them, then more, and then they were all thronging over the schoolyard and out to the gates, where a few teenage boys hovered. Craig appeared at his door, holding his phone menacingly as if he was at that very moment calling the police, and the last of the children melted away.

Beth slammed the door.

'How dare you!' she shouted at me. 'We could've had a riot! Begin,' she ordered Vanessa, as if Vanessa too was a naughty child.

So Vanessa explained what we'd been shown about the old ways of making flour for damper, and Rosa translated it into Djemiranga, adding on the way a great deal more detail about plants and their multitude of names and how each one used to be prepared. The children listened intently, even, I thought, proudly, with shining eyes and smiles. On the other hand, Beth didn't seem to listen at all. She was still busy with little pieces of paper. Then she looked up at me, oblivious to all but her thoughts, and spoke across Rosa's Djemiranga.

'You teach the next lesson, parts of the body. In their language,' she ordered.

This was going from bad to worse. I had to try to stop it.

I left my seat, walked around the outside of the desks and, once I stood near her, I whispered.

'I can't speak Djemiranga. I'll mispronounce the words. We need Libby to do this.'

'You should do it,' she answered. 'You're supposed to be the linguist.'

Just then, the door burst open, and Craig walked in. He held up his hand for silence, and his hand was obeyed.

'Good afternoon, children,' he said. The children stood. His eyes moved around the faces. He didn't look at all pleased to see so many children. He still gave no greeting to the ladies.

'Sit down. Proceed, Beth.' He sat and waited.

'We're doing parts of the body,' Beth told Craig. 'I've written parts of the body on these slips of paper. Our visitor, Kate, has agreed to be my assistant.'

Craig nodded approval and she shoved the little cards into my hand.

'Kate, you read the words,' she insisted loudly.

I looked at the first word, *Kapuju*.

I held up the card.

'Can anyone read this? Libby, can you help me?'

'Ask me,' said Beth to me. She smiled at Craig. 'I've worked with Indigenous people for ten years, as you know.'

She read the word. It wasn't a sound I'd heard, but what would I know?

'Say it after me,' she told the class.

The children looked at her blankly.

'Can't anyone read it?'

She pushed at my arm so I was holding the card higher.

Still silence from the children.

'You're probably mispronouncing it,' said Vanessa to Beth. 'They clearly think you're speaking a language other than Djemiranga, perhaps some sort of English they haven't heard before.'

'Of course I'm not speaking English!' cried Beth. 'I'm speaking Djemiranga.'

'But it probably doesn't sound like Djemiranga,' I explained, encouraged by Vanessa. I was turning out to be such a coward in front of Beth and Craig that I needed Vanessa's strength. 'I can hear sounds in it that aren't Djemiranga sounds. For a start,' I told Beth, 'their "u" sound isn't the same sound as the English "u".'

'What does the word mean?' asked Vanessa, turning to Libby.

Libby whispered it to her, so she wouldn't shame Beth publicly, and Vanessa left her seat and came to sit up the front, near Beth.

'Point to your arm,' she suggested quietly to Beth. 'Ask them for their word for "arm", and then show them the word you've written down.'

'That's not how they're to learn,' said Beth. 'They have to say it after me.'

She read it again, again mispronouncing it.

The faces of the children were closed. Are they laughing to themselves the way we did when someone can't get their tongue around our native language, or were they thinking: Here's another bit of white craziness? But they were polite children, and familiar with this sort of misunderstanding when their parents dealt with whites.

I was still holding up the card. It was my turn to try to rescue the situation.

'Libby – please tell me how to pronounce this word.' I felt that as a visitor, it was my right to invite her to speak.

Libby roused herself and said the word, and I repeated it. She nodded. There was a murmur from the children, so I knew that they recognised the sound.

I said to the class: 'Is *kapuju* –' I pointed to my leg and shook it high, my skirt flouncing, 'this?'

Suddenly the atmosphere changed, and everyone was laughing.

I pointed to my ear, sticking it out at an odd angle, clowning. 'This?'

More gales of laughter.

I pointed to my eye, walking around grotesquely, like a mad thing escaped from a pantomime production of *King Lear*: 'This?'

More laughter. Now, to my relief, the ladies were laughing, even crying with laughter. Craig and Beth were the only ones not laughing. One of the children hurtled out to rescue me and pulled at my arm.

'Arm! Arm!'

'This is getting out of hand,' called Craig to the class, but not to Beth. Everyone ignored him.

I tried to say *kapuju* again, but after all the laughter, I'd forgotten the sound of the 'u'. A little girl trained me to say it more accurately, while the laughter waned.

Now I held up the cards, one by one, each with their Djemiranga word and asked Libby to read it, and the children pointed to my body – my hand, my leg, my nose. Then I drew a stick figure of a large doll on the board and stuck on it the words on their little slips of paper with Blu tack that Kana handed me, carefully not meeting my eye.

'I'm sorry about this chaos,' Beth said loudly to Craig.

'It's a difficult situation,' he said. 'As always.'

Beth rose from her desk.

'Libby,' she demanded, in her most cutting voice: 'Which part of the arm is *kapuju*?'

She still mispronounced it.

Libby said nothing.

'Don't you know?' demanded Beth.

'Look, perhaps the children would like to tell us –' began Vanessa.

'Come on, Libby, tell us if you know, where exactly is *kapuju*?' repeated Beth. 'Elbow? Wrist?'

Still Libby said nothing.

'You're supposed to speak and read this language, so tell us.'

There was a horrified silence. No one could speak. No one could move. The children, confused but sensing the atmosphere, looked between Beth and Libby, like an audience at a tense tennis match.

Beth saw she'd gone too far.

'I was joking,' she told Craig, who inclined his head to show he understood.

'It's always difficult,' he repeated.

There was a deeper silence.

Beth stood at the front of her desk, leaning on it, assuming a relaxed stance. 'I've planned that we will play Simon Says,' she announced. 'Everyone. Including the elders.'

'We'll go,' called Vanessa, but the ladies didn't react. Perhaps in all the stress they didn't understand her, and then it was too late.

'Stand up, everyone. Except, of course, our headmaster.'

The children looked around, scared, waiting for their elders to obey. The ladies looked at each other, and slowly rose to their feet. Only then did the children follow.

'Simon says touch your *kapuju*,' Beth roared, still mispronouncing it, so no one moved. A child dared to correct her. Everyone understood the child's correction, and, touched their arms, though some of the children looked around at their friends to make sure it was an arm they should touch.

'Simon says touch your –' and she read out another part of the body from the little slips of paper on the board, but again it sounded like an English word, though one we'd never heard of.

Before anyone could work out what she meant, she yelled at Vanessa: 'You're too slow! You're out. Sit down!'

Vanessa sat, lost for words.

'Simon says touch your –' again, Beth roared, nominating another body part. Again, she mispronounced the word. Again, no one understood.

'You're all out,' she yelled at the elders.

The women stayed standing.

I roused myself. Somehow the horror of it had kept me spellbound.

'Thank you,' I said to her. 'We will go now.' I walked out of the room first, carefully avoiding Craig's eyes, praying the ladies would follow me, praying that Beth wouldn't rush out and grab hold of them, praying that nothing more shameful would happen.

'I'm sorry,' I said to each of them on the verandah as they emerged, one by one. I glimpsed Beth bursting into tears and Craig putting his arm around her heaving shoulders.

The women walked away, their straight-backed, dignified walk.

I didn't have the heart to ask anyone about the singer.

'How could the headmaster let his teacher behave like that?' cried Vanessa as we drove away.

'She was trying to get his love back,' I said.

We hadn't time to talk further because Adrian and Mandy were at our gate at home when we pulled in.

Adrian leaned in through Vanessa's window.

'Time for a cuppa before you go off to Alice? Mandy has asked me for something and you might be able to help. It's something they want. I've boiled the kettle.'

'I should've seen that situation coming,' I said to Vanessa. 'I was too distracted.'

Vanessa smiled kindly. 'Too hopeful.'

We sat outside on the white plastic chairs that I wiped every morning, and that turned pink with dust by dinnertime. Adrian had made tea in the big blue teapot kept for visitors, and pretended to pour himself a cup. Because I was sitting next to him I could see that it was full of pineapple juice.

I poured tea into the other cups. He'd remembered the pot but forgotten the milk and sugar, and I went inside to get them. I returned just as he was explaining to Vanessa that Mandy's car had broken down and she couldn't do the long drive to get the medicine plants her sick little granddaughter needed.

'And she's the gardener here,' he added. 'So I said that we could grow the medicine plant at the clinic. Not quickly of course,' he added to Mandy. 'It'd take time. But there's plenty of ground. We could have a forest of them.'

Vanessa turned to Mandy and quizzed her on the details of the plant; where it grew, what direction the land it grew on faced, at what time of the year they harvested it, and how many people needed it. She found out that all the settlement believed in its efficacy.

'It would be a very big undertaking,' Vanessa said to all of us. 'It'd cost a lot so we'd need to apply for a government grant, which I'm sure would be successful. All sorts of white people in town would need to be willing to help, to germinate seeds, to propagate them, to nurse them, to bring the fragile little nurslings out here, to plant them in orderly rows. And someone here would have to be willing to water the plants just as instructed, at first several times a day, then, when instructed, less often, for a couple of years, until they're really established.'

'I don't have staff that could promise that,' said Adrian. 'Even if I offered, I'm not here every day.'

'I don't think a white should do it,' she said.

'Me,' said Mandy. 'This is our good plant.'

'What about when you have to be away?'

'My daughters. They are good daughters.'

Vanessa said: 'Is it OK, you doing this?'

'Yes,' said Mandy.

'OK with your people?'

'Yes,' said Mandy.

We all stared down at the table surface, trying to imagine what might be involved in her undertaking. No one knew, but we all knew not to ask. This was a part of their culture that wasn't whites' business.

Vanessa asked Mandy to walk over the clinic land with her, to talk about where to grow the forest.

'It'll have to get the same sun, morning sun, afternoon sun or sun all day as it gets in its home.'

Mandy mused on this.

They both threw the dregs of their cups of tea on the dry ground beyond the verandah, the black woman and the white one. We all watched the arcs of the drops. They stood up together.

'I'll arrange it, the paperwork and all,' Vanessa said to us. Adrian stood up too, and together they walked away.

Chapter 19

That evening just before dusk, I saw women streaming down the street and off into the desert.

'It's ceremony time,' Adrian explained on a visit home. He had the fridge door open, and was gulping milk straight out of the carton.

'I want to join them,' I said. Perhaps I'd find the old woman.

'This isn't for tourists,' said Adrian, slamming the fridge door. 'They don't want to be observed.'

I slumped at the kitchen table, where Daniel found me when he came home for a snack. He asked me what was wrong.

'This is just the preliminary part of the ceremony,' he told me. 'They come back for a few hours then go out again. Dora will be coming back with them. Why don't you invite her in for something to eat with her grandkids? Everyone's always hungry. Then you could ask her to take you.'

I threw my arms around him and kissed his cheek. With him, complicated issues seemed to untangle. I rummaged in the pantry and, entirely forgetting myself in my excitement, I opened a big tin of salmon. I unfroze bread, fried strips of bacon and boiled eggs, all the time watching through the kitchen window. I boiled the kettle and made tea in the big blue teapot, letting it draw because everyone seemed to like tea strong. Then I sat on the verandah and just as Daniel had said, before dark settled in, the women returned, in twos and threes and family groups.

I ran and called to Dora and her grandchildren as they passed my gate.

'Come in and have something to eat.'

They devoured the bacon and eggs and bread but nibbled only politely at the salmon.

'We don't like the sea,' one of the children explained.

I'd already known that, but these things were so easy to forget.

I wanted to ask permission to go with them but even over a pot of tea, I was tongue-tied. Adrian's word 'tourist' seemed to brand me. But I didn't want to observe them, I wanted to be with them, I wanted to be included.

Daniel came back home from work and poured himself a cup of tea.

'Could disintegrate a spoon,' he said, checking the strength and grinning at me. 'Are you going to the ceremony?' he asked me in front of Dora.

'I haven't asked,' I said. I was red with shame, that they might think of me as a tourist.

'Kate wants to join you tonight,' Daniel said to Dora in his easy way.

'Bring a blanket,' was all she said.

And so it happened. Through the long dark evening, I stood with the women and children and watched the men dance. Dora stood beside me and ordered me when to watch, and when to turn my head. 'Look that way,' Dora ordered, turning my chin in the direction I must look. I instantly obeyed. It was very hard to see anything because they were black figures in a black night, so all I glimpsed was the gleam of feathers. I took her littlest grandson to give her a rest, and held him. He didn't notice me, he didn't look around. His little body was stiff with fascination. He'll always remember this night, I thought, it'll last him all his life, wherever he ends up living.

I assumed all the women were looking away when I did, but I didn't dare peek at anything, not men, not women, because I didn't want to see what I shouldn't see. I only wanted to please everyone, because after all, I was an appeasing person, and probably always would be. I must resign myself to that. But that time, the 'everyone' I wanted to please included the spirits, because if any spirits knew I was peeking, it would be sure to be the angry ones.

The men disappeared into the night, and the women lay down in their blankets. Dora told me to sleep next to her. I found I was lying on the outside of the group. Other women looked around at me and smiled, women I'd never talked to before. I suspected I was a human wall, because if there were bad spirits around, surely they wouldn't attack a white person.

We slept, and despite the cold hard ground just a blanket's thickness away, it seemed the most profound sleep I'd ever had, the sleep of my life, a sleep close to the sweet ease of death, but lulled by the soft air and the quiet breathing around me of hundreds of women. I woke twice, the first time to hear the men still singing. They were a long way off, away towards the almost-hills, over towards my right.

The second time I awoke, it was barely dawn. Birds began early there, in that last burst of cold when the night made its last grab to possess the earth, to freeze it into submission, before it surrendered and faded away. It was the moment before bird calls. A mist hovered over the blanketed bodies of the women, writhing into the distance above the flat earth. I'd never seen a mist in the desert before, wrapping its white angel wings around the boulders, frosting even the folds of my blanket. When I moved my head to another part of my pillow, the cloth was damp. Everything around me was still, the sand, the humped bodies of women under their colourful blankets, even the air. The ceremony was over, the fires had died. Like the toddler in my arms last night, I was spellbound, watching the desert dawn, the hovering angel mist. And then I heard it.

I'd never believed in the miraculous. People had told me about miracles they most fervently believed in and I'd nodded my head appeasingly, but secretly my mind searched for an ordinary explanation. There was always one nearby. Later that morning, I was to doubt what I heard, as I always have doubted myself. Later that morning I said: I must've fallen asleep and dreamed it. But at dawn when I heard it, I thought exactly that: I must be dreaming. I even pinched myself under my blanket, right on the outside of my left thigh. I pinched so hard, the next day there was a bruise. But despite all my efforts to deny it, I experienced the miraculous. This is what happened:

I'd sat upright in my blanket, the better to see the silent mist. Ice had crackled in the folds. I'd picked up a sliver of ice. And then I became aware that the ordinary world had a membrane across it, hovering above it like mist. On this particular dawn, the membrane broke apart. From under its tearing white tendrils a sound emerged, a sound like nothing I'd ever heard, like nothing I will ever hear again. The sound was singing. But who was singing?

The women were sleeping under their frosty blankets. And the men were sleeping off to my right, away off near the almost-hills. The singing came from somewhere else, over to my left, from where the sun would leap up any minute to stripe the sand with gold. I thought: it's an echo from last night! A delayed echo! Then I reasoned it couldn't be an echo, because there were no boulders or even trees to bounce an echo back to me – besides, it was too close, too immediate, too intimate. It wasn't male singing, nor female singing. It was a chorus, a whole chorus of voices, yet not voices, the sound was somewhere between a hum and the whining of wind. But the morning was perfectly still; there was not a breath of wind, not the slightest breeze. There was just the rise and fall of a chorus of not-quite-human voices arising out of the dirt.

I tried to reason it through: this was an ancient people, ancient beyond the ken of my culture, a people who'd been performing this ceremony every year for tens and tens of thousands of years, the same songs, the same movements, the same words, all exactly the same. Everyone knew every detail of the ceremony, everyone knew how to instruct me: 'You look this way, you look up, Kate, then you look this way' – even the watching audience was part of the dance, century after century.

I could only explain it this way: beneath my body was the red sand rippled with the prints of feet, the prints of bodies. The sand teemed with life and with death. It was crisscrossed with the footsteps, the bones, the spirits of this ancient people, their knowledge of each other, of their ancestors, of the animals and people they knew, and still commemorate. The very grit held their songs. Wrapped in my grey blanket, I'd been sleeping on the past, their bones, their stories, their ancient history with this ancient red earth, their songs. The very dust was rich with who they were.

All around me the old earth was singing, a rising and falling hymn to whom I did not know – a song that wasn't quite music but was more than sound, a rising and falling like the sea, like a cloud, like the slow march of humanity, like the inevitable, majestic movement of a river.

These people and their ancestors had taught the old earth to sing, I reasoned. Or perhaps, this most ancient earth had taught them.

By then the ice had long melted to nothingness on my fingers. It seemed that I lay awake for hours, enchanted by the song, but perhaps it was only minutes in that timelessness. I fell asleep at last in the midst of the earth's song. When I woke, the sun was fully up, and the women were on their feet, gathering up their blankets, speaking quietly to each other.

I blinked sleepily, not sure what was expected of me.

'Come,' said Dora. She was standing above me.

I had no words to tell her about the singing of the earth. Perhaps, one day, I would. Perhaps it would come as no surprise to her. Perhaps it sang to her.

We folded my blanket together, taking two corners each. As we moved, long side to long side, corner to corner, short side to short side, I felt that I could give any amount of love to this woman, I loved her large warm accommodating body, her contained, quiet authority, I loved even the way I couldn't predict her. But love wasn't what was wanted of me, though I hadn't worked out what was. And I wanted to thank her for the evening, but I didn't know how.

Her friend Daisy came over, and led me to a car already crowded. I shared it with a dozen other women I didn't know, who sat on each other's knees and wriggled over in a friendly way to make a little space for me to sit on the vinyl, not on another person as they were doing. Perhaps they knew how stiff and formal whites were. There was hardly any chatter, just smiles and a sleepy silence. I was dropped off first, a courtesy, I thought. They stopped right at my gate.

'Sleep now,' one of them said in English.

As I stumbled out, my blanket caught on the door, and in my struggle to free it, someone helped and everyone giggled, not at me, but in sympathy.

The next night Adrian knocked on my door.

'I'm not going to make the medicine forest wait for bureaucrats to decide whether to accept the paperwork,' he said. 'I've got a mate in Alice Springs who'll help us immediately. But he said the plants have to be picked before sun up and driven in right away. Want to come?'

I sat up.

'There's something I want to tell you,' I said.

I practised silently: I came to find out if your mother planned their deaths.

'It'll have to wait,' he said before I could continue. 'I've got to get the plants and come back to the clinic to help Gillian and Sister. A big day of health checks.'

I'd taken to going to bed in a tracksuit. It allowed me to walk out of my room, ready to go anywhere. Life here seemed to demand it. Now, all I needed to get ready for the journey was to splash water on my face, clean my teeth, go out to the kitchen and get water and pick up a box of apples that Daniel had brought from Alice Springs. Adrian was at the front door, holding large wooden trays for the cuttings, laughing at my sleepiness. I was always bewildered by the changes in his mood. I laughed back, but hesitantly.

Out in the dark air, we drove around from house to house, picking people up. Everyone was smiling and laughing as they climbed in, and soon there was a whole troopie of older women and young girls and children, some of them snuggled in their bright blankets on the floor.

'Is this legal?' I whispered to Adrian as the sixteenth person climbed in.

'It's the most popular thing I've ever done,' he whispered back.

Everyone slept on the three-hundred-kilometre journey through the dark bush to the medicine plants. I watched the headlights tunnel through the darkness, and saw how the track in the early morning light slowly became apricot gold, then tomato red.

In that huge distance we passed through two pastoral leases. I climbed out and opened the cattle gates, and closed them again. After my second gate, Dora and Mandy were laughing. They repeated what Gillian had told me when I was first here, that they used to say 'City Girl!' when I fumbled the locks.

'Now we say, City Girl knows those gates!'

It surprised me, the beauty of their precious medicine plant, its blue-grey leaves the colour an artist might choose against the red soil. But many bushes looked alike to my untested eyes. When we finished clipping the top-most leaves of one bush and moved to another, Rosa said: 'No, not this one. This one.'

I examined the leaves closely but they still looked alike.

'Wrong bush,' Rosa explained in English, laughing.

All around the women were gathering sheaths of the right bush to take to their families.

At first only Adrian and I worked on the cuttings. He clipped the tips of each branch with nail scissors, passed it to me and I poked it in the soil. Nearby, Dawnie was taking the opportunity to teach a group of younger women to track. She noticed me and politely switched to English.

'Here it landed.'

She pointed out the extra pressure in the sand of the first claw, tried to tell them in English why that was important to know but switched, with an apologetic smile to me, to Djemiranga. She talked to them a long time, with the girls squatting around her, eagerly quizzing her.

This was their sort of school, I thought.

'Hurry,' said Adrian, seeing me trying to follow the talk. 'The sun's coming up.'

He explained that the plant boxes had to be taken in to Alice Springs on the ambulance, which was to leave at lunchtime.

I went back to poking tiny cuttings in the soil.

I'd been concentrating so hard it was a shock to look up and see that the rising sun was already striping the red desert with yellow. Where a boulder blocked the path of the yellow light, the desert was creamy-grey.

'Work faster,' said Adrian. 'It isn't the time for looking around.'

Dora heard him.

'I help,' she said. She crouched beside me at the cuttings tray. Adrian said he'd hand her every second clipping.

'Little, little,' she said in surprise as he gave her the first tiny cutting. She rolled it around in her hand. Perhaps she was wondering why we were using such tiny cuttings, but she didn't ask and I couldn't explain, though I knew if I was her I'd wonder. However, we laughed as our hurrying fingers touched. My laughter was about shyness. I didn't know what her laughter was about; for a moment, I wondered if black women always laughed in the delight of being close, or whether being so close to a white woman was for her the surprise. But when we brushed fingers again, I found I could laugh more easily with her.

Working with her, it seemed to me that I was connecting to something much bigger than me; even with Adrian's impatience when I fumbled, I was filled with a rush of warmth for Dora, for the plants, for this red earth, for this moment.

Other women offered to join in. Adrian found another clipper in the toolbox under the seats of the troopie and taught Dora to clip the leaves, while the others helped me bury the tiny cuttings in the soil.

'Not too close together,' Adrian warned.

Then we found we were working in bright sunshine.

'Too late now. Home, everyone,' called Adrian. 'We've got to hurry.'

Everyone crammed in the troopie again, brandishing their sheaves of the medicine plant.

'How do you use it?' I asked my neighbour about her sheaf. She smiled at me and passed on my question to her neighbour.

'We –' she said, and mimed grinding for a long time, 'and cook it in oil.'

There was much laughter and chatter. I handed apples around. Despite the jolting, I dozed. Into my sleep, a familiar song trailed.

'One hundred green bottles hanging on the wall.'

I woke to find everyone singing, mature women and young girls alike, all chorusing it, a counting song that perhaps the older women had learned in their days of being maids in the households of pastoralists.

'One hundred green bottles hanging on the wall,
One hundred green bottles hanging on the wall,
And if one green bottle should accidentally fall ...'

But as they came to the fourth line, *'There'd be ...'* the song and the merriment jolted and stopped. I was about to tell them the next number, but I felt that would be insulting. If they wanted me to tell them, they'd ask. I saw Dora's lips moving and her fingers counting. I wondered if she was remembering her girlhood.

'Ninety-nine,' she found suddenly, and there were cheers.

'Ninety-nine green bottles hanging on the wall,
Ninety-nine green bottles hanging on the wall,
And if one green bottle should accidentally fall
There'd be ...'

And they all fell silent again. I was astonished at how much tension there was in the air. Something very big seemed at stake.

'Ninety-eight!' Dora at last called. There was acclamation and they were singing boisterously again. Then Mandy helped her at ninety-seven, ninety-six, all the way down to ninety-one. The two quavered at 'ninety'.

'Ninety green bottles hanging on the wall,
Ninety green bottles hanging on the wall,
And if one green bottle should accidentally fall
There'd be ...'

Another pause held the air. Again Dora's voice suddenly rang out. 'Eighty-nine!'

They all laughed, proud of her, it seemed, and they were off again, counting down through the numbers, but when they sang to 'eighty' there seemed as to be more than two voices, there seemed to be four or five.

But it was left to Dora to remember 'Seventy-nine!'

Then there was more happy, boisterous singing.

Dora and Mandy still needed to supply 'sixty-nine', but there were more voices at 'fifty-nine', and even more at 'forty-nine', so it seemed as if the whole troopie was beginning to learn the pattern. Now there was a sense of absolute determination to get to the end of the song.

'*Twenty green bottles hanging on the wall,*
Twenty green bottles hanging on the wall,
And if one green bottle should accidentally fall
There'd be …'

Someone tried 'ten-ty' but Dora shook her head.

'No,' she said firmly.

To everyone's relief, after a long pause, she found 'nineteen'.

She hesitantly led them through the teen numbers, paused dramatically at 'twelve', found 'eleven' after a long pause and much counting on her fingers, and there was a cheer when she led them to 'ten'. A few voices helped her down to five, but the whole troopie joined in and shouted triumphantly four, three, and two.

Everyone, even the little children, shouted:

'*One green bottle hanging on the wall,*
One green bottle hanging on the wall,
And if one green bottle should accidentally fall
There'd be no green bottles hanging on the wall.'

Then they all were turning to me, faces lit with wide beams, and I couldn't do anything else but burst into loud applause. Tears streamed down my face.

'Wonderful!' I shouted. 'Wonderful!'

* * *

'Thank you for your work,' said Adrian afterwards.

'It wasn't work,' I said.

'This morning, the women loved me.' We were in the kitchen. He had just showered, and he was wrapped in a yellow bath towel, his shoulders wet but still streaked with red dust. 'And you, too,' he added, grabbing a tea towel to sop the water from his grey ponytail still in its band.

'For what?' I asked, pleased to be included in their love.

'For caring,' he said.

'But do they believe the cuttings will grow?' I asked.

'Whether they do or not, they saw I cared.'

'They wouldn't doubt that about you,' I said warmly.

'Much of what I do, maybe that's just ordinary white stuff to them,' he said. 'What whites ought to do for them in exchange for taking their hunting land. But this morning, that was out of the usual, and they saw us as actually working for them. I'm part of the family now.'

'Who started the ten green bottles song?' I asked, explaining I'd been asleep.

'Dora,' he said.

'I had a feeling they were showing us something,' I said.

'Reciprocity,' he said. 'It's better than thank you, isn't it?'

There, in the kitchen, with a towel around him, and a tea towel on his head, I said to myself: Now.

'There's something I want to tell you,' I began. The words bulged in my brain.

I came to find out why you left, I should say.

But truth has many layers. That sentence had only one. I should also say: I came because I'd always longed to love you, because I wanted to be permitted to love you, I wanted to believe that you knew nothing of what was going to happen, I wanted to know if Diana killed my mother. I wanted to know if it was just an accident.

'Make it fast,' he said. 'I'm a busy man.'

He took off the tea towel from his grey head and laid it on the kitchen counter.

'It can wait,' I said.

Truth, I saw, was a great silencer.

Chapter 20

'It's time,' Adrian said through my door.

I was still in my dusty tracksuit, at work on parsing.

'To take me to her?' I was out the door already.

'To take you to my pink river.'

As I went to the toilet, I saw the bruise I'd made deliberately, purple now, halfway between my knee and my hip. I didn't tell him about the bruise.

It was a pink river of sand, almost a harbour of sand, so wide that I had to strain to see the far bank, then off up river and down river, off to infinity. Above us, pink geese-shaped clouds strained, necks outstretched, across a mauve sky that faded into a blue so full of light it seemed to hold silver foil behind it. The gums were so startlingly white in this pink land that they jolted the eye as they leaned into the river, as convivial as children, asking for food. Even the wrinkles in the gums' white bark were lit by pinkness. Then there was a shift in the sky, from pink to orange, and everything became lit now with pink-and-orange, and I wasn't sure if the light was from the sky or the reflection coming off the sand. My hands were lit by the pink-orange light, and the white evening-gowned trees glowed.

Adrian sat on the sand, his knees bent, hands grasping them.

'I thought you'd like it.' He was facing me, looking up. He paused. 'Nothing like the river you're used to,' he said.

'My river?'

For a moment I was winded, the breath taken out of me entirely. I was trying to remember when I'd forgotten myself enough to speak of my river to him, the river that was always in my mind. For a terrible second I thought I might have murmured too loudly while dozing on the long trip into town, or when I'd been very tired at the dinner table. Then I thought: perhaps he'd seen my photos after all, that first journey.

'My river?' I hedged.

'Ours,' he said.

I sat on the sand, which was surprisingly cool under my bottom. I bent my knees like his, clasped my hands around them like his.

'Ours?' I repeated. I could scarcely hear my own voice for the hammering in my heart.

'Remember when my mother cut our hair?' he asked.

When I was silent, he added: 'You don't remember?'

I couldn't speak.

'She was good with the scissors, she'd trained as a hairdresser, don't you remember?' he asked. 'She'd carry out the kitchen stools to the back path where no one would see us, and we'd have to take our shirts off.'

I found something to say. 'Why?'

'You don't remember this?'

He didn't wait for my answer, he'd given up on me, as if he had to do all the remembering for both of us.

'So she wouldn't have to wash the hairs off our clothes. She had no washing machine, remember. Anything that saved washing. So after the haircut, we'd just shake ourselves like puppies. Or dunk each other in the river. We both had to stare straight ahead at the tree to see if the eagle landed to steal eggs, that's what she'd say. "Watch out for the river eagle," she'd say.'

'What did the river eagle have to do with it?'

323

'I used to think it was so I wouldn't sneak a look at you. But that wasn't it. Watching out for it made our heads face the front. She'd do your hair first, working around the stool. You always were fussy, yours had to be higher than your ears and your fringe had to be level with the tips of your eyebrows. Mine was even more of a job because I liked my head almost shaved. Then she'd go back to you because the wisps took a while to drop and she had to get it even. I'd peep at you when you got off your stool. You looked specially made, like the template of all girls. Perfectly formed like a doll.'

His hands moved on the sand, though not near my hands.

'You had such pretty nipples. Like pink snowflakes.'

It was almost like a blow, a body blow, this revelation of his sexuality. I flinched under it.

'I remember nothing about haircuts,' I said.

'I blew it when I was about thirteen. You would've been about seven. You already had a cute indentation down here –' he drew a line between his nipples. 'I said something stupid, like, "She's getting breasts!" and Mum said quickly that you must be cold and to go and put your shirt on. She stopped being your hairdresser after that.'

He reached for my hand and touched it, though it lay beside him as flat as an oar.

'If I'd kept my big mouth shut it might've gone on forever.'

We sat in silence. Around us the bush settled into night.

'In your mind, do you talk to me?' I managed to ask after a while.

'What do you mean?' he asked.

'Like I do,' I said incoherently.

'I had a shock at first, thinking maybe I recognised you. You were always such a mouse! Why didn't you let on it was you?'

'There was a lot of sadness in our families.'

'You should've disguised yourself!'

I sighed.

'At any rate, you'd never be able to disguise your wrists.'

I was stiff with surprise, even as he lifted my left hand.

'I'd know your wrists anywhere. You remember – I was always watching you doing things with boats and ropes? Diana made me teach you. You were an awful pupil. I blamed the way you were built. Especially your hands. I used to wonder in particular at your wrists, your ulna. I looked it up in the dictionary, it was so different from mine. You looked like you'd break. You've always been built like a small giraffe. Uselessly. Then, and now, a giraffe.'

I was flushing with heat, with confusion.

'Did you come here to check up on me?' he asked.

'You know why I came,' I said. 'To impress my university. I'd been doing badly and wanted to make it up.' I swallowed. 'What's more – my life since you left never made sense. I had to settle something.'

'What?'

'You'd been everything to me. You and Diana. Suddenly you disappeared, as if you'd never existed. I wanted to know who Diana was. Who you were. What happened to my mother. What happened to Diana. She was almost my mother, too.'

He was moving his hands impatiently on the pink sand.

'I hated your father,' he said. 'I'm sorry – but I was so jealous! One night after they made love, it seemed, the whole night long, my mother moaning for more – I decided to get back at her and go looking for my real father. He cleared out before I was born. It was good for me to leave all that behind.'

'Did you find him?'

'No one remembered him.'

We both sighed.

'I came back to the river, years later. I didn't stay long.'

'There's something I've got to settle, something – the real reason –' I said, almost shouting above the persistent hammering of my heart.

'What real reason?'

'When –' I paused, I was so close to the pain, I could scarcely speak.

'When – what?'

'When you came back to the river, when you didn't stay long – when did you leave?'

'When did I leave? I stayed just a few hours.'

'But when?'

I was dizzy. I tried to reason it out: he wouldn't know my suspicions, unless he was guilty.

'I'd planned to stay with her, repair the past, that sort of thing,' he said, after a while. 'But when I got there, all she'd do was rant about your mother. I'd never even met your mother!'

'But Diana hadn't either, till the last day.'

'She was beside herself,' he continued. 'Apparently she'd asked your father for the thousandth time to leave your mother and come and die in her arms, that's how she put it, die in her arms. And he refused. Said he owed it to his wife, to die with her nursing him.'

I decided to tell him.

'I came to your house, as soon as your mother and mine had gone off in the boat,' I said. 'But you'd left.'

'Why did you do that?'

I couldn't speak.

'I left Mum at dawn, when the tide was high enough,' he said, not noticing the words that were blocked in my throat. 'She took me to the station. But I shouldn't have. I should've stayed. My lasting guilt. I could've prevented the death. Deaths. Somehow.'

'When, exactly?'

I lay down on the pink sand, limp with tension.

'When what?'

'When exactly did you leave?'

'I don't know why you keep asking that. But all right – we were so ruled by tides. It was one of the year's big highs. A 1.98

tide, I remember. Remember? We didn't have calendars. We had tide charts. I was so relieved to leave her, I've remembered that little detail all this time. I was counting the minutes before I could go. We left on the rise. If it had been a normal tide, we wouldn't have been able to get out in time for the train, and I'd have had a chance to reconsider.'

So I said at last the words I'd rehearsed.

'I came to find out what you knew.'

'You're right. I should've suspected. I was too self-engrossed,' he said, hardly noticing me.

'What could you have done?'

'Calmed her down. I don't know. Disabled the boat, maybe.'

'But you wouldn't have known her intentions,' I reasoned.

'Do you know what time she picked up your mother?' he asked and then I knew that he was completely innocent, that he had nothing to do with their deaths, that he was as much in mourning as me. I was ashamed of my suspicions, of the years I'd thought so badly of him.

'About an hour after the tide turned. They would've been heading towards the pylon when the tide was rushing out,' I said.

'She always said the running tide was the one we should be wary of,' he said.

'Terrible rips there,' we said together, in chorus, a line she taught us long ago.

We sat in sad silence.

'Do you think she planned it?' I asked.

He shrugged.

'Perhaps she wanted to punish me for leaving.'

After a while, he went on: 'What she hated most was that your mother knew how to keep him.'

'But he loved Diana. She was –' I swallowed, 'his anchoring love. He always said that.'

'But he chose to die with your mother.'

I sat up, and leaned into him. After a while, I said: 'Was my unassuming mother more potent than we thought? Like these people here? Unassuming but potent? You think they had a fight on the boat? Diana and my mother? Over who should nurse my father?'

'Would your mother have fought her?' he asked.

'No,' I said.

'Diana could get beside herself with jealousy,' he said. 'I'd seen her jumping up and down with rage, like someone possessed. She wanted to control everything, and here was something outside her grasp. You know what I think: she got beside herself with rage, and didn't keep her eye on the pylon.'

We were both sitting in the same way, bending forward in our pain, like twins.

'I don't think my mother meant to murder yours. I don't think she intended suicide. I think it was the rips. There are some things in nature no one can control.' He laughed. 'Not Diana. Not even me.'

He was sitting so close to me, I could almost watch the cells of my skin reaching out to him like tiny hands. I turned and found his mouth meeting mine. Fat, generous kisses. Healing kisses that promised that nothing would ever hurt so much again, sweet, moist kisses that lulled. Like a river, full of promises. I pulled away from him.

'I haven't been flirting with you, have I?'

'Why ask that?'

I couldn't tell him that it was a problem I'd had ever since he left.

'Why did you change your surname?' he asked.

'I got married. I wanted to put my past behind me. Why did you change yours?'

'I wanted to put my past behind me too,' he said.

'I tried to deceive you,' I admitted.

He caressed my face.

'So you could try loving me,' he said.

'Yes,' I said.

'Admit it; that's why you're here.'

As he kissed me again, our lips felt plump with emotions we had no words for. He'd planned that kiss. As he cupped the back of my head with his palm, my bird-like heart dropped out of its cage again. It was a long, long kiss, a drink after a long walk through an endless desert.

'We both needed that,' he said.

I pulled away again.

'Why have you been so nasty to me?' I managed to ask.

'When I recognised your wrists, I got angry. That you came after me. But you said nothing.'

'What should I have said?'

'You should've said: "I suspect you murdered both our mothers." You should've said: "I've always been hopelessly in love with you."'

He's loved you all the time, I thought.

Then it came easily to me. I held him. I held him for the sake of those poor tormented people. I held him for my own sake. We lay down on the pink sand, holding each other, two children lost in a mysterious dark forest.

Sex crackled between us. I tried not to notice it, but it was like forcing an exuberant dog to lie down. I couldn't give into it, I mustn't.

'I'll tell you where to find your old lady,' he offered suddenly. 'If that's what's still important to you,' he added.

I waited, silenced, except for the thumping of my heart. I was terrified, now that he was at last telling me, that I'd fall deaf, that he would be struck dumb, that I wouldn't be able to register such precious information.

'Where?'

'She's gone in to respite. Daniel took her in the other week. He can tell you where she is.'

'Tillie! Did Daniel know it was her?' I asked.

'No,' he said.

'Thank you,' I said, I breathed.

So I would ask Daniel to take me in. Daniel, who's calm, reasonable, patient, truthful. I didn't have to worry. If Adrian did one of his quicksilver changes of mind, I could still go to Daniel and say: take me to her.

The old lady from the outstation, I thought, but managed not to say. I was ashamed that I hadn't intuited it was her, that day when I lifted her into the troopie. I was ashamed that I'd still thought like a white, expecting that the singer of the oldest surviving song would be regal.

'Why haven't her relatives contacted me?'

He shrugged.

'You're just another white to them. A nurse, perhaps. Why should you be anything special to them?'

'Don't people ask why I'm here?'

'They accept you because of me.'

Then everything changed. Just like that. In an instant. Because of something said mildly, even though he'd said such a thing many times, in many ways.

I moved away slightly. My sexual attraction to him died.

'We should light a fire,' I said. 'Or we'll be cold.'

It was easier to get up and drag logs and sticks into an untidy pile than to think.

'Aren't we being extravagant?' I asked as he dragged a huge log that was most of a lightning-struck tree. 'This isn't the way they do fires,' I added.

'I'm building it to last all night,' he said. 'I want to sleep with you.'

I didn't speak. I worked at building the fire. All I was doing was building a fire, I wasn't thinking, nor feeling, I was just putting one stick on top of the other. And again, the fragile peace between us shattered.

'Not that direction,' he said. 'Crossways.'

I kept doing what I was doing.

'Crossways,' he repeated. 'So the fire is concentrated here.'

Of course he was right. I pulled the logs around so they were at diagonals to each other but his gaze was making me nervous, which the leaping flames were revealing, I was sure. I couldn't refuse his wishes because I was too polite, but worse, because when he chose, his melodious voice dragged my skin towards him, and winkled out the love I'd carried all my life for him.

'I know what I'm doing. At the river, I burned off a thousand times,' I tried to say. 'I set fires every winter night.'

He ignored me. 'Place that bough like this, not like that,' he said, miming boughs with his arms.

I attempted to follow his directions but the structure fell apart. His inspection of my work was making my lip twitch, and a tic was starting on my left eye which I longed for the darkness to hide. When on his order I yanked out a thick bough, it shot up a shower of sparks. His voice was so insistent, I was a prisoner inside it. He made it clear that he'd wait all night for me to build the fire in the way he wanted. I remembered a schoolteacher with a beguilingly soft voice making me try to trace the function of $f(x)$ through a labyrinth of logic that everyone else in the class could see. 'We're happy to wait for you all through our lunch break,' she'd said, while the class hooted with scorn.

'You should start again,' Adrian said.

But there were too many boughs to take off and change and I was flustered, clumsy, unable to follow his orders, even if I'd wanted to.

'Stop ordering me around,' I said.

Was this another thing he'd inherited from Diana? Is this really why he had to leave her?

*

On your boat there is a rubber bulb at the end of the fuel pipe from the fuel tank to the engine. One day when the boat won't start, Diana explains that there's no petrol in the engine, and shows me how to make the fuel flow into it.

'You put your whole hand around the bulb, and squeeze,' she says, explaining that the squeeze empties it of air so there's room for the fuel.

'It's like your father's hand, your hand,' Diana says as she watches me try.

I look at my hand on the bulb in surprise, for my father has long, tapering fingers, and I have my mother's hands, short and stumpy. I don't know how to tell her that.

'Your father holds my heart in his hand,' she explains. 'He's always squeezing my heart.'

Kookaburras have been making the krkrkr they do before they burst into laughter, as if they have to clear their throats and arrange their vocal cords while they consider all the absurdity in the world. Mocking laughter now erupts all around us. Then they stop abruptly or they stop in my memory of that moment, in case they miss a word we say. There are many things to listen for, many things I should say to Diana, gazing at the rubber bulb, but these moments come so quickly, like a cricket ball or a meteorite is said to, so that all you can do is reel with the impact. Minutes later, or years, it comes to you, what you should have said or done. Perhaps you only know how to react when childhood's over or, at least, when all the things are finished that could've been changed.

Take your heart away from him, I should say to Diana. You're hurting us all. My mother, your son, me.

I should say: You have your son's heart in your hand.

Such simple words, but I don't know how to say them, even how to think them. I should say that I've inherited my mother's hands, I'm from her, part of her, not part of Diana. I should say: What about my mother's heart in your hand? Don't you know you're squeezing the life out of my mother's heart?

But I say nothing. I don't love my mother enough, though I have her hands. Not at that moment, not when it matters.

I should say: You have your son's life in your hand, and there will come a moment when he won't allow you to squeeze his heart any more.

I should say: You have mine as well, and my whole life, for all the days I am on this earth.

I should say: Have you no shame, to do this to us all?

But I merely look down at her hand as she shows me again how to work the bulb. For the first time, I notice that though she'd painted her nails red, blood red, this morning, the red paint is already coming off in chips. Her chipped nails seem plaintive, as if a party is over.

But still I say nothing. Nothing at all. It's one of the burdens of childhood that a child has no words.

*

'Why are you crying?' Adrian asked.

'I've been building fires all my life,' I shouted. 'You're treating me like a fool.'

'Not out here, you haven't,' he said. 'Not to burn the whole night.'

'It's as if a fire must be made in a way that only you know, in a shape only you approve of,' I shouted at him.

He didn't shout back. He just talked gently, beguilingly, sweetly, as he did when he'd pushed me too far.

'It's got to blaze all night, to keep poisonous snakes away.'

I rallied for one last attempt.

'Where did you learn this only way to make a fire?'

'From them,' he said, glancing over his shoulder back to the Aboriginal settlement. 'They'd know. They've been doing it for a long time.'

He added: 'It has to keep us safe while we make love.'

I threw down the log I'd been holding.

'Finish it yourself.' I stalked off into the darkness alone.

'If that's what you want, we'll go for a walk up the riverbed,' he said. 'Together.'

I hurried in front. Everything was black, black soil, black trees, black sky, though I knew I was walking on pinkness. There was no moon, only stars.

'See with your feet,' he said, catching up with me. He tried to divert me by telling me how when the river came into flood, he saw the head of the river creeping across the desert.

'There are only seven permanent waterholes in this desert,' he told me, enjoying teaching me again. 'The river engulfed everything in its path. I was sure little animals must've drowned, they're so unused to a body of water. There are stories that the mob knew when it was coming, they'd know to get out of the way, they'd put their ear to the earth and hear its approach.'

I couldn't resist him, I never could.

'The river makes a noise?'

He shrugged. 'This riverbed has all the attributes of a river.'

'Except for water,' I spat.

We walked back to our fire together, which by then was roaring. He sat and tried to pull me down beside him but I went to the other side of the flames.

'There seems to be a glow over there, near home,' I suddenly noticed.

He groaned theatrically. 'You're lucky I'm with you. You've got no sense of direction at all. You're pointing south and we're east.'

Silence settled on us.

'We can't become lovers,' I said.

'Why not?'

He came over and put his arms around me and I sank into the pressure of his pink galah chest on mine, his strong shoulders against mine, his nipples against mine – his chest was so wide and deep it seemed it could enclose me, thigh to thigh, knee to knee. Our feet found a resting place between each other's, perhaps we even touched toes inside our shoes. I tried not to think of how he'd feel pulsing inside me.

'Anything further would be dangerous,' I said.

Unexpectedly, irrationally, I thought of Daniel. It was Daniel I wanted to be with, it was Daniel who felt like my home.

I shivered. Adrian disentangled himself, then went to the troopie and found a pillow and a tarpaulin. We lay down on it and he arranged it over us. He noticed one of my feet sticking out, and covered it up, endearingly. We held each other, merely held.

'Marry me,' he said sleepily. 'Aboriginal way. I'll keep you. You can make me food and a garden. Run chooks. Do womanly things. The mob will love you for that. In the morning, you'll – I don't know – you'll paint. You'll wake me. We'll have breakfast, you'll walk to the shop for, I don't know, milk. On the way back you'll hold babies, their babies.'

Even in the black night, I knew that the sand around us was still invisibly rosy.

'Not ours?' I asked, but he didn't hear.

I put my head on the pillow beside him and wept for the babies, the other women's babies, and mine which I thought I'd never have.

'I didn't get divorced,' I told him, but again he didn't hear.

'Women will visit you and sit on the verandah and drink tea with you. When I come home for lunch they'll fade away because they'll know what a man wants of his wife. Sometimes on weekends one of them will invite you to go out to a special place. They'll love you, that you left the city to be a desert woman with me and live with them.'

In his voice I heard his longing, like mine for Daniel.

'Why didn't you tell me about the old lady earlier?' I asked.

'Because I fell in love with you on first sight, and I wanted to keep you near me,' he said easily. 'We'll sleep near each other, get used to each other, tonight.'

'Go to sleep then,' I said.

I turned my back to him and allowed him to curve his body into mine, so we were like spoons in a drawer. He cupped my breasts.

'I should patent this position,' he said.

I accepted his cupping hands. I lay watching the black sky, a garden of flowers of light.

Then he stirred, and said sleepily: 'You're not the sort of woman an ordinary man would choose for here. But that's the point.'

'I'm not?'

'I'm a rare man.'

He had fallen asleep again. I gazed at the moon, now a full moon, beyond the very toes of my feet, the sort of moon that was considered romantic. But it seemed to be glaring at me, showing up my faults.

It was too difficult trying to reason; I drifted asleep. Cold woke me. The fire that would last all night was dying. I wriggled up, moving his hands away and being careful not to wake him with the crinkling of the tarpaulin, for now I was sure I didn't want him to be my lover, ever. I limped across twigs to put another log on the fire. Cold hit my bladder and I pushed my feet into my sneakers to go out into the desert for a pee. I was too cold to unlace them, so I walked inside them but on my toes, like a young girl in her first clumsy pair of high heels. That feeling of being young, vulnerable, unknowing, made me see that he was right, that I am odd. When I'd been a child at school, I had no friends, just people I tried to hang around with so the bullies wouldn't single me out. I felt the bullies could see something I couldn't see, something dark and horrifying. Bullies to me in those days were the seekers and finders of truth.

Tears were flooding my eyes. He seemed to be able to find and finger the hurt inside me, the hurt of not being the person I should be. Even E.E. Albert hoped I'd be someone else, someone she wanted.

For years, I'd felt unlovable, that I was a burden to every man I slept with.

All that I understood as my pee sank deep into the dry ground, watering it. I ran back, almost stumbling, and wriggled back under the tarpaulin again, against his warmth. It was then that I noticed that the moon had moved; it was now above my chest.

A voice was speaking inside my head. As I drifted, it had a chance to speak. It said: He loved you all the time. You've seen what love is to him. That was how he loves.

I fell asleep again, and at dawn I had to arch my body to find the moon, then pale, behind my head.

He awoke with a jump.

'We must go!' he cried.

But just before he eased himself back into the troopie, he turned and put his arms around me. My own arms stayed by my side until he pulled at them, placed them one by one around his neck. I felt the familiar thump of capitulation. I nestled my head against his shoulders though my face streamed again with tears. His hair smelled like a dead kangaroo that'd been left in the sun. The smell seemed to rescue me.

'Even your hair refuses to submit,' I said.

'You're not happy?' he asked in surprise. 'You get a proposal and you're unhappy?' And immediately: 'You're not standing properly. Sag your knees, so we're body to body.'

And it was true. I didn't seem to be able to put my feet in the right place.

'I don't think there's room for me,' I said.

On the drive back, he put his hand on my thigh, and we drove holding hands, in something that felt like peace. The prickly spinifex glowed silver in the new sun, as if the moon was still up. I thought of how many times I'd been tricked by the beauty of spinifex. I told him that.

He nodded.

'The sun keeps bleaching away everything you count on,' I said.

He suddenly swung the troopie off the road, and charged across the plain, mowing down saplings.

'My excuse for coming out here was to bring in a patient,' he said.

'A patient living alone in the desert?' I asked, but suddenly we'd arrived in a clearing.

In front of us was a group of lean-tos, maybe six, all with the blue smoke of cooking fires furling around them, and family groups watching over the cooking of dampers. They looked up, startled, at our approach.

'Is Nick here?' asked Adrian, dive-bombing out of the troopie to explain our presence.

I got out too, hoping I could pass for a nurse, hoping I wouldn't have to act as one.

'Nick here?' I repeated in faltering Djemiranga.

But when they replied in Djemiranga, telling me the whereabouts of Nick, correcting me – I'd left out the affix and more besides – I couldn't follow them. They laughed and gave up.

338

'No,' they told Adrian in English. They waved their hand towards the desert.

'Out.'

'Should we pursue him?' I asked Adrian.

'No,' said Adrian sadly. 'We can offer Western medicine but it's his choice.'

He thanked the people and got back in the troopie.

One of the women came to my window and spoke in Djemiranga. I made out 'fire' and 'Gadaburumili'.

'She's saying what I said – there's a fire at home,' I told Adrian.

'All women have a rotten sense of direction,' he said easily.

He wasn't at all in a hurry; on the way back he braked and pointed out a huge metal structure glinting behind the settlement.

'Another job-creation scheme. I told you the desert's littered with them. This one was for the mob to break in wild horses. You know the old men were once stockmen.'

'And what happened?' I asked, staring at the glinting metal.

'The stockmen are in their nineties!'

'And the young ones?'

'Why would they want to?'

'Did anyone ask them?'

'The whites would've come out, put on a barbecue, a few people would've turned up, the whites would've been hot and bothered and complaining about the heat and the flies, and if all that was needed so that everyone could go back home and be comfortable was a cross on a piece of paper, these are obliging people. Someone would've obliged.'

'Did the mob know what the whites were saying?'

'Probably not.'

'Did the whites speak Djemiranga?'

'Of course not!'

'Didn't they bring a translator?'

'Whites insist that the mob here speak English, and if they don't, that's their lookout.'

Bits of a lecture from E.E. Albert that I had scarcely attended to were drifting into my mind.

'The whites would've used abstract nouns,' I mused.

He looked impatient. 'What?'

'Aboriginal languages don't have many abstract nouns.'

Day by day, I was coming to understand E.E. Albert better.

Adrian groaned. 'Who cares about grammar?'

Love hadn't affected his opinion of my work. But I continued: 'So a lot of what the whites said wouldn't have made sense. Abstract nouns. Like "economy" and "independence" and "the future".'

'Democracy,' added Adrian.

'You've got it!' I cried, pleased that he'd remembered.

He gunned the troopie. In through the open cabin windows came the stench of fire.

'OK, so I was wrong,' he said. 'But it's no worry. They'll be burning off. They do it to make the grass grow again, and then the wild animals return to eat it, and to be killed and eaten. "The wild animals want to be eaten," the mob says. The pastoralists call the police, but the police can never find the culprits. And since some police are Aboriginal, perhaps they're sympathetic. After all, to people who care nothing about ownership, why should the pastoralists commandeer the mob's hunting grounds?'

We drove past a wrecked car on the side of the road.

'I'm amazed local people accept the white's right to run cattle,' I said. 'Any of these animals would make a meal for a week.'

'There's a dire history of the consequences of not accepting them,' Adrian said ironically.

The stench became stronger.

'Wind up the window,' he ordered. His voice was so cross, I took my hand away to do his bidding, and then I didn't give it back. He didn't ask for it.

'You keep putting barbs in my mind,' I said.

'We won't talk, then,' he said triumphantly.

I told him that Puig, an Argentinean novelist I loved, said that in couples there was always one who loves more than the other: the loved and the lover.

He reached over and touched my breast through the fabric of my blouse. Despite myself, despite the fabric of my blouse, my nipple prickled out into his blunt fingers.

He spoke to my breasts: 'You'll have to wait till she's ready.'

I laughed. 'The body's anarchic,' I said.

It was the wrong sort of thing to say: I so often nettled him.

'You're so needy!' he burst out. 'So spiritually needy! You're all like this, you come here with a gap in your lives, in your souls, and you want to feed on something. You're parasites!'

'And you?' I asked.

'I'm the loved,' he said proudly as if something was settled. But nothing was, not yet.

Chapter 21

As we turned into the settlement, smoke was billowing, and there was a knot of people on the road.

'Opposite the second doctor's house,' I said. 'It looks like a meeting.'

'They don't have meetings,' he said, sounding tired. But then all conversation ceased, for we saw that the second doctor's house was just a smoking, blackened ruin. Only the steel posts were in place, and even they had buckled. The roof had caved in, the walls had gone, the floorboards had gone. There was just a pit where I had once slept.

A few people looked around as we pulled up. Daniel emerged out of the crowd, and ran around to Adrian's window.

'There's a problem with the paperwork,' he said.

'Who cares about paperwork!' shouted Adrian. He dive-bombed out of the troopie, and headed over to the house. Daniel restrained him.

'Not yet, it's dangerous.'

'Danger? Who cares about danger?' Adrian demanded. He strode on. Daniel pulled him to a stop.

'The paperwork! The insurers!'

Adrian shook him off, but even he halted in front of the ruin.

'How did it happen?' I asked Daniel.

'I woke up this morning and found it. I didn't hear anything all night, what with the air conditioning roaring now the electricity's back. Or smell it, till I opened the door. The fire was out by then and just smoking.'

Adrian strode back.

'You should've cordoned it off to keep the kids safe,' said Adrian. He instructed me to keep everyone at bay while Daniel went for rope.

Daniel stood his ground.

'But the insurance – I got on to the insurers as soon as they started work. There seems a bit of a mix-up over which houses are insured. They can't cope with the way we have no street addresses, and no street numbers. I wasn't able to describe which house had the fire. They were counting houses on the plan and they couldn't find a mention of this one. They're on their way. They're bringing out their plan. They'll be here by late lunchtime.'

'What does it matter, which house it is?' I asked.

They both looked around at me.

'Bureaucrats,' spat Adrian.

'Not all the houses had up-to-date insurance,' Daniel persisted. 'This one mightn't have had.'

'You shouldn't have told them about the fire!' cried Adrian. 'We could've thrown up another house, you and me and a few blokes.'

Daniel paused, astonished. He seemed to shrink under Adrian's fury.

'You let me down over this!' Adrian cried.

When Daniel spoke, his voice was low. 'I'll go and look again for the paperwork.'

'You'll cordon it off first.'

Adrian stalked off into our house, pulled off his boots, lay on the sofa with his hand over his eyes, and fell asleep. I showered, changed into clean clothes, made a salad for lunch that might be only for us, or might also be for insurance agents from Alice Springs, and a pot of tea in the small teapot. I carried it out to the verandah, along with two cups. I sat gazing at the blackened house.

After a while, Daniel came down the street from the clinic.

He slumped down on a white plastic chair, entirely forgetting to wipe it clean.

'You stayed out,' he said, in that stumbling way people have when they can't think of a way to start a conversation that's necessary to them. I kept staring at the smoking house.

'We had to sort things out,' I said.

'Being at the river helped?' he asked.

'Being in the bush always helps,' I said. 'But if we'd come home earlier, we might have caught it,' I added after a while.

He'd finished his tea before he said: 'He's not right to blame me.'

'He's exhausted. In shock,' I said.

'It wasn't insured,' he said.

I poured more tea into his cup.

'Things might unravel from here,' he said.

We sipped our tea.

'When you're next taking patients into town, can I come too? Adrian has at last told me who I've got to record. It's Tillie.'

'Tillie! I'd never have guessed. Of course,' he said.

'You didn't know it was Tillie?' I checked. I wanted to believe in his empathy, I wanted to believe in him.

'Not a clue. He plays things so close to his chest. And Collins never mentioned it. But I was always busy, never had much of a chance to talk to Collins. Always wanted to, but things here, as you know, are often flat out. And the women wouldn't have mentioned it to me.'

Just then an unfamiliar troopie came down our street, with two strangers in the front seat. Daniel put down his cup.

'They got here fast! Wake Adrian,' he threw over his shoulder. 'It's not a good look, that the clinic manager sleeps on his sofa while Rome burns.' His voice was bitter with irony.

He ran out to the road and hailed the troopie as it rattled away down the street. The driver looked out the window, saw Daniel and backed up in a cloud of dust. I went inside and woke up Adrian, then served lunch.

'There's enough for us and our visitors,' I told Adrian.

'We're feeding them?' he grunted.

'It might sweeten them up,' I said.

He sat down at the table and began loading his plate.

'Don't you think we should wait?' I asked him.

'I didn't invite them,' he said.

'What do the people think?'

'I wish you'd call them the mob! That's what they call themselves! You sound like someone at a Darwin garden party. "The people".'

Another barb. But all I said was: 'I think they use it as a plural.'

When he looked uncomprehending, I explained: '"Mob". Like our "s". Book, books. Troopie. Troopies.'

He wasn't listening.

'To answer your question, the mob think it's boring,' he said. 'All this outrage over bits of paper.'

He shook salt on his food, slammed down the salt shaker and rubbed sleep out of his eyes.

'It was probably an arsonist. A white arsonist. Someone who knew it was the one house uninsured. An enemy.'

'An enemy here wouldn't have access to our records,' I argued. 'You mean some government official who wants to destroy you?'

He was already scraping his plate clean.

'You've made enemies at the school,' he said. 'You know Bruce and Craig are mates, and Bruce wanted to do me in. What have you done to Craig?'

'You're in shock,' I said evenly. But he'd put my heart in turmoil.

We heard heavy footsteps on the verandah. Daniel brought in the two men, both large, red-faced balding men, both with bellies spilling out of white shirts and barely buttoned away.

'Rotten roads,' they said, almost together. 'They need grading.'

'You did it fast,' I agreed, trying to make my voice pleasant and welcoming.

'We flew part way up, then borrowed a car,' one said.

I poured them iced water and they sat down, thanking me. I served salad.

'You think it was arson?' asked Adrian.

'We're here to investigate,' one said. 'Can't jump to any conclusions.'

'We should be able to tell this afternoon,' the other said.

'How?' I asked.

'Where it started, how it burned,' the first man said. 'It'll probably turn out to be an electrical fault. That happens often enough in the bush. Cowboys out here pretending to be electricians. Think they can get away with murder. Sometimes they do.'

'Heard you had trouble with your electricity,' said his mate. 'Then you got it fixed and kaboom!' The sound of their salad-munching could be heard, I was sure, all over the settlement.

That afternoon there was such a willy-willy of red dust that it spiralled higher than the telegraph poles, and all over the sky was a haze of red dust. I could see no further than the gate. Then the wild wind split a grey cloud and white Old-Testament-prophet light streamed through it down into our yard, lighting up the clothesline as if it, of all the earth, should be granted the honour of being singled out.

Lately, I'd taken to sitting on the verandah, working on my recordings, watching people go by, watching the weather.

Large black ants scurried to mock my slowness, almost instantly outlining the shape of things – verandah posts, the verandah edge and the chairs beside me. Even the table was ant-outlined. A well-fed dog I didn't know wandered into the yard, watching the sky with me, licking my hand. Rain began falling in thick drops, almost like jelly.

Daniel strode home from the clinic to get some papers.

'Out here, storms often come to nothing,' he said.

Birds began their exploratory peeping noises into the stillness – though it was more like a throat twitching. Drk drk drk. Everything seemed to come to a standstill after rain here – insects hid under leaves, dogs hid under houses, the donkey waited under a tree. Then the rain swooped again, in wild bird swoops of sound.

Two girls I recognised from Libby's house walked past. They stopped at the gate, nudging each other.

'Come in out of the rain. Have a cuppa,' I called.

They came timidly over the red yard, which would soon, because of the rain, be furred with tiny green weeds, I knew that by now.

They stood hesitantly, not daring to mount the verandah. One waited for the other to speak.

'Want a cuppa?' I asked.

The older girl, Rayleen, struggled with rain-saturated black hair and something she wanted to say.

'At least come out of the rain,' I said.

They paused, then, both using their right leg first, they mounted the verandah together.

'I'll get you both a towel,' I said. I was about to get up, when Rayleen spoke.

'The white men. They punish us?'

'Punish! What for?'

'The fire.'

I sat down.

'Did you light the fire?' I asked, trying to keep my voice calm so that they'd make a confession, if that was what was on their minds. It wasn't.

'No. But the government doesn't like Aboriginal people. Now, trouble. Maybe –' she had to find a way to express the enormity of the threat, 'maybe the government takes our land away.'

So that was the problem. That's why they'd come.

'That's not how it works. If someone set the fire, that person will be punished. Only that person. But if it was just an accident, no trouble at all. OK now?'

That set the girls talking in Djemiranga, while I strained to follow. I had the impression that Rayleen was explaining it to Kathy, the other girl. 'So,' I continued, pleased that I'd eased them enough so that now they sat down on the chairs. 'I'll go and get cups, and towels.'

I turned off the computer and went inside, humming to myself. I'm getting the hang of this, I thought. This would be my first real friendship. I'd be able to explain white ways to them, and they'd be able to tell me about their ways.

We drank tea and gazed across at the ruin of the second doctor's house.

'Our uncles been singing this rain,' one of them said.

For a moment my mind supplied a missing preposition. You sing to, sing about, sing with, sing at, sing under, sing over.

'Singing,' I repeated.

They nodded.

'They sang *up* the rain?'

They said nothing. Perhaps what I'd said made no sense.

We drank tea.

'Only white trouble,' Rayleen mused, still savouring her relief. 'Not trouble for us.'

'A missing paper is making trouble amongst the whites,' I agreed.

'My father said, why whites believe in paper? White culture not important enough to remember? Our culture important, so we remember.'

'You remember for generations. Maybe since the Dreaming,' I said.

They nodded solemnly.

'Would you like me to bake you a cake?' I asked. 'You come back in a while, you can eat cake. Chocolate?'

They talked to each other in Djemiranga, and Kathy nodded to Rayleen.

'We have shower?' Rayleen asked. 'No water at home.'

'The water's not connected at your house?'

'Doesn't work. Hasn't for –'

She swept her hand away from her body in a long gesture.

'Why ever not?' I asked.

'Bruce,' they said together, as if his name explained everything.

'Does Bruce know?'

They giggled again.

'I'll get you towels,' I said.

I heard them laughing and singing as they took turns to shower. Their happiness and our new friendship eased my foolish heart. I turned on the oven and mixed a batter for the cake.

I wondered if all women remember their mothers when they're doing these things their mothers did, turning on the oven in readiness, finding the right-sized bowl to mix the batter in, beating the yellow yolks into their transparent whites until they thicken, stirring in the sparkling white crystals of sugar, shaking in the flour that showers the working board like fine confetti and has to be wiped away, the sequence of stirring the batter, buttering the pan, pouring the batter into it, feeling the heat of the oven with the hand and setting the cake tin onto the warm shelf, sweeping the flour dropped on the floor into little white hills afterwards. But it wasn't my mother who was behind every move, it was the amber Diana, for her knowledge and her breasts and her laughter and her flirtatious eyes, and for her murderous jealousy. There between the oven and the table, as I swept up, I wrapped the tea towel around my face and crouched on the floor to be nearer the ground for that sad loss of them all.

'Are you OK?'

I looked up to see Daniel; he was crouching next to me.

'It's about you and Adrian, isn't it?' he said.

'Yes,' I said. 'No.'

He went to the drawer and found a clean, folded tea towel and passed it to me as if it were a handkerchief.

'Adrian and I grew up like brother and sister,' I wept.

'What?' he cried out. 'I never guessed! He's luckier than I thought. To be like your brother.'

'Lucky?' I gazed at him in the midst of my tears. 'Him? I was the one who was lucky. Not him. I was ordinary. He was,' I ran out of words, 'extraordinary.'

'It's true that he's still extraordinary,' said Daniel, 'but also extraordinarily lucky to have grown up with you.'

It came to me again how little I knew Daniel.

He startled me by adding: 'Is that why you stayed out last night?'

'It's why I came here,' I said.

Something seemed to settle in him. He stayed crouching beside me, his legs sticking out, like a giant frog. I shook with a fresh burst of sobs, and he took the tea towel out of my hands to wipe my face again.

'It's why I've done everything I've ever done,' I said.

But next to his warmth my crying seemed to ease, as if it wasn't the deep well of grief it'd always seemed, as if that well had begun to dry up. As if grief was finite, as if it could wane.

'Could you be in trouble too?' I asked him. 'Might you get the sack?'

He shrugged. He'd accept his fate, that shrug said.

'You've tried your best,' I said.

'So has Adrian.'

There came a new burst of laughter from the bathroom. I looked towards it and the girls' laughter seemed to slant down the hall in the same way the rising sun had done on the morning we picked medicine plants. The hallway seemed to be a striped pathway of gold.

'Thank you,' I told Daniel. I hoisted myself up, using his frog knees as a prop. I faltered as the warmth of his leg shot through my hand, up my arm, up and down my body. My errant vagina heaved; dampness fell between my legs. This was no time for lust, I knew, and anyway, whatever Daniel yearned for, a frivolous sexual approach wasn't it. He wanted something deeper, more elusive. I knew all this as if it was written on the wall, as I walked away from him down the happiness-striped hallway. He wanted, like my father, an anchoring love.

I only remembered Anastasia outside the bathroom door.

'Want me to put your clothes in the washing machine?' I called to the girls, my voice breaking. I tried it again and this time I was stronger. 'I'll find you something of mine to wear.'

There was a pause in the giggling, and then Rayleen opened the door, her face fat with smiles, and shoved out a damp bundle of their clothes into my hand.

Daniel was following me.

'What's happening over there?' I indicated the clinic, trying not to stand too near him and feel his heat again.

'It isn't good,' he said, as if he was remembering another world. 'I'd better get back.'

Afterwards I sat with the girls on the verandah to eat cake. They shook glossy wet curls out of their eyes.

'We come every day after school?' they offered. 'We teach you language?'

'I'll make you a cake every day for that. Let's cook it –' they discreetly pretended not to see that my eyes were as wet with tears as their hair, 'in a camp oven, out in the yard. You can tell me how. Not so very different from your mother's dampers. Just a different flavour, and sweeter.'

The insurance agents' troopie drove past.

'Only white trouble,' repeated Rayleen, watching my face for affirmation. I nodded.

Adrian was at the gate. He strode onto the verandah, his features taut.

'Official people are driving out here tomorrow – they arrive at ten – they must think it's so important that for once they'll leave their comfortable homes before dawn! They want a meeting with the mob.'

'The people don't have meetings.'

A wrong note. I shouldn't have taunted him. He was at the door. He wheeled around. And in that moment, at the mention of the mob, it came to me that I should tell him what the girls had told me, that a rumour was inflaming the settlement.

'The girls have just said –'

'What are you doing with them?'

'Having a cuppa,' I said, trying to smile at them to make them comfortable, but feeling very uncomfortable myself. 'But they said –'

'Send them home! This is my house! I need my peace! What they say isn't important! Send them home.'

They leaped up, Rayleen still with a slice of cake in her hand, looking between him and me, her eyes wide, Kathy with an open mouth full of chocolate cake. Adrian strode inside, slamming the front door behind him.

'But they *are* important!' I yelled at him through the door.

'I'm sorry,' I said to them. 'Come tomorrow. We'll have afternoon tea again.'

They'd already stepped off the verandah.

'Don't take any notice of him. He's in shock and exhausted.'

I went inside and found him lying on the sofa, hand over his eyes again.

'How dare you insult them!' I cried.

He was unrepentant.

'You give everyone credence,' he said. 'They're not important.'

I was just about to override him and tell him about the rumour they'd told me but he was in one of his vicious moods.

'Besides, you won't be able to make them your friends. You're no good at intimacy. You try but it doesn't work. People here are experts. They'll run a mile from you.'

This is how he loves.

Stung, I wandered back to the verandah. I tried to switch my mind away from him. I checked my watch. It was just before five, just before office closing time. Looking back, I should've stood my ground with him, I should've gone back inside and insisted on warning him. Or at least I should've told Daniel. But it was easier to think about the lack of water in Libby's house, and I let that distract me.

I was running away from my mind, which drummed: This is how he loves.

The council office was manned by a sweet-faced Aboriginal woman, and another on the phone. It was the first time in the settlement that I'd seen a local sitting in a chair. She pushed it out.

'Bruce?'

'Yes,' I said, smiling at her lovely face in spite of my heavy heart.

Bruce sat in an office papered with lists, names and phone numbers, his toy dog on his lap, his feet on the desk between stacks of paper. His dog was gazing trustingly at his face. I was moved by that gaze. I was full of self-pity and envy.

Neither man nor dog rose for me. But the look Bruce gave me, from my toes to my head, was like a long lick, except that his teeth were bared. I tried not to notice.

'Do you have a moment?' I asked. 'I know it's late.'

'Do we have a moment?' he asked his dog, but in a voice that was a mimicry of mine. 'Do we?'

I felt foolish, because his mimicry seemed to mock my politeness, as if politeness was absurd. I decided that he'd probably had a long hard day – he'd probably worked as Adrian did from five or six in the morning and now it was time for his little joke.

He spoke as if his dog had answered.

'We probably have a moment.'

He played at giving me all his attention, and even moved his dog's head around so that the dog could gaze at me, but the dog yelped at such a twist, so he shoved the dog's body around to face me properly.

'Thank you,' I said, not knowing if this was intended to put me at ease or to disconcert me. Bruce's face was deeply tanned and unlined, so his white curly hair was a shock, but as he leaned his head near the dog, its coat of white curls seemed like an extension of him. I asked if I could sit down, mainly so that I could hide my body and avoid a second lick.

He nodded, lifted his foot and kicked another chair in my direction.

I was determined to find nothing unusual in addressing four pairs of eyes, two of them canine. I wondered briefly if I should make small talk about whether the dog had been menaced by the other dogs when it had arrived out here, but words failed me and I came to the point immediately.

'Rayleen and Kathy were just visiting me,' I started.

'And who might they be?'

He asked this of the dog. The dog gazed at him unblinkingly.

'Oh, those young girls.' He replied, nodding to the dog as if the dog had told him. 'Pretty young things.'

I could've sworn the dog nodded.

'They're relatives of Libby. And when they asked me if they could have a shower, they told me there was no running water at Libby's house and hasn't been for a while.'

At that moment, everything changed. The game with the dog stopped. 'Why were they at your house?' he asked.

'I invited them. Also, most people don't have power – but you might already know that.'

'You had them in your bathroom? Were there men in the house?'

'The girls asked to have a shower!' I cried.

'Ha!' he snorted in disbelief. 'You got a permit to be here?'

I explained that I was invited to record a special song only women could hear. I told him that Collins had invited me.

'That happy-clapper!'

'Skeleton welcomed me. But that's not the point – I wondered if you knew the problem about the running water,' I said. 'And the power.'

'It is the point. You get a permit from Central Land Council, or you get out.'

'It's Skeleton's land,' I said.

'But it's Central Land Council's permit. Have I made my point?'

'Of course,' I said. I tried to mollify him. After all, I was here for Libby's family, not for an argument. I asked him for a permit application form, adding that I'd have to contact my university and ask them to apply.

'They'd better get a move on,' he said. 'Get them to fax it by the end of the week. Or you'll be out.'

I stood to leave.

I was surprised that he took his feet off the desk, and unfolded himself out of his chair, as if he still remembered how to be a gentleman. But in his sudden movement, the dog fell to the floor, yelping in a tumbled heap, its toenails scrabbling. It didn't seem to know how to get up.

I bent to help it. But I froze because he'd risen to the full height of his anger.

'How dare you speak to me without a permit!' he cried, his voice rising above the dog's scrabbling. 'You left-winger university types, no one knows what you'd get up to! Encouraging young girls to take off their clothes in your house! You live in your ivory tower but I have to deal with the real world. You want to know why these Indigenous people don't have running water? Or power? Because I give them three chances. Three strikes and they're out! I say, you throw disposable nappies down the toilets and block them – three times running – so I have to get plumbers out here – and you know what – you'll have no toilet! See how you feel about that! And if they don't pay their power bills, the same! Do you think the government gives me dozens of plumbers to run and fix their stinking toilets?'

The dog whimpered, but his voice overrode it.

'That family, I remember them well, I gave them three chances, and they took no notice of me. I'm a generous man – and on the fourth time, I switched off their water. Now – get out!'

I left his office, the dog still whimpering. As I walked out the door, the women politely downcast their eyes. On the way home, I glimpsed Adrian at the end of the street, talking to a black woman, and for the first time, I saw that he was only an ordinary man.

He stayed at the clinic all evening, and Daniel stayed with him. I forgot to mention the rumour.

Chapter 22

I worked in my bedroom late that night. When I looked out my window, Adrian's mattress glowed white in the moonlight, like a scar on the dark body of the desert, a scar that wouldn't heal. He didn't come to lie on it.

At breakfast, the phone rang. Adrian and Daniel were eating muesli, moodily. They were eating in unison, both spoons going into their mouths together, both spoons dipping into their bowls. Adrian passed the phone over to me.

'A friend of yours,' he said ironically.

It was Craig. We exchanged greetings, and then he said he was holding a meeting that morning to discuss what might be going wrong between the school and the settlement – if anything was wrong. He'd like as many whites to attend as possible – would anyone from the clinic be available?

I looked at the grim faces of Daniel and Adrian and said that no one was available today, only me.

'Don't stay out long,' said Adrian as I poured a second cup of tea.

'Why not?' I asked.

'If they sack me,' he said, 'I'll leave straight away.'

'How likely is another sacking?' I asked, keeping my voice light. 'Your twenty-first?'

'The mob love me, but can you always depend on love?' he asked.

There was no amusement in his laugh.

'And Daniel?'

'Daniel follows my orders,' said Adrian.

Daniel and Adrian walked together to the clinic, as they seldom did, in step with each other, and even that seemed ominous. I kept watching the road out my window, but no unfamiliar car had arrived by the time I was due to leave for the meeting. There was no one on the streets, and when I reached the school, no children. It came as a surprise to walk into a hubbub of voices in the staff room, a ring of people on chairs. Bruce was nearest the door, his white toy dog on his lap. I noticed for the first time how listless the dog was, how empty-eyed. Beside Bruce was Kana, the Japanese student, and next to her was Dudley, the teacher from the outstation whom I hadn't met. He was almost as young as Kana, still boyishly thin and lanky, with full red lips and a prettiness about the eyes, round-cheeked and shy.

Bruce didn't return my nod, as if he didn't remember me from last night. Beth emerged from a dark corner.

'Queen Kate has graced us with her presence,' she called to Craig, who was at his desk writing notes.

'I'm to take down proceedings,' said Craig, coming over with a notebook.

He turned the empty chair back-to-front and leaned over it to effect a casual air, while he thanked us for coming.

'My masters want me to find out why this community refuses education. I'm to ask you: is the school doing anything wrong? And to write down your answers. I'll ask each person,' he added.

'Should we watch our words?' asked Dudley hesitantly 'Might this affect our standing with the Department?'

'Not at all, speak out, say your mind, don't be timid,' said Craig. 'The Department wants your thoughts. But hurry. I've got higher duties,' he added with a proud smile, inclining his head towards his house.

'The baby has a temperature.'

He took a pen out of his pocket, clicked it, and tried it out on the notebook to check it hadn't dried up.

'I'll go first,' said Beth. She looked in Craig's direction, though not into his face. She was more grim and forbidding than ever.

'Though I've taught in Indigenous communities before, this one is more degraded than most,' she said to him, and we heard between her words the scratching of his pen. He bowed his head in agreement. 'Let's face it, education is boring, but the kids just have to accept it's boring. The parents don't accept that, so the kids don't.'

'Do you want me to write down that education is boring?' asked Craig, the pen hovering above the page. There was a hint of a smile on his lips.

'It's the people's fault. I want you to write that,' she answered.

Dudley had leaned forward, his natural shyness conquered by excitement and perhaps a sense of purpose.

'Dudley?'

'I've been approached by the mob.'

I was wondering where he'd learned to call them that – perhaps from Adrian. He was the sort of person who'd be sensitive to nuances, and he'd want to please.

'Your pupils' parents?'

'Yes – no, not entirely by the parents, mainly the grandmothers,' he said. 'You know how important they are.'

He was speaking quickly, his face shining. 'They want me to start a shop!'

'A shop? On school premises?'

'Not necessarily! I could do it under a tree! It's for when there's nothing around to hunt – when there's a bad season. Sometimes the kids have to go without dinner – they all do. Then they turn up exhausted and hungry – if they turn up at all.'

'You want to leave teaching and be a shopkeeper?'

Dudley seemed confused by Craig's line of questioning. It

came to me that perhaps he hadn't crossed swords with Craig before.

'No – not at all'

He tried a laugh. I was nodding vigorously to encourage him, but no one else was. Beth was looking out the window, and Bruce was glaring. Kana's eyes were swivelling between them.

'Just to help them. Lunchtimes and after school. Just flour and sugar and tea.'

Dudley took Craig's indrawn breath as sympathy.

'The mob out there, they don't have a Bruce to help them. And if someone doesn't help them, the kids can't attend school.' This he said with a flash of a smile at Bruce, who kept glaring.

Craig still said nothing, so Dudley felt he had to explain further.

'Look, I sort things out for them already, make phone calls for them to government departments, bureaucrats that need translating –'

'You speak Djemiranga?' I broke in, excited, hoping to improve his standing in the group's eyes.

'Bureaucrats don't speak English!'

I couldn't help myself.

'That'd be right. Bureaucrats are prone to using abstract nouns, and there doesn't seem to be any "could've been" or "should've been" here – no sense of how the future could've been different –'

No one was listening to me, not even Dudley.

'Or I sort out plumbing and fix things, like if something electrical breaks down, not that they have many electrical things –' He saw a storm in Craig's face and hurried on: 'It's in my own time, I assure you. I teach vocabulary while I do it, you know, because the kids are always around while I'm helping out – I have a good tool kit – it's teaching too but in a practical way – that's the way they teach kids – like, the other day I was using a spirit level, and it allowed me to teach the kids "level", "bubble", "flat" – oh I made a mistake at first and called it a spirit level –'

He laughed shortly, looked at our faces. 'I won't do that again ...' He wound down.

'That's why you're never here,' said Craig.

'Oh, I often sleep in the car – I've made it quite comfortable ...'

'You sleep in a government-issued car? The point is, your time is not your own,' said Craig. 'Teachers are given short hours so they have time to prepare and mark! You should be returning to your desk and marking!'

'But there's nothing to mark; they can't write –'

Craig ignored him.

'More importantly, we're not insured for this. There are health and safety issues here! What if you got electrocuted? What if you made a mistake with a government department – we could be in legal trouble,' Craig said. 'And you were planning to use your government car to transport your shop goods, weren't you?'

'If that'd make a difference, I could use my own car, though those rough roads –'

'I had no idea this was going on! If the people out there can't cope with everyday life, they should come back to this settlement.'

Bruce said: 'Craig's absolutely right. They should come back here, or better still, live in town where of course we'll provide them with all services.'

Craig checked his watch. Something about the time this meeting was taking place inspired him to soften.

'All right. Go ahead. But don't use the Department's car, don't use the Department's time, and don't expose the Department in any way to the threat of legal action. Or I'll have no choice but to inform the Department.'

Dudley bent double in his chair, so we could barely see his face.

'Yes?'

There was a long pause. His hands were clenched.

'I can't let them down,' said his muffled voice.

'Yes?'

Another long pause.

'Yes.'

The cry of a crow startled us in the playground, or perhaps it was the wail of a young child. Craig cocked his ear, looked at his watch, and though he spoke rapidly, his face had softened. He spoke to us all.

'My passion is to improve the IQ of these people, too – as you all know.'

His words were now coming so fast, he sounded like a horseracing commentator.

'Dudley – a noble, manly, egalitarian solution is to put on barbeques. You may use the Department car for Community Relations to transport the meat and equipment. While you're all eating together you can discuss problems, or do a bit of handyman teaching – and you'll have witnesses. I'll help you with the requisitions. We'll even put in for kangaroo tails. Kana?'

Kana declined to give her opinion about the school.

'I don't know any black adults here,' she said in a low voice. 'I don't know how to meet them. I've only met the children.'

'Bruce?'

His dog jerked as if it had been summoned, and panted while Bruce spoke.

'We fuss about them too much. We wouldn't mollycoddle whites like this –'

Bruce was drowned out by the crying of babies. The door swung open. Framed by the light was a very slight, very pretty teenager, the girl of the photo on Craig's desk, wheeling a stroller with a yelling baby and a toddler in it, like two noisy birds in a nest clamouring for food. She clearly was from

South-East Asia: Craig's land, I suddenly remembered, of the world's highest IQs.

Bruce stood up in an old-fashioned courtly way, smiling, holding his toy dog. Beth shrank back into the shadows. Only Dudley, beaten, didn't move a muscle.

But the girl looked nowhere but at Craig, as if she was unaware of us all. She frowned at him, her face still pretty despite the puckering around her smooth forehead, eyes and mouth. There was a long tunnel between them the way that sometimes when people are newly in love, the air between the two seems to sing with light. The only sound was the accusatory screams of the children.

'Darling, I'm sorry,' Craig said. His voice was hoarse, though somehow it carried across all our heads and above the screams. He was stuttering. 'We started late. I had to deal with complex issues – but they're over with.'

Under the gaze of all of us, he put his arm around her.

He bent his face to hers. 'I'm so sorry,' he said tenderly. 'How's her fever now?'

All the tension left her body, and she melted into him, her pretty face glowing. She nodded.

'Better?' he asked.

She nodded again. They seemed to fold into each other.

'I haven't spoken.' I got to my feet, toppling a chair. The crash startled them all, the lovers, the dog – who uttered a single yelp – and the screaming children. Even Dudley looked up. The older child's mouth slammed shut, and the baby girl, seeing her older brother startled into silence, slammed her little mouth shut as well. My voice strained thin.

'Was Libby asked to this meeting?' I asked Craig. 'She could tell us a thing or two. Or Quentin?'

'The meeting was for whites!' He momentarily dropped his arm from around Sabah. 'We were trying to work out what we whites are doing wrong – if anything,' he looked at his wife, smiling at her, and she smiled back, forgiving him. His smile was appeasing, I recognised, for I had smiled that way so many times.

'You invited me here,' I said, trying to clear my throat, trying to clear away the years of doing what was expected of me, speaking fast before the children began crying again. 'So you ought to hear me out.'

Then my mind went blank. I had no words.

'Well?' demanded Bruce, and both he and his dog were glaring at me. 'Get a move on.'

'The school –' I began, stumbled, began again. 'Dudley's right. We have to hold them, in reciprocity, now that they can't live in the old ways. If we want them to value our values, we can't at the same time hunt them away.'

Craig and Bruce both echoed 'Hunt them away?' Beth did the same, her voice higher, like a soprano soaring above the bass voices, 'Hunt them away?'

Only Dudley smiled.

There was a plop. The toy dog, forgotten by Bruce, after clawing at his trousers desperately, nails screeching, had slid to the floor. It landed in a whimpering scramble of back legs and front paws and tail, as it had the day before, except that even on the floor, its eyes were suddenly wide with life, almost whirring in their sockets, as if the mention of hunting stirred some long-forgotten memory.

'What do you mean, hunt?' demanded Bruce.

The toy dog barked, not a yelp but a hunting bark as if it was agreeing. The toddler yelled 'Hunt!', his baby sister glanced at him and tried to mimic him, but could only produce a gurgle. Then they both began howling. Sabah, seeing that Craig was distracted, pulled away from him, yanked at the stroller's handles and wheeled it in a U-turn but stopped as its wheels tangled in Beth's bag on the floor.

Craig sprang forward, eager to help, untangled the bag and hurled it away, where it slithered against the wall. Sabah wheeled her way out, and he hurried after her, forgetting to farewell us. Seconds later, he popped his head back through the door.

'What you're all saying is that we've done everything that can be done. Yes?'

He slammed the door behind him, shutting us in together.

'Can't you imagine how lonely it is for that girl?' Bruce roared at me. 'Craig does his best, but we've all got to help, or she'll go right back to her mother.'

I smelled the barbecue outside the clinic before I saw it. The sweet-faced woman from the council was turning over chops. As we exchanged smiles, there was uproar behind her. I pushed open the clinic door.

The waiting room was crowded with a hubbub of black people sitting cross-legged on the floor. I sat down next to Libby.

'Government woman,' she whispered.

Sister and Gillian were on chairs at the far side. At the door of the doctor's room were two white men in business suits and a woman, all sitting on chairs. The woman was answering a question someone had put to her.

'You people have to compensate the government for the destruction of property,' she said. A fair-haired white man I hadn't seen before listened to her, turned and spoke to the people in Djemiranga. He seemed to know them well because he was naming them in a comforting way. With a jolt I wondered if he was Collins, at last, brought back by the crisis. Beside him towered Skeleton in his cowboy shirt and jeans, now so thin that he seemed to hover, almost already a desert spirit. Then my heart thumped again to see Adrian slumped against the wall, folded in upon himself, head bowed so that his grey hair flared in the light, eyes downcast. I'd never seen him so still. It was almost as if he had given his energy to Skeleton. I knew it immediately: he was waiting to be hunted away.

The older of the businessmen cleared his throat. He was a tall man of about sixty, with a gnarled, beaten face.

'We haven't got all day,' he interrupted, just as Dora asked Collins a question in Djemiranga, merely a meaningless noise to the man, no doubt, so he ignored her. He leaned towards Collins, who glanced between him and Dora. Collins' mouth was open, ready to speak to her, ready to attend also to the white man.

'It's a long drive back,' the man said. 'We'd like to be home before midnight. Can we wrap this up?'

Collins said a word to Dora and then turned to the man.

'The people need to understand clearly what's been said,' Collins said to him. 'I'll translate it as fast as possible.'

'You're wasting our time. We've already stated our proposition as simply as it can be put,' the white man said, so I knew he hadn't brought Collins out to translate their proposals. As Adrian had explained, there was no cognisance of or sympathy for the local lack of English.

'This clinic manager before us is entirely unsatisfactory. The people must either pay for the rebuilding of the house, or they must agree to sack him,' the white man said.

'How much would they need to find?' Collins asked him.

'You know the costs around here. About $500,000.'

Collins turned back to the people, and explained in Djemiranga what had been said. It seemed to take a long time, to the businessmen's exasperation, the way they glanced at each other and eased their ties. I could only make out the odd word, but I heard the English clearly again and again in single digits, '$500,000.'

People interceded with Collins, and he turned back to the white men.

'These are poor people. They scarcely have money to feed their families. They don't have banks. They don't have mortgages. They can't possibly get hold of $500,000.'

The white man had a ready answer.

'We've made enquiries. Their land could be mortgaged for precisely that sum and, after due process of law, turned into a small pastoral lease,' he said. 'Or – I've brought with me –' he touched the shoulder of the man next to him, a sweating man who nodded at the crowd and stretched his lips in what he hoped was a friendly grin, 'a representative of a mining company that could well be very interested.'

The man nodded.

'We'd be very interested to help out,' he said in English. 'We've renewed our interest in mining this area.'

Collins turned back to the people and was part way through the translation, which caused an uproar, when Skeleton stepped forward. The uproar faded into silence, the silence deepened. The white men ceased their huffing.

Skeleton waited, majestic, commanding utter silence. He drew himself up to his full height. Even the air gave him its attention.

He half-turned to the white men, and half to the crowd. He had made a decision, and he wanted everyone to hear it. He spoke slowly and clearly, remembering, word by word, his English from his stockman youth.

'Adrian is a good man. A good friend to Aboriginal people. Done my people a lot of good.'

He took a deep breath, and looked back at Adrian, who seemed to slide further towards the floor. He knew even Skeleton couldn't save him, no one could save him now.

'A good, good man.'

Skeleton let the words linger, wrap around us all, around the government woman, the white men in their suits and loosened ties, around his people. He spoke with such gravity it made us all consider goodness, its nature, its worth, and most of all, its rarity.

'Very good. The best.'

Another silence.

'But –' He paused. 'Sadly, we give him back to you.'

There was a murmur from the crowd. But he hadn't finished. He stamped, a bare-footed, two-footed stamp that a white person would never do, almost as if he was about to begin a traditional ceremonial dance on a dark night. His long arms, his bare black feet with their pink soles, all of him made me think of the earth beneath the white man's floorboards, of the country of his ancestors, where his ancestral elders walked tens of thousands of years ago in the Dreaming, creating on their walk its rocks, its boulders, its mountains, its plains, its rivers.

'We give him back. Just –' He paused again, as any proud leader would do, and the air was cowed, electric with listening. 'Just give us the dirt.'

'The *dirt*?' the businessman called.

Skeleton had spoken. He didn't repeat himself.

There was utter silence, but I couldn't bear to stay. The door creaked like a scream as I left. I walked past the barbecue and over to our house where the donkey was trying to figure out how to get inside the gate. I gently pushed the animal out of the way, went inside, then stood at the gate and fed it the tufts of the soft grass it liked. Time passed; I didn't know how long we stood there, as I pulled at long grasses and fed a quietly munching donkey. After a while, Daniel and the blond translator were beside me.

'Adrian's got to go by nightfall,' Daniel told me.

'How did the people take it?' I asked him.

'They're grieving,' he said. 'Mandy in particular. She thinks that the bad spirits are punishing the community for her rebellion.'

'What rebellion?'

'Wanting a medicine plant forest, instead of going to gather it where it grows naturally,' said the translator. 'That's why I wasn't able to scotch the rumour.'

'What rumour?' I asked, my heart clamouring.

'People here were convinced those men were from the government, and they'd take away their land.'

'They weren't from the government?' I asked.

'Only the woman, a minor ex-bureaucrat who was sacked long ago. No, that was a little pantomime cooked up between the insurers and the mining company and someone's girlfriend. It was totally illegal. But I just couldn't get that through. I came too late.'

His fair hair rushed out almost upright from his scalp, as if it couldn't bear the turmoil in his mind.

'I couldn't convince the mob that they wouldn't be punished for the fire,' he added. 'That's why Skeleton exchanged Adrian for the land. I'm Collins, by the way. I'm sorry it's taken so long to get back. I had a family crisis but I knew I could leave Adrian to help you. I heard about what was happening and I raced out here to try to stop the disaster.'

We turned away from each other and watched the people stream down the road. They were walking slowly, not talking, almost the funeral march I'd seen when Skeleton fell sick.

'Does Adrian know?' I asked.

'I can't get through to him, either. The sacking's illegitimate, he doesn't have to leave. How did the recording go?' Collins thought to ask me.

'I've been getting, let's say, oriented,' I said. 'First.' I allowed myself to add: 'Adrian thought that was wise.' It was almost difficult to say his name, as if it'd become sacred.

Collins nodded. He had brown eyes that squinted in the desert sun, almost as bright as his hair, so my eyes moved distractedly between them, his brown eyes and his upright hair. But I settled on his eyes because they had kindly crinkles at their corners.

'I knew about the rumour,' I confessed. 'I tried to tell Adrian, but he wouldn't listen.'

'I know what you mean,' said Collins, 'but the old lady – don't put it off any longer,' he warned. 'She's near death, I'm told.'

'I'll take you in tomorrow,' said Daniel quickly, seeing my face.

'She's not in Alice Springs any more. Her family has taken Tillie home to die,' Collins told us both.

In the dirt road, I panicked. I tried to calm myself, but I couldn't let E.E. Albert down, I was her fieldworker. I must get there, I must get there today.

'The people like it that you didn't rush in, grab what you came for and rush away. Adrian advised you well,' Collins was saying. 'Getting to know them.'

Daniel and I avoided each other's eyes.

I walked into the kitchen. A troopie key dangled, waiting for me to take it and go to the outstation and record the dying old lady. But it was forbidden to take the troopie. Besides, Adrian's imperatives were more important than mine. He'd feel he had to leave by nightfall. He must go in the troopie. There were two troopies, it was true, but if I took one, he'd have to take the other, then what if there was an accident?

I wandered down the hall, trembling with indecision. Adrian was pulling things out of the high cupboard in my room. An avalanche had fallen around him, wads of paper, documents, old newspapers, press releases for new medical equipment that the clinic could buy.

'Sorry for the mess,' he said. 'But you won't need this room any more.'

I saw, amongst the papers, Medicare claim forms.

'I don't know when I'll be back,' Adrian was saying. 'I'll talk it over with you on the way in to Alice. Throw your things in your bag. We're leaving tonight.'

Daniel came to the door.

'Adrian – you don't have to go.'

Adrian kept rummaging on the floor, amongst the mess, ignoring him.

'I'll take the troopie,' he answered, making arrangements as he'd done for years. 'You'll need to come in with patients later on in the week, and then you can take someone to drive my troopie, to bring it back out.'

Daniel lingered at the doorway.

'I'm sorry –' he began, and dropped into silence. 'I don't know how –' He interrupted himself. 'The missing Medicare forms! I knew as much. And –' he was propelled into the room by his discovery, 'isn't that the insurance company letterhead? There! The missing form we never filled in!' His eyes were spots of light. His jaw slackened. I saw on his lips:

How could you do this to us, to me, to yourself?

How could I bear your stupidity?

You were my loyal friend.

But those words died. He swallowed the words, I watched his thick lips crinkle as he swallowed them.

Adrian, oblivious, kept rummaging.

But Daniel couldn't help himself. Though he hadn't been able to say anything about this rupture in their friendship, he could talk about the forms. He picked up the insurance paper.

'Why did you never send the paper in? They'd just about filled in all the difficult bits – look, it's just got yellow stickers saying "sign here" – look! Why didn't you? Or why didn't you let me?' He thrust them in Adrian's face, the toy-like yellow stickers with arrows. 'Why? Why?'

He allowed himself another sally: 'You blame me but it's all because of you!'

Adrian swooped along a shelf and another pile of documents fell down. Daniel had to jump out of the way.

'Aha!' Adrian shouted, deaf to all but his search.

'Listen to me!' Daniel's fists were raised, he was about to punch Adrian. But Adrian was gazing at a photo.

'It's him,' he said.

He gazed for so long that Daniel gave up and walked away, slamming the door. Adrian was used to slamming doors and took no notice. I looked over his shoulder.

It was the photo missing all those years ago from the drawer at our house: the photo of the miner with black people around him.

Greetings from Gadaburumili. Wish you were here.

'Where'd you get this?' I managed to mumble, the dusty drawer, the river, my mother's sad words all filling my mind so that I could hardly speak.

'Your father brought it round. Diana admitted it. It's him. It's my father. That's how I tried to track him down.'

'So my father took it to your place! Why?'

He glanced at my bewildered face.

'The man who sacked me was my father.'

I gasped, looked harder, tried to remember the man's face at the meeting.

'I can't be sure. I don't think so. But his name – did you see his card? Did you catch his name?'

His voice was high, angry. 'I'd know my own father, wouldn't I? What's it matter what his name is?' And then, even in his agony: 'I keep trying to get through to you – a name is only a word, and words don't matter.'

I heard the ordinary sounds of the outside world. I heard two women walking by on the road, talking. I heard a car driving by. I heard Daniel screaming in the hall: 'Bastard, bastard, bastard!' banging his fists, perhaps his head against the wall. I didn't know if life was the bastard, or if Adrian was the bastard, or if Daniel was cursing his disastrous compliance with Adrian's demands, or his enchantment, or his inaction. I suspected he was cursing himself. Because it so closely mirrored my own, his pain to me was greater than Adrian's. I couldn't move with the pain. My limbs seemed weighted.

'Could you follow him? Contact him?'

'What? Beg him for favours?'

'You followed him before.'

'He sacked his own son – for a scam.'

He crumpled it in his hand till it was a ball.

'No!' I shouted. 'Keep it.'

He laughed. I'd never heard such bitterness in a laugh. He threw the ball across the floor. 'Skeleton's love meant nothing.'

'But he showed how much he values you!'

He grabbed me.

'You know I've always loved you. We'll start again, just the two of us. You've got no reason to stay. This thing about recording the song for universities, in the long run it doesn't matter to the mob. It's our sense of history, not theirs. It's all just our temporary paper culture, not their eternal one.'

Remember how he loves, my mind said. My mind seemed stuck inside the words.

I turned and walked out the door, slowly down the hall, past the sloshing washing machine and out to the verandah where I sank in a plastic chair, exhausted.

At last I knew who the owner of our river house was, the owner of all the deserted river houses probably, the owner who I always expected to turn up, the owner who never turned up.

Diana was his wife, and you were his son.

Diana had owned and controlled all our lives.

Daniel stalked past me and up the road with such a weight on his shoulders, they were hunched. Rayleen and Kathy happened to be walking by at that moment. They stopped him, asking him questions. As I looked at the kindly, unassuming bend of Daniel's head, a flash of sheer affection went through me, a lightning flash.

Apart from Rayleen and Kathy, the rest of the settlement seemed deserted. Surely nothing else could go wrong for the next few hours? I thought of Daniel's lack of rebellion. I decided on mine. Once you lose your enchantment, rebellion is only a matter of a few simple steps. I stood, doubled back, went into the kitchen, and grabbed the forbidden key. I was walking out the door just as Adrian emerged from the bedroom and saw me. I folded my fingers around the key.

'You know I'm your anchoring love.'

I flinched. He'd remembered my father's phrase. He'd always remembered everything.

My mind hammered: Remember how he loves.

'Go and pack.'

It took a while for me to find my voice. It wasn't my usual conciliatory voice, eager to appease.

'I'm not coming with you.'

'But you owe everything to me!' he cried. He was standing so close, I realised how puny I was against him.

Nevertheless, I managed: 'That's probably true.' Before he could say another word, I headed out the gate.

Chapter 23

Only one troopie was parked at the clinic. I heard Sister inside, telling Gillian off for something. I opened the driver's door silently. It barely creaked on its hinges. The clinic door was flung open. I froze. Gillian happened to come out holding a bin. She didn't notice me. I turned the ignition key. The troopie roared. Gillian spun around, took in the sight of me as the driver and dropped the bin in astonishment, paper spilling.

She glanced back over her shoulder at Sister's voice.

'She'll kill you!' she hissed. The bin clanked down the driveway.

'Come with me,' I hissed. 'I'm recording the song.'

She wavered. She decided.

'OK,' she said. She ran over, hiked up her straight-skirted nurse's uniform and, almost bare-legged, clambered in.

'Fast,' she said. She thought to slip down below the level of the window, just in time.

'Want to keep my job, if there's a job to be kept,' she said as Sister, alerted by the engine, poked her head out the door. Sister opened her mouth to shout at me, but she was suddenly as ineffective as she feared, silenced by the motor that I gunned.

'She'll want to send the spare troopie after you, but Adrian will need it,' said Gillian. 'And she's bound to demand the police come after you but they'll only laugh.'

'Collins just told me that the old singer's at the outstation and about to die,' I said. 'It's Tillie.'

'So it's now or never,' said Gillian.

We bounced along the shortcut, across pasture land, across long shadows.

'Want me to drive?' she asked. 'It'd be more legal.'

'No,' I said.

'So I might as well enjoy myself.'

She leaned back, kicked off her shoes, planted her bare feet with their squared toes up on the dashboard.

'Got the recorder?'

I dared to take a hand off the wheel and pat my pocket.

'Always, these days,' I said.

'How long do you think it'll take?' she asked. She fished a pack of peppermints out of her pocket, poured a jolting pile into her hand and threw them into her mouth.

'Open up.'

She poured another pile of mints into my mouth.

'Maybe half an hour,' I said, sucking and crunching. 'Maybe all night. Depends.'

I asked her about Sister's daughter and found out that Sister always took her to desert settlements.

'She could have fun out here but she can't play with other kids. Fears anyone touching her, loud noises, all sorts of fears. Just a computer nerd.'

'Do you think I could visit her?' I asked. 'She might enjoy my parsing software.'

Gillian laughed. 'If Sister ever forgives you!'

We parked outside Tillie's house and waited at the gate, as Adrian taught me to do. Tillie's daughter was sitting cross-legged in front of a cooking fire in her yard, but the ashes were cold. She looked up, and smiled as she recognised Gillian.

'Hello, Carmen,' said Gillian.

Carmen gazed at me, then smiled slowly.

I showed her my recorder.

'Mother,' I said in her language. 'Sing.'

She nodded slowly. She must've been waiting all that time, since before the letter hung on the university noticeboard, since E.E. Albert decided that I was the one to send, since I came here almost four weeks ago.

'Where's your mother?' Gillian asked her in English. She spoke with the easy assurance that at least some of her English would be understood, at least the important words. She'd have learned that assurance from Adrian.

There was a table in the yard, a door on empty flour tins. Otherwise the yard was empty. There was no rubbish piled against a back fence, trying to free itself to blow across the desert, because there was no back fence.

'On the verandah?' Gillian peered around. It might be rude in their culture to peer like that, but whites were excused a lot because of our ignorance of their manners. There were mattresses on the verandah, with a tumble of blankets, but otherwise, just a broad stretch of cement, red with desert dust. 'Or inside?'

I dredged up the word in Djemiranga, so it was like an echo: 'Inside?' It seemed more polite in her language.

The woman, assuming I had more language than the odd word, as if she thought I was deliberately so monosyllabic – child-like, I remembered, if one didn't use the travel affix – spoke to me in Djemiranga while she got nimbly to her feet. She was still smiling, so whatever she felt about the long delay since her request, she wasn't showing it. Her bare feet raised little clouds of dust.

I scarcely had time to take in the central room, its cement floor bare of furniture, of clothes, or anything but red grit, its bare walls, darkened with children's prints of gleeful hands, before we were led into a room shrouded by blankets nailed up against the window light. There, on an old-fashioned mattress of the type that was covered in a black-and-white striped fabric, lay my singer, her old dress puckered up to her knobbly knees, her only comfort a blanket lying beside the mattress. Outstretched, she was almost the skeleton she was about to become.

Her daughter bent over her, took her limp hand, and gently spoke to her, again and again, calling to her, calling, calling, Djemiranga words I didn't know, perhaps her bush name, the name that whites aren't told. We stood on the other side of her.

'Is she in a coma?' I whispered to Gillian. I hadn't thought of Gillian's expertise in medicine when I invited her, not till that moment.

Gillian shrugged. 'We might be too late.'

Carmen, never quite taking her gaze off her mother, told me many things, but she spoke so quickly that I couldn't understand any of them. I heard the word for 'not', for negating, and I thought she was saying that her mother could not hear any more, could not eat, could not speak.

Gillian knelt down, smiled at Carmen as a request for her permission, then felt the old woman's pulse and put her head against the old woman's withered chest. She looked around at me.

'She's still with us – just.' She raised the old woman's head ever so carefully, and went to give her a sip of water from the bottle.

'No,' said her daughter.

She held her hand out for the bottle. Gillian handed it over, expecting her to lift it to the woman's lips and fearing it might make Tillie choke. But Carmen had done it many times that day, perhaps many times in the past hour. She lifted the water to her own lips as if she wanted a drink – but no, she didn't swallow but bent over her mother's face, brought her own face so close that they were almost kissing, and allowed a few drops of water to dribble from her mouth into her mother's mouth. The simple, practised gesture brought tears to my eyes. We waited through a moment of terrible suspense. Water ran down the old woman's chin, as if she'd been rained on. Then we saw her old throat moving, swallowing. The daughter bent over again, and again fed her mother the water. The mother again swallowed. Carmen looked around at us and spoke, though again, what she said I couldn't understand.

'Can she eat?' Gillian asked her. She mimed eating. 'Damper?'

Carmen shook her head: no.

'This way?' Gillian mimed food passing from Carmen's mouth to her mother's mouth.

Carmen nodded no.

Gillian sat back on her heels.

'Her singing days are over,' she said to me. 'Everything's over, or nearly.'

On my knees as well, I looked between them, at Gillian in her uniform, at the resigned, patient, middle-aged daughter, at the dying woman.

A word popped into my head. It seemed an order, but Dora had taught me that orders aren't necessarily impolite – besides, I couldn't manage any complicated language.

'Sing,' I said to Carmen in Djemiranga.

Carmen looked startled.

'What are you saying?' asked Gillian.

'I'm asking Carmen to sing,' I explained.

'Carmen won't know the song,' said Gillian reasonably. 'That's the whole problem, isn't it, that the song hasn't been passed on.'

'But she might have heard some of it,' I argued. 'In her childhood, maybe. Just a line or two.'

'This isn't like white culture, where a mother might be blithely humming a song while she does the washing-up, and the children overhear it,' said Gillian, speaking with passion and certainty.

'These songs are shrouded in secrecy. They control things, they're magic. That's why men mustn't hear them. That's what I was telling you, it mustn't fall into the wrong hands. It could even put the wrong listener in danger. Tillie must've been through the ceremonies and earned the right to sing it. For whatever reason, Carmen didn't go through the ceremonies. She may regret it now but she has no right, not even to ever have heard it –'

We were interrupted by a sound. We looked around. Carmen was leaning over her mother, so that she was almost lying on top of the old woman. At first I thought that she was feeding her mother more water. I could only see the side of her head, her profile against the old woman's. She seemed to suck air loudly in through her teeth in a way I hadn't heard before. Then, from her mouth came not water, but what seemed to be almost a wail. She was wailing for her mother's death, I thought, but suddenly the wail changed note, then became a rhythm. There were words I almost recognised amongst what I heard as a stream of sound.

Carmen was singing.

I turned my recorder on. At least, I thought sadly, I'd record this fragment of a daughter's memory. At least that would be something to give E.E. Albert for her belief in me. And the Dean, of course.

Carmen paused, took a breath, kept singing. I was checking my recorder, checking the digital numbers, so I wasn't quite watching what happened next. What I was aware of was another sound, a creaking, breathless, whispering but more practised sound. I whirled to see.

From her bare mattress, the old lady had begun to sing. I watched her throat, not taking in water then, but giving out her song, the song she had been born to sing. Her voice swelled, she found her notes, it was like no music I'd ever heard except for the night of the ceremony. It wasn't just notes she was singing, she was singing a song full of remembered words, and perhaps amongst them was the ancient grammar that might or might not have changed, that might tell whites many things about her language, the way of life of her ancestors, about their ancient beliefs. Daniel's face and his words flashed through my mind. The oldest surviving song!

The old woman paused, took a rattling breath. I thought she was going to stop, but no, she kept going, more notes, a new stream of notes and words. Carmen's voice had dropped away, perhaps she didn't know any more, perhaps she was ashamed or fearful of the little she knew, but her job was done. Her mother kept singing. Gillian reached over to me and held my hand. I dared to reach across the old woman's body and hold Carmen's hand. Tears were sheeting down all our faces.

There was a movement in the old woman's legs, more than a twitch, almost a jump.

Gillian started, almost jumped as well, and mimed to Carmen to help her lift the old singer's body.

'No,' Carmen said.

'We must help her up,' whispered Gillian over the singing.

Carmen explained in Djemiranga that Tillie couldn't get up, couldn't walk – I followed that much, and then I lost the sense. But the old woman's legs still jumped. It was as if she was already walking over her country, though she was lying on her back. We had no choice but to lift her, we all lifted her, but one of us could easily have done it on our own, for she was such a slight, pitiful weight, scarcely a human weight at all, she was more like a long, heavily boned, fragile bird. We all yearned to help this fragile bird to fly. We all put our arms around her.

The song faded. Perhaps it wasn't the end of the song, perhaps it was just that the old woman couldn't make the huge effort to stand and sing at the same time.

Then, another miracle. She was lifting one emaciated, bare arm. We all looked to where she was pointing. She was pointing to the window with its blanket, to the yard, to the light, to the sky, then growing dark. We carried her, somehow upright, to the verandah. She winced away from what was left of the light, as if it was a slap, then, blindly, put her leg forward, to take a step. Everything in her creaked.

We lowered both her feet to the floor. With all of us holding her, she took another step, creaking so much that it would've drowned out her singing, but her song had ceased.

Her daughter cried out, her daughter didn't want her mother to walk, to make that huge, that fateful effort. But the old lady was oblivious to us all. She could barely see us, could barely see anything but the light, and her eyes were screwed up against it. She took another step, then another. Gillian loosened her hands from around the old woman's body. I did as she did, though I was fearful that Tillie would fall to an instant death. They somehow made it off the verandah's edge, they were in the yard, walking in the dust, with only Carmen holding her upright. They moved slowly, gingerly to the back of the house, where the endless desert rippled away into the purple sky of dusk.

Somehow the old woman freed herself from her daughter's clasp, perhaps by a word I couldn't hear, couldn't understand. Just as Carmen let go, the old woman's body drooped, but though she collapsed, like a rag doll, she didn't fall, she was down on all fours. Carmen helped her again to her feet, looking around desperately at us for help. We started forward, but the old woman was crawling on all fours, on her own. Then, somehow, she straightened, and walked. Carmen stood back, watching her mother. The old woman resumed singing. She walked, singing, one foot slowly after the other, into the desert. Carmen hovered, at a distance, silently, reverently.

Gillian looked at me, eyebrows up questioningly. I knew her enough to understand that she was wondering if I planned to follow them, to record the walk.

'No,' I decided. 'This isn't whites' business.'

She squeezed my hand.

I switched off the recorder.

'What's over in that direction?' I asked.

'Her mother's country.'

Then it came back to me, something that I'd been told when I first arrived.

'Her mother's country yearns for her. She yearns for it, but it yearns for her.'

'You translated that?'

I shook my head no. 'Adrian guessed what the song was about at the beginning.'

Together we stumbled back to the troopie, our shoulders rubbing together, consoling each other.

'I'll drive,' she said. 'You've got a lot to think about.'

Chapter 24

We drove back to the settlement through the moonlight, a silver desert now, the silver of a much-used coin.

'I'd like to stay on, if they'll have me,' Gillian suddenly said as we mused separately, but conscious of each other's company. 'And you?'

'I'm of no use,' I said.

After a few more kilometres, I asked: 'Will Daniel stay on, do you think?'

'That's why he's broken it off with Anastasia.'

I cried out, 'When?'

'A few days ago. He said losing her was easier than leaving this country.'

All around us the desert gleamed with silver light, as silver as ever my river had been.

'I know what he means,' I managed to say.

We drove on and on through the silver world.

'What do you think of Graeme?' Gillian's voice broke into my tumbling thoughts. 'Don't you think he's a fine figure of a man?' she added, and when I paused, trying to remember him, she prompted: 'Graeme, who sacked Adrian last time.'

I dragged my astonished eyes away from the silver to her face, also silvery around the nose and forehead, and her innocent letterbox mouth, though her cheeks had dark shadows.

'Yes,' I said. 'He is.'

'He keeps dropping into the clinic for a cuppa when Sister's not around. What I'm trying to say is – would I be betraying Adrian to like him?'

In her moonlit self, she seemed part of the desert.

I floundered. 'Does Graeme believe in Western medicine?'

'No.'

We drove on silently for a few minutes.

'But what do you think of Graeme and me?' Gillian persisted.

'I know you'll think, "Of course she'd say that" – but I think you should learn his language first,' I said.

'But his English is perfect.'

'That's not the point. You need to know what he means when he speaks English. And ask Collin Collins.'

'Collins! So linguists are, on top of everything else, experts in romance?'

'With their language, he's probably as close to the hearts of these people as any white could be.'

She dropped me off at my house. In my exhaustion I saw the signs of Adrian's rapid departure – piles of paper still strewn around my room, piles of clothes abandoned on the floor. But my bed looked sumptuous. It had been made with sheets that promised they'd furl around me. I never make my bed, but tonight it was smoothly done, the end of the sheet folded down evenly over a light summer blanket, and with envelope corners. It came to me that he'd made it for me, just like he had when I first came here. A farewell present, to show he loved me. That simple, caring act brought tears to my eyes. So that I would think, after all, that I'd been wrong: that this is how he loved.

But tears stop.

I went to the toilet, made myself go to the kitchen, drank water to give myself time to think. Then, in case I slept in, I wrote a note to Daniel and left it on the table in the kitchen.

My fault about the troopie.

Out my window, Adrian's mattress was still there, a white scar on the red earth.

I woke when the sun was high. The house was silent. Daniel had had a shower and gone to work, I could tell because of the damp bathroom and the bowl and spoon drying in the washing-up rack on the sink. He was always considerately tidy. My note had gone.

It took me just a few minutes to walk to Dora's house, rehearsing what I was to say. Everywhere was the blue smoke of cooking fires, with women cooking dampers in the ashes. Dora's family, like everyone else, was gathered around their fire. She must've started earlier than most, because everyone was already eating. I waited at her gate. They all looked up, startled.

Dora came over.

I held out the recorder, complete with its recording.

'The old song,' I said slowly in Djemiranga, trying to get the grammar right, although I couldn't use, and still didn't know, the affix I'd come to record. 'The song of the mother of Carmen.'

As I spoke, she corrected me. She was probably correcting my tenses, she might even be adding in the travel affix, because what I was saying must sound like the babble of an uncooperative child.

'I want – you – to hold it,' I managed. Annoyingly, I was crying. I dashed away tears. I switched to English.

'The song is not white people's business,' I said.

We both looked down at the ground.

'The university sent me to record it,' I said, again in English, only English. 'But whites haven't been through your ceremonies. They don't know Aboriginal ways. You hold it. You decide.'

She took it. Her pressure on my fingers was slight, a small caress. She nodded, turned away. I turned away.

'Kate,' she said.

I turned back.

'Hold it,' she said.

It came out of my mouth in Djemiranga. 'Me? You want me to keep it? To take it back to the city?'

She indicated the desert of her country.

'Stay here. Hold it.'

She'd spoken in English.

I took it from her, I broke the rules, I gazed at her.

'Stay,' she repeated. It seemed an order.

I thought of the day she cleaned our house, her cleaning of all those silent receptacles and arrangers and administrators of Western possessions, the cupboards, the filing cabinets, the shelving, the drawers, the wardrobes, the benches, even the ironing board. I thought of Tillie's house, empty of furniture. Dora's probably was, too.

'You want me to be – a bank? A museum?'

But she'd already turned back to what was much more important: her family, and her country.

There was no film music then, no sign that said Destiny. All I was doing was making a path into the desert, as if I'd never walked there before. That day it was the colour of the earth that elated me; it changed as I walked between apricot – gold – orange – rust – russet – crimson – pink – mauve. These were the colours of my new life. In comparison, the grey mud of my river seemed alien and dismal. Oh, my river had gleamed with silver light, but why hadn't I ever realised before how grey the earth was? I'd taken its greyness for granted; I'd assumed all earth was grey or black.

But a childhood in that Bay of Shadows had made me a person easily moved to tears over a landscape. Even now, my eyes glossed with tears over the particular bend of the white gum's bough, and over the powdery yellow acacia blossoms that had fallen gently on the red sand. I wanted to go back and show them to Daniel, Daniel who I'd never deceive, would never have to deceive. But there would be time for that.

As I walked, it was as if I'd never seen beauty, this or any other. The desert and its people had reached into new chambers of my heart and pushed them wide open. I could almost hear the swinging open of the doors. As if I had to learn over and over how beautiful the world's possibilities were, as if I hadn't been concentrating hard enough before.

I sat for a minute, and then I lay down on the red earth and embraced it. When I got up, my sweaty skin, now faded of its bronze and only my ordinary skin, was dusted with red. I didn't brush it off.

All this I started to tell you, all of this story.

But then I stopped talking to you, because I needed to drop into silence. The desert was singing to me.

Acknowledgements

Into this book have crept the thoughts and phrases of many favourite novelists; I can't deny this, nor wish to. They have seeped into me, they're part of who I am. Further, I want to thank all the people in the Northern Territory, black and white, who talked and sat and walked with me and took me hunting. Each in their own way patiently educated me in what became a pilgrimage; from the very beginning, for example, before I spent the better part of two years in the Territory, Alice Springs's Craig San Roque took my breath away by telling me that I had to learn to sit in the dust and listen – not to him, but to the enigmas unfolding before me; that there are many ways to learn, that my inquisitions only yielded answers to my particular line of thought.

I also am deeply indebted to many scholars. David Moore and Susan Moore were among the first to explain to me the new world I was entering; I kept returning to them again and again for advice, and they were unstintingly generous and patient. My colleague Dr Michael Walsh, Honorary Associate in Linguistics of Sydney University, talked to me hundreds of times, and sent, at my request, fascinating papers that he'd published, or was about to publish. He kindly laboured over an early version of the manuscript. I also attribute to him, to Dr Joe Blythe, now of the Max Plank Institute for Linguistics, and to Dr Linda Barwick from the Conservatorium of Sydney University, the story of this novel. When I was despairing of the whole endeavour – by that time the manuscript was just a collection of sense impressions –

they allowed me to accompany them on a fortnight's field trip to Wadeye, on the west coast of the Northern Territory, where I watched Joe poring over a recorded fragment of the local language, syllable by syllable, Michael examining a hand-written collection of local words and their meaning compiled by a priest seventy years ago, and Linda recording local songs; because of this experience, as we bumped back on dusty roads to Darwin in the hired troopie, I mused aloud: 'What if my heroine is sent to a remote community to record an ancient song known by only one old woman who's on her deathbed – and my heroine can't find her?' Few stories arrive like that, flying in, fully-formed, through an open window.

I also drew on the knowledge of Associate Professor Claire Bowern, historical linguist in Australian Languages at Yale, who generously sent me precious material about women's songs, and I followed the fieldwork of ethnoecologist Dr Fiona Walsh. I had hours of conversations with other scholars, including Ron Williams, Iain Davidson, Emeritus Professor of the University of New England, and Dr Diane Austin-Broos, Professor Emeritus of Anthropology at Sydney University who read an early draft and contributed pivotal ideas that became whole scenes.

Other readers of at least one of the dozen drafts of the manuscript include Libby Hathorn, Gordon Graham, Kathryn Heyman, Con Anemogiannis, Kiriaki Orfanos, Vidya Madabushi, Sarah Bedford, Gary Marshall, Jenni Ogden, linguist Sally Dixon, Susan and David Moore, Blair McFarland and Jenny Turner-Walker; many Alice Springs people took me into their homes and cooked me marvellous dinners and introduced me to their friends: again I must thank Susan and David Moore, Blair McFarland and Jenny Turner-Walker, Craig San Roque and Judith Pritchard, Cait Wait and the late Paul Quinlivan.

However, I must emphasise that after the help from these scholars, advisors and friends, I put aside all I'd learned in order to create this work. The people I've thanked are in no way responsible for what I've done with their assistance; all errors are entirely mine. I also must stress that no one in the Northern Territory or anyone I've ever met, or any government body, figures in this story, nor does the story reflect anything that anyone has done, or should have done. If anyone imagines themselves in these pages, they are flattering or denigrating themselves. This is not a factual account of 'real life' experiences. It's a work of the imagination. I observed and listened to thousands of stories and rumours and many dusty kilometres of gossip, and then I put it aside and told the story I wanted to tell. I made it all up. That's my job; that's what novelists do.

I must thank Sydney University for employing me as a teacher of creative writing during the seven years I took to write this work.

The manuscript was given a warm welcome by my publisher, HarperCollins, in particular by Jo Butler and Sue Brockoff, and became what you've read because of patient and always insightful editing by Linda Funnell. Jo Butler asked Josie Douglas of the Northern Territory to take on the responsibility of final cultural advisor.

As he's done during the writing of my previous novels, Gordon Graham, my life partner, kept listening to all my fears and uncertainties, and urging me on.